Despite being an avid reader and closet writer her whole life, **Erin Knightley** decided to pursue a sensible career in science. It was only after earning her B.S. and working in the field for years that she realized doing the sensible thing wasn't any fun at all. Following her dreams, Erin left her practical side behind and now spends her days writing. Together with her tall, dark and handsome husband and their three spoiled mutts, she is living her own Happily Ever After in North Carolina.

Visit Erin Knightley online:

www.haveyourcakeandreadittoo.blogspot.co.uk
www.twitter.com/ErinKnightley
www.facebook.com/ErinKnightley

Praise for Erin Knightley:

'Endearing characters, eloquent writing
and a spoonful of charm'
Under the Covers

'A witty and engaging love story'
Lydia Dare, author of *Wolfishly Yours*

'Charmingly sweet and tender'
Publishers Weekly

The Duke Can Go to the Devil

Erin Knightley

piatkus

PIATKUS

First published in the US in 2015 by Signet Eclipse,
an imprint of New American Library, a division of Penguin Group (USA) LLC
First published in Great Britain in 2015 by Piatkus

1 3 5 7 9 10 8 6 4 2

A CIP catalogue record for this book
is available from the British Library.

ISBN 978-0-349-41067-8

Printed and bound by CPI (UK) Ltd, Croydon, CR0 4YY

Papers used by Piatkus are from well-managed forests
and other responsible sources.

Piatkus
An imprint of
Little, Brown Book Group
Carmelite House
50 Victoria Embankment
London EC4Y 0DZ

An Hachette UK Company
www.hachette.co.uk

www.piatkus.co.uk

*To my fellow writer friends Tammy, Mindy,
Máire, Dana, Val, Ash, and Anne, who not only
keep me going, but keep me sane. Mostly ;).
Thanks for sharing the journey with me!*

*And to Kirk, who is my true definition of home.
From high school sweethearts in Kentucky to living
our happily ever after here in North Carolina,
wherever you are is where I want to be!*

Acknowledgments

Can we all just stop for a moment and gaze lovingly at this beautiful cover? Once again I tip my hat to the New American Library art department for giving me yet another swoon-worthy image. A big thank-you to my intrepid editor, Kerry Donovan, and to my agent, Deidre Knight, for taking such good care of me. The proper care and feeding of an author is tricky business!

This is the last of the three books that were plotted in one extraordinary weekend with my friends and fellow writers Hanna Martine, Heather Snow, and Anna Lee Huber. I'm so grateful for your insights and unique perspectives, which really helped to make this series into something I'm proud of. We must do another plotting retreat, stat!

Finally, I am ever thankful for you, dear reader. Thank you for taking the time to read my stories. I certainly hope you enjoy them! I especially love hearing from you. Please join me on Facebook, Twitter, or via e-mail. The links are at my Web site (erinknightley.com) along with a gratuitous shot of Colin Firth giving me a hug. You can also sign up for my newsletter to stay up-to-date on new releases and the like. Happy reading!

Chapter One

To most, Mei-li Bradford's aunt was known simply as Lady Stanwix, second wife and widow of the old earl. To a very select few, she was referred to as Victoria. To the servants, she was called something not entirely fit to repeat. But in May's mind, her father's sister—with whom she'd be living until Papa returned from his current voyage—was more often than not The Warden.

An entirely fitting title, given how often she required May to stay buried in the suffocating opulence of the grand house the older woman had called home for the past two decades. The rooms were large, but that didn't make the place any less confining. Especially since, thanks to her aunt's uninspired sense of design, the place was as dark and dreary as a mausoleum.

Fortunately, May was nothing if not resourceful.

And while she prudently avoided clashing with her aunt whenever possible—she had made a promise to her father to behave in his absence, after all—she was not above exploiting The Warden's weaknesses.

Which was precisely why May had been sneaking out every morning for the past three months. She had a routine to keep, and after a lifetime of tropical living, she refused to do her morning exercises within the olive-and-brown-walled confines of the lifeless old house. Although, to be fair, it was hardly *sneaking* when one walked straight out the front door. If her aunt chose to keep to a rigid routine that consisted of being awoken at nine o'clock sharp every morning—and not one minute before—then that was her prerogative. Just as it was May's to rise before dawn and start her day.

Smiling, she breathed in the cool morning air as she pulled the door closed behind her, more grateful than ever for the quiet solitude of the city this early in the morning. Unlike many of the cities May had visited in her life, Bath had a certain laziness to it this time of the day. This was a city that came alive in the evening, with the monied glow of hundreds of beeswax candles lighting the rented homes and public gathering places that were packed to overflowing come sundown.

Walking along the deserted streets in the timid predawn glow, one would never suspect the thousands upon thousands of visitors filling every available inn and town house, nearly all of whom had flocked to Bath for the first annual Summer Serenade in Somerset music festival.

The festival, and the new friends it had brought her, was the only thing making this forced visit bearable. *Until last night.* Her jaw tightened at the memory of the disastrous evening she had endured thanks to the combined efforts of The Warden and one self-entitled, pompous visitor in particular. As quickly as the thought had popped into her mind, she mentally shoved it away again.

Coming to the park by the river today wasn't about her aunt, or more specifically, defying her aunt. Nor was it about the encounter last night, as infuriating as it had been. Coming here today was about *her*. It was about doing what she had done every morning for years, whether she was in the Far East, the East Indies, on the open ocean, or right here in Bath.

And she'd be damned if she'd let her aunt's dictates or last night's confrontation spoil it for her.

Arriving at the park at last, May slipped out of her shoes and stepped onto the soft, dewy grass. *Bliss.* Next she shed her dull gray pelisse, letting the ugly fabric fall in a heap on the damp ground. The coat had been the first thing Aunt Victoria had commissioned for May upon her arrival this past spring. It had seemed a nice enough gesture, until she realized it was The Warden's attempt to cover May's bright and exotic wardrobe. Still, its dreary color did come in handy this time of morning, when she wished to avoid notice if, by chance, someone did happen to be about.

Sighing happily, she stretched her hands over her head, reveling in the loss of the restrictive garment. God bless the English and their propensity to sleep in. Not only did she actually have some time to herself each morning, but there was no one around to dissolve in a fit of vapors over the thin silken tunic and trousers she wore.

The soft whisper of the fabric was nearly lost in the muted sounds of the flowing River Avon as she walked toward the clearing beside the water, limbering up her body as she went. Rolled shoulders, windmilled arms, a few neck stretches—just enough to get the blood flowing for her routine. The light was particularly lovely this morning, all pinks and purples with the blushing promise of a new day. In this light, the greens of the trees and grass and shrubs and, well, *everything* in this bloody country, wasn't quite so overwhelming. Truly, it was as though the king had ordained exactly one shade of green for every plant, leaf, and blade of grass in the country, and the flora, being good little English subjects, had obliged.

She caught herself sliding down the familiar path of negativity and firmly banished the thoughts from her mind. She was here to find peace. To be centered for the day, to start off the morning on the best possible foot.

Breathing in a long, slow lungful of the fresh morning air, she cleared her mind of all the clutter it had accumulated over the past twenty-four hours. And there was a *lot* of clutter, thanks to yesterday's debacle. Getting her body into position, she closed her eyes, imagined her favorite place on Earth, and began her routine.

Each movement was slow and controlled, gliding effortlessly from one position to the next. She took slow, measured breaths and focused on the feel of the air as her hands swished through it, on the gentle sound of the river flowing against its banks, and on the soft, spongy grass beneath her feet as she slid from one step to the next.

Yes, the routine that she'd learned from Suyin, her friend and lady's maid, was technically a form of martial arts, but it could more accurately be described as meditation in motion. The movements were so familiar, it was as though her limbs moved themselves, following the age-old rhythm that she'd learned years ago. The sleeves of her tunic slid along her arms like cool water, pooling at her elbows before slipping back down to her wrists. Again and again the silk caressed her skin as she went through the routine, a sort of silent lullaby.

As the minutes ticked by, the knotted muscles of her upper back loosened and her body became more and more relaxed. The tension caused by the day before melted like candle wax. Her mind settled as well, letting go of all the negativity that had plagued her since yesterday.

Just as she had reached the perfect place of quiet clarity, the sound of a cleared throat startled her from her peace, wrenching her back to the present. She straightened abruptly and swung around, her heart pounding.

She saw the interloper at once, standing only a dozen feet away with arms crossed and lips raised in a slight sneer that she was beginning to think was the only expression he was capable of. His strong, aristocratic jaw was tipped up in a look of superiority as his decidedly disgusted whiskey-brown eyes raked her over from the top of her head to the bottom of her bare feet. May silently cursed.

In four different languages.

The Duke of Radcliffe, it would seem, was not as easily forgotten as originally hoped.

The previous evening

"You look beautiful. A gemstone come to life."

May glanced away from the mirror and grinned to Suyin, who was not only her lady's maid, but her friend and companion. "Thanks to you, of course," she said, giving a little wink.

Suyin nodded once. "Yes, I know," she said, her dry humor making May laugh. Her English was much better than May's Chinese, but she always spoke with an economy of words. Tilting her head to the side as she regarded May's reflection, she smiled softly and said, "So like your mother. More every day."

May drew in a swift breath, the unexpected comment making her heart squeeze. Joy and sadness mingled within her chest at the thought of her mother, who had died last year. Smiling past the emotion, she nodded her thanks.

Outward beauty was such a subjective thing—a truth learned over the years as May had encountered different cultures and their varying definitions of what was appealing. May never put much stock in comments, be they positive or negative, about her looks. But to be compared to her mother? It was enough to bring uncharacteristic moisture to her eyes, which she quickly blinked away.

"This was her favorite color," she said at last, sliding her hand over the cerulean silk of her gown. Papa had bought it for May during their last trip to Java, and Smita, one of her dearest friends in India, had embroidered the bold design at her waist, a colorful two-inch-wide band with stylized flowers in varying shades of yellow, pink, and blue. Another band trimmed the gown's hem, which was just short enough to show a hint of her magenta silk slippers. It was an ensemble she knew her mother would have loved, which in turn made May love it that much more.

Suyin nodded. "Blue silk makes blue eyes sing."

"How very poetic," May responded with a light-hearted shake of her head as she got her emotions back under control. "Although, at the moment, I'm much more concerned with making my fingers dance than my eyes sing."

Her friend's beautiful almond-shaped eyes widened incredulously. "Mei-li? Nervous? It cannot be."

May chuckled at the teasing. "Not so much nervous as excited. This is the last time we shall play as a trio—I want to do well." It had been an unexpectedly lovely summer, thanks to Sophie, Charity, and the little trio they had formed.

They had found one another quite by accident over a month ago during the first days of the festival, when one of the organizers had insisted there was room for only one more in their Tuesday evening performances. Not to be thwarted, they had impulsively joined together into a trio that turned out to be the best thing that could have happened to May. Being able to play her guzheng in concert with such wonderful musicians had been a treat, but it was their friendship that she truly treasured. When her father finally came to collect her, she had every intention of writing them copiously, no matter the cost.

The clock in the hall tolled seven o'clock. Devil take it—May was late. Rushing to grab her wrap, she turned and gave Suyin a bright smile. "Enjoy your evening! And do wish us luck—with that crowd, we may well need it."

"*Zhù hao yùn,*" Suyin dutifully called after her as May rushed out the door.

Aunt Victoria was as fastidious about time as a clockmaker, so this wasn't the best start to the evening. May hurried down the stairs, lifting her skirts halfway up her calves in an effort to keep from tripping. As she reached the landing, the butler smoothly pulled open the door, his dour expression unchanged despite the breathless female racing past him.

"Thank you, Hargrove," she called as she rushed to the waiting carriage. Her aunt's profile was just visible through the closed window of the carriage, her elegantly sloped nose lifted despite the fact she was alone. Perhaps that was her natural resting position after all.

The evening sun flashed across the black lacquer door as the footman pulled it open and assisted her up. She smiled briefly to him before settling onto the seat beside her aunt. Arranging her skirts as carefully as she could, she said, "Good evening, Aunt Victoria. My apologies for my tardiness."

Instead of answering, her aunt rapped on the roof, signaling to the driver to be off. It was only after they had merged into the slow-moving traffic headed up the hill that she deigned to turn to May, her gray eyes disapproving. "Punctuality is a virtue. Particularly when a duke is present."

Her aunt would actually have been quite attractive, if she could ever relax now and then. Her cheeks were smooth and softly rounded, but her mouth and forehead were lined from the scowl that seemed to weigh down her features more often than not.

Inwardly sighing, May nodded. "Hence the apology. I have no wish to be late to the gala." She cared not at all for a duke she had never met, but she had no intention of wasting any of her remaining time with her friends, especially on such a big night.

"Do not take that tone with me, young lady. If I had my way, we wouldn't be attending at all."

May's eyebrow lifted, despite her intention to remain impassive. "What tone? I was merely—"

"Oh yes, you are forever 'merely' doing one thing or another. I've gone above and beyond in my attempts to teach you proper comportment, yet you steadfastly cling to your habits." She adjusted her shawl, aggravation making the movement jerky. "Which is precisely why I will not be introducing you to the duke. I will not allow your poor manners to reflect ill upon me in his presence. Heaven knows you've done enough damage already."

May's excitement for the evening abruptly fizzled in the face of her aunt's censure. She had been all of one minute late, for God's sake. Leave it to The Warden to snowball that small infraction into something so dire.

Her spine stiffened as she cut her gaze to her aunt. "Yes, so much damage that the committee saw fit to invite the trio to perform for the vaunted duke."

Aunt Victoria's lips pinched together, emphasizing the wrinkles that radiated from her mouth like the spokes of a wagon wheel. May could practically see the steam building behind her ears. "One more impertinent comment, and you will find yourself back home the very moment the performance is over."

It was May's nature to rebel against her aunt's authoritative manner, but for perhaps the thousandth time that summer, she bit her tongue and took a deep breath. Her father had implored her to respect his sister's authority. May had done her best to honor his wishes, for more reasons than one. It wouldn't be forever, and she didn't wish to make either of them more miserable than they already were with the living arrangements. Still, it galled her not to defend herself.

After a few moments of silence, her aunt nodded, apparently pleased that she had won that round. They carried on for a few minutes with the tentative ceasefire, each of them staring out their respective windows in the increasingly stifling heat of the small space. For some ridiculous reason, her aunt felt it was more dignified to travel in a closed carriage.

Finally, the horses slowed to a stop, and the butter yellow limestone of the Assembly Rooms came into view. Without waiting for the groom to assist them, May pushed open the door and stepped out, grateful for a breath of fresh air. She pulled off her wrap and lifted her arms. She sincerely hoped no dampness marred the silk bodice.

Her aunt alighted from the carriage, her brow ominously furrowed as she took in May's gown. Before she could say whatever sour thing was perched on the end of her tongue, May held up her hands. "Please, may we just enjoy a pleasant evening? I won't say or do anything to embarrass you. I will speak with Charity and Sophie and consider the evening a rousing success for not having conversed with anyone else. I honestly have no wish to draw any attention outside of our performance."

The Warden looked none too pleased with May's little speech. "Is that so? One wonders at your choice of gown if it is not attention that you seek." Shaking out the voluminous skirts of her lavender gown, she sighed and said, "However, I shall take you at your word. Do not make me regret it."

An hour later, May was valiantly attempting to recapture her earlier good mood as she stood off to the side of the Ballroom with Sophie during intermission. Sophie, who was now the Countess of Evansleigh and still very much a blushing newlywed, had that certain gleam in her eye as she looked past May's shoulder, which warned her of Sophie's intentions before she even said a word.

"Don't look now, but you are being watched most intently."

May grimaced. She had been right: Sophie was matchmaking. Letting out a long-suffering sigh, she sent Sophie a stern look. "I have absolutely no problem not looking. In fact, I shall continue to not look for the rest of the evening."

She kept her gaze where it was, idly watching the milling crowds of music lovers all here for the extravagant gala honoring the arrival of the festival's patron. Everyone seemed to be decked out in their absolute finest, with jewels glittering every which way one looked and cravats reaching their most absurd heights yet.

Sophie merely grinned, her enthusiasm not dimmed in the least. Of course, when it came to Sophie, very little ever managed to dim her enthusiasm. It was one of the things May liked best about her. "Yes, I know, being gawped at is a completely normal experience for you, blond goddess that you are, but it's not the staring that is unusual; it's who is *doing* the staring." She leaned forward, clasping May's hands in excitement. "It's the Duke of Radcliffe!"

Ah, the patron himself. Lord High-and-Mighty, whom Aunt Victoria deemed too lofty to be tainted by May's lowly presence. The awe in Sophie's voice was unmistakable, and May didn't wish to trample her excitement, but it was difficult to keep her cynicism at bay. "That's nice," she said diplomatically, though with no real enthusiasm.

Though she was technically English, many of the social customs here were still foreign to her. The incredibly strict rules relating to a lady's behavior was at the top of the list, but the tendency to practically worship peers of the realm was a close second.

That's not to say that she didn't enjoy some peers on an individual level—Sophie's new husband, the Earl of Evansleigh, was quite lovely, as was Charity's betrothed, Baron Cadgwith—but elevating the group as a whole merely because of the lucky circumstances of their births seemed beyond absurd. Particularly when the peer in question couldn't even be bothered to attend the very festival he was patronizing until the very last week—a fact that everyone seemed to be tactfully ignoring.

Undaunted, Sophie rolled her eyes and said, "It's not nice—it's tremendous! He is young—but not too young—handsome in a reserved sort of way, obscenely wealthy, unmarried, and as close to royalty as we could hope to find outside of the palace grounds. And believe me," she added, looking around as she lowered her voice, "he is *much* more attractive than any of the royal family."

Despite herself, May laughed at her friend's less than shocking revelation. "From what I hear, most anyone is more attractive than the royal family."

"What have you two got your heads together about?" Charity Effington, the other member of their little musical trio, approached with three punch glasses precariously balanced in her slender hands. Her cheeks were about as red as her hair, no doubt thanks to the overly warm and crowded hall.

Sophie grinned, her dark eyes sparkling every bit as gaily as her yellow-and-white diamond necklace in the Assembly Rooms' dazzling candlelight. "The Duke of Radcliffe has fallen for our May. Perhaps if we can match them up, we can keep May from leaving us when her father returns."

"He most certainly has *not* fallen for me," May cut in, widening her eyes at Sophie. "And I most certainly will not fall for him. Just because you two find yourselves rather happily impaled upon cupid's arrow does not mean I am similarly inclined."

"You only say that because you haven't *seen* him," Sophie said, irrepressible as always.

Charity chuckled as she handed out the crystal punch cups. "He is rather handsome, in a tall, dark, and imperious sort of way."

"Charity!" Sophie exclaimed as she playfully bumped her arm. "You are not helping."

"Oh yes, she is," May responded, flipping open her fan with her free hand. It was hot as hades here tonight thanks to the two unusually hot days they'd had in a row. Perhaps she was losing the immunity to heat she had spent a lifetime acquiring in the tropical climes in which she'd grown up. That thought did not sit well. "I've no interest in any of the men here, and dukes in particular. If I wanted to spend time with someone unaccountably superior, I'd seek out Miss Harmon."

"Touché," said Charity, laughter buoying the word. Miss Harmon seemed to go out of her way to belittle every female in a half-mile radius, and not a one of the three of them had been spared her barbs.

Speaking of unaccountably superior, Mr. Green, one of the festival coordinators, squeezed his way through the crush, his pale eyes looking down at them all the while through the smudged lenses of his spectacles. "Pardon me, ladies. I thought it prudent to remind you that you are scheduled to be the first performance after the intermission. Please be at the stage in five minutes."

There was no love lost between the trio and Mr. Green. He'd been so insufferably rude the first time they had met, it was hard now to address him with any amount of respect. May smiled with all the sweetness of a sack of coal. "Not to worry, kind sir. We shall be punctual or die trying."

"Well, there is a first time for everything," he retorted before turning on his heel and marching away.

Before May could form a properly cutting insult for the man, Charity sighed and shook her head. "One must wonder if he has ever known a moment of joy in his life. Such a shame to go through life with such a sour outlook."

Ever since she and the baron had come to know and later love each other, Charity had begun to look at others with a kinder eye. May, however, was not so afflicted. "If you ask me, he takes quite a bit of pleasure in spreading misery wherever he goes. Now then, shall we make our way toward the stage? I should hate to give Mr. Green the satisfaction of seeing us late."

The others nodded, and they quickly finished off their drinks. May couldn't have cared less about the duke's supposed interest in her, but his patronage had made the festival possible, and for that she could be no less than grateful. And in any event, she and the other girls were always happy for an excuse to perform together, even if May's aunt did so hate exposing the tender ears of their fellow festival-goers to May's Chinese zither. Relinquishing their cups to a passing footman, they smiled to one another, linked hands, and headed off toward the stage.

Chapter Two

"Congratulations on attaining the ripe age of thirty, old man. Many happy returns, et cetera, et cetera."

William Spencer, Duke of Radcliffe, turned away from the lovely blond vision in blue silk below and nodded in acceptance of his friend's felicitations, such as they were. Lord Derington was one of the few people in the world who dared speak so familiarly to him. Although, anyone who could legitimately claim to have saved William's life at one point or another was certainly welcome to the same privilege.

"Thank you, Dering," he said dryly, lifting a sardonic eyebrow. "Your tidings warm the soul."

The man grinned as he came to join William at the balcony railing. "Quite a gathering for your royal self. I'm beginning to wonder if elephants and tigers will be next."

Following his gaze, William had to agree. As the guest of honor, he was seated on the balcony enclave where he could best view the performances and, by extension, the attendees. It was better than mingling below, but this wasn't how he had envisioned his first night in Bath. "Honestly, I find this whole exhibition quite unnecessary."

He'd been so furious when he'd received word of his stepmother's latest exploits, he didn't think of the ramifications when he sent word of his intention to attend the last week of the festival. He'd been focused on arriving as quickly as possible in order to curtail her activities, not on the fact that his arrival would set off the inevitable series of events leading to just this sort of evening.

Yes, he had provided the initial funding for the first Summer Serenade in Somerset music festival, and yes, he had used his connections to help populate it with some of the best musicians in the country, but that didn't mean he had expected or wanted such a display in his honor.

However, someone on the committee had known it was his birthday and they had taken it upon themselves to surprise him with an event fit for, well, a duke. So far, they'd trotted out half a dozen of the festival's finest, from opera singers to lute players, and though they themselves were tremendously talented — England's best and brightest, to be sure — he didn't particularly like being displayed in a manner not unlike the exhibits at the tower menagerie.

Actually, he took that back. Being on display was ten times better than being at the mercy of the attendees. This was not some London event, where those present were more or less of the same social status and with an ingrained knowledge of propriety. Here, there was a much more diverse population, and his arrival had caused quite an uncomfortable stir.

In fact, in the half hour or so before he'd taken his place of honor, he'd politely ignored at least three eager young women who, despite their lack of proper introduction, had rather baldly attempted to catch his attention. As though *that* were the way to win the heart of an unmarried duke.

He did understand their enthusiasm—the honor of his station had been engrained in him since birth—but it was difficult to endure such breaks in protocol. In his family, there was nothing more sacred than pomp and circumstance. Whenever he did finally choose a duchess, it would be a woman who understood and respected such things.

His friend scoffed at William's declaration. "Of course you find it unnecessary. Which is why it is such great fun to watch you endure it." Dering's dark gaze glinted in the candlelight as he gave William a devilish wink. "It's even greater fun to know that, now that you've entered your fourth decade, calling you 'old man' takes on a frighteningly accurate new meaning."

"I believe now is a good time to remind you that you are precisely one year younger than me, Dering. Barely perceptible difference, really." It was good to banter with his long-time friend again. William had been preoccupied— obsessed, really—with his project for too long and had made time for little else.

His friend snorted in amusement. "Perceptible enough for those of us young enough to still be in possession of all our faculties." A bit of the humor dimmed as he took in William's appearance. "What's happened that should bring you here at this late date? I remember you stating quite clearly that you were entirely too busy working on getting your new mill up and running to attend the festival."

The muscles of his shoulders instantly tensed. "I'll give you precisely one guess."

Understanding flooded Dering's features as he shook his head. "And what is dear Lady Radcliffe up to now?"

It was a testament to their friendship that Dering knew exactly what might bring him here. Since the day the old duke had announced his plan to marry Vivian a decade ago, she and William had clashed with each other. His father had been blinded by his lust for the Parisian beauty, and she had wisely kept him dangling after her like some sort of rutting stag by refusing to consummate their relationship until marriage. Once the deed was done, her true colors had been revealed, and William's poor opinion of her had been vindicated.

She had always been her own top priority. She brought no money, no connections, no pedigree to the union. Nor did she bring respect for either the old duke or William. The only positive thing that he could say about her was that the affairs didn't start until his father had died. Once she was a widow, all efforts of keeping up appearances had been tossed to the wind, and he'd been left with the continual task of damage control ever since.

He'd have disowned her from the family years ago if it weren't for Julian and Clarisse, his young half siblings. He'd been raised without his mother, and he'd be damned if he'd allow the same to happen to them. At only five and seven years old, they still had need of her, even if she rarely had need of them. He was literally counting the days until they reached their majority and he could cut ties in good conscience. "She is a master at turning the screw. It's diabolical, really."

"A new lover, I take it?"

"Not just a new lover," William said, the words as sharp as his lingering anger. "She's bloody well taken up with Lord Norwich."

As understanding dawned, Dering's eyes widened and he dragged a hand down his jaw. "Bloody hell. She really is a piece of work. As is he, for that matter."

William nodded grimly. He had spent the last six years spearheading the fight to break the East India

Company's trade monopoly so that English textiles could get a toehold in the market. Though William had been largely successful, the Company's exclusive trade rights to China remained firmly in place, so there was still more to fight in the next session. His strongly held philosophy was and always would be that the more work was kept in England, the better off her citizens would be.

Norwich, whose fortunes were integrally tied to the Company, had been his biggest opponent in the House of Lords. Who better for Vivian to take up with, then? She seemed to savor her ability to infuriate him.

"So you are here to keep an eye on her?"

"More or less. She could bed the whole of His Majesty's army, for all I care. But I intend to force her to be discreet about it."

Dering quirked a brow, his faith in such a feat clearly lacking. "How, exactly, do you plan on accomplishing that?"

"Same as every time she does something like this," William said, the frustration rising in his throat like bile. That woman needed attention like most people needed air. "As soon as I personally confront her, she always backs down. It's the most tiresome cycle in the world, but I can't seem to break it."

The master of ceremonies climbed the four steps onto the stage then, and the hum of the crowd quieted. William drew a long breath, setting aside his renewed annoyance as best he could.

Dering started to turn toward the stairs, but William called him back with a wave of his hand. "You might as well stay. Ox that you are, you'll cause a commotion if you try to make your way back to your seat now."

They settled onto the elegant, almost thronelike wooden chairs and listened as the man on the stage announced the next performance. William straightened in his seat as he realized the trio included the tall blond woman of nearly otherworldly beauty that he'd spotted a few minutes earlier.

The interest that had been diverted by Dering's arrival surged back to the forefront, and he leaned forward for a better look. He was in no mood to be bothered by the fairer sex just then, but exquisiteness such as hers demanded a man's notice, whether he wished it or not.

With her regal bearing, golden skin, long limbs, and an inherent gracefulness that could rival any prima donna, she was exactly the sort of female with whom the *ton* clamored to associate, yet he was positive they had never crossed paths. Given the company she'd kept this evening, she was clearly of the higher echelons of society. How was it they had never met? She should have been on every gossip's tongue and included in every betting book in town as to when and to whom she would marry. She should have been invited to any number of exclusive balls, and danced with only the most eligible of bachelors, including William.

Especially William. He was England's most eligible bachelor, if the gossip rags were to be believed. So how had this diamond of the first waters managed to escape his notice?

The three women climbed the steps onto the stage, which was already outfitted with a pianoforte as well as another long, wooden instrument William couldn't place. He recognized the other two women. The ginger-haired girl was Viscount Effington's daughter and the short brunette was one of the Wembley girls. Both decent families with good connections, so it was unlikely they would cleave themselves to someone who wasn't good *ton*.

"Ah, I see you've noticed Miss Bradford." Dering's

low voice reflected a shared appreciation for the lady in question.

So she was a miss, as opposed to a lady. "Bradford, you say?" The name didn't sound familiar.

"Indeed. She's new to Bath. Staying with her aunt, Lady Stanwix."

William leaned back in his chair, nodding slowly. Lady Stanwix. Quality relations, then. The dowager countess was the epitome of a proper English matron. There hadn't been even a whisper of scandal associated with her or her family since he'd been alive. Now that he was thirty, he did need to start thinking of the future. Producing an heir was his number one duty, after all, and he was nothing if not committed to the title. He made a mental note to add her to the list of acceptable candidates for when he was ready to consider such things.

On the stage below, the girls turned to face the crowd and curtsied. He kept his gaze on Miss Bradford, curiosity about the woman burning even brighter now that he knew a bit of her family.

He liked what he saw. The way she held herself showed innate confidence. A comfort in her own skin. Her chin was raised slightly, a soft smile gracing her full, rose-hued lips. And those high, pert breasts that were so tantalizingly swathed in silk? *Perfection.* "Perhaps an introduction is in order."

He surprised himself with the declaration, but apparently not as much as he surprised his friend. Dering made a suspicious noise—was that choked laughter or just a cleared throat?—but by the time William looked back at him, his face carried only an expression of mild helpfulness. "Absolutely. I shall be more than happy to oblige."

William narrowed his eyes. Dering was definitely

amused. The tight waver of his voice was a dead give-away. But before William could question him to ascertain what he was up to, the music began. Shaking his head, he reluctantly turned back to the stage. As clear, resonant notes began filling the hall, he settled back to enjoy the performance.

The Effington girl was at the piano and was performing a solo as the other two appeared to wait for their cue. William blinked, realizing then that Miss Bradford stood behind the odd instrument he had noticed earlier. Its many strings stretched almost the entire length, an odd combination of harp, guitar, and zither.

She raised her fingers over the strings, and he found himself leaning forward, waiting to hear the beautiful music he was certain someone as lovely as she would produce. Already he could imagine a sort of heavenly and ethereal harplike music, fit for God himself. Her hands descended, as graceful as gull wings soaring on the breeze, and then . . .

What in the world?

Twanging, foreign noise—certainly not music—came pouring forth from the instrument, mangling the otherwise impeccable performance of Mozart's masterpiece. It was an abomination. He cut a glance toward Dering, whose fingers were tapping gaily against his thigh as he bobbed his head in time with the beat.

"You can't possibly be enjoying this performance," William hissed. "It's rubbish!"

His friend's expression changed not at all as he continued to tip his head from side to side. "I knew that would be your reaction. I think it's bloody brilliant, but you, my friend, are a purist."

He couldn't be serious. "It was written by a master of the art; of course I'm a purist."

Dering chuckled, the sound a low rumble in his chest. "Well, you are virtually the only one who thinks so. The trio has been quite popular, hence their performance tonight."

William sat back and crossed his arms, disappointment washing away his interest of only moments ago. Anyone who could take the work of an absolute master and mangle it beyond recognition — not by poor playing, but by willful disfiguring — was of no interest to him.

For several long minutes, he listened with distaste as the twanging notes continued to rake across his nerves. Dering must be mistaken about their popularity. How could anyone think this fine music? But even as William scowled, the audience's approval quickly made itself known as the song came to an end, and muffled, enthusiastic clapping of a thousand gloved hands erupted throughout the room.

After letting out a shrill and highly inappropriate whistle, Dering turned toward William and grinned. "Still looking forward to that introduction?"

"I should think not," William replied firmly, refusing to be drawn in by his friend's ribbing. He was well aware that many of his peers felt him too conservative by half, and took great pleasure in teasing or even mocking his rigid ways. He cared not a single iota. He took his title and his standing in society exceptionally seriously, and he would not see it tarnished under his watch. When it came to those he associated with, he preferred those with reserved intelligence and a respect for the natural order of things. As far as he was concerned, Miss Bradford's performance was indicative of a lack of appreciation for the English way.

Dering relaxed against the chair back and smiled. "You are definitely missing out, my friend, but such is your prerogative. I imagine many here would breathe a sigh of relief to know of your disinterest."

The trio curtsied as one, and from his elevated vantage point, William was treated to a delectable view of Miss Bradford's décolleté. Against his will, his body took notice. Turning away from the display, he shot his friend an appraising glance. "Are you to be included in the count?"

Dering gave a shrug of his massive shoulders. "I think Miss Bradford and I are very well suited for friendship. I like her quite well, in fact. She's unlike any woman I've ever met."

Of that, William had no doubt. Already his mind dismissed the girl, pushing aside her startling beauty and unconventional music. "I shall take your word on that."

"This may be the last time we play in public, but it shall *not* be the last time we play," May declared, giving her dear friends a three-way hug. It was oddly emotional, knowing that the festival was soon coming to an end and the girls would be going their separate ways. As opposed as she had been to coming to Bath in the first place, it was strange to think that she would actually miss it.

Stepping back, Charity shook her head. "Of course not! You must promise to play at my wedding breakfast. Assuming we ever get all the details sorted out."

"Well, you had best get them sorted out quickly," May said, giving Charity's arm a teasing little tap with her fan. "I am determined to be there, but once my father returns, there's no telling where we will be off to next."

Perhaps back to China or Indonesia. Java was a frequent stop for her father, so it wasn't unreasonable that they might head back there. The thought filled her with excitement, but at the same time, it broke her heart to think of leaving her two friends for so long. Lord knew the post was unreliable at best when one was traversing the seas.

Sophie flashed a sly smile and tipped her head toward their friend Mr. Thomas Wright, who was wending his way through the crowd half a dozen feet away. "You could always marry by special license. I know a good vicar who can do the deed for little more than a please and thank you."

His attention duly captured, Wright flashed a broad smile and veered from his original path. "Did I hear somebody mention a vicar?" His blond brows lifted in teasing mischief. "And to be clear, my fee is a please, a thank you, and an exceptionally good wedding break-fast. Or dinner, I suppose, depending on the time."

May chuckled at his cheek. He was as fun and affable a fellow as she had met in Bath. "Ever the benevolent soul. Charity, you should consider yourself lucky to be offered such a bargain."

He nodded, his lips quirked up in that irrepressible smile of his. "Well, for Hugh and his bride, I can certainly make an exception. If you throw in a fortnight at that magnificent oceanfront estate down in Cadgwith, I'll forgo the meal. Need to visit my sister and the new baby soon, anyhow."

Charity's smile broadened. "I cannot wait to meet Fe-licity and little Isabella. I know she's only Hugh's sister-in-law, but that's close enough to be called family, as far as I'm concerned. And you are most welcome to visit any time, but I'm afraid my parents have insisted that the wedding be held up north at our longtime parish. Are you terribly upset?"

He pretended to consider it before shaking his head. "I suppose, in time, I shall get over the heartbreak.

Though Miss Bradford, when it is your turn to spring the parson's mousetrap, I fully expect to be allowed to do the honors."

The comment caught her off guard, making her laugh. "Parson's mousetrap? I certainly hope you won't be holding your breath, as you will likely be waiting a very long time." It wasn't that she was against marriage—indeed, she was wholeheartedly for it—but the idea of finding someone whom she not only loved, but with whom she could share a meeting of mind, values, and personality seemed altogether unlikely. Particularly when one took into account her love of world travel.

"As long as it takes, Miss Bradford, though I can't imagine you'll be unmarried for long. You're delightful in both wit and countenance, neither of which has gone unnoticed, I assure you." He tipped his chin to indicate the room at large. "Half the men in this room are watching you as we speak, in fact."

Sophie slipped her arm around May's elbow. "Yes, but only the best for our May. We won't let just anyone have her." She gave a little wink, then abruptly straightened. "Oh drat. I hate to be the bearer of bad news, but it appears as though your aunt is on the warpath."

May didn't even attempt to suppress her disappointed groan. If her aunt was headed their way, then the evening was about to be cut short. As sour as the woman's mood had been on the way over here, it was a given that listening to May perform on her guzheng would have only worsened her disposition. No doubt she looked forward to nipping any enjoyment May might glean from the evening in the bud.

"How far away is she?"

Charity's gray gaze flicked over May's shoulder. "A minute, two if you are lucky."

Damn it all. After the contentious nature of the ride there, the last thing May wanted to do was abandon her friends and subject herself to what was sure to be a miserable ride home. If May could evade her now, it would be easy enough to get lost in the crush again.

Her mind made up, she sent a meaningful look to her friends. "I have a sudden and overwhelming desire for a spot of tea. Rest assured, I shall return shortly."

With a quick wave, she hurried away toward the closest door, which she knew led to the Octagon. Traveling along the perimeter, she slipped through to the crowded hall, keeping her gaze to her feet and her walk to a brisk, purposeful pace meant to discourage interruption. The door across the way put her into the Tea Room, where she skirted along the back wall to the farthest possible spot from where her aunt had been.

Pausing to take a breath, she glanced across the sea of finely coifed heads, making certain Aunt Victoria wasn't in pursuit. "Blast," she muttered when the bobbing purple ostrich feather came into view. Making a split-second decision, she pulled open the side door and darted into the warm, damp night air, quickly closing the door behind her.

Exhaling, she turned and surveyed her surroundings. She'd never been on this side of the building, which was significantly less polished than the elegant front entrance. A long row of waiting carriages lined the pavement, standing at the ready for whenever their owners should decide to leave. Several surprised drivers glanced over to her, but quickly averted their attention. Obviously well trained, to a man, if they knew not to question the sudden appearance of a gowned and bejeweled young woman dashing from the Assembly Rooms this time of night.

"May I help you?"

May jumped sideways, startled by the clipped words that were chilly enough to freeze the English Channel. Standing in the shadows to the left of the door was a lone figure in dark clothes, a lit cheroot held idly in his left hand.

"I require no assistance, thank you," she responded, automatically lifting her chin with regal disdain. It was a gesture she hated in her aunt, but it came naturally enough when confronted with a tall, dark, and unwanted stranger.

In the dim light, his eyes narrowed. "I don't believe it. Did Dering send you out here?" The words were ripe with accusation.

Dering's name gave her pause. What the devil did he have to do with anything? She was certain she didn't know this man from Adam. She was also certain that she did not care one bit for the way he spoke to her. "Not at all," she said coolly. "Why, did he send you out here?"

He threw the half-smoked cheroot to the pavement and ground it beneath his heel. "Nice try, Miss Bradford. You may tell our mutual friend that I was in no way ex- aggerating when I said I was not interested." A flick of his eyes communicated his aloof dismissal of her.

Affront flooded through her as she grasped his mean- ing. Why the conceited, self-centered jackass! How was it that he even knew her name? She had no idea who the man was, and more to the point, she had no desire to know who he was. Her hands went to her hips, heedless of the fact that she was crushing the delicate fabric of her gown. "And *you* may tell our mutual friend that he needs to be more discerning when choosing his acquaintances. Had he actually arranged this little rendezvous, I would have told him quite plainly of my intention not to associate with arrogant, conclusion-jumping Englishmen."

He stepped forward, revealing himself to the weak lamplight behind her. Chiseled jaw, long arrow-straight nose, wide, full lips—he wasn't overtly handsome, but he certainly had an aura of power and authority. Doubtless, he was used to females falling at his feet. Well, she was no ordinary female, unfortunately for him. She stood her ground, glaring right back at him.

One disdainful dark eyebrow lifted as he shook his head slowly. "So the cat hisses when her schemes are ruined. You do yourself and your aunt a grave disservice, Miss Bradford. Now then, turn around and march yourself back inside like a good little debutante. With any luck, perhaps your aunt will never learn of your machinations."

Machinations? "First of all, you have me at the disadvantage, sir, as I haven't the least idea of who you are—*not* that I wish to. Secondly, I have as much a right to be out here as you do. If you have a problem with it, I suggest you march *yourself* back inside like a good little gentleman."

"Your Grace," he bit off.

"My grace ... what? Leaves you in such awe you cannot finish sentences?"

His eyes narrowed further so that they were little more than dark slits against his pale skin. "You misunderstand. As the Duke of Radcliffe, you should address me as Your Grace."

She cringed inwardly, only just managing to keep the surprise from her expression. Damnation, *this* was the Duke of Radcliffe? It would be her luck that she would inadvertently lock horns with one of the most powerful men in all of Britain. The very man, in fact, whom Aunt Victoria had been so worried May would offend.

She took a deep breath, willing herself to close her mouth against his insufferable arrogance. Heaven knew what her aunt would do if she ever learned of this meeting.

Just when she was about to turn and walk away, at the very moment she had convinced herself to ignore the man and his loutish ways, she made the mistake of meeting his gaze. The amount of pure, unadulterated conceit and imperiousness she saw there was like a dagger to her pride. He thought he had put her in her place!

Almost before she even knew what she was about, she crossed her arms and said, "One would think that as duke, you would have a better grasp of proper grammar. Given your sentence structure, you just referred to *me* as the Duke of Radcliffe."

It wasn't a horrible thing to say. Just a little prick to that massive ego to let him know that he had in no way cowed her. Granted, her rejoinder might have been grasping at straws, but in all fairness to herself, it was hard to put together a proper retort when he was looking down his dukish nose at her. The man seemed to radiate authority and power the way coal radiated heat.

"Proper grammar?" he repeated, incredulous. "Perhaps before you devolve into schoolroom lessons on word choice, you might attempt to remember your clearly lacking tutelage on etiquette. Society takes no umbrage at a grown man out alone on darkened streets. Females, on the other hand, should have a care for both their reputation and their personal safety."

May scowled. Did he think to lecture her like a wayward child? "I have survived darkened streets the world over, *Your Grace*. Not to mention darkened ships, darkened jungles, and darkened villages. I sincerely doubt a moderately dim street in the middle of Bath shall get the best of me now."

Speaking of the street, it had gone noticeably quiet. The grooms and drivers who had been chatting among themselves were now avid witnesses to her confrontation with the duke.

Judging by his flexing cheek muscles, Radcliffe wasn't pleased by her riposte. "Such pridefulness for what sounds like an exceptionally base existence." He swept his hand out, encompassing the elegant limestone buildings and well-paved street. "We are not on a ship, in a jungle, or near a village. We are in a thriving metropolitan area where the greatest danger lies in the wagging of a gossip's tongue. Given your behavior, however, it is entirely possible that such a fate is exactly what you hope for."

And there he went again, accusing her of those *machinations*. "Of course it is," she retorted without missing a beat. "Subjecting myself to that delightful personality of yours is just a bonus." The man's ego probably required a separate carriage in which to transport the sheer mass of it.

"Sarcasm is very unbecoming on a lady, Miss Bradford." His patronizing tone was enough to make her teeth grind. The duke and her aunt must have had the exact same tutor for their "How to Talk Down to Others" lessons.

Fluttering her eyelashes innocently, she said, "Is it? Please, enlighten me further about how I can be a proper lady." She said the words even as she knew that she was allowing things to get out of hand. The prudent thing to do would be to close her mouth, turn away from the man's infuriatingly arrogant self, and retreat back inside

Prudence, however, had never been her strong suit.

They stood there in silent deadlock, neither one willing to leave and allow the other victory. The warm night air began to feel the slightest bit suffocating and she could feel a flush rising up her neck and blooming across her cheeks, but she held her ground, staring back at the maddening duke.

She knew his type. Arrogant, powerful, accustomed to respect no matter how he treated others. He was everything she couldn't stand about the aristocracy. A person should earn respect by his actions, not by his birth. Her father hadn't started life with a silver spoon in his mouth. He had worked hard for years to prove himself worthy of promotion after promotion.

He was a captain because of a lifetime of bravery, work, and determination. This man, on the other hand, had done nothing more than survive birth. And yet he clearly thought himself superior to her, and probably every other person he encountered. Straightening her spine, she met his piercing gaze with a smile of pure innocence. If he thought to outlast her, he was about to find out that she was prepared to wait all night.

After a long, pregnant moment, the duke reached into his jacket, pulled out another cheroot, and walked the half dozen steps to light it on the nearest coach lantern. He had to know the figure he cut when viewed from behind. May had always preferred men with strong, capable physiques, and somehow this pampered duke managed to possess just that. Rather annoying, really.

The cut of his lavishly expensive jacket, with its shiny silver-and-gold buttons and silver threaded hem, showed off every inch of his broad shoulders and long, lean torso. It was so close fitting, in fact, the fabric seemed on a mission to prove that there wasn't an ounce to be pinched anywhere on the man's body.

Not that it mattered to her.

After taking a long, surely exaggerated pull, he exhaled a cloud of smoke and turned to face her, his head tilted slightly to the side. "Do you know, I believe you actually did speak the truth when you said that Dering did not send you after me. He would never wish for a friend to endure one of such boorish manners."

"Precisely," she said with a decisive nod, her lips curling into a triumphant grin. "He likes me far too well to play such a prank on me."

Aha! She'd won that round. His smug expression fell just the slightest bit as he realized how neatly she had appropriated his insult. Knowing she had the upper hand, she manufactured a small yawn. "And now I find that I'm bored to death with those manners and this conversation. I do *so* hope you enjoy the remainder of your evening, Your Grace."

Turning on her heel, May took two victorious steps toward the building before the door suddenly swung open, and the very last person May wished to see stepped outside.

Bloody, bloody hell.

Chapter Three

Things had not gone well for William following the concert. When he'd descended the stairs after the final performance, two of the young women he had evaded earlier had been lying in wait. They'd pounced as soon as his foot touched the last step, and had proven to be relentlessly forward. When he'd finally disentangled himself from them, a pair of men from the continent had set upon him, apparently eager to meet the highest ranking person in attendance.

He'd managed to escape outside, but he hadn't been there five minutes when Miss Bradford had so thoroughly and gleefully shattered his peace. For that reason, the satisfaction William felt at the look on Miss Bradford's face was almost sinfully good. It might have been petty—very well, it most certainly was petty—but he welcomed the surge of gratification that raced through him in that moment.

"Lady Stanwix," he said, dipping his head in greeting. "A pleasure to see you again."

Surprise registered in her narrowed gaze as she jerked her head toward where William stood. Her eyes widened almost comically and the look of fury was quickly replaced by a one of muted horror. "Your Grace! I beg your pardon, I didn't realize you were out here. With my niece," she added, obviously confused.

"I daresay she had a similar reaction upon discovering my presence," he replied dryly. He directed his attention to the interloper herself and said, "My apologies for having intruded on your solitude, Miss Bradford. It is never my intention to be where I am so plainly not wanted."

The girl scowled at him suspiciously. Wondering if he was purposely calling her out for her conduct, perhaps? William offered her the same look of innocence she had bestowed upon him earlier. There were consequences to one's behavior, something that she'd do well to realize sooner rather than later now that she had joined society.

Lady Stanwix's lips compressed into a thin, ominous line as she sent an icy look toward her ward. She no doubt could guess just how welcoming the girl had been. Returning her attention to William, the countess shook her head. "You must excuse my niece. She was raised in the wilds of the East, and despite my best effort, has yet to understand the fine nuances of civilized behavior. If she has been anything less than gracious, I hope you will accept my most abject apology on her behalf."

William was fully aware of the rudeness of speaking of the girl as if she wasn't standing right there, her eyes hot with fury and her lovely white teeth no doubt grinding. If she hadn't already been so spectacularly rude to him, he might be inclined to feel badly about it. But she had, and he wasn't.

Shaking his head gravely, he offered the countess his most commiserate look. "Such a terrible burden for one with such impeccable manners and station. You have my sympathies, madam."

The older woman dipped her head regally, causing the purple feather at her crown to sway precariously close to his forehead. "Thank you, Duke. You are most understanding. Now I think it best that I escort my niece home before she can cause any more offense."

Just as William suspected, the girl couldn't keep her mouth shut for long. Stepping between them, she said, "Offense such as speaking of a person as though said person were not present?" She lifted a single blond brow. "Yes, such a thing would be egregious, I agree."

The countess's eyes narrowed ominously. "May," she said, her voice sharp with warning, "I strongly suggest you keep your tongue behind your teeth for once. We shall talk more when we are home."

William's impassive expression almost slipped. *May?* Such an innocuous name for such an overbearing female. Make that an *unwise* female. Despite her guardian's unmistakable threat, he could already see the retort forming on the girl's lips.

The last thing he needed was the pair of them descending into a squawking match sure to draw the notice of gossips. Stepping forward, he grabbed May's hand and lifted it toward his lips for a civilized dismissal that was intended to shock her into silence. "Good evening, Miss Bradford," he said firmly before pressing his lips to—

Thin air.

The impertinent chit had snatched her hand back! She smiled blandly despite the daggers in her gaze. "And to you, Your Grace."

The movement had been subtle enough that it was likely she thought it would go unnoticed in the dark, but he saw the countess's eyes widen briefly before narrowing to angry slits. Whatever was about to transpire between the lady and her ward was none of his concern.

Straightening, he nodded tightly to Lady Stanwix before stalking to his carriage. He had endured quite enough of the dramatics of bothersome females for one night and he intended to put as much distance between himself and the blond vixen-turned-shrew as possible.

It was only when he'd vaulted up into the dark, sumptuous interior of his carriage that he realized that he'd just allowed her to win their little standoff: He'd been the one to walk away.

The vacuum of silence left by the duke's departure was all the more deafening for what she knew was coming. His blithe words had virtually guaranteed her aunt's fury, drat the man.

Straightening her shoulders—preparing for battle, really—May turned to face her aunt. She was momentarily taken aback. The older woman's eyes glittered menacingly in the dim light, as hard and cold as the diamonds draped across her throat. She nearly vibrated with the fury and tension that stiffened her joints. She looked as brittle as glass, as though a single tap would shatter her control.

There was a more than fair chance that her aunt had witnessed May tugging her hand away, despite the dim light. She hadn't intended to do such a thing, but everything in her had rebelled against the thought of that insufferable man's lips upon her hand, gloved or otherwise. Lifting her chin, May said calmly, "Shall I collect my wrap so we may leave?"

Aunt Victoria made a low sound of disgust in her throat as she closed the short distance between them. "First, you lead me on a merry chase through the whole of the Assembly Rooms. *Then* you make a fool of yourself *and* me in front of one of the most highly ranked men in the *ton*. Why in heaven would I let you out of my sight now?"

The ostrich plume quivered as she shook her head. "No," she said, slicing a hand through the air, the glint of diamonds flashing like bottled lightning. "No, you will not collect your things. No, you will not speak to your friends. No, you will not embarrass me again, you ungrateful child. You will leave with me this very moment. You will confine yourself to your chambers, and you will think about what you have done."

May knew she should keep her mouth shut, she really did, but she also couldn't bear not to defend herself. "I have done no more and no less than the duke himself has done. If you are not angry with him, then why should you be angry with me?"

Her aunt's finger wagged perilously close to May's nose. "I'll not have any back talk from you. That man is the Duke of Radcliffe, one of the most powerful and respected men in not only England, but in the entire world. It is not my concern how he chooses to comport himself. In any event, I very much doubt he behaved as anything other than a gentleman."

"But—"

"Moreover," she continued, rolling right over May's attempt to speak, "whatever did occur between the two of you was entirely your fault for having come out here in the first place. What were you *thinking*?"

May very nearly told her exactly what she'd been thinking, but some long-dormant sense of self-preservation kept her lips sealed for once. Her aunt had always been unyielding and disagreeable, but May had never seen her quite this furious before. She thought of her father, and his heartfelt pleading for her to be on her very best behavior for his sister, no matter how difficult it seemed.

Swallowing her pride and anger, she lowered her gaze

to the stone pavers at her feet. "I suppose I wasn't. My apologies." That last word stuck in her throat like day-old toast.

Her aunt was quiet for a moment, no doubt suspicious of May's capitulation. Finally, her lavender skirts rustled as she turned toward the street. "John Coachman?" she called, despite the likelihood that most of the men out there responded to the exact name. "We wish to leave."

Remarkably, the appropriate Stanwix servant promptly responded, "Yes, m'lady."

Dread gathered in May's chest, and she took a long, slow breath. No doubt every servant out here would be buzzing with gossip when their employers arrived. She didn't give a fig what the people of Bath thought of her, but the more people knew of it, the more her aunt would punish her.

Not that Aunt Victoria needed an excuse. The woman had been critical of May's every move since the moment she had arrived to stay with her. Her clothes were too exotic, her vocabulary too vulgar, her manners too coarse, and her skin too tan. She was overly tall and inadequately educated in the exceedingly important British societal hierarchy.

To be fair, May would give her that last one. What use did she have for a system she never planned to be a part of? By the time her father returned, he would have recovered from his grief enough to realize leaving her here had been a dreadful overreaction. Not that she could really blame him. Mama's death had been indescribably difficult for them both. But it had almost been a year, and May was more than ready to go home.

Home. Even the word brought a pang of sadness to her heart. Her mother had always said that home was where one's heart resides, not necessarily where one's head lies at night.

The carriage arrived then, its shiny black paint and gold coat of arms somberly reflecting the firelight, even as the interior seemed as dark as pitch.

Within minutes they were on their way, the steady tap of the horses' hooves counting off second by uncomfortable second. After what seemed like hours, Aunt Victoria finally cleared her throat. "The Duke of Radcliffe is an ally we cannot afford to offend. I don't know what possessed you to behave so abysmally, but it is an error in judgment that shall not be repeated."

May clamped her teeth together and nodded. If she valued what little freedom she might have left, it was the best tactic . . . no matter how much she wanted to argue. Besides, she had no intention of ever talking to the man again, so it was unlikely she would offend him.

"As for your behavior tonight, I don't know what you said before I arrived, but it was clear to me that the duke had taken exception. You will apologize to the duke— *sincerely*—and do whatever it takes to earn his forgiveness."

May was perfectly amenable to apologizing to the duke. Just as soon as he apologized to her. After all, he was the one who set the tone of the encounter by accusing her of those vague but dastardly machinations. She almost laughed, imagining him apologizing.

Pigs would fly before Radcliffe ate crow.

Aunt Victoria continued on, unknowing and likely uncaring of May's thoughts on the issue. "Until such time that you are able to accomplish this goal, you are to be confined to your chambers. No visits from your friends, no constitutionals, none of the festival events. I won't even have you visiting the music room until you've made things right. Is that clear?"

May's stomach tipped at her aunt's words. Good God, the woman could not be serious. Sentences for smuggling had been less harsh than this. "And how, exactly, am I to gain the forgiveness of the man if I'm never to leave the house again?"

"When you are ready to speak with him, I shall send a note requesting his indulgence in calling upon us."

May was exceedingly grateful for the inky darkness. She could hold her silence, but hiding the outrage from her face would have been impossible, which would have only served to further anger her aunt. And even as she mentally rebelled against the thought of facing the duke with her proverbial hat in her hands, there was one thing that kept the situation from being unbearable: her aunt's rigid schedule.

As far as May was concerned, her aunt's dictates stood only while the woman was awake. There was nothing to keep May from waltzing out the door in the morning for her normal routine. Aunt Victoria was an unpleasant woman to live with, which meant that the servants were not particularly loyal to her—a fact that May happily and frequently exploited.

Still, this was not the life of freedom she was accustomed to. The weight in her chest that had been so familiar since her father left swelled again, leaving her a little breathless. She craved that old freedom that came not from lack of walls, but from lack of oppression. Her parents had always respected her, even when she was very young. They had listened to her, and talked with her, not at her. They had loved her unconditionally, regardless of what clothes she wore or how she spoke.

It was becoming more and more apparent to her just how unusual her upbringing was. Not the sailing or the exotic locales—though those too were unusual—but the love and support she had received.

"Well? Answer me, child," her aunt demanded, yanking May from her thoughts. "Have I made myself clear?"

Staring straight ahead in the darkness, May nodded once. "Crystal clear, Aunt." Closing her eyes, she settled back against the squabs and allowed the rocking of the carriage to remind her of the rocking of the ship that would soon be taking her home.

"And here I thought you didn't indulge in spirits."

William's hand tightened around the crystal tumbler at the sound of his stepmother's low, overly sensual voice. "I'm not certain why you should think of me at all." He didn't bother to clarify that it was only white wine. He preferred a clear mind to the oblivion strong spirits offered. "Or why you are here at such an unseemly hour."

It was nearly midnight, well past the time for paying a proper visit. Something he was certain she knew full well. Vivian gave a delicate Parisian shrug and sauntered toward him, her ruby lips lifted ever so slightly at the corners. She moved the way water slipped around rocks in a shallow stream, fluid and graceful at every turn. It was all calculated, of course. Custom-designed to make men of power weak at the knees.

Luckily for William, it only ever made him weak of stomach.

She stopped less than a foot away and reached for his glass. He readily surrendered it, unwilling to allow her fingers—or any part of her—to brush his skin. Lifting the tumbler to her lips, she took a small sip, her eyes never leaving his. "Wine?" she said, one auburn brow lifting. "Your father preferred brandy."

He was not in the mood to discuss anything with her, especially his father. "Was there something you wanted?"

"I heard you had arrived, and thought perhaps you would wish to see me." She ran a finger along the rim of the cup, then licked the moisture from her fingertip. She was beautiful in the way a panther was, sleek and grace-ful, but with a danger to her that meant he could never let his guard down around her.

Again, he silently amended. Never let his guard down around her *again*.

Casually, he took the glass from her and stepped over to the sideboard. It was more an excuse to put distance between them than anything else. He exchanged the used tumbler for a fresh goblet and filled it with red wine. Without looking up from his task, he said, "And why would I wish to see you?"

She gave a little chuckle. "Because you always wish to see me when you leave Clifton House."

He replaced the crystal stopper on the decanter and swirled the liquid in his glass, watching the way it smoothly coated the sides. "Indeed. So let us dispense with the needless subtleties. You've gotten my attention, as I'm sure was your intention. Once again, I'm forced to implore you to show some discretion, both in your activ-ities and your choice of companions."

"A bit jealous, are we?"

His lip lifted in disgust. "I won't justify that with a response."

"So you haven't changed your mind?" There was the ever-present invitation in her pouty voice, but no real hope, thank God.

"There is a better chance of me moving to France than there is of me changing my mind."

He looked up in enough time to catch the tiny flare of her nostrils in the oval mirror on the wall over the sideboard. Good. His barb had hit its mark. Still, there was no way Vivian was going to give up that easily. She met his eyes in the mirror and fingered the Radcliffe rubies at her neck. "You would like France. The weather is so much more pleasant than England, especially in the south."

It was more than he could ever remember her saying about her homeland, but he was too preoccupied with her necklace to care. He hated that she wore his mother's jewels. His father had given her the few pieces that weren't entailed, in addition to showering her with new jewelry. She seemed to prefer the old ones, however. The ones William remembered catching glimpses of in his childhood on the rare occasions he'd seen his mother dressed for parties before she had died when he was six. Turning abruptly, he settled his unamused gaze directly on her. "It's late. You don't have to go home, but I don't want you here."

She smiled then, not her real smile, but the angelic one she always reserved for those who didn't know any better. "But I wish to see my children. Surely you didn't leave them in the country like so much cattle?"

If William was a man given to dramatics, he would have rolled his eyes. "They are at Clifton House with their nurse and governess. Bath is no place for children."

"Mmm," Vivian murmured, nodding. "I suppose I can ride back with you when you return after the festival. When should I be ready?"

She was attempting to manipulate him, of course. But he would never punish the children by keeping them from their mother whenever she decided they were convenient.

"Why not go now? They'll be delighted to see you."

She gave a dismissive flip of her hand. "Too many engagements between now and then. I wouldn't want to back out on my word."

Yes, he could just imagine how much she'd hate that. "I'll send word next week," he said, taking solace in the fact that he would at least be riding on horseback while she rode in his carriage. Her pleased smile grated, but he refused to let it show. "Now if you'll excuse me, I believe I shall retire for the night."

Her hazel eyes seemed to suddenly smolder in the low firelight. The flickering shadows served to highlight the lush swell of her bosom and the small waist beneath her sheer gown as she clasped her hands behind her back. "Would you like some company?"

For the space of a single breath, the image of Miss Bradford flashed in his mind, her eyes sparkling with passion and her exquisite figure only inches away. When he blinked, it was gone, and only his stepmother remained. "Go home, Vivian. I'll let you know if your company is ever desired."

If she counted on that, she'd spend the rest of her life waiting.

Chapter Four

William had been to Bath enough times to know that his early-morning rides were unlikely to be interrupted. It was one of the things he liked about the city. If, by chance, he did happen to see another person about, it was almost certainly a servant or business owner, rushing on to his duties with head down and brisk, no-nonsense strides.

So when he happened upon the figure in the park before the sun had even crested the horizon, it brought him up short. For a brief moment, he thought it might be an apparition; some sort of beautiful, ghostly presence gliding along the mist-cloaked shores of the River Avon. But as he'd drawn closer, he'd realized it was no specter—it was the spectacularly rude chit from last night.

Immediately his jaw tightened, displeasure turning down the corners of his mouth. With the possible exception of Vivian, Miss Bradford was the last person he wanted to see this morning. And what a sight she was, outfitted in the most bizarre, scandalous ensemble he had ever laid eyes on. What did she think she was doing, traipsing about in the park this time of day, dressed like that?

Her long, lean legs were on full display, encased in

some sort of silky, loose-fitting trousers. The matching tunic was high-collared but only just covered her bottom. Scratch that—it *almost* covered her bottom. The curve of it was visible as she moved from one position to the next.

And that wasn't the only curve he could see.

As she moved, the fabric of the tunic momentarily pulled taut across her chest, giving him a tantalizing glimpse of the swell of her breasts before she transitioned to a different stance.

He swallowed, remembering the moment she had flashed through his mind the night before. *Would you like some company?* Almost as quickly as that thought surfaced, the memory of her sharp tongue and appalling manners crowded it out. And really, the woman must have some sort of death wish. What kind of mad fool must she be to be out here looking the way she did, completely vulnerable and alone?

Sliding from his saddle, he flicked the reins around a nearby branch and marched toward the clearing. He might hardly dislike the girl, but he was too much of a gentleman to allow her own folly to cause her harm. Her aunt couldn't possibly know she was here. What if some blackguard set upon her? Not only was she vulnerable, she was practically bait.

He stalked toward her, waiting for the moment that she looked up and realized she was no longer alone.

Only she didn't look up.

It was as though she was lost in her own world, totally focused on her odd, seemingly pointless movements. A sweep of her hands here, the slide of her foot there—each move seemed to segue directly into another with such slow, deliberate movements, it was like watching time at half its normal speed.

It was strangely mesmerizing.

Almost against his will, he slowed and watched her. She kept her body low, with her knees bent even as she stepped forward and back, then side to side as though creeping through an invisible labyrinth. With each step, her arms moved in a different way: reaching for the ground, sweeping along her sides, extending straight out in front of her. The silky fabric of her clothing responded to each step, slithering up and down the delicate length of her forearms and sliding along her long, slender legs.

His eye naturally followed the line of her calf, and when he reached her ankle, his brows rose in surprise. She wasn't wearing any shoes. That realization snapped him from his trance. A grown woman, barefoot in a city park, was beyond the pale. Straightening his shoulders, he stepped a few feet closer and cleared his throat.

She started violently, snapping upright and turning her wide and incredibly blue eyes toward him. He stared straight at her, allowing the full force of his disapproval to saturate his gaze and weigh the corners of his mouth. Miss Bradford stared right back at him, her own gaze frosting over with displeasure.

At the very least, it was safe to say she recognized him.

A hundred questions darted through May's mind as she glared at the disapproving duke. How had he found her? Had he been looking for her? An even worse thought assailed her: Did her aunt break her normal routine and know that she was missing? She valiantly worked to keep her expression even, refusing to give him the satisfaction of seeing her flustered.

With deliberate insolence, she straightened to her full height and put her hands to her hips. "See something of interest?"

His dark eyes were cool and calculating as he raked his gaze up and down her silk-clad form. In that moment, despite being covered much more thoroughly than she would have been in a normal gown, she felt practically naked beneath his scathing inspection. Exactly as he intended, no doubt. When he'd completed the inspection, he met her eyes and shook his head. "Not in the least."

Liar. She'd been around men her entire life. She certainly knew interest when she saw it. She also knew when she wanted nothing to do with it. Still, with her pride smarting, she couldn't stop herself from responding. "And yet here you are, intruding on my private time."

The sharp, arrogant slant of his cheekbones hardened as he flexed his jaw. "You are in *public*, Miss Bradford, where any poor soul may be subjected to your presence. I strongly suggest you dress and act accordingly next time."

Subjected to her presence? She wasn't a leper, for heaven's sake. "I shall always act as myself, whether I am in private or public. Just as you, I suspect, shall always act the overbearing ass."

Apparently the duke wasn't accustomed to hearing the truth. His nostrils flared with affront, but he kept a tight rein on the flash of anger she saw in his eyes. "Such a pity you were never taught proper respect for your betters. Resorting to name-calling only serves to highlight your own ignorance and lack of decorum. As does this exceedingly inappropriate . . . ensemble." He nodded toward her as though she wore rags instead of the world's finest silk. "What is it that you were doing, dressed like that?"

There was that interest again. Disdain, yes, but it was clear he was also intrigued.

"Ever heard of martial arts? Or is that too base for your civilized English sensibilities?"

A light gust of wind blew up from the river, daring to ruffle the hair that flipped out from beneath the rim of his hat. That made at least two things he held no power over: her and the elements. The thought almost made her smile. Once upon a time, her mother had likened her to a force of nature.

He took a slow step toward her, his expression dubious. "I am aware of martial arts. They are techniques used in combat or defense, and in no way resemble what you were doing just now."

Because he was obviously such an authority. He'd likely never even rolled up his sleeves before, let alone engaged in combat of any sort in the whole of his pampered life.

"Martial arts is more than fighting. It's communing with one's body, mind, and soul. There are the hard versions—the ones that concentrate on defensive and offensive moves intended for protection. But some forms also have a soft version, like what I engage in. The purpose is to focus the mind solely on the movements in order to bring about calmness and clarity."

He lifted an eyebrow. Had she surprised him? For a moment, something dangerously close to respect hinted in his eyes, but then it was as though a shade was dropped, and once again he was regarding her as though she'd just claimed to have been to the moon. "Calmness and clarity?" he scoffed, amusement lightening his words. "Keep practicing. It's fair to say the point of the exercise has been lost on you."

Yes, of course. Far be it from him to acknowledge that

she might actually know what she was talking about. The level of condescension that he exuded must have taken a lifetime to develop. Did they give lessons for that sort of thing? In between world history and literature lessons, perhaps? She could just imagine him as a six-year-old practicing his patronizing stares in the mirror with a tutor nodding approvingly behind him.

"I would, but *someone* decided to interject himself into my practice. Might I suggest you take yourself somewhere you're actually welcome? I'm sure there are dozens of young ladies around who would simply love to bask in the glow of your magnificent ego."

His dour expression remained intact as he said, "I sympathize for your poor aunt. Attempting to mold a person of such advanced age and stunted manners into something respectable must be an incredibly thankless pursuit."

Crossing her arms, she glared at him. "Of course you sympathize. You and your ilk are always threatened by that which you cannot control. It threatens your perceived superiority that I do as I want, how I want, without bowing to your opinions or dictates."

His eyes narrowed slightly. "I do believe it is your *aunt's* sensibilities that you should be worrying about. For I am absolutely certain that she knows nothing of this little rebellion of yours. I hate to imagine how such a shock would affect the poor woman." The implication was clear.

May's brows shot up. "Is that a threat? Do you plan to run and tattle on me as though we were children?"

He pursed his lips as though considering it. "No, I think not. However, once again there is clearly a matter of safety here. Since you show so little regard for your own well-being, I see no choice but to take up the task myself." She could practically see the smugness rolling off him in waves. He knew he had the upper hand here.

The silk of her sleeve slipped across her skin as she jabbed a finger at her own chest. "The task is mine, and mine alone. Your only task is to leave me be."

He shook his head slowly, as though regretful, but she knew full well he was enjoying this. "The choice is yours, Miss Bradford. Either I escort you home, or I send word to your aunt that it is necessary for her to provide an escort."

The spleeny rats-bane. Why the devil did he care? There was absolutely no reason he should be taunting her like this, other than the fact that he could. Was he happy only when he was compelling others to bend to his will?

"Your choices are absurd," she bit out. "I am perfectly capable of taking care of myself."

"Oh?" he said, tilting his head disdainfully. "You think yourself capable of withstanding an attack on your person?"

"Absolutely. I was raised among sailors, my lord; I know a thing or two about how to look after myself." In fact, she could fight both dirty and fair, depending on the situation. Hopefully, he would consider himself warned.

He stepped closer, far too close for her state of mind, but she refused to retreat. "It's 'Your Grace,'" he corrected, his warm breath licking faintly across her cheek. "And I think you vastly overstate your abilities. You may be tall for a woman, but you are still dwarfed by a man of my size."

God, but he smelled good. Even through her frustration, even though she could have happily smacked the smug grin from his perfect lips, some part of her recognized the elemental maleness of him. He smelled of strength and barely leashed power, like a racehorse poised at the starting line.

The fact that something inside of her responded to him made her want to rebel only that much more. She lifted her chin, never so thankful in all her life for her height as she was at that moment. "If you are asking for a demonstration, I will happily oblige."

He shook his head slowly, his eyes still locked with hers. "Your bravado would be impressive, Miss Bradford, if it weren't so clearly just that: bravado. As it is, you are no match for a man who—"

And just like that, the lofty Duke of Radcliffe went over her shoulder.

Chapter Five

For the space of three seconds—an eternity, at least—William lay flat on his back, stunned. One moment, he had been conversing with the Bradford chit, and the next, he was blinking up at the pale pink sky.

She leaned over him, her face little more than a dark outline against the brightening sky. "Well, I did warn you," she said, her voice utterly matter-of-fact.

He closed his eyes and rolled onto his side, drawing a deep breath in order to reinflate his lungs. He would have never, ever guessed she was capable of something like that. Threads of irritation, grudging respect, embarrassment, and pain tangled in his chest as he sought to compose himself.

So she was right about taking care of herself. But that didn't negate the fact that someone of her station simply couldn't be out here like this. And what if more than one person set upon her? Both her reputation and her person were still vulnerable, and now that he was invested, he felt responsible for her.

Shaking his head, he pushed himself into a sitting position. "I could have you thrown in gaol for that, you know."

She rolled her eyes and leaned down to grab his arm. "Oh, do go on. You were pushing me to show you I can take care of myself, so I did." Her grip was strong despite her long, delicate fingers and she had him to his feet before he could even protest.

He could not believe she had just thrown him over her shoulder like a sack of potatoes. As though he wasn't at least four stone heavier and a good five inches taller. He'd never condone such behavior, but he really was impressed. Of course, she had the element of surprise on her side—who on earth would have anticipated such an action?

Pulling his arm from her grasp, he took a deliberate step back. "Apparently 'taking care of oneself' in your eyes means assaulting the very person who was attempting to assist you."

"Assist me?" she repeated, doubt liberally coating the words. "You were attempting to *intimidate* me."

True enough. It was a tactic that had served him well his entire life. "Because you were being obstinate. How else was one to get through that exceedingly stubborn head of yours?"

"But that's the point! You didn't *need* to get through. I am perfectly safe out here on my own."

Based on her little stunt, he was inclined to agree with her. The male population of Bath would do well to steer clear of her. But after how the encounter had gone, he absolutely was not about to let her simply waltz away, thumbing her nose at him and every civilized person in this city. He was committed to this now.

"But you clearly know that your presence here, at this time of morning and without the benefit of a chaperone, is wrong. Why else would you fear I would 'tattle' to your aunt? You may have been raised outside of society, but

you must submit to its rules now that you are part of it."
God knew he did. Everything he did was deliberately
aligned with what was expected of him.

"So you keep telling me," she said, unimpressed. "But
I'm not harming anyone, and it's not as though I'm running some sort of smuggling ring. I'm simply enjoying a
bit of morning exercise."

It was remarkable that someone of her beliefs and
manners could look so regal. Despite her scandalous
clothing and her simple braided hairstyle, she looked utterly self-assured and almost irritatingly beautiful. As
much as she was frustrating him, she also intrigued him.
Her behavior was as far from feminine as he could imagine, but still his body responded to her. There was an
undeniable attraction there, whether he admitted it or
not.

And if he was taking that much notice of her, he certainly wasn't the only one.

He shook his head, exasperated. "You can't possibly
be that naïve. You worry that your aunt will learn of your
outrageous behavior, yet you are not even attempting to
be discreet. Even if your physical person is not under
threat, your reputation most certainly is."

"Once again, that is none of your concern. Why don't
you turn around, collect your horse, and carry on with
your morning ride? Pretend we never met." There was
no more anger in her voice. She was speaking matter-of-
factly now, as though she'd already dismissed him.

"Would that I could," he muttered. He bent to retrieve his hat from the ground, brushed off the moisture,
and set it back on his head. "I cannot call myself a gentleman were I to leave you here. Gather your things, I'm
taking you home."

"No, I—"

"Allow me to rephrase," he said, his patience at an end. "I am going to Lady Stanwix's home one way or the other. Either you accompany me and I deposit you before the front door, or I go alone and demand an audience with your aunt."

All at once, her eyes went huge. "An audience? With my aunt?" She wilted before his eyes, groaning aloud. "Bloody hell," she murmured, smoothing a hand over her hair.

Stiffening at the curse, he regarded her censoriously. "Is there a problem, Miss Bradford?"

Oddly enough, for the first time she seemed genuinely distressed. That flippant little grin of hers was noticeably absent, and she started walking toward where her things waited in an untidy heap on the ground. "Yes, there most definitely is," she said over her shoulder.

The woman was an enigma. He waited while she lifted her jacket and jammed her arms through the sleeves. "I don't suppose there is something you are lacking in this life, is there Radcliffe? Money, baked goods, or perhaps a bodyguard?"

What on earth was she talking about? Walking toward her—cautiously—he shook his head. "I have everything I could ever need or desire and then some," he answered, honestly. "Why do you ask?"

"Are you certain?" she replied, stepping into her shoes. "Everything? There's absolutely nothing you could wish for?"

A loaded question if he'd ever heard one. Everyone in the country assumed he had everything he could ever want. The envy and jealousy of those below him was palpable nearly everywhere he went. In their eyes, he held all of the cards in life, and they held none. He had worked hard to prove himself worthy of the respect and wealth the title held, but he couldn't change the way some people were determined to see him.

What they didn't seem to see was that he was still human. Money and power would never fill all of his needs or even wants. But he was a duke, and a duke did not discuss that which might or might not be lacking in his life. Deflecting the query, he said, "Is there a point to this line of questioning, Miss Bradford?"

She turned to face him fully, her extraordinary eyes momentarily distracting him. Surely the sky had never been so blue as that sapphire gaze of hers. "Sometime today you will receive a missive from my aunt inviting you to visit. She has it in her mind that I have wounded your tender sensibilities and wishes for me to apologize."

His tender sensibilities? If she was attempting to ingratiate herself with him, she could use some work on her approach. "And you refuse to do so."

"Not at all," she said, pulling a pair of gloves from a hidden pocket in her coat and working them on. "I fully intend to throw myself upon your mercy. I'm only telling you this now so that you can be prepared for the encounter. A simple 'I accept' from you, and I shall be out of your hair forever."

"If that is all it will take," he said, conspicuously brushing a blade of grass from his jacket sleeve, "consider yourself pardoned." The woman was more or less a scandal just waiting to happen. She was exactly the type of person he typically strove to avoid.

That bravado of hers slipped even more as she shook her head. "I'm afraid you must wait until the apology has been issued before you accept."

His eyes narrowed a bit. What was she up to now? "Why would I do that? I have no desire to go through the ceremony of it all. That would defeat the purpose of having you out of my hair, as you put it."

She looked to the ground a moment before sighing and meeting his gaze again. The frankness he saw there was disconcerting. "I'm afraid my aunt won't believe it, otherwise. She is determined to see you accept my groveling apology."

He crossed his arms. "I like your aunt well enough, Miss Bradford, but to be quite blunt, I don't have time for indulging the whims of others."

Something rather close to anxiety tightened her fine features as she flexed her jaw. Why was she being so strange about all this? It wasn't as though either one of them wished to be in the other's presence any more than necessary at this point. Impatient, he said, "If that's all, come along. I haven't all day, and I am going quite out of my way to deliver you home."

She stayed stubbornly in place, her hands setting on her hips. "The thing is, Radcliffe, that until such time as my aunt is satisfied, I am to be held prisoner in her dreadful house."

He raised an eyebrow, not impressed with her hyperbole. "If you are currently a prisoner, you are a remarkably well-traveled one."

It might have been the morning light, but he would swear her cheeks reddened just the slightest bit. "There is a difference between sanctioned leaves and opportunistic ones. The latter is a specialty of mine."

He nearly snorted. "Of that, I have no doubt. Be that as it may, whatever trouble you have caused for yourself is none of my concern. In fact, both I and my grass-stained jacket are in agreement with your punishment." He was only half-serious. But he was starting to wonder if she really was being sincere. Could her aunt honestly be restricting her until such time that he accepted her apology? It seemed a little far-fetched, but why else would she say such a thing?

"Again, you practically begged me to demonstrate my capableness," she said, completely unrepentant. "And don't be bitter. I would think you would relish the opportunity to show grace to one so far beneath you. It is why you are called 'Your Grace,' no?"

Gesturing for her to start walking, he detoured to where his horse was tied and freed the reins. "I am called 'Your Grace' as a show of respect, actually. Not that I imagine you care."

They fell into step with each other, with Gray following obediently behind them. The sun had just begun to flirt with the horizon, brightening the sky as they walked. It wasn't unpleasant, walking along with her at his side. Though he'd certainly not call themselves friends, the bitterness between them had definitely faded.

Beside him, Miss Bradford kept her eyes trained on the ground ahead. "I am not a stranger to respect. I simply believe that it is something one earns."

As a man who had worked tirelessly in his role as both a political leader and landowner, he didn't appreciate her assumption that he hadn't done anything to earn the respect he demanded. "Oh yes, I'm certain you consider yourself very much above the British social hierarchy. Yet I doubt you have any concept of how much responsibility those born to a title must bear. I have a century-old dukedom I am charged with, which must be maintained not only for the future dukes, but for the livelihoods and well-being of the hundreds of people dependent upon the estate."

She nodded, making a soft sound of sympathy. "Mmm, that does sound tough. Such a pity that you have only tens of thousands of pounds to make up for the inconvenience of hiring people to do everything for you. I do hope you keep a few banknotes on hand with which to dry your tears."

He cut a censorious gaze her way. Could she take nothing seriously? "I have always found sarcasm to be the lowest form of wit."

The smile she sent him was as wicked as it was unexpected. "You find me witty? Well, I must figure out a way to work that into a conversation with my aunt."

He started to reply, but realized she was only baiting him again. Instead, he shook his head and turned his attention to the road ahead of them. It wasn't yet seven and the city was beginning to awaken. A few pedestrians rushed past them while the occasional cart lumbered by. Though William wasn't willing to allow her the triumph of escaping his escort, he certainly hoped no one would recognize them.

After several blocks, she gestured to a grand old townhome that was about a hundred paces ahead. "This is my aunt's house. I think I can survive the walk from here."

He gave a crisp nod of his head as he came to a stop. She was a singular human being. Half the morning he had wanted to throttle her, and the other half . . . well, the other half he had still wanted to throttle her. But she was without doubt an interesting woman. Few people had ever managed to successfully draw him into an argument, and in the space of just a few hours, she had somehow sucked him into several. She had also somehow managed to show a different side of herself, revealing glimpses of humor and intelligence.

Still, she was trouble and he'd do well to remember it.

She paused beside him, turning to face him fully. "I do

hope I didn't hurt you when I gave my little demonstration."

It had certainly not been pleasant, but nothing on earth could compel him to admit it had affected him even that much. "I would think you'd be disappointed to learn that I'd been unharmed."

She smiled up at him, her face so angelic it almost made him laugh. "I need you in one piece when you accept my apology. Wouldn't want my aunt asking questions, should you show up in a sling."

For the first time since he'd met her, he allowed a slow, earnest smile to stretch his lips. He had every intention of answering her aunt's missive in the affirmative, but Miss Bradford didn't need to know that just yet. The uncertainty could be her penance for tossing him to the ground like a sack of potatoes.

"Yes, that apology." He paused and mounted Gray before looking down on his companion. "Having given due consideration to the topic, it's possible I'll be entirely too busy to find an opportunity to call in the short time I'll be in town. Do give your aunt my best though."

With that, he flicked the reins and rode away, leaving a gaped-mouth Miss Bradford in his wake.

Chapter Six

The low-down, no-good, toad-eating bounder! May stared after the retreating form of her adversary, completely blindsided by his parting words. Just when she had started to like the man—almost—he had to go and reinforce her original opinion of him. Too busy, her foot. She'd seen the pleasure in that handsome little grin of his. He enjoyed making her sweat.

Blowing out a harsh breath, she turned and stalked back to the house. She had really misjudged the softening she had thought she'd seen in him. There was a moment, when the sun had crested over the trees and illuminated those amber eyes of his, that she had thought she'd seen a bit of who he really was, behind all that imperious posturing.

And he had taken being thrown to the ground remarkably well. It had been impulsive and certainly not the wisest thing she had ever done, but she wasn't sorry for it. It had broken the building tension between them, allowing them both to step back from trading those rather sharp verbal barbs.

She had been so sure he was softening toward her plight, so certain he would show a bit of grace and decency by accepting her apology. Yet here she was, back to square one and the uncertainty of how long she would be trapped in her aunt's dreary house.

He hadn't said he *wouldn't* come, at least. Still, she certainly couldn't count on him. As she approached the front door, she paused to take a long, deep breath of the morning air, much as she had on the way out that morning.

It was back to the dungeon with her.

William did not go back to his townhome.

He should have, as he really did have things that needed his attention, but he was far too preoccupied with his encounter that morning to have the patience for them just yet. Instead, he exercised Gray for an hour before deciding it was late enough to call on his old friend.

He wanted information, and no one was better for that than Dering. Even if William didn't already know of his friend's acquaintance with May, he would have sought him out anyway. Dering knew everyone in the country one way or another. He had one of those easy, open personalities that, combined with his status as heir to an earldom, seemed to draw others toward him. And thanks to his exceptional memory, he was a veritable treasure trove of gossip and secrets—including many of William's.

It was remarkable that he couldn't seem to shake May from his mind. He was generally quite accomplished at such things. But she was singular in every way. He'd both seen and felt her sharp side, where her lack of both respect and manners bordered on legendary, yet she'd also revealed her softer side. She possessed humor, even wit, and certainly she was honest to a fault.

Dering had spoken rather fondly of her. The Effington and Wembley girls both thought well enough of her to play side by side with her, and the Selection Committee had allowed her to participate in festival events. He couldn't help but wonder: Had they seen both sides of her, or was there something about him that brought out the worst in her? He readily admitted that she absolutely had that effect on him.

Ten minutes later, William was seated in his old friend's drawing room and, just as he'd suspected, Dering was awake, if somewhat the worse for wear. He yawned hugely as he strode into the room and dropped into the nearest chair. The angled morning light pouring through the room's two windows readily betrayed the redness of his eyes and the purple smudges beneath them.

"Still burning the candle at both ends?"

Dering gave a short brusque laugh and nodded even as he reached for the steaming pot of tea a maid had brought in a few minutes earlier. "Some things never change. Far too many delights to be had at night, yet I never can seem to sleep past dawn. As curses go, it's a relatively mild one. A few cups of tea and I'll be good as new."

Cracking a small smile, William said, "You do realize that our youth is behind us, yes? You don't actually have to stay out that late."

"*Your* youth. You are the one who just turned the corner into the next decade. I, on the other hand, am still in the prime of my life." He raised his cup in a mock salute before taking a hearty drink.

William chuckled, the sound rusty after his contentious morning. "Yet of the two of us, you're the one who looks like something the cat dragged in."

"Mmm, I'll concede the truth in that. So, my bright-

eyed friend, what is it that I can do for you?" He leaned
back in his chair, cradled the oversize cup in his hands,
and waited for William to get to the point.

A point that, now that William was face-to-face with
the man, seemed somewhat less pressing than it had been
a half hour ago. Why had he let the woman get so thoroughly beneath his skin? The only other female who
ever managed such a feat was his stepmother, and that
was not a favorable comparison. Still, he was here now,
and there was no point beating around the bush.

"While out for my morning ride, I encountered Miss
Bradford in the park by the river. *Alone*," he added,
though he kept her state of undress to himself. "I must
say, I am at a loss as to how you, or any other sane and
reasonable person, could find the girl to be suitable for
society. Based on my two encounters in the last twelve
hours, I cannot imagine how she hasn't embroiled herself
in scandal by now."

Dering's black eyebrows lifted as he drained the rest
of his tea. "Not mincing words, I see. And what the devil
do you mean, 'two encounters'? Is that why you disappeared last night? It wasn't very well done of you, leaving without a word. I was expecting you to lose good
money to me in the Card Room after the performances."

"Let us just say the first encounter ended less than
amicably. Now then, answer the question if you please."

Running a hand through his dark hair, Dering sighed.
"In my experience, she has been interesting, friendly, and
witty with a good sense of humor. Quite charming, in an
unconventional sort of way, and certainly refreshing."

For a moment, William just stared back at his friend.
"We are talking of Miss May Bradford, yes? Blond hair,
exquisite features, vocabulary and comportment of a
dockworker?" It was a little harsh, but really — *charming*?

He'd accept *interesting*, and possibly the *good sense of humor*, but *charming* and *friendly* seemed completely ill-fitting for the woman.

An unmistakable spark of interest flared in Dering's dark eyes, along with a smile that quirked up one corner of his mouth. "One must wonder what exactly happened during those two encounters. You must have offended her royally to elicit such a response."

"Quite the reverse, I assure you," William replied, shaking his head wryly. "Honestly, I find it hard to reconcile the fact that she is related to Lady Stanwix. What do you know of the girl's history?"

Dering paused to rub a hand over his eyes before answering. "The countess is her father's older sister. From what I understand, Miss Bradford was raised overseas for most of her life, particularly around India and the Orient. I believe her mother died recently. The father is a ship captain, and presumably because of his wife's passing, he left his only daughter with her aunt before departing for his latest voyage. I gather Miss Bradford is *not* happy with the arrangement."

Not difficult to believe, given her personality. He imagined she wasn't the sort to sit back and allow others to make decisions for her. "A ship captain?" he mused, settling back in his chair. And she'd been raised in the Far East?

He sat up straight as the obvious conclusion flashed in his mind. "Don't tell me her father is a Company man." That would just be too perfect. After the way they had butted heads personally, of course her father would stand for everything William had been fighting against politically since before he'd even inherited the title.

Dering's tired laugh was a little raspy. "He is. No wonder the two of you get on so well. You and the girl, that is. Obviously not her father. Damn but I'm too tired to make sense just yet." He leaned forward and poured another cup of tea, this time adding a splash of what looked to be scotch. "If further conversation can wait—and I imagine it can—then feel free to call again at a more civilized time."

"Yes, yes, I'll let you be. Just one more question."

Dering raised his eyebrows, inviting William to speak.

"Do you think she knows of my role in spearheading the legislation to strip the Company of its monopoly?" It was possible, given her strong negative reaction to him initially.

"Contrary to popular belief, I don't actually know *everything*, old man. A woman's mind is at the top of that list." Though he gave a careless shrug, William didn't miss the flash of sadness in his eyes. He was thinking of *her* again, no doubt. But since that was a topic William had solemnly sworn not to mention ever again, he simply stood and nodded.

"Fair enough. Enjoy your morning, and thank you for the audience."

He started for the door, but paused when Dering said his name. "Yes?"

"I'm not sure what exactly happened between the two of you, but try to cut her a little slack. She may look like a proper English rose, but she's about as far from home as one can get."

Keeping his dubiousness to himself, William gave a curt nod before striding from the room. Miss Bradford might be far from home, but she did *not* need coddling. He rubbed the back of his neck, where the first hint of soreness was taking root. She had proved she could take care of herself.

He idly wondered what else she had learned on her

travels throughout the world. That thought stuck with him as he navigated the now-steady traffic. Why had her father left her here after a lifetime abroad, especially when it was evidently against her wishes? Were Captain Bradford's trade routes tied to textiles? If that was the case, the man must have seen the writing on the wall.

Dering might think that Miss Bradford was very far from home, but William suspected that Bath might very well soon be her new home.

Dear Charity and Sophie,

My kind and benevolent aunt has tossed me in the clink and thrown away the key until such time that I properly apologize to the Duke of Radcliffe (a very long story), which essentially means I shall be here for the duration. Please send a metal file, extra linens that are sturdy enough to be knotted together, and biscuits. Chocolate ones, if you please.

Sincerely,
Your Hardened Criminal Friend, May

Dear May,

The injustice of it all! We couldn't find chocolate biscuits, but hopefully the gingerbread will suffice. No file yet, but Charity swears she saw a grappling hook in the labyrinth, if she could only find her way back to it. In the meantime, though we are raven-ously curious about what exactly transpired be-tween you and the duke, we shall endeavor to give him the cut direct, should he deign to look our way.

Yours in Solidarity,
Sophie and Charity

Settling back against the plush cushions of the divan May had dragged out onto her balcony for a small taste of freedom, she took a bite of the smuggled biscuit and sighed. It had been only a day and a half since Radcliffe had abandoned her to her punishment, but she was already chafing at her confinement. Thank goodness for Suyin. Not only was she able to smuggle notes to and from the bedchamber-turned-prison-cell that May would call home for the foreseeable future, but she was the only person allowed to visit. Apparently The Warden believed that even a lady in confinement should be dressed in her finest.

So far, in addition to the notes from Charity and Sophie, May had received a long letter from her friend Smita. May had spent several years in India during her early adolescence, before Mama had become ill. Smita's family was well-known for its exquisite embroidery, and her father worked closely with May's for many years. Being of an age, the two girls had quickly fallen into friendship. Even though May had moved away and visited infrequently, they still maintained a fairly regular correspondence.

Smita's note was actually the first piece of mail May had received since coming to Bath, and her spirits had momentarily soared. Unfortunately, the news was not so encouraging, as Smita's family's business was declining and they were beginning to worry for the future.

The letter served to make May only that much more disheartened that she was half a world away from home. Any comfort she could offer in her response would take months to make it back to her friend.

Polishing off the rest of the biscuit, she crossed her arms and tried to figure out what to do with herself. Carrying two cups of tea, Suyin padded out onto the balcony and sat beside May on the settee. Handing one to May, she said, "Your aunt is like a great dragon. Terrifying in her threats, but full of hot air."

May hooted in laughter, loving her friend's refreshing candor. She always did seem to know what to do or say to make May feel better. Originally from China, Suyin possessed lovely, delicate features and a small stature that belied the strength beneath.

"I agree wholeheartedly. Still, I must find a way to slay her—metaphorically speaking—if I am to enjoy the last bit of the festival. I may not have wanted to come to Bath, but the festival has been absolutely wonderful." And damn the duke for being such a poor sport. She had thought he was simply toying with her when he had said he might be too busy to bother with it all, but it had been more than a day since he'd left her. There was no other way to interpret her continued confinement: He had left her to rot.

She stewed just thinking about it. As self-important as he was, one would think he'd take great pleasure in wielding his power in order to release her. It was hard to believe she had ever imagined he was softening toward her. Their walk home had been much more lighthearted, hadn't it?

"So, apologize to the big-headed duke and be free. A sting to the pride is perhaps better than no nose?"

"No nose?" May asked before realizing what she was saying. "Oh! Cutting off my nose to spite my face. Yes, of course you are right, but in this case, I don't have a choice. I already offered to apologize, and he looked down his long, aristocratic nose at me and declined."

At least that's what she imagined him doing when he'd decided to ignore her aunt's letter. Sighing, she threw a halfhearted smirk to her companion. "It is a good thing that expression isn't literal. I would have gone through half a dozen noses by now at least."

"Is that all?" Suyin's innocent expression made May laugh all over again.

She was right. May was stubborn, and it didn't always work out in her favor. Her mother once had told her that she used to dread punishing May whenever she needed correction. She'd talk back so much, before all was said and done, the final punishment would have been ten times as bad as the original. Her mother had admitted that she had sometimes cried afterward, feeling the worst sort of brute, but she'd known she had to hold firm if May was to ever grow up to be a reasonable and respectful adult. Looking back, May conceded that her mother had been right, but that didn't stop that stubborn streak from rearing its ugly head from time to time.

And look where it had gotten her. If she could just learn to walk away from situations that got under her skin, she wouldn't be in this predicament.

Groaning aloud, she faced Suyin with her nose wrinkled in displeasure. "Fine, fine. I'll write the man directly. Hopefully by now he feels that I've learned my lesson."

Delicate raven brows arched ever so slightly. "Have you?"

May gave a soft snort. "The only lesson I have learned in all of this is to avoid arrogant noblemen like the plague." Although, it wasn't exactly a *new* lesson. Still, it had certainly been reinforced since she'd met him.

Humor glinted in Suyin's dark eyes. "Remember, a little groveling goes very far in a man's heart." Flashing a quick grin, she stood and retreated back inside. Her feet were soundless on the thin rug as she walked with short but graceful strides.

She had once explained that her name meant "plain or simple sound," which seemed completely ill fitting. To May, she was the epitome of a strong and purpose-filled woman. With her many talents, she could have taken any position she wished, but she chose to stay with May after Mama had died. And thank God for it. Without the meditation techniques Suyin had taught her to deal with her mother's illness and death, it was hard to say what state May would be in now.

Never one to procrastinate, she headed inside to her escritoire and pulled out the necessary writing implements. She had actually expected him to come to the park this morning just to be contrary, but she'd seen neither hide nor hair of him or the big gray beast he rode. Having given it some thought, she decided that his *not* showing up was actually more contrary. He had to know that she'd be waiting to argue her case, as well as to give him a piece of her mind for ignoring her aunt's request.

Dear Radcliffe,

It would appear that my aunt's missive may not have been to your standards. Perhaps you require an engraved invitation? Given my cloistered state, I haven't the means to provide one at the moment, but do take note of how very careful my calligraphy is. See? Crossed T's and elegantly dotted I's fit for even the most discerning duke. If you had seen my normal penmanship, you would know what an impressive effort this is for me. Now then, I beg you: Please have mercy on my humble self so that I may be set free. Lesson learned, et cetera, et cetera.

Awaiting your response with bated breath,
MB

Three long hours later, a tap at the door preceded Aunt Victoria, who swept into the room in a cloud of mulberry bombazine and overly aromatic perfume. "The duke sent round a note," she announced without prelude, her stern features showing none of the satisfaction that May would have expected. "He spoke of his intention to attend the Ackerman's farewell soiree, and indicated his hope that he would see us there."

Relief washed through May as she blew out a pent-up breath. "I'm glad to hear it. I'm eager to speak with him again." The sooner she met with him, the sooner she could be done with this nonsense. Best of all, she was certain Charity and Sophie had planned to attend the ball, so she would have support.

Her aunt pursed her lips. "I'll warn you now, young lady, that you'd better be on your very best behavior. I am in no way exaggerating when I say you will spend the rest of the summer in this room if you offend the duke further."

Biting her tongue, May smiled tightly and nodded. She would treat him so sweetly his teeth would ache. It would be at least another month or so until her father returned, and she refused to spend that time withering away in a dungeon. Besides the fact she wanted to make the most of the time she had left before her friends went their separate ways, May was simply a social person. She thrived on the company of others.

Depending on the "others," of course.

Aunt Victoria tilted her head as she inspected May's appearance. "Wear one of the dresses I had made for you, and we'll have Upton do your hair. I hate to give up my own lady's maid, but I won't have that maid of yours doing you up exotic."

Little bursts of pain in her tongue told her she was

biting too hard, but May didn't relent. Again, she nodded.

"Don't speak unless spoken to," The Warden continued, her chin raised in that special way of hers that allowed her to look down upon those who were taller than she. "When you do converse, stay to acceptable parlor talk: the weather, the festival, music. Do *not* refer to that *thing* you call an instrument. Before he departs, apologize sincerely and concisely. Your freedom to interact with your friends is directly dependent on his favorable response.

"If, by the time you finish conversing, I do not feel the incident at the Assembly Rooms has been forgiven and forgotten, well," she said, offering a cold smile, "you may forget showing yourself in public again for the duration of the festival."

So many words longed to come forth, threatening to break free of May's attempts to keep them in check. She forced a nod one more time.

Without another word, her aunt turned and swept from the room, leaving nothing but the cloying scent of her perfume behind. Wrinkling her nose, May moved to the divan and let out a long, frustrated breath. She was not meant for this life. She was going to rupture something if she kept holding words in like that.

Closing her eyes, she laid her head back against the uncomfortable cushions. Thank God the duke had responded favorably to her note. She could only hope it meant he was ready to relent. And if he didn't accept her apology?

May dismissed the thought out of hand. This time, she wouldn't let the man out of her sight until she got what she wanted.

Chapter Seven

With its brightly burning candles, low roar of conversation, and finely dressed attendees, the Ackerman ball was not unlike any other ball William had attended that year. Servants served, musicians played, and gossips had their heads together, their keen eyes sweeping the room in hopes of catching some fresh bit of scandal.

There was, however, a subtle difference in tone here when compared to similar events of the London Season. It was . . . lighter. Less jaded, even. Despite the gossips and occasional sour-faced matron, the attendees appeared to be genuinely enjoying themselves. With the end of the festival only days away, people seemed anxious to squeeze every drop of enjoyment from their time here.

Even though his arrival had caused the usual stir—nothing made heads turn quite like the word *duke*—he felt substantially less hunted here, which was a relief. As he'd made his way through the room, greeting friends and nodding to acquaintances, he'd found himself scanning the women in attendance, searching for the tall blonde who would inevitably hunt him down the moment she saw him.

Her note had made him laugh, almost against his will. It was obviously impossible for her to show him any real respect, but her words hadn't been sharp, at least. Odd, but not sharp.

Lord Wexley spotted him then, and quickly parted from his companion and made his way over. "Good evening, Duke," he said, the words crisp as he offered a short nod. "How fortuitous that you were able to join the festival after all. I hope that means all is well with your little venture." His lips stretched into a thin line that could be interpreted as either a pained smile or uncommitted sneer.

The viscount had never done anything to call into question his integrity, but William still didn't particularly like the man. He had a disingenuous air about him that made every word he said suspect. The fact that Wexley referred to it as his *little* venture irritated him, but it wasn't worth allowing the man to get beneath his skin.

"I am more than satisfied with the project." William wasn't about to share more than that about the implementation of his years-long plan to build a textile mill on his estate. They had encountered several issues early in the summer, but things were running sufficiently well now that he felt comfortable leaving it behind for a fortnight or so.

"Excellent. Ah," he said, raising a hand and lifting his brows. "I see my daughter has returned from the terrace."

William automatically turned, but instead of Wexley's daughter, Miss Harmon, he saw Miss Sophie Wembley blink in surprise, then raise her hand and wave in return. Behind her, a blonde approached, but unfortunately it was only Miss Harmon.

"Oh, for God's sake," the viscount said, his voice

sharp and loud enough to carry. "She can't possibly imagine that I would ever address her. Evansleigh may have been duped into marrying the chit, but everyone here knows she's little more than a glorified adventuress."

Anger pierced straight through William's chest, especially when he saw Sophie's face drain of color and her bright smile go brittle as glass. He had spoken with her only a few times before this, but she had always been very sweet, if a bit loquacious. She possessed the kindness of spirit that was impossible to counterfeit. If Evansleigh had chosen her for his wife, it wasn't because he'd been tricked or fleeced into it. William wasn't any great friend of the man, but he knew the earl well enough to be sure of that much.

Straightening slowly, he turned cold, hard eyes on Wexley, pouring every ounce of his contempt into his expression. The other man shrank back, uncertainly lowering his brow. After several beats of pointed silence, William turned his back on the viscount and walked straight to the new countess.

Her eyes were perilously large, her nostrils flared, but she had the good manners to remember to curtsy. "Your Grace," she croaked, clearly flustered.

"I have just discovered your happy news, Lady Evansleigh. Please allow me to extend my most heartfelt felicitations to you and your new husband. And please," he said, forcing a gentle smile to his lips as he leaned the slightest bit forward, "you must call me *Duke* or *Radcliffe*."

Her relief was palpable as she breathed out a slow breath and nodded. "Thank you, Duke. I'm … I'm exceedingly grateful you are here."

"I'm delighted to be here. Tell me, is your husband

also in attendance?" He had no doubt the man would be keen to know what had just transpired.

"He is, indeed. I only just left him to, um, have a moment's respite from the crowd." She sounded somewhat uncomfortable, but William's attention had been momentarily diverted when he had caught Miss Harmon's censorious expression out of the corner of his eye. He purposely didn't acknowledge her, despite the fact she was only a handful of feet away.

The sooner he could get Sophie away from these people, the better. "May I escort you to your destination, Lady Evansleigh?"

Color infused her pale face and she smiled hugely. "I'm afraid I may have been a smidge too tactful, which truly is rather unusual for me. To be completely honest, I was headed toward the ladies' retiring room, and while I certainly don't mind the escort, you very well might. Fear not, however, you shall still be my hero should you choose to rescind the offer."

He bit back an unexpected grin. She was honest to a fault, which was a trait he rather admired in a person. If he hadn't been distracted by Miss Harmon, he would have realized what she had been trying to say. Extending his arm with the elegance that had been drilled into him since he was in leading strings, he said, "A gentleman never goes back on his word. Shall we?"

Her dark eyes danced with humor and delight as she very purposefully laid her gloved hand upon his sleeve. "By all means, lead the way."

May stood arrested several feet away, hardly able to believe her eyes. Surely this was not the same man who had purposely left her languishing in her gilded prison for a day and a half. Or who had looked down his nose at her from the very moment he had first laid eyes on her. Or who had attempted to reprimand her in the park, before ending up flat on the ground at her feet.

Having arrived only minutes earlier, she had been following in Sophie's wake, attempting to catch up to her when she'd seen the exchange. She hadn't been close enough to hear Lord Wexley's words, but the look on Sophie's face had told her all she needed to know. She'd struggled to push through the crush to reach her friend, but the duke had beaten her to it.

It had been . . . incredible. Based on the way Sophie had spoken of him, he was a passing acquaintance at best, and yet, he had defended her. May would have never, ever thought to use the words *Radcliffe* and *gallant* in the same sentence, but the proof was right there before her and the roughly three hundred other souls filling the ball to capacity. She swallowed, attempting to reconcile his kindness with the way he had behaved during their previous encounters.

It was all very vexing.

Regardless, any enemy of Lord Wexley and his daughter couldn't be that bad. Drawing a fortifying breath, she struck out after them, weaving her way through the jovial people conversing around her. By the time she caught up to them, Sophie had curtsied and disappeared into the room designated for the ladies' retiring room. The duke turned and stepped forward just as she approached, and suddenly they were face-to-face, much closer than she had intended.

His clear, tea-colored eyes registered a moment of surprise before he efficiently wiped his expression to neutral. She hastily took a step back. It wouldn't do for him to think she was stalking him.

Pasting a smile on her lips, she tilted her head. "Do I

know you?" she asked, coloring the words with perfect innocence. It was best to be on the offensive in these sorts of situations.

His eyebrows lowered as he regarded her cautiously, obviously suspicious of her intentions. "How I wish I could reply in the negative."

"Ah, yes. It *is* you. I thought for a moment I was witnessing the chivalrous actions of the Duke of Radcliffe's lesser known but much more agreeable twin brother." She kept her tone light with just a hint of teasing. It was an admittedly backhanded compliment, but it would be a lie to say she didn't enjoy the flicker of uncertainty in his eyes as he decided whether to be offended or flattered.

"Might I suggest, Miss Bradford, that since you were the one who requested an audience with me not more than a handful of hours ago, you might have a care how you speak to me." Even though he sounded as imperious as a king, there was definitely a seed of humor nestled between the stern words.

She was entirely at his mercy and he knew it. Even so, and in spite of the fact she had been determined to be as complacent as possible in order to gain her freedom, she found it almost impossible to ignore the desire to spar with the man.

The orchestra, which was situated in a small alcove twenty paces away, signaled the start of the next dance, and men and women all around them started for the dance floor. Within moments, the two of them were left stranded like seaweed on the shore of an outgoing tide. "Remarkable," she said, lifting a single brow. "No one can clear an area quite like your ego."

He came as close to rolling his eyes as she imagined he ever had. "Or this is a ball, and people wish to dance."

"Is that an invitation? How positively unexpected. Peasant girl that I am, I never expected to be asked to waltz by the great duke himself." Her smile was both teasing and wicked, meant to show that she wasn't intimidated by him in the least, despite the fact that she needed him. She had seen the kindness he had shown Sophie. He might have little regard for May's pride, but he had protected someone she loved. It made him that much more interesting, and even more appealing than he had a right to be.

Something very much like determination flickered in his eyes. Or was it exasperation? Whatever it was, she didn't have time to examine it before he thrust out his hand, palm up. "Absolutely."

She blinked, then stared down at the supple leather encasing his outstretched fingers. "I beg your pardon?" He couldn't truly wish to dance with her. She had only been needling him.

Leaning close enough that she could smell the crisp, classic sandalwood scent of his shaving soap, he looked her dead in the eye. "I'm calling your bluff."

Without waiting for her response, he clasped her hand in his and towed her toward the dance floor. She was so surprised, she didn't even protest. Her heart stirred with anticipation as she contemplated the feeling of her hand tucked firmly within his. If she was honest—and she always was—it wasn't an altogether unpleasant sensation.

"You think to shock me, but it won't work." His voice was even, controlled to a fault. Nothing in his manner would have tipped off a casual observer to the battle of wills that was brewing. "If you can make it through this dance without causing a scene, I shall escort you to your aunt afterward and proclaim your apology accepted.

This is your one and only chance, Miss Bradford, so I suggest you be on your very best behavior."

Her very best behavior, indeed. Did he think she would fall on her face? Embarrass herself before their peers? Did he *want* her to? By now he should know better than to try to put her in her place.

Increasing her pace, she pulled ahead of him, effectively taking the lead. She led him to the very center of the ballroom before abruptly coming to a halt. Turning to face him fully, she arched a brow in challenge. "You do realize that by dancing the first waltz with me, you are effectively showing your approval for me, yes?"

The music cued, and he snapped her into position, holding her not a single inch closer or farther than society demanded. It was almost as if an invisible box was placed between them. "Don't underestimate the power of a cut direct. Now behave yourself. If you attempt to lead, I will gladly allow you to carry on without me."

He stepped forward then, propelling her along with him in time with the music. He was a competent dancer, sure-footed and graceful, yet wholly masculine. *Too* masculine, really. The way he was holding her, her feet hardly even touched the floor.

She wiggled a bit in his grasp. "I am capable of dancing, you know. My mother was adamant I learn the ways of English courting, though God knows why."

Though his posture never changed, he allowed his gaze to meet hers. "Forgive me if I don't believe you. I heard what you did to Mozart, after all."

Oh, he thought himself clever, did he?

"Glorious, wasn't it? So refreshing not to hear it played as boring as written."

"Boring? His work is art," he exclaimed. Then his eyes narrowed, and she knew he'd realized she was baiting him. Lifting his chin an inch, he said, "Although personally I prefer England's own Thomas Linley, the younger. His talent transcends the generations."

"Oh, rubbish. You only say that because he's English. I imagine you prefer black pudding over curry soup, because congealed pig's blood is so deliciously English," she said, wrinkling her nose despite the fact she didn't really mind black pudding. "But the fact is, Linley is known as the English Mozart, yet Mozart has never been called the German Linley. Food for thought," she said, flashing a knowing smile.

Pleased with having parried his point, she redoubled her effort not to allow him to control her movements. His strides were long, but thanks to her height, she had no trouble keeping up. They swooped past couple after couple, spinning and turning with exactly the precision she would have expected from the man. The other couples whirled past them in a blur of brightly colored gowns and jackets. With her dreadfully dull pale pink gown and his dour charcoal jacket, they must have looked like an inkblot in comparison.

His hand tightened against her back, reining in her efforts. "I do, in fact, prefer black pudding to curry anything. Now then, if you don't quit attempting to outpace me," he said, his words stern, "we will end up spinning right out of the room."

It was as close to hyperbole as she could probably ever expect to hear from him. He was, however, quite right. She slowed her pace until he was guiding her along once more. As they glided past the corridor, she spotted Sophie as she emerged from the retiring room.

"I'm curious," May said, peering back up at the duke's unarguably attractive countenance. "What did Lord Wexley say to Lady Evansleigh?"

His bronze gaze flickered down to meet hers for a moment before settling back just over her shoulder. "I can't imagine you'd think I would gossip, so I shall assume the question was rhetorical."

The retort was a prick to her conscience, devil take him. "I have no interest in gossip, Radcliffe. Sophie is a very dear friend, and I have a vested interest in her happiness. It was obvious without hearing a word of the exchange that the viscount said something disparaging."

The duke remained silent for a few beats as the music moved them along. He could be so blasted stubborn when he put his mind to it. After several seconds, May shook her head. "Oh, never mind, I'll get the details from Sophie. Whatever they were, I feel it only fair to say that I thought it very well done of you to take her side." She wouldn't begrudge him the credit for his kindness.

He raised a dubious brow. "A compliment, Miss Bradford? I may perish from the shock. Regardless, I did not take anyone's side. As a duke, it is beneath me to involve myself in such a thing."

Speaking of shocking, was that *modesty* she heard? She shook her head. "Yet as a human being, you were kind."

"It was nothing, I assure you."

She blew out an exasperated breath. She'd seen too many people be cruel to Sophie to allow him to discount his actions. "It *wasn't* nothing, for heaven's sake. Quit deflecting my praise and let me acknowledge your munificence, you contrary lout of a man."

At that, his gaze cooled. "You seem more intelligent than most. I cannot imagine why you insist on demeaning yourself and others with your off-color vocabulary."

There was that extraordinary haughtiness with which she was so very familiar by now. For the first time that evening, he seemed truly annoyed with her. She rolled her eyes, not caring a whit if any of the other dancers witnessed her reaction. "And I suppose you never speak out of turn? Never swear at all?"

"Never." The single word was so decisive, it actually made her blink.

"Never?" Surely he couldn't be serious. He was a duke, not a saint. "Not even in the dark and mysterious dens of debauchery known as a gentlemen's club? I find that rather unbelievable."

The corners of his lips curled into a small, reluctant smile as he shook his head. "Where do you get such outlandish ideas? Whoever told you a gentlemen's club was anything less than civilized?"

If there was one thing of which she was most certain, it was the subject of a man's baser existence. Men, as a rule, descended into the maturity of twelve-year-olds when left to their own devices. She had witnessed more than one sailor be sent to the ship's doctor with wounds resulting from some ridiculous bet or dare. Though she had never seen her father participate in such things, he was the exception that proved the rule.

Lifting her chin knowingly, she said, "I have spent a great deal of time in my life in the company of men. I know very well how they can be when they gather en masse."

He was obviously amused now. "Such wisdom. I think perhaps you failed to take into account the difference in station of the men you have been around in the past and the men who frequent the fine, old establishments of London."

"Yes, I'm certain they would never make ridiculous bets about everything under the sun, drink themselves silly, or tell stories as tall as fishermen's tales about their supposed conquests."

He gave a decisive nod. "That is exactly correct."

Her laugh was as unexpected to her as it was to him. "Oh, do go on. Either you've never actually been to one, or you are simply the boldest liar in the room."

The music came to an end far sooner than she expected. How had time managed to get away from her so completely? He halted their motion and immediately stepped away. "I'll leave it to you to decide which. Now then, which way to your aunt, if you please?"

"By the refreshments, last I saw."

He started that way, but she tightened her hand, causing him to look back at her in question. "Before we part for good, let me just say thank you for accepting my apology. I don't handle forced confinement very well."

He looked down at her as the people around them streamed past, his eyes unreadable. "You're welcome. Contrary to what you seem to believe, I do not wish you or anyone else ill."

After their rather teasing tit-for-tat dance, his response touched a nerve. Dropping his hand, she stepped backward to put some space between them. "Don't you? You *did* abandon me to my aunt's censure. Not exactly the most gentlemanly thing I've ever heard of." She couldn't quite figure him out. Yes, he had been exceptionally nice to Sophie, but he had purposely left May to suffer.

Instead of allowing her to have her distance, he grasped her elbow and said evenly, "Follow me, if you please. This is not the conversation to have in the middle of a ballroom."

It was then that she noticed the heads turned in their direction, the many curious gazes bright in the golden candlelight. With a firm hand, he guided her toward the garden doors, which were left open to the night air. She could have protested, but decided to keep her tongue in check as they made their way across the limestone patio to the well-lit gravel pathway beyond. Gossip about her behavior was the last thing she needed. The night was surprisingly humid, and only a handful of other guests wandered the garden. It was as private a setting as they could hope for.

"Now," he said, his voice maddeningly composed, "you were saying?"

She pulled her arm from his grasp and turned to face him, ignoring the way the torchlight turned his eyes to molten gold. "You claim to be a veritable paragon of good English manners, but it seems to me that could not be further from the truth. I had already shown that I was more than willing to apologize. To ignore my aunt's letter and instead allow me to fester in that dreadful old house was downright cruel.

"And then," she continued, gaining momentum, "when you do finally deign to reply to my groveling letter, you have us come here where it must be done in public instead of permitting me the modicum of dignity apologizing in private would have allowed."

He didn't look the least bit affected by her words. Lifting a single eyebrow, he said, "Are you finished?"

Something about the way he spoke gave her pause. "Yes?" she replied, suddenly cautious.

"Then perhaps you'd like to know that I suggested meeting here so you could see your friends. I didn't respond to your aunt's summons because I never *received* anything from her, and didn't feel it would do you any favors for me to show up unannounced, proclaiming I was ready to accept the apology you so graciously offered when we were alone in the park together."

She stood there, feet rooted to the pebbles, probably

looking like a startled owl as she blinked at him in surprise. "You . . . didn't hear from my aunt?" How was that
possible? She had specifically said she wanted May to
apologize, and wouldn't allow her freedom until she did.
Surely her aunt would have wanted her to do so as soon
as possible. Wouldn't she?

No, she wouldn't. She probably wished to leave May
tucked up in the house for a few days, where she wouldn't
have to worry about her. May gritted her teeth at the
thought.

Crossing his arms in a very un-dukelike fashion, he
shook his head once. "No, I did not."

"Oh," she replied lamely, at a loss of what else to say.

"*Oh?* A whole soliloquy about how cruel and terrible
I am, and all you have to say for yourself is '*oh*'?"

She shifted her weight, beginning to feel a bit foolish.
Perhaps she had jumped to conclusions. But even as she
thought it, she realized that wasn't right. She had been
guided to the wrong conclusion. Purposely. "Pardon me,
but how was I to know your intentions? I believe your
parting words were that you would be entirely too busy
to see my aunt, and for me to give her your best."

He didn't look the least bit guilty or contrite. "I believe I was entitled to a little ambiguity. You had just
thrown me to the ground for no reason at all."

Yes, well, there was that. Nodding, she dropped her
hands to her sides and offered a wry grin. "Oh, sure, use
that for your justification. I suppose we shall simply have
to call it even."

"Yes, gladly," he said, unfolding his arms and stepping
forward. "Now if you don't mind, I'd like to escort you
back to your aunt so we can be done with it." He held
out his elbow, his features relaxed for once.

Oh, Lord. When he wasn't scowling, he was actually

attractive. Quite, quite so. Particularly with the torchlight dancing across his angled cheekbones, roughing up his normally polished facade. A small shiver danced down her spine as she reached out and placed her fingers against his sleeve. Her pale glove stood out against the dark fabric of his jacket, momentarily holding her attention. The two of them were as different as black and white. Night and day.

Swallowing, she looked up into his bronze-colored gaze. Perhaps it was the reflected fire, but in that moment, his eyes looked warm. Inviting, even. No, that couldn't be right. There was no love lost between them, as it should be. Licking her lips, she offered a brusque smile. "The sooner, the better."

Hopefully he wouldn't notice the odd hoarseness to her voice.

Chapter Eight

S ome things in life are best left unanalyzed.

 Like the unexpected rush caused by a single touch, or the sudden pounding of the heart when one's eyes locked with another's.

Guiding them forward, William steadfastly ignored both of those reactions, concentrating on taking measured, calm steps back toward the house. He was a reasonable man who kept tight control on both his emotions and his body. There was no reason Miss Bradford, of all people, should challenge that.

It mattered not that her floral, sultry scent made him want to pull her closer. It was enchanting, putting him in mind of hothouses and warm tea. Or that, instead of simply laying her fingers upon his sleeve like any other female, she allowed her fingers to tighten on his forearm almost possessively, as though she had every right to claim him.

She wasn't, of course. Claiming him, that is. She was as unnerved and exasperated by him as he was by her. Nothing about her fit into the neat molds by which he categorized people.

What was most unnerving was that he found himself liking that about her.

As they stepped onto the limestone pavers, he stole a glance at her. She was luminescent, despite the drab pink gown that hung shapelessly from her frame. Her cheeks were lightly flushed, her eyes exceptionally dark blue in the low light. Her skin was still golden, as though illuminated from within.

A movement ahead of them caught his eye, breaking the spell. He turned in time to see a couple emerge from the shadows near the edge of the house. Before he even saw the woman's face, he recognized her fiery red hair. *Of course.* He came up short, jerking May to a stop beside him.

Vivian turned, meeting his gaze as though she knew he would be there. Which, undoubtedly, she did. Slowly, deliberately, she allowed her lips to curl into a catlike grin. "Radcliffe, darling," she purred, her soft Parisian accent caressing the words. "What a surprise, finding you out here. You remember the earl, yes?"

William could feel his muscles harden one by one as he turned to acknowledge the man who had long been his political opponent. "Norwich," he said, dipping his head in the shallowest manner possible.

The other man returned the gesture. "Duke. And Miss Bradford, what a pleasure to see you again." He offered a wide, surprisingly honest smile to May.

She grinned right back at him, as though they were old friends. "And you, Lord Norwich. I didn't realize you were back in town."

He had never heard such welcome in her voice before. Something uncomfortably close to jealously flashed through William and he clenched his teeth against it. It was utterly ridiculous. She meant nothing to him. Entertaining at times, but even those were few and far between.

Still, the earl's overly friendly expression was just this

side of vulgar, as far as William was concerned. He was easily five-and-forty, old enough to be May's father.

"Only just," Norwich replied, then patted Vivian's hand. "Lady Radcliffe here convinced me it was worth returning for the last week."

May's eyes went huge, and she took a quick step away from William, taking the warmth of her hand with her. "*Lady* Radcliffe?" The confusion was clear in her voice. Her gaze slipped back and forth between William and his stepmother, accusation furrowing her brow.

"My father's widow, Miss Bradford," he replied coolly, not wanting her to give his stepmother any more ideas than she probably already had. He continued with the introduction, all the while wondering why May would have reacted as she did. They were merely acquaintances, weren't they? Straddling the line between friend and opponent since their tentative ceasefire.

Vivian looked May over from head to toe, interest sparking in her pale blue eyes. "How very lovely to meet another friend of Radcliffe's. I feared that for him, there was nothing but the estates and his little projects."

May turned her attention back to William. "I didn't realize you were so industrious. What are your projects?" Was that a hint of admiration, or just surprise? She probably had been imagining him lazing about his days, sipping tea and riding aimlessly across the countryside.

Straightening in a way meant to convey impatience, he said, "I won't bore you with the details while there is a ball to be enjoyed. Speaking of, I must return you to your aunt. She'll be wondering what became of us."

"Ah, yes, mustn't keep Lady Stanwix waiting," Lord Norwich replied, his attention on May. Stepping forward, he captured her hand and lifted it to his lips. William's jaw clenched as she allowed the earl to press a kiss to the top of her hand—something she had denied William not two days earlier. "I do hope there's room on your dance card for one more this evening."

"Alas, I am without a card this evening, as my aunt doesn't intend to stay long. Another time, perhaps?"

Norwich had barely nodded when William turned and led May back inside. His body was still tense, and he was agitated in a way he didn't wish to scrutinize.

"Your stepmother seemed lovely. Where is she from?"

"France," he responded, purposely curt. Vivian was *not* lovely, not in the least. She was a master of manipulation, and he was not looking forward to her accompanying him back to Clifton House.

"Aha. No wonder you don't like her."

He slanted a narrowed look toward her. "I beg your pardon?"

"You don't exactly hide your opinions of others. It's clear you dislike her, and if she had the audacity to be from France, I imagine that explains it."

A rebuttal perched at the tip of his tongue, but he refused to allow her to draw him into yet another argument. Nodding to where Lady Stanwix stood beside the small section of chairs to their right, he said, "There is your aunt. Have you in mind what you wish to say?"

"I have all sorts of things I wish to say, but yes, I have rehearsed the required apology."

"Excellent. It's been"—he paused, attempting to find a word that could possibly describe their encounters— "*interesting*."

She smiled, clearly not taking offense. "My sentiments exactly."

Aunt Victoria looked as though she couldn't decide whether to be pleased or furious with May. With her nostrils wide and shoulders rigidly straight, she stayed where she was as they approached, a queen awaiting her subjects. The good news was, with Radcliffe beside them, she would at least keep a civil tongue.

"Lady Stanwix, do forgive me for detaining your niece." Radcliffe was back to his stiff, imperious self. One would never know the heated manner in which they had spoken not ten minutes earlier. "The dance may have overheated her, I'm afraid."

The suspicion was still evident in her narrowed eyes, but she nodded graciously. "You are too kind to have escorted her, Duke. Thank you for your attentiveness."

"Yes, thank you," May echoed, offering him a purposely effusive smile. "And once again, I hope you can accept my most *sincere* apology for how I behaved when we met the other night."

"Of course. I believe it is safe to say that neither one of us was quite ourselves that evening." He didn't smile, but then again, she didn't expect him to.

Her aunt shook her head, her face grave. "Thank you for your understanding and forgiveness, Duke. I can only hope my niece has learned her lesson. I must say, I'm relieved the festival will be over soon. My nerves need a break from the constant worry that being her chaperone has caused me."

"I'm certain you are both looking forward to her father's return," he replied, cutting a knowing glance in May's direction.

Her forced smile melted into a real one. She could have kissed him for that response. Sometimes her aunt needed to be reminded that May didn't want to be here any more than her aunt wanted her here. "Very much so. I'm not sure what I will do with myself once the festival is over, as he won't touch English soil for a good month yet."

The thought was thoroughly depressing. Without Charity and Sophie, or the many distractions the festival offered, she couldn't imagine how she would keep from going mad. Her aunt would happily have her seated in the drawing room, embroidering samplers and writing letters and knitting whatever it was proper young English women knitted.

He laid a reassuring hand over her fingers where they rested on his sleeve. "You'll find plenty to do in Bath once the crowds have gone. No more balls or concerts, but the city has much to offer."

It wasn't his words that held her attention, but his gesture. May's gaze fixated on his hand as his warmth seeped through the leather separating their skin. It was a familiar gesture, one that she might expect of an old friend or family member, certainly not of an uptight and proper peer.

"Indeed," Aunt Victoria said, oblivious to May's wandering thoughts. "I much prefer the city without the crowds. I wonder, will you be staying past the closing concert?"

His hand quietly slipped away from May's as he shook his head. "I'm afraid I shall exodus along with the masses. I have much to tend to at Clifton House."

His answer wasn't a surprise, but the fact that it was a disappointment was. She assumed they would go their separate ways, but the thought of him leaving seemed to make the remainder of her time in Bath that much more lonely. Who else would she have to argue with when he was gone? "I'm glad you came," she said, surprising herself. "It has been an eye-opening experience, meeting a duke."

He gave a short laugh, making May's eyebrows hitch

up her forehead. She hadn't been entirely sure he was capable of actual laughter. She rather liked the sound of it.

"I am quite sure that it was, Miss Bradford. It has been eye-opening meeting you as well." He smiled then. Not a patronizing or condescending smile, or even a pitying one, but a true grin that May felt all the way to her toes. "And now, I shall leave you ladies to your evening." He bowed his head regally to each of them, winked subtly but unmistakably at May, and walked away.

She watched him as he disappeared into the crowd, her lips pressed together against a telltale smile she didn't want anyone around them to see. Devil take it, she actually hated to see him go.

"Tell us *everything*."

May was impressed. Her friends had waited all of ten seconds before springing the question on her. The only thing that surprised her was that Charity had been the one to speak first.

Sophie, however, didn't keep quiet for long. "More than everything. I want to know every last detail, and if he didn't kiss you, then lie to us and tell us he did."

"Sophie!" May exclaimed, laughing at her friend's obvious enthusiasm. "You have a much more active imagination than I even realized. And you Charity—I would have expected a bit more levelheadedness from you."

From her place on the wrought iron bench flanked by potted lemon trees, Charity shot her a rueful look, her gray eyes full of mischief. "Oh please, you expected no such thing. Having borne witness to the dour Duke of Radcliffe laugh aloud in front of an entire ballroom of people because of something you said, I am as determined as Sophie to squeeze every last detail from you.

Especially after we were under the impression that he was to be boycotted following your last encounter."

Smiling, May settled back onto the comfortable cushions of her lounge chair and tipped her face to the sun. It felt wonderful to have her freedom back. They were only in her aunt's garden, but it was a vast improvement over the house. "Now, now, I'm sure such a thing isn't *that* unusual. It's not as though he swept me from my feet and carried me from the room, *Sophie*," she said, sending a teasingly pointed look to her friend.

Dark eyes widened as Sophie sat up straight. "What? That worked out quite well in the end, thank you very much. And really, if you can ever persuade a man to do such a thing, I highly recommend it." Her cheeks were bright red even as she said it, but her grin was absolutely irrepressible.

May couldn't help but laugh—an old married matron, Sophie still blushed like a girl fresh from the schoolroom. "I shall keep that in mind."

"Don't think I haven't noticed that you neatly dodged our questions," Charity said, reaching up to adjust her bonnet to better keep the sun from her cheeks. Already her freckles where becoming more apparent, but in May's opinion, they served to make her look only that much more lovely. "You promised to explain how you came to be imprisoned, and what the duke had to do with it."

Acquiescing, May recounted the night she'd met him and the encounter the following morning. Sophie's eyes went round as portholes as May related their increasingly sharp barbs, culminating in the duke ending up on the ground.

"Oh dear heavens, I think I might just have my very first fit of vapors," she said, her hand at her throat. "You aren't being metaphorical, are you? You flayed him so effectively with your sharp-witted comebacks that he was left figuratively on his back, gasping for air?"

"No, I'm being quite literal. I imagine he still has the grass stains to attest to it."

"Right then. Good. All right. Carry on." Sophie's normally pale skin seemed slightly green. Doubtless she and Charity both thought her mad as a loon by now.

May laughed, shaking her head at the pair of them. "It was all for the best, I assure you. If I hadn't shown him what I was capable of, we might still be locked in verbal combat. The man is as thickheaded as he is stubborn."

Charity lifted a dubious brow. "Oh really? So he was perfectly fine with the, um, maneuver?"

The image of his almost comically shocked expression as he stared up at the sky flitted through her mind. She should probably keep that to herself. "Sort of. Not at first, perhaps, but I think, deep down, it made him feel something."

"That 'something' may have been a flattened spleen," Sophie said, obviously torn between laughter and horror.

Even though May laughed, she shook her head. "He's made of sterner stuff than that. And really, I think I am an oddity to him. He's used to people either fearing him or fawning over him, and obviously I'm not one to do either."

"That is an understatement," Charity teased, flashing a grin, "but as you say, it must have ended well. Forgiveness given, transgressions forgotten, ways parted?"

"Indeed."

More or less, anyhow. They didn't need to know that she hadn't been able to properly concentrate this morning during her exercises, preoccupied as she was with the man. She kept imagining she heard a horse in the distance and had looked around over and over again, until she had finally given up on finding her inner peace for the day and had made her way home.

"And what if you see him again?"

She pursed her lips, giving Charity's question due thought. "Supposedly he is headed back to his estate soon. Since there's only one more major event, I don't imagine the likelihood of running into him is very high. The park will probably be packed to capacity."

Sophie sat forward on the divan, her smile absolutely wicked. "All the more reason to have a plan in place to ensure that you *will* see him. Now that you've caught the duke's attention, it's only fitting you should add 'kissed a duke' to your list of accomplishments during your world travels."

"Sophie!" May and Charity exclaimed in unison, for once the both of them equally shocked.

"What? You've obviously piqued his interest. I've never seen him show any interest at all to any one female before, and Lord knows I would have read about it in the scandal sheets if it had happened. Everyone wants to guess at who will catch the bachelor duke's eye."

May shook her head, quickly dismissing her friend's ridiculous suggestion. "I can assure you, the only thing I have caught is his censure. Thankfully, we parted on good terms, as my aunt would have thrown away the key otherwise. I don't need to jeopardize my freedom by attempting to kiss the man."

The other two had no need to know that her heart was suddenly pounding away in her chest like the beat of a kendang drum. The thought of his surprisingly strong arms encircling her and those gorgeously masculine lips of his pressing against her own was much more enticing than it should have been.

Unconvinced by her protest, Sophie crossed her arms over her generous bosom. "And here I always assumed you were the most adventurous of the three of us. This is to be a summer to remember, one that we shall all look back on fondly when we are old and gray and wishing to relive the escapades of our youth. Don't you want to say that the first man you ever kissed was a handsome duke universally sought by others but felled by you?"

"Don't be silly—I've been kissed before. And I don't need to make a conquest of one of your famous peers."

Charity nodded in agreement. "Yes, I think perhaps you're right. Kisses are to be reserved for someone you actually like, for one thing."

"I do like the duke. I simply see no need to corner the man." He could certainly be infuriating when he put his mind to it, but she meant it when she said she liked him. Most of the time.

Sophie's grin bordered on sly as she sent May a sideways look. "Oh, I saw the way he looked at you during that dance-to-end-all-dances. I can assure you, cornering will *not* be necessary."

It was absurd to pay any mind to Sophie's words, but that didn't stop the spark of awareness that danced though May's belly. It made no sense that Radcliffe, of all people, should cause that sort of reaction in her. He was self-important, condescending, heavy-handed ... kind, forgiving, and on the rare occasion, witty. He possessed power and confidence in spades, and whether she liked it or not, it was a potent combination.

For one indulgent second, she imagined that wink that he gave her and swallowed. No matter what she wanted to think of him, he was attractive to her contrary self. Lifting her chin, she said, "The concert is for music and a farewell to friends. Let us leave it at that."

Sophie and Charity exchanged glances, then looked back at her in unison. "Mmhmm," Sophie murmured, her lips turned up in a knowing grin. "And let us hope some farewells are more exciting than others."

Chapter Nine

The lanterns were already lit by the time William arrived at the park for the final concert of the festival. There were thousands of them strewn from every branch and bush, sending their colorful glow over the whole place, making it feel as though one were walking though a prism. The bright colors added a jubilant air to the event, the perfect atmosphere for the last evening of the festival.

Tonight, in keeping with the Farewell to Bath Musical Masquerade theme, the festival-goers wore brilliant, jewel-tone clothes with fanciful masks playfully obscuring the wearers' identities. Of course, as with any masked event, one could generally recognize those with whom one was familiar, but it always lent a bit of mischief and mystery to the occasion. William knew from experience that those present would be more daring, more honest to their true selves.

Adjusting his own mask, which was covered in unembellished midnight-blue satin to complement his jacket of the same color, he peered out over the crowd, gaining his bearings. Most of the activity was clustered around the pavilion, where a full orchestra was arranged in a sweeping half-moon, their dark and somber clothes serving as the perfect backdrop for the dull shine of their instruments.

The amphitheater was divided into several dozen temporary boxes, each one separated by bright fabric panels and boasting between six and ten seats. Some were attended to by servants, and featured tables of food and drink, not unlike the boxes at Vauxhall Gardens.

Since the concert had yet to begin, many of those present were still milling about, conversing with great enthusiasm, if the level of noise was any indication. William ignored those clustered on the lawn and instead scanned the boxes for Dering, who had invited William to join him. In a matter of moments he spotted his friend's huge frame, which stood head and shoulders above those around him. He was at the center of a small group of people, gesturing widely as he no doubt relayed one of his many stories.

William plunged ahead into the throng, keeping his attention straight ahead as a means of discouraging interruption. He was well aware that masked events did nothing to hide his identity, and instead seemed to make him only more approachable to those who were normally too shy or prudent to speak to him.

Tonight would be no different, it seemed. He'd made it only halfway to his destination when someone snagged his arm, bringing him to an abrupt stop. He swung around, prepared to give a cutting remark, when he spotted the golden hair of the woman whose fingers still clutched his sleeve. For a moment, his heart leapt to his throat, but then he realized she was far too short to be his lovely rival. He released his breath and scowled at the light brown eyes behind the shimmering gold mask. "I beg your pardon," he said curtly, tugging his arm from her grasp.

She gave a sultry little chuckle. "I thought that might be you. It's Miss Harmon, Your Grace. I'm positively crushed we missed each other at the ball the other night."

He had to work to keep his annoyance in check. It was just like her to presume that he would wish to speak with her. Despite the come-hither glint in her eyes, there was something very calculating about the way she looked at him. He was willing to bet that was why one with her beauty was still unmarried. It certainly wasn't for lack of trying on her part.

"Is there something I can do for you, Miss Harmon?"

Her smile never wavered as she leaned in close. "Perhaps you wouldn't mind escorting me to my father's box? I fear I've grown weary of standing about with no decent conversation to be had."

He had absolutely no desire to escort her anywhere, but he lived and breathed proper manners, and he was going that direction anyhow. Inwardly sighing, he offered a shallow nod. "Very well."

At his invitation, she snaked her arm fully around his, as good as claiming him. "My hero," she purred as they started down the footpath toward the pavilion. "I can't tell you how delighted I was that you'd decided to join the festival, however briefly. In all honesty, though it was rich in musical diversions, I found it alarmingly devoid of proper society."

"Interesting. I have found perfectly acceptable company thus far."

"Oh, do go on," she said, as though they both knew he was putting her on. "Why, I saw you speaking with Miss Bradford at the ball, you poor thing. Despite her handsome face, she has all the wit and manners of a dairymaid." She gave a commiserative chuckle, shaking her head. "And now I feel as though I've insulted dairy-maids."

The surge of anger that the comment brought took William by surprise. Yes, he might have thought the same thing only a few days before, but that didn't mean that he would sit by and let Miss Harmon spread her venom. "Miss Bradford is not used to society, I daresay. She has proven to be a unique and interesting individual, despite her shortcomings."

Why was it he felt as though he were betraying her simply by mentioning her shortcomings? Lord knew she had many.

"How very diplomatic of you, Your Grace. I confess I wouldn't be nearly so kind if she had spoken to me the way she spoke to you. And on your birthday, no less." She tutted, shaking her head.

His shoulders tensed as he realized that she was speaking of their argument outside of the Assembly Rooms the night they met. It was too much to hope that the incident would have been ignored. Wexley's coach-man must have been one of the witnesses. "How she and I speak is of no concern to you, Miss Harmon."

His voice was heavy with censure, but she didn't seem at all concerned. "Of course you are right," she said air-ily, flipping a hand by way of dismissal. "But should you desire the company of one with the utmost respect and admiration for both you and your rank, I do hope you'll know where to look."

He didn't wish to pursue the topic any longer, and he certainly had no intention of taking her up on her offer, so he said simply, "Indeed."

Her eyes brightened behind her shimmering mask. "I know what a great music lover you are, and that various obligations kept you from attending much of the ball. As an exceptionally accomplished pianoforte player, I would be more than happy to give you a private performance before you depart."

She put so much husky emphasis on the word *private*, it was impossible to mistake her meaning. Yes, he could imagine her father would just love that. "I'm afraid I'll be returning to my estate by week's end." He paused just at the edge of the first row of boxes. "I imagine you can find your way from here?"

"Oh, yes, I'm aware," she said, making no move to disengage her hand from his arm. "Lady Radcliffe was telling me only yesterday of her plans to accompany you to Clifton House. Why, with the two of you, it would only take a handful more to make it a house party. No need to keep such a fine estate all to yourselves."

If she thought that implying friendship with his stepmother would gain her any favors, she was sorely mistaken. "The solitude is its greatest asset, Miss Harmon. If Lady Radcliffe feels otherwise, she is welcome to avoid it."

Her smile turned hard, as though she were gritting her teeth. "If you should change your mind, I trust I'll be the first to know."

Instead of answering her honestly, which was impossible to do without being overtly harsh, he pulled his arm from her grasp and tipped his head. "I hope you enjoy your evening, Miss Harmon."

Dipping into a pretty curtsy, she looked up at him through the slanted holes of her mask. "And you, Your Grace. I do hope I'll see you again soon."

To say the words were ripe with promise would be a tremendous understatement. It made him very, very glad that he hadn't been here for the whole festival. It was also clear warning that he should be on his guard tonight. He didn't want to find himself alone in her clutches somewhere.

Turning on his heel, he headed straight to Dering's box.

"He's here!" Sophie dropped her opera glasses onto the blanket and turned back to May, her dark eyes huge against the pale yellow of her mask.

"If by *he*, you mean your husband, then yes, I'm here," Lord Evansleigh said, cutting a teasing grin to his wife. "*Right* here."

It was probably a good thing that they were positioned so far from the rest of the concertgoers. May sat in the middle, Charity and Sophie on either side of her, and their respective significant others beside them. In order for Charity's betrothed to join them, they had claimed a spot on the lawn well away from the orchestra. Lord Cadgwith rarely joined them for festival outings, but he seemed quite content. With the distance from the rest of the attendees, it allowed their small group to relax and truly enjoy themselves. It also allowed them to tease and laugh as much as they pleased.

Sophie rolled her eyes. "Oh, hush, we're not talking to or about you," she replied tartly, before laughing when he grabbed her by the waist and tugged her against him. "And besides, I know *exactly* where you are: at my side where you belong."

Evansleigh nodded as though perfectly pleased with his wife's possessiveness. "Very well. Back to your spying, then."

May grinned. The pair of them were exactly what she thought a good English married couple would never be: completely in love and uncaring of who knew it. Wasn't that why her mother had run away with her father?

Theirs was a match that was looked down upon by Mama's family, and to this day, May had never spoken to or written with anyone on her mother's side.

Charity leaned forward. "The duke is here? Where did you see him?"

Sophie handed her the glasses and pointed to the left of the stage. "The third box from the front. He's with Dering and a few of their friends."

Pushing her mask up onto her forehead, Charity squinted through the lenses. "Oh yes! I see him. Very dark and dashing tonight, I must say."

"I can hear you," Cadgwith deadpanned, never taking his eyes from the stage.

"That's nice, dear," Charity replied, winking to May and Sophie. "And your coloring is much too fair to ever be dark and dashing. You will have to settle for rakishly handsome." After Cadgwith's chuckle, she held out the glasses to May. "He does look rather lonely, if you ask me."

May crossed her arms. "Oh no, I am not participating in this."

Her pulse might have kicked up at Sophie's announcement, but she was determined not to be their little project tonight.

"Mmhmm," Sophie murmured, exchanging a glance with Charity. "Don't think that we didn't notice that you wore your most gorgeous gown yet tonight, which is really saying something, given the caliber of your wardrobe."

"First of all, I wore this gown because I was *allowed* to wear this gown. My aunt would never normally allow me to leave the house in scarlet red," she said, waving to the bold silk and satin creation, its hem and high waistline skillfully embroidered with shimmering gold thread.

It was by far her favorite gown, and it had been moldering in her trunks since she arrived. Paired with the glittering gold mask Sophie had commissioned for her, May had to admit that she felt special. Powerful. More like herself than she had in a long time.

"Is there a second of all?" Charity asked, her gray eyes wide and innocent. Too innocent.

May narrowed her eyes. "Second of all, whatever I choose to wear has nothing to do whatsoever with any man, duke or otherwise."

Sophie scoffed, unimpressed. "Other than the fact that you look absolutely exquisite, and any unmarried man under the age of ninety would take notice, including one handsome and available Duke of Radcliffe."

May chose not to respond. It was clear her friends had their hearts set on pairing May with the duke, so she knew she'd be wasting her breath. Besides, he *had* been on her mind when she had slipped into the gorgeous gown, but she would have worn it whether he was here or not, so technically her claims held truth.

Still. If she did happen to run into the man, a part of her hoped he'd take note. There was absolutely nothing wrong with that, even if she didn't wish to share that particular fact with her friends.

Pulling off her mask, Sophie turned to Charity with raised brows. "Not another word. I think we may have just won."

They were absolutely incorrigible. "The two of you may think what you like. I am here to enjoy the marvelous music, and to spend time with you both before you leave next week."

"So here is my plan," Sophie said, obviously ignoring May's protestations. "After the concert, we shall all go over to greet Radcliffe, and I'll convince him to walk with us. Once we naturally break up into pairs, you can lead him to the copse of trees beside the canal and voila! A stolen kiss with the duke."

May shook her head and laughed. The woman's imagination was positively legendary. "Absolutely not. Not only do I have no interest in kissing the man, that is the most convoluted—"

Charity grabbed May's hand, cutting her off midsentence. "He's leaving!"

The wave of disappointment that washed from her chest all the way down to her toes proved May to be a liar. Parting with her aunt standing there watching their every move had not given her the chance to properly say good-bye. Her stomach twisted anxiously at the thought of him simply walking out of her life forever. Swallowing her pride, she snatched the opera glasses from Charity's fingers and peered through them.

There he was, exiting the box with his shoulders wide and straight and his strides long and confident. Damn it all, she might not want to ambush the man with kisses, but she did want to see him one more time before he left for good. After all, he hadn't seen her dress, and she hadn't told him how very ineffective that mask was at concealing his identity. His composure and self-assurance branded him as the man of power he was, regardless of some piece of fabric stretched across part of his face.

Dropping the eyepiece to the blanket, she came to her feet, startling all four of her companions. "If you'll excuse me, I have an errand to run. I'll be back shortly."

"Miss Bradford," Evansleigh started to say, his mouth turned down in a very chaperonelike expression, but Sophie stopped him with a light tap to his chest.

"She's fine, Evan. She simply needs to stretch her legs for a moment, and if she can travel the world in one piece, I'm certain she shall be fine in Sydney Gardens. Right, May?"

May sent her a grateful look, suddenly very, very glad that she had managed to find such wonderful friends. "Yes, quite. I shall be back before you know it."

Drawing a fortifying breath, she set off across the lawn, aiming to intercept the duke before he reached the boundary of the park. She had no idea what she would say to him once she caught up to him, she knew only that this was her chance, and by Jove she was taking it.

Though the music had been remarkable, and the evening exceedingly fine, there was nothing that could compel William to stay once Vivian and Norwich had joined the box beside them. It was as though the woman had a sixth sense about where she wasn't wanted.

He'd recognized her flaming red hair in an instant, piled atop her head and draped with the distinctive diamond tiara his father had given her on the occasion of Julian's birth. She wore a sheer silvery gown with an even sheerer gossamer overlay and an open décolleté that dipped appallingly low across her chest. It was an outfit better left to the bedroom, as far as he was concerned.

He was extremely displeased that she was continuing to see the earl, and he had no intentions of sitting beside them as though he was perfectly amenable to their pairing. He stalked along the grass, taking the most direct route back to his horse, heedless of the state of his shoes. This was *not* how he'd envisioned the evening progressing. He was much too dignified for this sort of thing, but once again, the woman had gotten beneath his skin.

A movement in the bushes ahead snapped his mind back to the present, and he took a quick step to the side.

"Who goes there?" The lanterns were few and far between this far from the concert, and he squinted into the darkness.

A gold-masked blond woman appeared from around the foliage and whispered his name.

He gritted his teeth against the curse that came to his tongue. Of course Miss Harmon would pounce on the chance to get him alone. Extending a stern finger in her direction, he said, "Perhaps I wasn't clear enough before, so let me be *very* plain. I have no interest whatsoever in you. *Go away.*"

Even with the dim light and the mask covering her features, he could see her eyes go saucer wide. Good. Perhaps he'd finally gotten his point across. She pressed her lips together, straightened to a surprising height and said, "Thank you for clarifying. I have no intention of being where I'm not bloody well wanted."

His heart slammed to a stop in his chest the moment she said "thank you." *May!* He started forward, determined to correct his mistake. "Miss Bradford, I—"

But she held up her hands, cutting him off. "And for the record, if you had wanted me to go away, all you had to do was say so. I'm not a blasted mind reader, you know."

"Miss Brad—"

"Furthermore, you need to work on your communication skills," she said, her finger pointing back at him just as he had done to her. "One can't smile and wink at another without said other feeling as though their company is at least somewhat welcome."

She was in full dudgeon now, her eyes flashing like black diamonds in the darkness. He could just make out the rest of her, outfitted in a superbly fitting gown that had just enough sheen in the moonlight to hint at its silkiness. The color was impossible to determine, but it was dark against her pale skin.

"I—"

"Good evening, Your Grace. Or better yet, good life." She turned sharply on her heel and took one magnificent step forward.

"May," he exclaimed, grabbing her hand in a bid to halt her escape.

That got her attention, to say the least. She snapped her mouth shut as she whirled back around to face him, her eyes piercing in their intensity. Yes, he'd taken drastic measures, but she'd be halfway across the park by now if he hadn't stopped her momentum.

Taking advantage of her shock, he tugged her toward him. She stumbled forward, stopping only inches from his chest. Awareness washed through him, pooling in his gut as he realized just how alone they really were in that moment. Drawing a calming, floral-tinged breath of air, he said evenly, "I thought you were Miss Harmon."

It was the wrong thing to say. Whatever spell that had held her in thrall abruptly shattered. She drew back, her face screwing up beneath the mask. "Miss Harmon? How on earth could you confuse me with that earth-vexing woman?" She yanked her fingers from his grasp and crossed her arms, waiting expectantly for his explanation. She looked every bit as imperious as a disapproving Greek goddess.

Waving a hand vaguely, he said, "Gold mask, blond hair, dark night. Mostly, I had no idea you were even here, and I most certainly knew she was, much to my dismay."

"Oh," she said, dropping her arms back to her side.

He chuckled softly, shaking his head. "And once again, all I get is an 'oh.'"

"Yes, well, it was an honest misunderstanding on both our parts."

He let the comment go without challenge. To challenge her would only get her back up again. Purposely relaxing his stance, he tilted his head to catch her eye. "Were you looking for me?"

She gave a little shrug, her lips lifting in an enticing little smile. "Yes, though I'm having a hard time recalling why."

Across the park, the orchestra started a new song, this one slower, more languid. It was the perfect backdrop to the warm and slightly humid night.

"Are you?" he replied, his voice slightly rough. He pursed his lips, hating that she still looked like the distasteful Miss Harmon. "One second," he said, moving closer so he could reach the strings of her mask. Thanks to the delectable cut of her gown, he saw the rise of her breasts as she inhaled sharply. He realized how unseemly their position was, but it seemed best to just be done with it instead of making it seem as though he were retreating from her. Swallowing, he tugged the strings and pulled the mask from her face. *Much better.*

Stepping back quickly, he cleared his throat and returned to the conversation. "Perhaps you wished to say good-bye without a ballroom of people as witness?"

She was more beautiful than she had a right to be. Her skin looked as pale and smooth as fresh cream in the silvery moonlight, her eyes as dark as the night sky. Why had she come after him? She had followed him into the darkness, wanting to speak with him in private. His pulse kicked up at all the reasons why she might wish to do such a thing.

"Perhaps." She gave a delicate shrug, arching one impish brow. She stepped forward then, closing the distance he had just made between them. Slowly, she reached up one hand behind him to untie his mask. He'd knotted the ribbons himself, and it didn't give way as hers had. Instead of giving up, she slid her other arm up into something that very much resembled an embrace and worked the knot free.

She smelled so incredibly good, he fought not to draw a long deep breath. Through force of will, he held very still until she was done. It was sweet torture, something he never would have imagined he'd feel with her.

"There," she said quietly, pulling the mask free. He exhaled. *Finally.* She allowed her hands to slide down the front of his chest, her touch little more than a skim. "I much prefer being able to see you."

He smiled, a lopsided lift of his lip. "After the way things started off between us, I never would have expected to hear those words from your mouth."

She chuckled. "Touché."

She didn't step away, and neither did he. Of their own volition, his eyes fell to those full, beautiful lips of hers.

"Won't you be missed?"

Surely she had come with others, so it stood to reason that they'd be wondering where she was. The last thing he needed was indignant chaperones making an appearance.

"Soon. But not yet." She wet her lips, sending anticipation burning through his chest. She was brash and forward, irreverent and impulsive—everything that he thought he didn't like—yet in that moment, he had never wanted to kiss someone more in his whole life. The desire was as strong as gravity, making it near impossible for him to pull away from her.

He was a gentleman, he reminded himself. It wasn't right to kiss an innocent like her. It was up to him to do the right thing. Closing his eyes, he drew in a breath, trying to find the strength to step away from her.

"Radcliffe," she breathed, the longing palpable in her voice.

Shaking his head, he opened his eyes. "I can't. There are rules in society that cannot be ignored."

He was a duke. He didn't misstep; he didn't dabble in scandal. He held the moral high ground because he lived his life according to the rules. Kissing her would hardly be a cardinal sin, but it would compromise the strict code that he lived by.

"Damn the English and their ridiculous rules," she muttered darkly. She was silent for a moment, and he imagined he could hear her heart beating as loudly as his was. "Did you know," she said at last, "that there are many acceptable ways to say good-bye, depending on where you are from?"

He blinked, doing his best to follow where she was headed. "Oh?"

She nodded, her eyes never leaving his as she stepped back. He hated the distance she put between them, even as he willed her to step back farther. "In China, they bow, but differently from the British." She demonstrated, bending forward with one hand fisted and the other wrapped around it. "In India, one doesn't bow. Instead, they press their hands together and dip their heads slightly." Again she showed him, murmuring, "Namaste."

Straightening, she said, "In America, shaking hands is more common, or so I hear." Reaching out, she slipped her right hand into his and moved their combined hands up and down a few times. When she stopped, she didn't release her hold. "And in Italy and France?"

She tightened her grip and slowly pulled him to her. He could have resisted—should have—but he allowed her to draw him close. Lifting onto her toes, she pressed her lips to first one cheek, and then the other. "They kiss. It's not only acceptable, it's expected."

"Good to know," he said, struggling to keep the desire from his voice.

Offering a slow, challenging smile, she turned her head, presenting him with the impossibly smooth skin of her cheek. "So tell me good-bye, Duke."

Chapter Ten

May held perfectly still, with even her breath frozen in her lungs, waiting for Radcliffe to lean down and press his lips to her. She couldn't even say what had happened. One minute, they were arguing and teasing again, and the next, her heart was thundering with anticipation. She stood there, hoping, *wanting*, waiting for the man to break out of his own bonds and seize what he so clearly desired.

To give them both what they wanted.

He leaned forward, then hesitated, his breath warming the skin at her neck. She shivered with the sheer delight of it. The smell of his sandalwood soap mixed with the unnamable yet intoxicating scent of his breath, drove her mad. He would taste like that; she knew he would. Despite her resolve to stay still, she swayed toward him an inch or so, encouraging him to take what she offered.

Then, just when she was sure he would give in, he exhaled deeply. He leaned back—the wrong direction, damn him!—and lifted their still joined hands. "And in England," he said, his voice as rough as sandpaper, "this is how we say good-bye." Holding her hand as gently as if it were made of bone china, he leaned down and pressed a kiss to her curled fingers. The warmth of his mouth easily penetrated the thin leather of her glove, but still she cursed the thing to perdition. She wanted to feel *him*, damn it, not the sterile suggestion of him.

But it was not to be. Straightening, he released her hand and stepped away. She immediately felt the loss of his warmth, and cursed him for his blasted manners. "I knew there was a reason I so disliked this country."

A small ghost of a smile graced his lips. "It's been a pleasure, Miss Bradford. I wish you all the best."

"Do you? I'm not certain I should say what I wish for you right about now."

He chuckled then, the sound half mirth, half regret. "I can imagine."

There was nothing different about the way the park looked that morning. The trees were still heavy with damp leaves, the grass still cool and wet beneath her feet. The river still swooshed by quietly within its banks. The light was less than inspiring, with the dull gray clouds hanging low and ominous above, but even that wasn't unusual in this soggy little country.

It was all as it had been, but yet somehow empty. Heartless. The festival was over, and the exodus of its attendees was under way. Other than Charity and Sophie, who would both be leaving on Monday, two days hence, there were only a handful of people she would truly miss. Dering actually lived in Bath, part-time at least, so she wouldn't be completely bereft of company. The vicar had proven to be an entertaining companion, so she would truly be sorry to see him leave.

But none of these impending departures explained the hollowness that settled heavily in her chest that morning. It darkened her mood and dulled her enthusiasm for the exercises she generally loved. She, Mei-li Bradford, strong and independent person of worldly experience, was missing a man.

It was ridiculous. Galling even. But absolutely true. Which was even more galling. Blowing out an exasperated breath, she got into position and began her routine. She eased from one movement to the next, slowly and methodically, concentrating on the hum of her energy and the gracefulness of the move. Still she pictured him, his bronze eyes burning through her as they had the night before.

She paused midmotion and stood. She had to get out of her own mind. Shaking her limbs, she drew another long breath and settled back into the position she had abandoned. Closing her eyes, she pictured the dramatic, cone-shaped mountains of Thailand, rising out of the deep blue waters of the Indian Ocean. She imagined the many shades of green, the fierce reds and oranges of the flowers, the familiar call of wildlife. White sand, gentle waves, Radcliffe standing barefoot in the surf, shirtless, as the ocean breeze tousled his sun-lightened hair.

Gasping, she opened her eyes, her heart pounding. What in the world was wrong with her? She rubbed her cool hand over her face, trying to get ahold of herself.

"A bit off this morning, are we?"

She gave a little shriek of surprise and whirled around to find the man of her imagination standing there behind her. He was properly dressed, hat in place and hair neatly combed, but her belly still flipped at the sight of him.

Not wanting him to guess her thoughts, she set her hands to her hips and lifted her chin. "Can I help you?" It still rather smarted that the man had refused to kiss her yesterday. She'd spent much of the night before lying in bed and thinking of the encounter, all the while toying with the ribbons of his mask.

He smiled at her insolent tone. Taking off his hat, he set it on the heap of her jacket and walked over to her. "I certainly hope so. There is nothing so bothersome to me as a squeaky conscience."

What the devil was he talking about now? "If you are looking to confess, I know a very good vicar to whom you can speak." Lord knew his wounded conscience had nothing to do with her. If it had, she would have slept much better last night, satisfied with a proper kiss goodbye.

"A vicar cannot help, I'm afraid." He clasped his hands behind his back and paced before her, the damp grass softening his footfalls. "I find I cannot bring myself to leave you here alone in Bath, with only your aunt for company. It wouldn't be fair to either of you.

"Further, it occurred to me that you have formed quite an unfair opinion of this country, which sorely needs to be corrected. What better place to do so than at the finest estate in all of England?"

Something fluttered deep in her chest, but she couldn't help teasing him a bit. "In your humble opinion, I suppose?"

"My opinion is never humble," he said decisively. Now that was something she could believe. He stopped his pacing and pinned her with a look that was unnerving in its earnestness. "I'll write to your aunt this afternoon. There is no reason for you to be miserable until your father returns. Lady Stanwix can come on and keep my stepmother company, and I shall take about the task of demonstrating to you why England is the greatest country on Earth."

"Again, *so* very humble," she said dryly. His offer

thrilled her, but she chafed at his high-handed manner. Did it ever occur to him to ask instead of decreeing?

Just to be contrary, she said, "I'm not convinced the company would be such a vast improvement over my current situation." Still ... it was extremely tempting. She had no interest in hearing more about the wonders of the British Empire, where men like him were handed riches and respect without so much as lifting a finger, but if it meant getting out from beneath her aunt's thumb, she was willing to go along with it.

He quirked a brow. "You wound me."

"I'm intrigued enough to consider it ..." She trailed off, straightening as a thought occurred to her. "But if I am to submit to your lessons, I would ask you to submit to mine."

Something flashed in his eyes, and she sincerely wished she knew what he was thinking. "I can't imagine you'd think I'd submit to anything."

She smiled at him, taking in his perfect appearance, covered from wrist to neck to the soles of his feet. The image of him as she had imagined him on the beach slipped back through her mind. What she would give to see him loosen up a little. To drop the driving need to be proper at all times, and actually live a little. "I agree to go with you to your estate—assuming my aunt agrees—and to listen to whatever predictable, inflated thing you have to say about this country and its customs, but in return, I'd like something from you."

"You do realize that the entire invitation is for your benefit, yes?"

"So you say. But if you want me to come, I want to share my morning routine with you. I can easily teach you a few basic moves."

His brows shot up his forehead. "Here? You must be

mad. If someone were to see me involved in such a thing, I'd never live it down. It's bad enough that I am here alone with you now."

Yes, of course—an unpardonable sin to have a conversation with a female acquaintance. "Fair enough. At your estate, then. I'm assuming you have a lake or stream on your property, yes?"

He nodded, crossing his arms over his chest. "Several of both."

"Excellent. Do you agree to my terms?"

His smile bordered on devilish. "I have no reason to. I could easily say no and leave you to your aunt's lovely company until your father returns."

"But you won't," she said confidently, flashing him a knowing smile. The fact that he had invited her at all spoke volumes about the way he thought of her. Anticipation wended its way through her veins, a very heady sensation indeed.

He sighed heavily and shook his head. "But I won't. Be ready at noon, two days hence. I'll take care of speaking with your aunt."

Without waiting for her response, he turned, retrieved his hat, and took off into the morning gloom.

"I must say, I am at a loss, old man."

William nearly raised his glass to that. Dering wasn't the only one feeling that way. "Is that so?"

His friend swirled his drink round and round his glass, peering thoughtfully over the rim. "That's so. Am I to believe you have developed an interest in Miss Bradford since the last time we spoke?"

William took a long drink of his wine, considering the question. "I wouldn't say that."

"So you have no intentions toward her? Marital or otherwise?"

If William hadn't already swallowed, he would have choked on his drink. "I *definitely* wouldn't say that."

Setting down his glass, Dering met his gaze squarely. "Then what would you say?" There was a distinct edge to his voice. A warning, unless William was mistaken. In all their years of friendship, he couldn't recall ever hearing that particular tone directed toward him.

He didn't appreciate the implication. "I would say it was none of your business."

"I'm well aware that you look down on the girl, Will, but I won't allow you to hurt her." He was serious. It had been years since Dering had called him Will. With his hulking shoulders tensed and his dark eyes narrowed, he would have been uncomfortably intimidating if William didn't know him as well as he did.

Actually, it was still intimidating.

Dering leaned forward, earnestness outlined in his every feature. "I *will* show up on your doorstep if I believe your motives are less than gentlemanly. And I assure you, I am not an easy person to move."

This was *not* the visit William was expecting when Dering had shown up unannounced shortly after supper. The man was a friend, but William had no intention of being interrogated by him or any other person. Setting his goblet aside, he came to his feet. "I meant it when I said it was none of your business, but you of all people should know I am a man of integrity. Your interference is both unwelcome and unneeded."

Dering rose as well, then crossed his arms as he looked down on William. Though the study was spacious enough normally, Dering's censorious presence seemed to dwarf the room and its fine antique furnishings. "That girl has no father or brother to speak for her at the moment. I will not apologize for being concerned for her welfare."

"For heaven's sake, it's not as though I intend to accost her. Furthermore, if you were such a great friend to her, you would know that if it was needed—and it is not—Miss Bradford is more than capable of taking care of herself." In fact, if she had any inkling of this conversation, she'd be livid.

Dering shook his head. "You are discounting how easily passion can get the best of a person."

"I'm not a man controlled by his passions." In fact, William was more in control of his baser needs than any man he knew. If he wasn't, would he have walked away from the kiss he so desperately had wanted the night of the concert? He bit the inside of his cheek, remembering just how much he had yearned to take her in his arms. Perhaps that wasn't the greatest example.

"That's what you think," Dering said, pulling William back from his thoughts. "When you truly fall for a woman, you will know how absurd that statement is. *Every* man is a man controlled by his passions when the right woman is about."

The fervor with which he spoke belied how personal the issue really was. Once again, William knew he was thinking of a different time, a different female.

Shifting uncomfortably, he nodded. "If it makes you feel better, I give you my word as a gentleman that Miss Bradford will be perfectly safe in my presence."

Blowing out a sigh, Dering set a wide hand to William's shoulder. "There is one thing you are forgetting, old friend. Women can be ruled by their passions as well. Be careful, or you will have me to answer to."

Giving him an uncomfortably firm pat to his back, Dering brushed past him and headed for the door. "Safe travels, my friend. When in doubt of how to behave, just imagine my fist in your face." The last was said with a wink before he disappeared into the corridor.

William stared after him, hardly able to believe the odd conversation. Despite the wink, he had the distinct impression the man meant what he said. Lucky for William, he had every intention of keeping his word. May was a friend, of a sort, and he intended to keep it that way.

And if she was the first female friend he had ever invited to his estate, well, that simply spoke to how well he thought of her. He sat back down and rubbed his jaw. Perhaps Dering's threat wasn't such a bad thing after all.

Chapter Eleven

The sun shone bright and hot as May, Charity, and Sophie walked along the riverbank, their moods reflective as they followed the same path they had taken the day they met two months earlier.

It was hard to believe so much had happened since then. In fact, it was hard to remember how lonely she had been before they had become friends. She stopped walking, and the others followed suit. "If you two don't promise to write me with frightening frequency, I swear to you I shall hex you both."

Sophie laughed even as her eyes shimmered with threatening tears. "And if you don't swear to visit us at least once a year, I shall hex you right back. Or at the very least, send copious stern letters, although I have never been very skilled at coming across as stern, in letters or in person, but I shall do my best."

Shaking her head, May swallowed her friend up in a fierce hug. "I can't believe you are an old married lady now. And a countess, at that! I shall never call you anything but Sophie, no matter how respectable you are."

She turned to Charity, who was biting her lip against

the myriad emotions May could see in those sweet gray eyes of hers. "And you. Do please hurry up and set your wedding date. I want to be sure I can be there."

Sighing, Charity shook her head. "It may be some time yet. We are taking things as slowly as Hugh needs. Still, I shall be utterly heartbroken if you are off sailing the world when we finally do marry."

Sophie linked arms with the both of them. "Which is why I am pinning all my hopes on this trip of yours to Clifton House. I hereby demand that you fall head over heels for the man so that you can marry him and spend your days within carriage-riding distance from us. I am a countess now, so you have to do what I say," she added with a mischievous grin.

May groaned. "I knew I shouldn't have told you about it. I assure you, it is merely a diversion until my father comes. Since the two of you couldn't see fit to stick around and rescue me from my aunt's company, I had to make do with the next best thing."

"Oh, pish," Sophie said, giving May a teasing bump of her hip. "Don't go ruining our fun. Now that we are both settled, we need to live vicariously through your romantic escapades."

"Sophie!" May couldn't help but laugh. "You are absolutely incorrigible. There are no escapades in my life, romantic or otherwise."

Charity's copper brows lifted. "Oh? Then why, I wonder, are you suddenly blushing?"

"The heat, of course," May responded promptly. "Now then, in all seriousness, I love you both to pieces and I am so glad my father left me here for the summer. No matter what I think of your soggy, stuffy little island, I am tremendously glad to have met you both."

The tears flowed then, and the three of them were hugging and wishing one another well, demanding again that they write one another often.

Finally, May sighed. "I suppose I need to get back if I'm to meet His Grace's stated time line." Despite her sadness at leaving her friends, a little spark of excitement flared to life at the thought of the coming fortnight.

Drying her eyes on a dainty lace handkerchief, Charity nodded. "And Grandmama and I need to tour the town house to be certain the servants haven't overlooked anything."

Sophie nodded as well. "And Evan wants to make it to the estate by dinner, so I'd best be getting back as well."

Linking arms again, they started back down the trail. "But just so you know," Sophie said out of the blue several minutes later, "I'm still close enough to make it to the duke's house in less than half a day. If you need anything—*anything*—send word and I shall be there in a trice. All right?"

"Duly noted." The promise did actually make May feel marginally better. Knowing Radcliffe, she didn't foresee any great dramas occurring under his watch, but it was good to know she wasn't completely without friends.

"Good," she said with a decisive nod. "Which means I can also be there in a trice should you have need of a special license and vicar. Obviously I know how to procure both."

Their shared laughter filled the air around them, warming May's heart more effectively than the late-summer sun ever could. "*Don't* get your hopes up."

By the time May returned to the house, though, anticipation had begun to build low in her stomach and was spreading with each step. She really didn't want to get her friends excited about something that was never going to lead to matrimony—God knew she'd never cleave herself to a landlocked Englishman—but it would be a lie to say she wasn't looking forward to the trip.

Particularly the lessons she still couldn't believe Radcliffe had agreed to. And if she could loosen him up enough to steal the kiss he had denied her at the concert? That would definitely be something to remember the trip by.

Grinning, she let herself into the house, where servants were rushing this way and that in preparation for their departure. As May walked past the drawing room, her aunt's voice stopped her in her tracks.

"Where have you been, young lady?"

Drawing a long-suffering breath, May backed up a few steps and looked to where Aunt Victoria sat on her favorite chair, already outfitted in her olive green traveling costume. The older woman's mouth pinched as she surveyed May's appearance. "The duke will be here any minute, and you look as though you have been hiking through the hills like a farm girl."

May glanced down at her rumpled and tearstained morning dress. "What, is the windswept look not as popular here as it is on the islands?" The quip was out before May could think better of it, as usual. It probably wasn't the best way to start a day that would include the two of them being trapped in a carriage for several hours together. Still, she had just said good-bye to her two closest friends and she wasn't in the mood to be criticized.

"Do not make me regret accepting the duke's invitation. It is not too late for me to beg off due to sudden illness."

As threats went, it was rather toothless. May knew her

aunt well enough to know that she would not risk disappointing the duke.

She forced a contrite smile. "Fear not, I'll be perfectly presentable in no time."

She started to walk away, but her aunt wasn't finished. "It was against my better judgment to accept in the first place," she said, her mouth turned down in a frown that seemed more worried than chiding. "If I think for one moment you are making a fool of either yourself or me, I will not hesitate to return home. It's precisely why I insisted we travel in our own carriage."

Whether May liked it or not, the threat got her attention. Aunt Victoria genuinely believed that May would be an embarrassment to her, which gave a sound thump to her conscience. There was no love lost between them, but she needed to rein in her tongue and show a little restraint when it came to her aunt. Lifting her shoulders, she nodded once and continued up to her chambers to change. This was not an opportunity she was prepared to lose.

Nervousness was not an emotion William was accustomed to. He generally went through life with the sureness that came from knowing one's place at the top of the social ladder.

Yet that's exactly what he was feeling as they turned the final corner on the road to Clifton House. He slowed his horse and maneuvered to the side of the carriage where he knew Miss Bradford sat. She readily opened the window and smiled up at him, her brilliant blue eyes glittering beautifully in the afternoon sun. "Am I to assume we are almost there?"

"Less than a quarter mile to go. Would you like to walk the rest of the way, or would you prefer to ride?"

"I would gladly pay you to get out of this carriage right now," she replied, earning a pained sound from Lady Stanwix.

William smiled. Exactly what he thought she would say. He nodded and called to the coachman, who promptly pulled back on the reins. Dismounting, he tied Gray to the back of the carriage and hurried around to assist Miss Bradford to the ground. He gestured for them to go ahead, and within moments they were alone.

He drew a deep, contented breath as he looked around the familiar oaks and neatly trimmed hedges that lined the lane. "I confess, nothing is ever so great as the feeling of returning home. How are you faring?"

Her pretty blue traveling costume was slightly the worse for wear, and she gave the skirts a good shake before smoothing a hand over her hair. "Anything disparaging that I ever said about you, I take it all back. Any man who would rescue me from the clutches of The Warden has my undying admiration."

His eyes widened. "The *Warden*? A little dramatic, don't you think?"

She shrugged, not at all concerned. "Perhaps, but it suits both her personality and my mood. It's a shame Lady Radcliffe went on ahead of us. I would have been better off sharing her carriage."

William didn't comment. She would form her own opinion of Vivian over the next fortnight. A small bur of worry slid between his ribs. He hoped Vivian would behave when she saw the children later that evening. She was never cruel to them, merely indifferent, but he wasn't sure one was necessarily worse than the other.

Setting aside his worry for the time being, he extended his arm to Miss Bradford. "Shall we continue? I imagine you're anxious to rest up after such a long journey."

She chuckled softly, shaking her head. "That was little more than a jaunt. If you wish to speak of long journeys, I'm more than happy to tell you all about sailing halfway across the world."

They fell into step with each other as they walked along the lane. Pride welled within him as they approached the point where the manor would come into view. For the second time that day, a hint of nervousness tightened his chest. "I will leave the world travel to you, as I am absolutely content right here in Codford. In fact," he said, gesturing ahead as the trees gave way to the full glory of the house and grounds, "I give you my home, Clifton House."

Miss Bradford followed his direction and gazed out over the view. He'd been gone only a short while, but the scene was enough to make his chest ache. The grounds were meticulously groomed, the huge gates impressive, the house absolutely majestic. The afternoon sun reflected gloriously off the gold leaf sashes of all one hundred windows lining the west-facing facade, making the whole house shimmer. The grand fountain that was centered before the house sparkled as well, the water shooting up two stories into the air before cascading back to its huge oval pool.

Exhaling with pleasure, he turned to see her reaction, to observe the moment when he finally impressed her. But her face wasn't lit with awe or wonder. She didn't even look mildly impressed. What he saw in her expression was a blow to his pride: She was indifferent.

"It's big," she said, stating the obvious.

Big? That's all she could say about his ancestral home, the single most celebrated privately owned residence in all of the country? About the building that was an architectural wonder, updated with the very latest in modern conveniences and the envy of all who saw it?

"Yes, it is big," he replied, his words clipped. "One hundred and eleven rooms, to be exact."

She turned to him, one blond brow arched high. "I had no idea you had so many family members. Christmases must be chaos at your house."

First she was indifferent, and now she was offering sarcasm? His eyes narrowed slightly as he pinned her with a chilly stare. "Do you think to insult me, Miss Bradford?"

"Not *you*," she replied, extending an arm toward the house. "But I have to wonder, what on earth is the point of a house this size? What does one do with all those rooms? And please tell me I am imagining that your windows are lined with gold."

He clenched his jaw, glaring at her and her impertinence. "Gold leafing is extremely durable and is a practical solution to weatherproofing so many windows. As for the size, the majority of the rooms are for guests, should a house party or ball be thrown. Social functions are expected of a duke."

"Are they? You don't strike me as the type to host house parties and balls. When was the last time you held one?"

Why did he suddenly feel the need to defend his own estate? The house—as well as all his other homes—constituted both his birthright and his legacy. The wealth of his family reflected centuries of good stewardship and good favor from half a dozen monarchs.

Refusing to be bated into defensiveness, he turned and stalked forward, uncaring if she followed or not. If she wished to tag along, that was her prerogative. After a moment, the quickening tap of her half boots on the packed earth indicated her choice.

"I'm sorry," she said, her voice more long-suffering

than sincere. "I just have never seen anything so overtly grandiose. I can't seem to fathom why a single person would need so much."

"Tell me, Miss Bradford. In all of your travels, where was it that you learned to insult your host's home? India? China, perhaps?"

She slowed to a stop, and he swung around to face her. She actually looked a little guilty. "You're right of course. It's never acceptable."

He was just about to thank her when she said, "But in my defense—"

"Oh no," he said, holding up a hand. "You don't get to qualify bad behavior. Either you offer an apology for being wrong, or you keep your tongue behind your teeth."

Her eyes narrowed as her fists went to her side. "Did you just tell me to close my mouth?"

He crossed his arms. "I'd rather you apologize, but I'd accept the other as well."

She opened her mouth, tilted her head, then decisively closed it. Smiling mirthlessly, she started walking again, her pace just this side of trotting. He started after her, his long strides closing the distance between them as he shook his head all the while. "Stubborn to a fault. Very well. I could certainly use a quiet walk on a lovely summer day."

She had to be the single most vexing woman he had ever met. What on earth was it about her that still managed to draw him in? She seemed dead set against everything that defined him. At this rate, the visit was sure to be an exceptionally long one.

After a few minutes of silence, she slipped her hand around his arm, surprising him. As he slowed to a stop, she released her hold and sighed. "Please accept my apologies. I've upset you, and that wasn't my intention. The house is lovely, the grounds are lovely, and you have every right to be proud of them. I was . . . shocked, and I reacted poorly."

This time, she seemed in earnest. He nodded, accepting her apology. "Thank you. I'm sure it can be overwhelming to some the first time they see it. And for the record, it was built long before I was born, so I had no say, but it's part of who I am."

She pursed her lips, glancing back over to the house. "It's hard to imagine having that sort of connection to a house. I've lived in several, and sometimes without one at all, when we lived aboard my father's ship for long stretches."

"How unusual. I cannot imagine not having a place to truly call home."

A gentle smile softened her features. "My mother once told me that home was where one's heart resides, not necessarily where one's head lies at night." It was a telling statement. She spoke quietly, reverently, when she mentioned her mother.

"She sounds very wise."

Miss Bradford nodded, keeping her eyes trained ahead. "She was. I miss her very, very much." She seemed to wilt a little right before his eyes. It was clear the grief was still fresh in her heart.

He reached out and captured her hand to give her a consoling squeeze. "It never goes away completely, but it gets a little easier to bear as you figure out how to live with it." The ache, he knew, would always be there.

For the first time since he'd known her, she seemed almost fragile. It made him want to tug her into his arms and comfort her. He couldn't, of course, not with the unseemliness of such a thing, and certainly not with them in full view of the house, so he simply rubbed his thumb along the top of her hand.

She met his gaze, her own questioning. "Are you thinking of your father or your mother?"

"A little of both, I suppose, but more so my mother. My father was a decent man, but very distant. My memories of my mother are all very . . . warm." It was the best word he could think of to describe the feeling her memory gave him. Most of the actual memories had faded, but the emotion was still there.

"How old were you when you lost her?"

It might have been an intrusive question at any other time—he never spoke of his mother to anyone—but in that moment, it seemed natural. "She died when I was six."

"So young," she said, her voice soft. "I'm sorry."

He cleared his throat, attempting to stop the unexpected upwelling of emotion. The conversation needed to be returned to safer subjects. "Yes, much too young. But I survived, and I am certain that you will heal in time as well."

Releasing her hand, he nodded toward the house. "Shall we? The others will be wondering what became of us."

For a moment, she looked as though she might argue the change in topic. He kept his expression as neutral as he could, willing her to let it go. Finally she nodded and offered a resolute smile. "Yes, of course. I'm positively rapt to see the inside. I do hope it comes with a map."

He released a breath and chuckled. "I'll see what we can find."

Chapter Twelve

The house was a hundred times grander up close than May had feared it would be. Marble floors, statues, and tabletops, crystal sconces and chandeliers, frescoed ceilings and velvet-covered walls—it was really quite overwhelming.

Gold frames here, silver tray there, bronze figures crowding the mantel . . . It was as though the treasure from a dozen pirate ships had ended up in Radcliffe's public rooms. How did one live among so much stuff? It was gorgeous, all of it, but the clutter of it all was almost suffocating.

"It's very nice," she said, as diplomatically as she could. After the way he'd reprimanded her, she was determined to be polite about the place. And after the surprisingly emotional turn of their conversation earlier, she wanted to show kindness toward him.

"Thank you," he said wryly, obviously not fooled. "Would you like to be shown to your chambers now, or would you prefer to sit for a moment?"

She sent him a mock look of trepidation. "The way you say that makes me think that it's another quarter mile to my room from here."

"Don't be ridiculous. It's a fifth of a mile, at most." He was teasing her again, which was a good sign. "Would you like some tea? Or lemonade, perhaps?"

She followed him into what she imagined must be the drawing room, although it was big enough to fit a whole herd of elephants. She wouldn't be surprised if he considered the space cozy. "Any brandy?"

He shot her a look. "Perhaps. Not exactly the most refreshing beverage after our walk."

"Yes, but tremendously refreshing after my carriage ride with Aunt Victoria." Her father had never minded sharing a sip with her growing up—for medicinal reasons, he always claimed—so the drink was sometimes comforting to her.

Chuckling, he headed for the heavily laden sideboard. "Fair enough. Do you prefer vintage?"

"What do you think?" she replied, lifting an eyebrow. It wasn't as though she was used to having a huge selection to choose from. In fact, she was lucky her aunt stocked it at all, though it was entirely possible it had belonged to the old earl.

"The best of the stock it is." He poured a small amount into a crystal tumbler and brought it back to her.

She accepted the glass and settled onto a plush settee that looked as though it had been borrowed from a museum. "None for you?"

"I'm not one for spirits."

Of course he wasn't. It probably topped the list of Things a Duke Did Not Do. "No cursing, no spirits, no kissing willing females in the dark. At least I know you indulge in tobacco, or I might very well have had to turn around and go back to Bath."

He rested a hand on the high wooden back of the impossibly rich-looking sofa and shrugged, very much a master of his domain. "I do enjoy the occasional cheroot. One must do something at one's club."

As intimidating as the room was to her, he looked very much at home in the space. He seemed exceptionally confident here, but still more relaxed than usual. He owned this space, literally and figuratively. He fit in among the rich baubles and furnishings, like a puzzle piece slipping into place.

It raised the question, if she had met him here, how differently would things have gone? Would she ever have guessed that there was more to him than the sum of his wealth and influence? In all honesty, she couldn't imagine she would have ever said a word to him.

She took a sip of her drink. Lud, it was as smooth as warm satin, rich and full of flavor. She made a soft sound of pleasure and leaned back onto the cushions. "I've smoked a cheroot."

He crossed his arms. "Only one?" Humor sparkled in those golden eyes of his. Or perhaps it was the reflection from the weatherproof windowsills.

"Only one. Papa may condone a bit of brandy now and then, but I thought he might actually toss me overboard when he discovered me on deck one night, attempting to smoke my first one."

"And that was enough to prevent you from trying again?" He seemed completely dubious. Apparently, he was truly getting to know her.

Smiling at the memory, she shook her head. "Not at all. But the feel of the grit coating my lungs was."

He gave a small laugh, shaking his head. "Why is it I find myself sympathizing with your poor father? The trouble you undoubtedly gave him must have turned him gray years ago."

"Only his head. His beard was still plenty black the

last time I saw him," she replied archly. She opened her mouth to say more when a crash erupted from the corner of the room, startling them both.

May wrenched around in time to see white-and-blue porcelain skittering across the marble floor and onto the enormous plush rug arranged beneath the conversation area in front of the fireplace. She put a hand over her wildly thumping heart as she turned to Radcliffe. "Bloody hell, that scared me near to death."

A little blond-headed boy popped up from behind the sofa, his eyes huge. "You said a very bad word!"

May could not have been more surprised if a mermaid had appeared in the room. Who was this child, and where the devil had he come from?

Radcliffe, on the other hand, seemed completely unperturbed. Straightening, he settled his hands at his waist and said, "Have you been spying, young man?"

The boy was immediately contrite. "Yes. I know it is wrong and I'm ever so sorry." Even as his chin dipped to his chest, his brown eyes darted back to May, his gaze bright with curiosity. He couldn't have been more than six or seven, and he bore an unnerving resemblance to Radcliffe.

May's own curiosity was piqued now. Surely the duke didn't have *children*. Wouldn't Charity or Sophie have said something? She turned a questioning gaze to the duke. He, however, paid no attention to her. Addressing the back of the room, he said, "Clarisse, I know you must be part of this as well. Show yourself, please." His tone was stern but gentle.

Another head popped up from behind the sofa, this one belonging to a very mischievous looking little girl with strawberry blond curls and bright hazel eyes. "It was Julian's idea," she said, the words completely matter-of-fact. Pointing her finger at May, she added, "Who is she? And which word was bad?"

Radcliffe gestured for them to come closer, and the children did so without fear or concern. May's eyes darted to the broken porcelain on the floor, which thankfully had broken several feet to the left, and had sprayed out in the opposite direction from where they had been hiding. She bit her lip, squinting at what she felt sure was the remains of a priceless vase. It was probably an antique. And royal. And worth more than her father's ship. Yet, to the duke's credit, he didn't seem angry at all.

When the two children were standing guiltily before him, he said, "What are the rules about spying?"

The boy, Julian, spoke first. "Only at the bequest of the king, and only to save the country from traitors."

May had to press a hand over her mouth to stifle a laugh. Is that what Radcliffe had taught them? He answered the unspoken question when he nodded gravely. "And do you have good reason to believe that a traitor is in our midst?"

Julian shook his head, but Clarisse turned and pointed to May again. "What about her? She could be a twaitor."

It was the duke's turn to bite back a smile. He turned to May then, pretending to size her up. "Hmm. Perhaps you are right. She does have a bit of a strange accent, in addition to saying bad words. And she came here on a great ship that had sailed the seven seas all the way from China."

Both of the children's eyes went wide as saucers, and Julian muttered an appreciative, "Whoa."

Tilting his head, Radcliffe said, "How shall we discover if she is a traitor?"

"Ask her!" Clarisse shouted, bouncing up and down excitedly.

Julian thrust both hands straight into the air. "Throw her in the dungeon and feed her crusts of bread!"

Just then, a woman came skidding into the room, wearing a plain gray gown and a white apron, her hair frazzled and her eyes wide with alarm. "Your Grace! I—"

But he cut her off with a single raised finger. "In a moment, Nurse Plimpton." Turning back to the little girl and boy, he said, "Since she has not yet been charged with a crime, I think perhaps Clarisse's idea holds the most merit. Would you like to do the honors?"

She nodded with huge enthusiasm and stepped right up to May. Tugging on the dusty skirts of May's gown, she said, "Are you a twaitor?"

Bending down to the little girl's level, May looked her right in the eye. "No, I don't think so."

Radcliffe pursed his lips and squinted his eyes dramatically. "Are you certain? I seem to recall that you dislike this great country of ours."

Julian gasped, as though such a thing was the worst of crimes. "To the dungeon!"

Holding up her hands in surrender, May said, "I'm innocent, I swear it. I may not be a great lover of England, but I haven't a single state secret to betray, and I wouldn't know to whom to betray it even if I did."

"Hmm," the duke said, rubbing his jaw thoughtfully. "I suppose she is telling the truth. Very well, Miss Bradford, you have escaped the dungeon this time, though watch your language or you may find yourself there yet. Which means you," he said, pointing a finger back and forth between the children, "have no excuse to be spying. Nor do you have excuses for abandoning Nurse Plimpton and breaking that very ugly vase."

Even as they tried to look contrite, they giggled at his

description of the vase. Little Clarisse looked up at him with those big lovely eyes of hers and said, "But you didn't come for us. We waited forever and ever."

"Five minutes is not forever, Clarisse. Exaggeration is unbecoming of a lady. Now, come give me a hug before you go back to the nursery. I'll be up in a few minutes." He held out his arms, and embraced both the children at once.

"But William," Julian said when he'd been released, "isn't it rude not to introduce us to your guest before we go?"

William? So definitely not his offspring, thank heavens. "I believe he has a point," May said, winking in commiseration to the boy.

Sighing, Radcliffe stood and gestured to May. "Miss May Bradford, may I present to you my brother, Lord Julian Spencer, and my sister, Lady Clarisse Spencer."

"I'm five," Clarisse volunteered. "And my *real* name is Lady Clarisse Fleur Diana Dubois Spencer." She said each name with careful enunciation, as though she had been practicing.

"Nice to meet you, Lady Clarisse. I'm twenty, and my real name is Miss Mei-li Britannia Bradford."

Out of the corner of her eye, she caught the duke's raised eyebrows. He likely had never heard such an exotic name for an Englishwoman.

"Twenty? William is thirty, so he is older, but you're still old," Julian said, matter-of-factly. "I'm only seven."

"All right, that's enough." Radcliffe herded them toward the waiting nursemaid. "I want you to apologize to Nurse Plimpton for running away, as well as to Mrs. Curtis, since she will have to see to the mess you made. In the future, any spying will require a personal letter from the king, and in no circumstances will that spying involve me. Understood?"

"Yes, William," they replied together before scurrying off in the nurse's care.

For a moment, they both listened to the receding sound of their excited little voices, buzzing about the adventure they had just had. When the duke turned back to May, it was with a raised brow. "Mei-li?"

"Are we now on a first-name basis?" she asked, all innocence.

"How could I not know that was your name?"

"How could I not know that you had siblings?"

He glanced back toward the corridor a small smile on his lips. "They are my half siblings. Vivian—Lady Radcliffe—is their mother, which is why she accompanied me back to the estate."

"She doesn't live with them?" May uttered the question before she considered how very intrusive it was. Cringing, she said hastily, "I beg your pardon. That is none of my business."

Sighing, he shook his head. "No, she doesn't live with them. They are more or less my responsibility."

"And you adore them. And they you." She still could hardly believe the change in him when he spoke to them. Such kindness and gentleness, even when correcting them. She would have never imagined him having such a tender side.

"Yes. They are my family, and I am theirs." A simple yet telling statement. Turning fully to her, he pinned her with a playfully reproachful glare. "And as such, I must implore you to refrain from cursing while you are here. I won't have you corrupting them."

She winced. She did feel rather bad about that. "Yes, my apologies. However, if you had warned me that there would be children present, I would have been more careful."

"Or, you could simply refrain from such language at all, so such an issue would never arise." There was that holier-than-thou tone, creeping into his voice again.

"Now what would be the fun in that? A life that re-quires no censure in the company of children doesn't sound like much of a life at all to me."

"And there, Miss Bradford, is our fundamental differ-ence."

"I couldn't have said it better myself. In fact, since you and my aunt have so much in common when it comes to life philosophy, and you apparently suffer from a lack of family, I am more than happy to lend her to you."

His lips twitched with repressed humor. "Thank you, but no. Clarisse and Julian aren't my only family, per se. Simply the closest, and the ones who matter most to me."

Volunteering more information, was he? She leaned forward a bit, wanting to know more. "Oh?"

He nodded. "I also have two half sisters from my fa-ther's first wife. They are quite a bit older, however, and are both married with families of their own. Mary lives near the Scottish border and Elizabeth is in Belgium. There are also cousins, aunts, and one eccentric bachelor uncle, but I've never been particularly close to any of them."

So his father had been married three times? There was no telling how old he had been when Julian and Cla-risse came along. It was sad that he had passed away when they were so young. That thought made her think of how young Radcliffe had been when his mother died, which in turn made her think of the sweet, reassuring caress he had given her hand when he had comforted her.

A short, stout, and efficient-looking older woman bustled into the room then, dismay clear in her well-lined face. Shaking her head, she turned her attention to Radcliffe. "Welcome back, Your Grace. My apologies for the delay. Lady Stanwix has been seen to, and I'll have this cleaned up in no time. Shall I show Miss Bradford to her rooms?"

In a heartbeat, he was suddenly all business again. Nodding briskly, he took a few steps back from May. "Yes, please Mrs. Curtis." As he turned to May, she could see that his impersonal, detached facade was firmly back in place. "Dinner is at eight. If you wish to rest, you may request a tray for your room."

She had a sneaking suspicion he would continue to pull away from her after having unintentionally shown her so much of himself today. "What about tomorrow morning? Where can I go for my sunrise exercises?"

Nodding toward the back of the house, he said, "There is a dirt path that diverts just past the conservatory. If you follow it for a half mile or so, it will take you to the folly beside the lake."

"Thank you. I look forward to seeing you then." Without waiting for him to attempt to beg off, she swept past him toward the waiting housekeeper.

Today had been a very eye-opening experience. She could hardly wait to see what tomorrow would bring.

Chapter Thirteen

William lifted up on the reins and surveyed the grassy knoll beside the folly. The mist was thick, but it was easy to see May's slowly moving, crimson-clad form as she transitioned from one position to the next. And she was "May" to him now. As much as he attempted to remain proper and correct, he found that somewhere between their arrival and when he'd gone to bed, he began thinking of her by her given name.

Which made it doubly mad for him to be here. He wouldn't have come at all, but he had given his word—foolishly—so here he was, participating in an early-morning assignation on his own property. Unlike Bath, his household was up with the sun, so he could only hope that none of the groundskeepers or gardeners had reason to visit the lake this morning.

Dismounting, he left Gray's reins loose and set off to face whatever ridiculous thing May planned to have him do this morning.

She paused when he was only fifteen paces away and looked over her shoulder. Spotting him, she abandoned her pose and smiled at him. "You came."

What was it about the early-morning light that seemed

to make her so appealing? She looked refreshed and re-laxed, with her cheeks lightly pink from her exertions and her eyes entirely too welcoming. He nodded, keeping his expression as neutral as possible. "I said that I would."

"Yes, but in my experience, people do not always do what they say. Regardless, I'm glad to see you."

Had others often broken their word to her? In his book, that was one of the greatest sins of all. "If there is one thing you may count on, it is my word. Now then, let's get this over with."

"Such enthusiasm," she said wryly, rolling her eyes. "First of all, you cannot participate in this type of exercise dressed as though you're headed to a dinner party. Take off your jacket and cravat, if you please."

"I do *not* please. I am perfectly comfortable, I assure you."

"You won't be, not when you need full mobility of your arms and legs. Now do please cease being a prude and shed the jacket at the very least."

A *prude*? He glowered at her, setting his hands to his waist. "For propriety, at least *one* of us should be properly dressed." He still couldn't believe she would ever wear such scandalous clothing outside in the light of day. A true lady would never dream of wearing trousers. Not that she had ever claimed to be a lady, but still, there were rules about these sorts of things for a reason.

Instead of being insulted, she grinned. "You'll be jealous of these clothes in a few minutes. Now then, the fish and birds are all very impressed with your modesty, but we are wasting the morning light by arguing. Take the jacket *off*."

She spoke with such authority, he momentarily imagined her taking it off for him. The thought held much, much more temptation than it should. Blowing out a breath, he pulled the buttons free and yanked the thing off.

"And the cravat."

He scowled at her. "I have reached the limit for compromise, Miss Bradford. It's this or nothing." The woman was not going to get her way with him at every turn.

She narrowed her eyes as though considering whether or not to keep pushing, but finally gave a short nod. "Very well. If you wish to constrict your chi, that is your prerogative."

"My chi?" He was questioning his decision to agree to this more and more.

"That's what this exercise is all about. The Chinese believe that within each of us flows our life force, which they call our chi." She paused and tapped her chin thoughtfully. "Do you know, now that I think about it, the cravat stemming the flow may explain a lot when it comes to you stuffy Englishmen."

That last sentence was issued with a challenging lift of her brow, but for the rest of it, she spoke as though she was serious. She looked so earnest, yet he couldn't credit that she actually believed such foolishness.

"The lady proves to be both impertinent and improbable. I have never heard such nonsense in all my life."

She sighed and shook her head. "I knew you would say that. But nothing has helped me quite so much as this routine. All the time my mother was sick, and then . . . after, and when Papa left me behind like so much baggage, nothing else came close to providing the peace and healing that I needed. Now close your mouth, open your mind, and pay attention."

He wanted to argue with her, but he was learning just how pointless such a thing was. "Fine. The sooner we get through this, the sooner I can get on with my day."

Her sapphire eyes sparked with the first signs of irritation. "Which I'm sure is going to be so *very* busy. A nice ride, a full breakfast, the idle entertainment of your guests, followed by a sumptuous dinner and a drawn bath. I can't imagine how exhausting it will all be."

His jaw tightened in annoyance. His day was indeed packed to overflowing. The mill would require most of his attention, followed by the incredibly tedious task of going over the backlog of correspondence for the time he was in Bath. And yes, he had houseguests to entertain, though at that particular moment he was having difficulty remembering why he had invited them in the first place.

However, what he wasn't going to do was bicker with her about the subject. If she believed him to be a lazy, self-indulgent lord of the manor now, after all she knew of him, then that was her own issue.

Crossing his arms, he said simply, "Yes, terribly. As such, may we hurry up and be done with it?"

She stared back at him, her brows drawn together in displeasure. She almost looked hurt, as though she had any foot to stand on. Didn't she even see that she was the one who was disparaging him? Throwing up her hands, she said, "Never mind. If you don't want to be here, then I don't want you here. You're bringing bad energy with you anyhow."

He worked hard not to roll his eyes at that bit of rubbish. Instead, he gave a curt nod. "Very well. I bid you good day, Miss Bradford." Collecting his jacket, he stalked back to his horse. This had certainly not gone as anticipated. Chi? Life force? She must have been mad to think that he would go along with something like that.

And honestly, of all the people he knew, she was the

least likely to be an authority on finding peace. And on giving peace, for that matter.

As he mounted Gray and wheeled back toward the house, he resolved to throw himself into the many important things he needed to focus on. Heaven knew he'd already spent entirely too much time thinking of May.

"Why, Miss Bradford! How nice to see you again."

Lady Radcliffe smiled wide as May emerged from her chambers later that day just as the duchess was walking by. The older woman was immaculately dressed in a handsome pale blue-and-white-striped gown that perfectly complemented her deep red hair. She wore a choker adorned with diamonds and rich blue aquamarines, which might have been a bit much for a morning gown, but was so pretty, May couldn't fault her for wearing it.

So far during their time at the estate, they had managed to miss each other, since both May and her aunt had chosen to take their suppers in their rooms last night. It was well past noon now, but May was only now venturing back outside her chamber after her rather disappointing morning. Suyin was good company at least, telling her bits of gleaned gossip about the duke's staff, but Aunt Victoria had finally sent word of her insistence that May come down.

Returning the duchess's smile, May said, "And you, Your Grace. I trust you are recovered from your journey yesterday."

"Yes, certainly. I've just enjoyed a bit of luncheon, and I was on my way up to the nursery to greet the children." Her gentle French accent made the words seem almost musical.

May's polite smile transformed into an honest grin. "I

met Lady Clarisse and Lord Julian yesterday. They were absolutely adorable, and I quite enjoyed seeing them vex the duke."

Lady Radcliffe shook her head and sighed, not looking at all charmed. "I am not surprised. They tend to be very good at vexing people. However, he has only himself to blame. He is far too lenient with them both."

Oh yes—it had completely slipped May's mind that he had said the duchess had little to do with the children's upbringing. Such an odd situation. Surely no mother would have purposely chosen such an arrangement. "Regardless, they were a delightful surprise. I do hope I can see them again soon."

Her perfectly arched eyebrows lifted delicately. "Truly?"

"Yes, of course. I know frighteningly little about children, but they were wonderful company."

"Well," the duchess said, gesturing down the corridor, "in that case, why don't you come with me? I am certain they would enjoy seeing you again."

May didn't hesitate. "Absolutely." No matter what, they were bound to be better company than Aunt Victoria.

They made their way to the wide stone staircase that led to the third floor. As they ascended, the duchess gave her arm a little pat. "It is such a pleasant surprise to have you here at Clifton House. William—or Radcliffe, I should say, though it always makes me think of my late husband—is notoriously stingy with his invites."

It was as much a question as a statement. Keeping her eyes on the elegant wrought iron banister, May gave a little shrug. "It was certainly a surprise to us, but we are most grateful. With the festival over, there will be little to do in Bath until my father returns. This is a pleasant diversion before I leave England behind in a month or two."

Her hazel eyes cut to May. "Leaving England? Where will you go?"

The nostalgia for hot, humid breezes laced with the scents of spices was suddenly so strong, May couldn't help but sigh. "Home. My father is a captain with the East India Company, so much of my life has been spent overseas. I have enjoyed the summer here, but I am anxious to set sail again."

She could almost taste the salty ocean air, practically feel the rolling of the deck beneath her feet. If she was lucky, they would head to Java first. It was one of her father's main routes, and she had many friends among the locals. She couldn't wait to share her stories of her time here in England, especially about the lovely musical trio and how they had thwarted both the pernicious festival clerk and lofty viscount who sought to prevent them from playing.

The thought of her friends was bittersweet. If only they could have remained in Bath a little longer. May would have happily chosen more time with them over the troublesome duke.

The duchess made a sympathetic sound in her throat. "I certainly understand *nostalgique*, er, that is, being homesick. I am glad that you will soon find your way back home. And here we are," she said brightly as they reached a set of double doors just off the landing. "I will apologize in advance for any poor manners the children might have."

Releasing her grasp on May's arm, Lady Radcliffe pushed open both doors and swept inside. The children squealed with delight and ran for their mother, despite the nursemaid's admonishments to show decorum. Their sheer joy made May smile as she slipped into the room as unobtrusively as she could.

The children were talking fast and loud, one over the other. The sweet cacophony filled the spacious and bright room all the way to the twelve-foot-tall ceilings. The afternoon sunlight poured in through several wide windows, each one covered with cream-colored sheers. There were art supplies and books lining shelves and toys spilling from chests placed all about the room. There was a great globe in one corner, plus several maps papering the wall, each one dotted in dozens of pins. A huge orange cat lounged in the sunbeams on the thick wool rug, seemingly unperturbed by the wide purple ribbon tied in a bow around its neck.

May exhaled happily, soaking in the cheery atmosphere. This place was a little slice of heaven. She let her attention wander as the children chattered to their mother, happy to allow them their time. However, when snippets of the conversation began to reach her ears, she came to a rather disconcerting realization: This was the first time they had seen the duchess since her arrival several hours before May yesterday.

As that sunk in, she also noticed other things: the duchess standing before her children, nodding and smiling at what they said, but not really engaging. She never bent down to hug them or speak to them on their level. May shifted, unsure of what to make of the scene. Her movement caught Julian's attention, and his whole face lit up. "It's the traitor!"

Lady Radcliffe gasped. Her hand shot out quick as a whip, grabbing her son by the chin and pinching hard enough to make the boy wince. "Julian, what is the matter with you? Apologize to Miss Bradford this instant, you naughty boy."

Rushing forward, May pasted an apologetic smile on

her face, though really she was gritting her teeth. "No, please, it's all right. The duke teased with them yesterday about the possibility of me being a traitor. It was all in good fun, of course."

But the duchess didn't soften. "Such things are nothing to tease about. People have been killed for less. Apologize, young man."

With wide, bewildered eyes, Julian blinked up at May. "I'm sorry, Miss Bradford. I didn't mean it."

"It's quite all right, Lord Julian. No harm done." She wanted to hug the hurt from his expression, but she settled for a reassuring smile.

Lady Radcliffe released her hold at last and rubbed her hand down her skirts. "Let's hope you've learned your lesson. Now, Clarisse, what do you say to Miss Bradford?"

Clarisse, who May now realized was a sweeter, paler version of her mother, turned to May, her hazel eyes huge. "I'm sorry, Miss Bradford." Confusion coated her words, the poor thing.

"No, no, you silly child. You should say, 'How do you do, Miss Bradford.' "

Dancing nervously from one foot to the other, she dutifully repeated her mother's words. May knelt down and smiled as wide as she could. "I am very well indeed, Lady Clarisse. Is that your kitty over there?"

The little girl darted her gaze over to the monstrous feline, then looked back to May and nodded shyly. After meeting her yesterday, it was hard to imagine she would ever be so reserved. May concentrated on not glancing toward the duchess, for fear of the look she would give the woman.

"Well, I've seen tigers smaller than him. What's his name?"

She giggled into her hand, and Julian's hands went to his slender hips, his arms akimbo. "Are you serious?" He looked as though he couldn't decide whether she was teasing him or not. "He's fat, but tigers are as big as carriages!"

"Well, he's certainly as big as a few tiger cubs I've seen. And tigers are closer in size to small donkeys than carriages."

Clarisse ran over and scooped the animal up, throwing his front legs over her shoulder before carrying him over to May. The cat, remarkably, simply yawned broadly before allowing himself to drape there like a stole. "His name is Orangey. His favorite color is purple, just like mine."

The duchess clucked her tongue disapprovingly. "Put him down, Clarisse. He'll get fur all over your pretty dress." She glanced over to Nurse Plimpton, who promptly rushed forth and plucked the cat from Clarisse's arms.

"What a coincidence," May said brightly, gaining the little girl's attention once more. "Purple is my favorite color as well." It was a bald-faced lie, but worth it when she saw the toothy grin Clarisse gave her.

"Purple is for girls," Julian volunteered, taking a step closer to May. "I like blue. Nurse Plimpton says it's the color of the ocean, and I want to be in the navy someday."

"Well," she replied, doing her best to sound suitably impressed, "that is a *very* respectable goal. I know the duke mentioned that I had sailed here from China, but did you know that my father was the captain of the ship?"

She might as well have said her father was the king of the world for all the awe that crossed the boy's face. "A *real* sea captain? Has he ever fired a cannon?"

Before she could reply, Lady Radcliffe clapped her hands together softly. "I think we have imposed upon our guest long enough. Say good-bye, children."

They groaned in unison, but did as they were told. The duchess kissed each of their cheeks before sweeping from the room, pulling May along with her. Waving to the children over her shoulder, May decided then and there that she would visit them as often as she possibly could. She had never really been around children, so she had no idea what one was to do with them, but from what she could tell, it didn't matter. All they seemed to need was someone to show a bit of interest, and perhaps share a few smiles.

The second thing that she decided as she descended the stairs beside the beautiful but heartless duchess was that she would spend as little time with the woman as she could manage. As far as May was concerned, the duchess and Aunt Victoria were practically made for each other, so she hoped to leave them to each other's company as much as possible.

Thank goodness Julian and Clarisse had Radcliffe.

Thinking of the way the duke had treated the children yesterday, her heart suddenly ached with tenderness. No matter how much he had aggravated her this morning, she could just kiss him for being the lovely brother that he was. Anyone that could make those two light up with laughter and mischief had to be someone worth giving a second chance.

Chapter Fourteen

It was nearly dinnertime when William finally returned to the house, tired, hungry, and covered in soft white cotton fibers. It had been a good day, and he was relieved to find that things seemed to finally be running somewhat smoothly. His supervisor, Wallace Perkins, was proving to be as capable in the job as William had hoped. With the arrival of their biggest order of cotton yet, the mill had a huge amount of work ahead of it for the foreseeable future.

As dirty as he felt, however, he was anxious to spend a little time with the children before they went to bed. Yes, he should have been a better host to his guests today, and yes, he should be hurrying to clean up and head to the drawing room, but his siblings were, as always, his priority. He knew from experience that whenever their mother was in residence, their initial excitement would always descend into disappointment.

He hated it, but there was little to be done. A detached mother was better than none at all, however, which was why he continued to support her visits.

As he reached the top of the stairs, he was surprised to find the nursery door ajar. Not a good sign. If they had snuck out again, there was no telling what sort of havoc they would cause with their guests. He hurried forward, but paused when he heard a peal of laughter from Clarisse, followed by Julian's exclamation of, "Do it again, Mei-li!"

Mei-li? William kept his footsteps light as he crept forward to peer into the nursery. Sure enough, May was standing—or rather stooping—in the middle of the room, both children at her feet. Her posture was completely at odds with her tidy golden curls and lovely blue-and-gold-trimmed white gown. Her chin rested against her right shoulder as she swung her right arm back and forth with slow, deliberate swoops. She lumbered across the carpet a few steps before raising her arm and letting out the most unladylike sound he had ever heard.

His eyebrows inched up his forehead. *What on earth?*

The children dissolved into laughter, falling against each other as they giggled uproariously. The sound brought a begrudging smile to William's lips. Had anyone ever made them laugh so hard? At that moment, he didn't care that she had allowed them to call her by her first name, or that she had come up here without his permission. She had made them laugh when he had expected sadness, and for that he was grateful.

May straightened and grinned at them. She looked as luminescent and happy as he had ever seen her. "Your turn!"

Clarisse and Julian bounded to their feet, and began what he could now tell was supposed to be an impression of an elephant. They giggled as they plodded around with their hands dangling to the floor, pretending to knock over invisible trees and trample hedges.

"Very good," May exclaimed, clapping her hands. "Now let me hear you trumpet."

Squeaky, high-pitched bellows filled the room as they

gave it their best try. It was the most pitiful imitation he had ever heard, and he loved it.

"You two must be part elephant," she teased, tickling Clarisse. "Did you know that in many places, they use those great, big, huge elephants as pack animals? I've even seen whole families riding them at the same time."

"But aren't the people heavy?" Julian asked, his arm still swinging back and forth. "Why doesn't the elephant just knock them down like this?" He threw his arm out straight and spun in a circle.

May laughed and shook her head. "I suppose they are heavy, but elephants are very gentle, most of the time. It's just like when you ride Lemon Drop. They are much stronger and bigger than us, but we trust each other."

She knew the name of Julian's pony? How long had she been there, anyway? It was obvious she'd come to play with them, all on her own. Something tightened in his chest, watching her being so kind to them. They were lapping up the attention like kittens with fresh milk, practically glowing with their excitement.

All the frustration he had felt toward her at the start of the day began to soften and slide away as he watched her, a mindless smile tugging his lips.

"And did you know," she said, bending down to speak to Clarisse, "that sometimes people dress them up? I've seen elephants with vests and headdresses and gold-trimmed blankets that jingled like bells when they moved."

His sister's eyes went wide with wonder. "Do they ever wear purple?"

May nodded. "Purple, and green, and orange, but most of all, red."

"What about blue?" Julian asked, leaning against May's shoulder.

"Sometimes. Not the same blue as the naval uniforms, but more like this," she said, pointing to the trim on her gown.

William shook his head. She'd been here less than a day, and she already knew their favorite colors, what Julian hoped to be when he was older, and how to make them laugh. He debated for a moment clearing his throat and letting them know he was there, but decided to let them have their special time with their guest. Plus, he didn't wish to dim May's enthusiasm with his presence. He was feeling worse by the minute about the way he had acted this morning.

He would come by after his bath to tuck the children in. As for May, well, clearly he had some making up to do. No matter how silly he thought her ideas about her exercises, she had just proven herself worthy of all the patience and respect he could possibly give.

The duke's house might have been overly large and frustrating to navigate, but the grounds were proving to be an absolute delight. Where the house felt cluttered, the land seemed expansive. She felt free here.

The area that he had designated for May's morning routine was particularly picturesque and peaceful. The lake was well protected by the surrounding woods, and the surface was mirror calm this time of the morning. The folly had a certain gracefulness to it that was appealing in its symmetry: ten fluted columns, a domed ceiling, and a perfectly circular shape that must have been measured within an inch of its life.

Slipping out of her shoes, she savored the cool, damp grass against her bare feet. The lawn around the folly was well manicured, so she had plenty of room to move around without worrying about becoming mired in the

tall grasses farther out. The low clouds overhead threatened rain, but she wouldn't mind that either. After
spending so much of her life on the ocean, she was well
used to the elements.

She walked to the center of the lawn, breathed in
deep, then exhaled long and slow. She was just about to
begin when movement on the path from the house
caught her attention.

William.

The name came naturally to her. Since playing with
the children yesterday, she had begun to think of him
that way since that's how they referred to him. And refer
to him, they did. In their innocence, they had no idea
how much of him they were revealing to her. They had
been full of anecdotes about him, and only too eager to
share. Stories of fishing and rowing in the lake, playing
games, lessons on the pony, and her favorite of all, how
they had come to have their cat.

She smiled. Only a softhearted brother would have
brought his young sister a guard cat to protect her from
the monsters beneath her bed. Especially when Orangey
apparently made him sneeze like a donkey. How a donkey sneezed, she hadn't a clue, but Julian had been most
emphatic in the comparison.

And now he was here, despite everything that had
been said between them. She laced her fingers and
waited, all the while wondering what he could want with
her. Here to reprimand her, perhaps? Or demand that
she cease her exercises? He'd spoken very little to her at
supper last night, content to allow the others to fill the
silence.

Still, she had caught him watching her more than
once. He hadn't seemed angry or even mocking of her,
but she couldn't say what he was thinking. For her part,

she was still unhappy with how things had gone yesterday morning. His mind had been shut more tightly than a prison cell, closing out any possibility of trying something new and different. Not that she was surprised. He had a set idea of how things should be done, and any divergence from that path had to be bad.

When he finally made it to the edge of the lawn, he paused instead of approaching her as she expected. She furrowed her brow. What now? But just as she opened her mouth to ask what he wanted, he began unbuttoning his jacket.

Her eyebrows shot clear up her forehead. What the devil was he doing? She waited, head tilted in a mix of surprise and confusion, to see what he was about. Without saying a word, he pulled the jacket off and laid it across the little stone bench beside him.

And then he started in on the cravat.

Her heart gave a little leap as she hurried forward. "What exactly do you think you are doing?" She sounded like a reproving nursemaid, but really, how was she supposed to think properly when he was disrobing before her?

He continued working at the fabric, his chin lifted. "Loosening my chi."

May narrowed her eyes. Either he was mocking her, or he was walking in his sleep, because the duke she knew would never consider doing such a thing.

"Why?"

"Because you asked me to." He spoke so matter-of-factly, it was rather thwarting.

She crossed her arms, unconvinced. But then the cravat came off, and she found herself quite distracted by the naked length of his throat and the small but tantalizing glimpse of the hollow where his neck met his chest.

Goodness. All this time of wishing that he would loosen up a bit, and when he finally did, she was the one who was at a loss for words. Which was ridiculous, given the number of men she'd seen in various stages of undress during her travels.

Swallowing, she rallied. "But that was yesterday. A solid and solitary twenty-four hours have passed, and I have quite moved past it."

He smiled blandly. "As you can see, I have not. It simply took me a little time to think it over."

"Are you really so bad at making decisions?" she countered. "If so, it's little wonder parliament never gets anything done."

His amber eyes showed nothing but calm determination. "Decision-making is something at which I excel. Apologies are not. As a gentleman, I must apologize for not showing proper respect to you yesterday." He dropped the neck cloth on top of the jacket and gave her his full attention. "Shall we proceed?"

A man who could apologize and make good was a rare breed, indeed. She couldn't imagine what would have brought about such a change in him, but if he was truly willing to try this morning, she certainly wasn't going to turn him away. Biting her lip against a pleased smile, she nodded.

If nothing else, this promised to be interesting.

Turning on her heel, she led them back to the center of the lawn. "I know it may sound excessive," she said, diving right into the lesson, "but each move of the routine I do took a full week to properly learn. They aren't complicated, but it is important for one to be able to perform them with an absence of thought. It should be so natural, one could go through the entire set with their mind in a whole different place altogether."

She was momentarily distracted as he began to roll up his sleeves, revealing inch by tantalizing inch of this forearms. What was it that kept him in such good shape? Did he make a sport of riding each day? His arms were leaner than those of the sailors she was so accustomed to, yet she could see the clearly defined muscles as he moved.

"I am willing to give you today, Miss Bradford," he said with a small, droll curve of his lip. "Perhaps we could speed up the process."

"Yes, obviously. I'm merely pointing out that it is impossible to impart the full experience in one small session. Still, we'll be able to go over a few of the basics so that you'll be able to get the feel of it."

He nodded. "I am at your command."

Now that was a phrase a woman could get used to. She didn't even try to contain the smile that came to her lips. Doing her best to ignore how rakishly handsome he looked standing in the grass, his shirt loose at the neck and his embroidered forest green waistcoat cinching nicely at his waist, she clapped her hands together. "Very well. Let's begin with a few of the stretches to limber the joints and increase the pulse." As though she needed anything to increase her pulse just then. "First, stand with your feet shoulder-width apart."

He followed her lead. The buff-colored buckskin breeches fit him like a second skin, showing the flex of his muscles as he adjusted his position. Yes, he definitely must spend all his free time in the saddle, holding his body taut as Gray raced over the countryside. It was the only thing that could explain an idle peer having such an impressively toned physique.

"Good," she said, forcing her attention to the task at hand. "Now, with your elbows straight but not rigid, lift your arms in front of you until they are straight out from your body."

She slowly demonstrated the move, then nodded to him. His arms came up much too quickly and with an unsurprising lack of grace. She shook her head. "You're not picking up a stack of firewood. Try to be more graceful. Like the way you dance."

He quirked a brow as he dropped his hands back to his sides. "You thought me graceful, did you?"

"I said *more* graceful," she countered with an exaggerated roll of her eyes. "You're perfectly adequate as a dancer when you're not bullying your partner about."

Humor flickered in his bronze gaze. He knew she was a liar.

She pressed her lips together. It was best not to linger on times spent in his arms. "All right, now try again, and slowly."

This time, his movements were much more fluid. He was a very quick study, it would seem.

"Very nice," she said, keeping her voice smooth and low the way Suyin used to do when May was learning. "Turn your palms upward, and then bend your elbows and pull the air toward your face, dropping your arms as you move."

He dutifully copied her every move.

"Now turn your hands and push the air away."

They continued on for a few minutes, rolling through the moves the way storm clouds roll through the sky. He didn't do every move perfectly, but he was genuinely trying. It meant more to her than it probably should have. She wanted to think all of this was for her, but it was most likely simply his gentleman etiquette getting the best of him. God forbid he insult a person and not make amends.

Still, after a while, it really didn't matter what his motivations were. She liked having him there. She liked watching the way those long limbs of his worked through the sequences, slow and meticulous in his execution.

It started to drizzle, but she ignored it and he didn't complain. Imagine that—he wasn't afraid to let a little rain dampen that well-groomed hair of his. With her own tresses secured in braids around the crown of her head, the moisture wouldn't bother her.

As they completed the stretches, she straightened and offered him a small smile. "Very nice. I think we are ready for the first sequence."

Once again he nodded. It was such an odd experience, having him be so malleable to her instruction. More than a little heady, in fact.

Refocusing on the routine, she showed him the beginning position, then slowly worked through the whole move. "Be sure to breathe slowly and deeply, drawing the air fully in and pushing it back out again. Normally, this is where one clears one's mind, letting go of the stress and clutter of their day."

Instead of immediately complying, he tilted his head slightly to the side and said, "Do you often find yourself under stress?"

She paused, taken off guard by the question. "Sometimes. It was very stressful moving here. I looked more like those around me than ever before, yet I've never felt so out of place. And then there's my aunt," she said, a fleeting, wry smile lifting her lips.

"Yes, I know how well you get on with her." He crossed his arms loosely, his expression pensive. "Why do the two of you have so much contention?"

Why, indeed. She pressed her lips together, not even sure how to answer that question. "She lives her life within very defined boundaries," she said at last. "Everything about me is outside of those lines. I imagine she's embarrassed to be related to me."

That much had been clear within the first day of her arrival. Every word from her mouth was disparaging of something: May's clothes, her manners, her vocabulary. She'd been on a mission ever since to attempt to corral her wayward niece into her definition of acceptable.

He nodded slowly, appearing to ponder her answer. "Why, then, did she agree to bring you into her home? She had to have known about your unusual upbringing."

May shrugged. "I imagine because my father asked her to."

She hadn't given the topic much thought. It was a very dark time, when she'd discovered his plans. She'd felt angry, hurt, but most of all betrayed. Her family had always been a unit: her father, mother, and her. First her mother died, and then her father had abandoned her against her wishes with an aunt she barely knew.

It still stung. May could hardly wait to wrap her arms around her father when he finally returned, but she still wanted to give him a piece of her mind.

"Nevertheless, it had to be a significant sacrifice for her." William lifted his chin, thoughtful. "I've known your aunt for years, albeit peripherally, but she always seemed to be a good woman. It's hard to imagine her being so difficult for the sake of being difficult."

She scowled. She wasn't in the mood to be told of her aunt's virtues. She especially wasn't in the mood to be thinking about her now, during the time of day when she was completely free of the woman. Why would he even bring it up?

Pinning him with a narrowed gaze, she said, "If your

reason for coming out here was to lecture me on my aunt, you may turn around and leave right now."

He held up his hands in surrender. "Simply thinking aloud. It wasn't my intention to upset you." Lowering his hands, he shook his head. "Believe it or not, I dislike the thought of you feeling distressed or upset. You've been through much, and you deserve contentment."

The wind went right out of her righteous sails. There was just enough exasperation in his voice to lend credence to his words. "Why would you care one way or the other? Why bring me here at all, in fact?" She gestured vaguely around them, encompassing the estate as a whole.

His home, his sanctuary. Why invite someone so clearly at odds with his beliefs? Did he view her as a challenge? Entertainment? Someone to be pitied? He sure as hell didn't seem to view her as a woman.

His hands hooked on to his hips as he gave a little shrug. "You are one of a kind, May. You have a talent for holding my attention, whether I like it or not."

One of a kind. She liked that, though she wasn't as sure about the second part of his answer. "That doesn't sound very flattering," she said with a wry laugh. "Am I the squeaky wheel then? Just bothersome enough to make it impossible to ignore?"

He ran a hand over his hair, pushing the dark, damp tresses from his forehead. "More like a candle in a darkened room."

Oh. There he went again, surprising her. The comparison was a nice one and she rather liked the image it elicited. Still, she didn't want to appear overly sentimental about it. That wasn't the sort of relationship they had. Raising a teasing brow, she said, "So, I'm useful when wanted, annoying when not?"

He nodded decisively, knowing he had effectively defused the tension. "Yes, that was exactly what I was saying. And did you know, your other talent is twisting words? It's really quite diabolical."

"Oh, he believes I have *two* talents. Where will the compliments end?"

He chuckled, the sound deep and rich. "And at least one more. You have a talent for making people laugh. Speaking of which, my brother and sister seemed to delight in the time you spent with them yesterday, and for that I am grateful."

That one caught her off guard. "How did you know that?"

"I went up to see them when I returned to the house. Instead of the somberness I expected, I was greeted with two irreverently giggling children and one terrible excuse for an elephant."

He had seen that? A flash of self-consciousness zipped through her as she tried to remember if she'd done something embarrassing. Well, more embarrassing than impersonating an elephant. He already knew she wasn't a lady, so it shouldn't have been too great a shock.

She set her hands to her hips, not quite sure whether to laugh or chide him. "Well, I didn't see you stepping in to offer a better one. And by the way, didn't you just reprimand the children for spying? Not one to lead by example, I see."

"They were having a wonderful time, and I didn't want to interrupt." He glanced to the grass for a moment before looking back up to her. "I did want to say thank you, however. You are a good person, and I'm glad you are here."

Warmth flooded her chest. Wasn't he just full of surprises this morning? That was effusive praise indeed coming from someone of his high standards. Her heart lifted at the knowledge that he really did appreciate her in all of her unconventional glory. Her smile was small and sincere as she met his amber gaze. "I'm glad I'm here as well. I like your siblings." She paused, then decided to be completely honest. "And I rather like you."

He didn't mock her for saying so. He simply returned her smile briefly before straightening. "Shall we continue? I fear the rain won't hold off much longer."

Yes. Good. Back to business.

Resolutely steering her mind away from the giddy feeling in her chest, she drew a deep, cleansing breath and nodded. "Right. I believe I had been saying that one would normally clear their mind at this point, but for now, we'll just be focusing on the moves themselves."

She forged on, showing him the proper positioning, all the while struggling to draw her mind away from their exchange. It at least explained why he was here this morning. It was also revealing. She would have thought he'd be disapproving of her silliness. Was there even more whimsy within that proper dukish heart of his than she even realized?

She transitioned into another position, waiting for him to copy her. The move was a little more complicated than the others, and while he mimicked her hand motions well enough, his feet were all wrong. She stepped forward to correct him.

"Be very deliberate when you move your feet. Heel, then toe. And when you bend, your knees should never go over your toes. Good. Now imagine you are holding an invisible ball as you pivot into the next position."

This elicited a wry smile. "Imagination is not my strong suit."

"Oh? You'd never know that, were you to speak to

your siblings." She gave him a little wink, letting him wonder about what exactly they had told her. "Step back to your left foot, heel first."

Even as he followed her command, he raised a brow in her direction. "You can't believe a word they say. I don't think I want to know what they told you to convince you to come up to the nursery and play."

"Trust me, they were the best company to be had in the house." That was the God's honest truth. Evaluating his position, she said, "Sink down into the stance again, then pivot on your right toes."

His center of gravity was clearly off, and she tapped his arm to stop him. "Go back to the position before. Good. Now this time, when you pivot, on your toes follow it up with a pivot of your waist. Like this." She went slowly through the move, exaggerating the movement of her middle. "Try again."

Still, he couldn't quite get the right movement. It was as though his torso was glued to his hips. "You can't be that inflexible," she teased, stepping forward to place her hands on either side of his shoulders in order to guide him through it.

As soon as her bare fingers touched the damp lawn of his shirt, she knew it was a mistake. She could feel the warmth of his body, feel the tension of his muscles. The fabric was so fine, she might as well have been touching his skin directly. She swallowed. It was an incredibly tempting thought.

Her gaze flickered to his. He was watching her, holding completely still. For once, he wasn't Mr. Propriety. It was as though he was waiting to see what she would do. Her pulse soared at the thought. Would he stop her if she leaned forward for a kiss? Would he allow her to lift up on her toes and press her mouth to his? Her fingers slid around the firm curve of his shoulders, testing him.

As if summoned specifically to thwart her, the skies opened up then, pouring down cold rain hard enough to make them both squint against the splashes. Damn it all, that would be her luck. Despite the downpour, she hated to release him, to lose the feel of his warm body beneath her questing fingertips and, perhaps more to the point, his willingness to allow it. But the rain was cold and relentless, and he was already looking off toward the nearest refuge. Sighing, she pulled away so that she could shield her face from the onslaught.

"Come on," he said, holding his hand out to her. "We can take shelter in the folly."

Nodding, she slipped her bare hand into his and hurried forward at his side. The rain was absolutely torrential, far and away the heaviest storm she'd seen since she'd been in the country. She cursed it with every step they took, frustrated to have lost the moment of intimacy.

By they time they reached the relative dryness of the open-air building, both of them were fairly soaked. She reluctantly released the warmth of his hand and shook off her arms. Water rained down, but the silk clung to her despite her efforts to loosen it.

William ran both hands through his hair, pushing it back from his forehead. It rebelled against his attempts to tame it, curling up at the ends. He looked more disheveled than she'd ever seen him. It was a very, very good look for him, as far as she was concerned. It reminded her of her little daydream with him standing on the beach with tousled, sun-kissed hair.

His shirt, bless it, lay damply against his skin, hinting

at the contours beneath the fabric. Blowing out a breath, he set his hands to his buckskin-clad hips and smiled. "I'm not sure Mother Nature approves of me divesting myself of my jacket."

She gave an unladylike snort. "Actually, I think it was an endorsement." She was only half teasing. He had never looked so virile or approachable. So attainable. Gone was the polished duke, and in his place was a real man.

His smile dimmed a little while his eyes seemed to darken. "Regardless, I think the lesson has been learned." His gaze flitted down her figure before darting back up. "Perhaps I should fetch our jackets. I wouldn't want you to catch your death."

And just like that, the duke was back. Sighing, she gave him a wry grin. "They'll be far more soaked than us by now. Besides, this is naught but a gentle rain. You should have seen some of the monsoons I've been through." She shook her head, thinking of the days and weeks of rain that had seemed to go on forever. "Sometimes, during the rainy season, you begin to dream about what it would feel like to be dry again."

"And yet you miss it there." His words held a hint of bafflement, as though it was a concept he couldn't quite comprehend.

Glancing heavenward, she blew out a long sigh. "I do. Very much." She rubbed her hands over her arms idly, more for comfort than because of any chill.

"Are you cold?" Without waiting for her to answer, he stepped closer and set his hands to her upper arms. The warmth was immediate, and she allowed herself to lean into it. The smell of sandalwood flooded her senses, and it was all she could do not to close her eyes and draw a deep breath.

"You're surprisingly warm," she murmured, unwilling to admit that she wasn't terribly cold. Not when it would result in the loss of the delicious feel of his hands upon her. The dancing of her heart seemed to make it hard to breathe correctly.

His eyes wrinkled at the corners, betraying his humor. "Did you think me cold-blooded?"

Oh, how to answer that question. She looked up at him, challenging him. "Well, you did refuse to kiss me in the park. If that's not cold-blooded, then I don't know what is." Her stomach flipped at the mere word *kiss*.

She probably shouldn't have said it, but they were so close, and his hands so warm, and his scent so enticing, all she could think about was . . . "What would you do if I asked you to kiss me?"

He froze, all humor fleeing his features. "A lady—"

"Isn't here," she interjected, knowing exactly what he would have said. *A lady wouldn't say such a thing. A lady wouldn't speak of kissing. A lady wouldn't allow herself to be alone with a man in broad daylight.*

"Still, it wouldn't be right."

"Says who?" She looked around pointedly at the empty landscape through the curtain of rain. "I see no one here to judge."

"Except myself. I'm the one whose opinion matters most to me. I strive to live up to my own standards." As retractable as he sounded, she could see the battle taking place within him. He wanted to. If she knew nothing else, she knew that. Why wouldn't he bend a little? Why must he always be so rigid?

Except . . . he *had* bent. By coming here, by divesting himself of his armor, by submitting himself to her unusual hobby, he had pushed himself far beyond his usual limits.

Perhaps it was time she met him halfway.

Stepping as close as she dared, she gazed up at him, wanting him to see her honest desire. "And what would you do if I said I wanted to kiss you?"

His fingers tightened, the movement tiny but significant. "May," he breathed, shaking his head. "Please."

It wasn't a no.

His pupils had widened until they resembled gold-rimmed inkblots. It was one thing to test his own will-power. It was something else altogether to attempt to police hers as well.

"Please, what?" she returned, her voice dark and husky above the roar of the rain. She watched the battle rage on, his conscience at war with his desire. He was almost unbearably attractive at that moment, so beautifully raw and natural and honest. No stuffy clothing, no finely coiffed hair. No imperious attitude or invisible title hung from around his neck like the lead weight it was.

He swallowed, then wet his lips. "Please don't make this harder."

She lifted up on the balls of her feet so that her eyes—and lips—were level with his. "Will you tell me no?"

She waited for one second. Two. Three. Four. But he didn't say a word. He just stood there, his chest rising and falling rapidly with each breath, clenching his jaw shut.

When she was sure he wouldn't speak, she slid her hands around his back, took a deep breath, and leaned forward.

Chapter Fifteen

He could stop her. He knew he could. His hands were still wrapped around her upper arms, and it would take hardly any effort at all to push her away.

But he didn't. He *couldn't*.

His heart was hammering madly in his chest, his blood roaring even more loudly than the rain. He wanted this kiss. Needed it. Waited for it like a starving man awaited his first morsel of food.

She drew closer, and closer ... and then her lips touched his.

The sensation of her warm, damp mouth pressed against his sent hot sparks showering through his body. It took everything in him not to pull her tight against him. This was her doing. He couldn't find it in himself to fight, but he couldn't simply give in, either.

Her fingers tightened at his back, pulling him the slightest bit closer. Close enough to feel the heat of her body, and to be enveloped in the exotic smell of her skin. The rain poured down all around them, and for a moment, he could imagine they were in another place, another time. Some place where rules could be broken, or at the very least suspended.

She kissed him again and again, driving him mad with the temptation of it all. He kept his lips pressed together, trying to maintain that small amount of control, but even that will crumbled when her tongue slid along the seam of his lips.

With a groan, he gave in fully to her exploration, opening his mouth and pulling her flush against him. Their wet clothes proved to be no barrier at all to the contours of their bodies fitting together. She was slender, but the press of the small swell of her breasts against his chest sent his pulse pounding.

He'd kissed plenty of women in his life, but he couldn't even remember being so thoroughly kissed. She was in control, boldly exploring his mouth, eagerly twining her tongue with his. Her fingers scraped lightly across his lower back, making him shiver.

For endless minutes, he indulged in the pleasure of the moment, taking everything he could, knowing he couldn't ever allow it to happen again. It made him want far too much, and this was a woman he could never make his own. Nothing about them was compatible, other than the raw desire that burned between them now.

By the time they finally broke the kiss, they were both panting. He leaned against her, forehead to forehead, attempting to gather the strength to move away.

"Before you say anything," she whispered, her voice raspy, "know that I will kill you if you apologize, denounce, or say that that should not have happened."

She pulled away a few inches, looking him straight in the eye, so close that he could see the faint green streaks in the sea of vivid blue. "Because it most definitely should have. And I am not and will not be sorry for it."

Despite all the emotions and doubt rioting in his gut,

he found himself smiling at her command. "Then let us just say that it cannot and will not happen again."

She pursed her reddened lips and looked off to the side as though seriously considering the comment. After a moment, she shook her head and grinned. "*You* are free to say whatever you'd like."

"May," he said, drawing out the word.

"William," she responded, shocking him. No woman had ever called him by his first name, not since reaching his majority. It very nearly reignited the spark he had so resolutely extinguished.

He exhaled and set her away from him. "You are my guest. I cannot take advantage of my position of host. If you will not agree that we cannot forget ourselves again like that, then I will be forced to steer clear of your company. Something I really don't wish to do," he added, because it was true. She captivated him as much as she vexed him. He felt well and truly alive when he was with her, something he wasn't prepared to give up just yet.

"I think you are bluffing."

"I beg your pardon," he said, lifting a single authoritative eyebrow. "Dukes do not bluff."

"Which could just be another bluff, since I've no other experience with dukes." Her smile was downright wicked.

He crossed his arms. She was the absolute embodiment of trouble. "I have much to do around the estate. It would be very easy to leave you to your own devices. Perhaps Lady Radcliffe would be happy to entertain you."

"Now you're definitely bluffing. You wouldn't dare leave me at the mercy of the duchess and my aunt."

He wasn't prepared to give on this. He had his own self-preservation to think about, in addition to the preservation of her reputation. "Promise me you'll not attempt another kiss."

"I will not." Her legendary stubbornness was returning in spades.

He spread his hands. "Then you are on your own." Bowing shortly, he turned and strode into the rain, welcoming the cold sting of the water on his heated face.

It was for the best. The more time he spent with her, the more time he wanted to spend with her. It was a dangerous cycle that could lead only to pain. The fact was, they would be parting soon enough, and he didn't want any regrets between them.

Any *more* regrets, that was.

She might think that she would be gone from this country for good once her father returned, but given what he knew about the state of the Company thanks to his own legislation, he suspected she would be in for a rude awakening.

They might well find themselves stuck in the same social circle for the foreseeable future, and it was up to him to be sure there wasn't any sort of expectation between them. No matter where she lived, she could have no part of his future.

Sometimes there was nothing worse than a man of his word.

Dropping her book to her lap, May glanced to the window for perhaps the tenth time that hour. Unfortunately, the lane was still free of any stubborn men on gray horses.

Where the devil had he been all day? The downpour of that morning had abated to a steady light rain, but it still seemed highly unlikely that he would be riding for pleasure in this weather.

"It appears that you are nearly as restless as I am, Miss Bradford," Lady Radcliffe said as she laid down her slender volume of poetry on the cushion beside her. "I do wish Radcliffe would have invited more people so we could have a proper party. We can't even have a card game with these numbers."

May glanced to the settee, where her aunt had fallen asleep while knitting. "I daresay we are not the most exciting guests in the world," she replied, sending the duchess a wry grin.

"In this rain, no one has hope of excitement. I would say we should take the carriage to town for shopping, but by the time we slog through these roads, all the shops will have closed."

Coming to her feet, May walked to the elegant pianoforte tucked into the back corner. She suddenly wished Charity was here to play for them, and Sophie to keep them all entertained with her boundless energy. "I don't suppose you play?"

The duchess wrinkled her nose just enough to convey her displeasure for the idea. "I do, but I haven't any great love for it."

Drat. "It's a shame my aunt would not allow me to bring my zither." Nothing made her feel more relaxed or at home than her guzheng. It had followed her wherever she lived, and the sound always took her to a better place.

In this enormous house, built with little more than leisure in mind, surely there was something that would hold their interest. She thought of the children and brightened. "Perhaps we could devise an indoor scavenger hunt with the children." The sheer vastness of the house would make for quite an impressive hunt.

Lady Radcliffe recoiled, her brows knitting. "Heavens, no. The two of them would tear apart the house, to be sure."

May's first instinct was to defend them, but the place *was* filled with an ungodly number of priceless baubles, and the sound of that shattering vase her first day here was still fresh in her mind. "Perhaps a visit to the nursery would be more prudent," she allowed.

"They are most likely having dinner right about now. I know," the duchess said, glancing at Aunt Victoria before coming to her feet. "Why don't we take a turn about the conservatory? It will give us a chance to have a nice chat." She gave a close-lipped little smile and waited for May to join her.

Just what she needed: more English greenery. Besides that, the duchess wasn't her first choice for a companion. May didn't dislike the woman, but there was something about her that made one wonder how much of her true personality she was presenting, although it might have just been a cultural idiosyncrasy. May had heard several remarks about the temperamental French since arriving in England. More likely, it was the odd detachment to her children that May found bothersome, though to be fair, that seemed to be how most of the upper class interacted with their children.

Regardless, with nothing better to do than watch out the window like some sort of love-struck fool—which she was *not*—it was as good a suggestion as any.

In order to avoid the rain, Lady Radcliffe took the long way, winding through the maze of corridors that seemed to go on for miles instead of cutting across the garden. At last, they reached the door leading to a short covered walkway out to the conservatory. May had passed by the huge, mostly glass building several times on her way to and from the lake, but she hadn't paid any real attention to it. Therefore, she was shocked when they ducked through the doorway into a veritable wonderland.

The transition from traditional English gardens outside to vast tropical paradise inside was nothing short of incredible. She closed her eyes and breathed in the warm, damp air, savoring the fresh earthy scent. There were other scents, as well. A hint of citrus, a bit of floral sweetness, the pungent aroma of dirt and mulch—it was all so inviting.

"This is fantastic," she said, turning with delight to the duchess. "I had no idea it would be like this. With the sound of the rain pattering on the glass and the warmth of the air, it feels like a jungle."

The huge wall of glass on one side was fogged, blurring the surrounding landscape into indiscernible shapes. It made it possible to imagine they really were somewhere else. Somewhere that felt *familiar*. Nostalgia twisted around her heart. The only thing that was really missing was the hum of insects and the cry of distant animals. Even birds chirped throughout the space, some of which flitted back and forth around the nearby branches.

"It is lovely, no?" Lady Radcliffe plucked a tiny white flower as they started down the stone path. She spun the bloom between her fingers for a moment before tucking it above her right ear. The white petals contrasted beautifully with her brilliant red hair. "It never fails to impress visitors. Neither my husband nor the current duke show any interest in it, but its beauty is undeniable."

May slowed to a stop, incredulous. William had no interest in this glorious place? Beauty aside, it must have cost a small fortune to keep the space maintained. Not only was there the care of the plants and the fuel for the boilers, but the number of windows lining the place must have made for a terrifying tax bill. Why bother if he was uninterested in enjoying it?

"I can't imagine not wanting to spend time here. With so many hours to fill in the day, why not surround yourself with such beauty?" Knowing him, he probably felt it was far too exotic for his taste. Just like her.

The duchess arched a single thin eyebrow. "Hours to fill? Oh my dear, if only that were the case. William is not like his father. He insists on toiling like a fool, day in and day out. It is unnervingly common of him."

What? May gaped at her, completely taken aback. "He . . . works? Do you mean when parliament is in session?" Some men did tend to take their politics seriously, and he was just duty-driven enough to do so.

Lady Radcliffe shook her head. "He is well-known for his pet projects. He spends months, and often years researching, organizing meetings, and uniting his fellow peers for whatever legislation has caught his interest. In fact, he was heavily involved in politics before he ever officially inherited the title."

"How interesting," May murmured. How could she not have known all this about him? It wasn't as though they'd known each other long, but they had spent quite a bit of time in each other's company. She *felt* like she knew a lot about him.

Sighing, the duchess started forward again, trusting May to follow her. "Not so interesting. He lives a very tedious life, in my opinion. All his rules and talk of propriety. He's always so afraid of scandal disrupting his efforts." She fluttered her fingers dismissively. "Such a dull existence."

May's gut twisted a little with guilt. Was that why he was so determined to act a gentleman? And why he was always pestering her about rules and proper behavior?

When they had been in the park that last night of the festival, he had been adamant that they behave appropriately. She had seen it as a challenge, and later a disappointment. But if he'd worked for years toward something that might have been damaged in the blink of an eye ... She shook her head, inwardly groaning.

She was a fool.

Smiling thinly, Lady Radcliffe slipped her arm around May's elbow. "Perhaps that's why he invited you here. He is so busy, I think he worried I might be lonely otherwise."

Now that caught May's attention. She cut a surprised glance her way. "Oh?" After the kiss this morning, it was hard to imagine him having her tag along to play companion to his stepmother. The tension had been building between them well before the invitation. "I just thought he was interested in showing off a bit more of the English countryside before I left."

"Trust me, he is not that considerate. Everything he does is with purpose, and since he has not seen fit to entertain this week, one can deduce his purpose." She belatedly offered a sympathetic smile, as though she hadn't just implied May wasn't worth his time or interest. "Although, I suppose it was considerate of him to have thought of my comfort."

May bit down on the inside of her cheek. It was pointless to argue with the woman. Of course she couldn't know that May's refusal to meet the duke's demands had resulted in her being left alone—something she was regretting right about then. And she sure as hades wasn't going to tell the duchess about the unbelievably passionate kiss they had shared earlier. Honestly, her toes curled just thinking about the way the duke had responded to her.

Still, the suggestion chafed. Pasting a polite smile on her lips, she said sweetly, "Whatever his motives, I'm happy to be here."

"And we are so happy to have you. I will admit, I have half a mind to invite some more guests. If he insists on ignoring us in favor of his duties, what should he care if we find a way to entertain ourselves?" There was a slight edge of petulance to her tone, as though she were personally exasperated with him.

The scrape of the opening door interrupted the conversation and they both turned to see who had entered. The devil himself strode inside, his clothes and hair dripping with moisture. His eyes found May's immediately, and she was hit with a dizzying rush of awareness.

He possessed a dastardly ability to appear more handsome every time she saw him.

Pulling off his hat, he swiped the moisture from his face before offering them both a shallow dip of his head. "Good afternoon, ladies. I thought I saw the pair of you slip in here." He held his shoulders stiff and straight despite the exhaustion she saw in his eyes.

The duchess gave a delicate sniff. "What else had we to do? We have been confined inside with little hope of entertainment. How nice that you could finally see fit to join us."

There was that edge again. May slid a curious glance toward the other woman. Why would she be so short with her stepson? There was a certain sulkiness in her voice that May was determined not to echo.

Offering a small, neutral smile, she lifted her chin and said, "I'm so glad Lady Radcliffe suggested we come. It was an astonishing surprise to walk through those doors into such a place." She left the part about the duchess attempting to undermine May's confidence to herself.

Though he didn't quite return her smile, his jaw did soften as his gaze wandered over the trees and ferns filling the space. "So you have discovered the famous Radcliffe Conservatory. My father's contribution to the ducal legacy."

May tilted her head, confused. "But I thought your father had little interest in it."

"For visiting, yes, but when it came to showcasing the estate's wealth, he was terribly proud of the place." He shifted on his feet, squishing a little as he moved. How was it that he was soaked and tired and yet still looked so self-possessed? "I won't keep you. I need to change into something dry before dinner. Until then." He offered another abbreviated nod before retracing his steps back outside.

May let out a disappointed little sigh. Damn it all. The encounter was much too short and impersonal. Surely he wasn't as unaffected by her as he acted. It was impossible to reconcile the man with such passion from this morning with the staid and detached peer who had just left them. She watched him for a moment as his blurry figure slipped through the yard toward the house. He didn't bother with the covered walkway. It was unlikely he could be any wetter than he already was, the poor man.

"Do you see?" the duchess said, her mouth pinched in displeasure. "He has precious little time for anyone else in his day."

May ignored her. What she saw was a man who bore the evidence of a very long day. She suddenly was ravenously curious to know what he had been doing with his time. What projects could have sparked his passion and elicited such dedication? She wanted to hear more about it from him, not the duchess with all her negativity. Moreover, the older woman was obviously attempting to establish some sort of subtle dominance, and that was one thing May had no intention of bowing to.

She didn't plan to stir the pot, so to speak, but she wasn't going to give the duchess any power over her. Smiling blandly at her companion, she said, "I should probably go see to my aunt so that we may make preparations for dinner as well. Will you excuse me?"

At the duchess's nod, May hurried back toward the house. There was a whole other dimension to the duke, and she was determined to discover more about it. More than that, she needed to apologize to him for being so flippant with his concerns. And, more selfishly, she needed to get back into his good graces so he wouldn't leave her to the duchess's company again.

May groaned aloud. She really, really hated the taste of crow.

Dinner had been surprisingly enjoyable. Or rather, May had been enjoyable, and her aunt neutral, for lack of a better word. Vivian had been sulky, but that had little bearing on him.

William hadn't been sure what to expect from May. Of course, he *never* knew what to expect from her, but after she had kissed him this morning and he had left her to her own devices for the day, it was impossible to predict whether she would be angry or not.

Fortunately, she had been pleasant. Demure, even. Which, now that he really thought about it, was rather suspect. What was she up to now? Softening him up so that she could blindside him later? Or worse, softening him up so that she could push his boundaries again?

He had spent the entire day attempting to push that kiss from his mind. It had proved to be an impossible task. No matter how busy he was, his mind seemed to reserve some small niche in which to examine it. To turn it over again and again, to revisit the feel of her lips upon his, the heat of her body pressed fully against his. Clenching his jaw, he drew in a long, slow breath. The woman was custom-made to drive him to distraction.

A soft tap at the door caught his attention. As he glanced up, he already knew who would be there, and he was right. May stood framed in the oversize doorway, a tentative smile lifting those beautiful lips.

Of course, who else would it be other than his own personal tormentor?

Her femininity had never been more apparent, juxtaposed as it was to the masculine inner sanctum that had served each of the last three dukes of Radcliffe. The study was intended to exude power and wealth, and its wide, substantial furnishings, austere portraits, and gold fixtures accomplished exactly that. Standing before them in her shimmery pink-and-ivory gown, with her wheat-blond hair entwined with ropes of pearls and the single gold cross hung from a slender chain around her neck, she looked the very picture of loveliness.

He came to his feet and nodded, keeping his expression neutral. "Good evening, Miss Bradford. Is there something you require?" He didn't want to sound too curt, but he definitely did not need her battering away at his defenses now, when exhaustion weighed like stones on his shoulders. With all of the rain, the canal downstream from the mill had become blocked with a fallen tree.

Wallace Perkins and he had spent much of the day frantically directing the workers as they tried to clear the blockage. It was the sort of disaster where rank had no place—all available hands had been needed. Though it had been cleared, it was plain that they needed some sort of spillway in place should something like that happen again.

"No requirement," she replied, her smile firmly in place. "I merely wished to say, with as much privacy as I could find without compromising propriety, that I agree to your terms."

His eyebrows lifted before he could think better of it. Why would she care about propriety all of a sudden? She was the least concerned about respectability of any female he had ever met, outside of the demimonde. As for the second part of her statement, he probably should have known what she was talking about, but he was drawing a complete blank. "Those terms being?"

She backed up a step, glanced in both directions down the corridor, then made her way toward the desk. "That I wouldn't try to kiss you again." Her voice was hushed and furtive, and she barely more than breathed the word *kiss*.

Why was she acting so strangely? Leaning forward, he said, "Why are we whispering?" He used the same quiet voice as she, teasing her.

Her hands went to her waist. "I am trying to be discreet."

"I wasn't aware that you were familiar with the concept."

Her scowl was immediate, but its effect was softened by the humor that pulled at the corners of her lips. "I beg your pardon. I am *attempting* to behave in the manner in which you have repeatedly requested of me."

So indignant, as though he didn't know how out of character that was. He came around to the front of the desk, leaving a good three feet between them. "Which only serves to inspire wariness as to your motives."

"What kind of logic is that? A person attempts to play

by your rules, and becomes suspect because of it?" She made a *hmph* sound like a disapproving old maid. "Not exactly the most fair-minded person on the planet, are we?"

"If such behavior is so far from said person's nature, then, whether it's fair or not, it is generally warranted." He grinned then, happy to see that he had drawn her out of the odd demureness.

She threw up her hands in a show of vexation. "If I have failed to mention in the past just how exasperating you can be, allow me to remedy the oversight now." Her eyes flashed brilliant blue in the dim light of the lamp by his desk. He had to bite back a smile. She was happiest when she was arguing, he'd wager his horse on it.

"Duly noted. Back to your original point, then. Are you saying that I have your word that you will not attempt to take advantage of my person for the remainder of your stay?"

"Take *advantage*?" She rolled her eyes, but didn't stifle her small chuckle. "For God's sake, listen to you. I had no idea you were such a shrinking violet. And by the way, I distinctly recall participation from both parties, but, yes, I hereby give you my word."

William didn't feel nearly as much relief as he would have hoped. Instead, he found himself recalling the moment her lips had finally touched his, and the cascade of sensation that had raced through him at the time. They echoed through him now, in fact, just thinking about it.

Clearing his throat, he dipped his head in a single munificent nod. "Very well, I am glad to hear it." He really wished he would have put a little more space between them. Three feet was more or less an arm's length away, a distance so very easily bridged.

She smiled then, easily and with that very un-English

openness that he was slowly getting used to. "Does that mean that you will rescue me from having to spend the day with Lady Radcliffe and my aunt again tomorrow?"

He pretended to consider it. Everything within him wanted exactly that, but he wasn't going to allow himself to look so eager. "Possibly. I have much to do, but perhaps I could give you a tour of the estate, weather allowing? After breakfast, we could set aside a few hours to ride to the north end and back." Assuming he didn't receive word from the mill. Things were well in hand when he left, but nature was unpredictable.

The idea of them riding across the grounds, side by side and alone on the lands he had loved since childhood, held great appeal. He wanted to show her the beauty of the land, the vitality of the soil, and the crops it supported. He wanted to see her eyes widen with the vastness of his holdings, of all that he was steward of.

She worried her lip, not appearing at all excited by the prospect. "I don't exactly ride. There wasn't much need growing up, and I never learned."

"Really? Well then, I suppose we could saddle one of the ponies and have a nice slow trot. I imagine it wouldn't take but an hour or so for you to feel comfortable in the saddle." They wouldn't be able to see as much of the property, but it could still be a nice outing.

Brushing at a speck on her gown, she shook her head. "No, thank you. I didn't bring anything appropriate to wear. And it could be raining again tomorrow, for all we know."

He tilted his head, eyeing her suspiciously. He might be wrong, but he was fairly certain he heard what she wasn't saying. "Don't tell me that the fearless, brash, and headstrong Miss Bradford is afraid of a *horse*."

It was immediately apparent that he'd guessed correctly as her cheeks actually flushed. *Flamed*, really. "Of all things to be afraid of, having a fear of horses is completely rational. They have the ability to bite, kick, throw, and trample a person at will. They are huge beasts of uncommon muscle mass and they are too bloody fast for their own good."

He just barely managed not to laugh out loud. He was so amused, he wasn't even bothered by her awful language. "This from a woman who lived among lions and tigers and elephants her whole life? Or God forbid, monkeys?" He gave a shudder just thinking of the clever, shrieking little beasts.

Her hands went to her waist, inadvertently diverting his attention to her figure. "Where did you learn your geography? I've never seen a lion in my life, let alone lived among them. Elephants are generally quite gentle, and I've never once heard of them kicking or biting a human. As for tigers, they are mostly skittish of humans, and more important, no one would ever try to *ride* one."

"Yet, I would take horses every time over any of those others." He shook his head slowly, as though terribly disappointed. "I must say, you have just gone and ruined your entire image. I'm not certain I will ever look at you in the same light again. However, I am nothing if not a thoughtful host, so I'll not force you to ride. Would you rather go to town tomorrow instead? We could take a nice, leisurely carriage ride."

Codford was a lovely little town, with almost anything he ever had need for. He didn't spend a lot of time there himself, but he was perfectly willing to accompany her.

She set her jaw, staring back at him as though he'd just thrown down a gauntlet right there on the priceless Persian rug. "Oh, for the love of Triton, don't patronize me.

If you want to ride the estate, then we will ride the estate. Just be aware that it will be an exceedingly slow ride."

Ever unpredictable, as always. Even as he was taken aback by her response, there was no denying the swell of pride that she would be willing to face her fear like that. "No, no. If the lady wants a carriage ride, we shall take a carriage ride."

She looked around her as though searching for something. "And where is this lady you speak of. Lady Radcliffe perhaps?"

He made a face. "*No.* Let me see if I have this straight: You wish to climb atop a large, muscular beast full of sharp teeth and iron-plated hooves simply to prove a point?"

"Absolutely." She nodded for emphasis.

He laughed. He couldn't help it. The woman was absolutely incomparable. "Very well. We can depart after breakfast tomorrow morning. If you lack appropriate clothing, I'm certain we could find something here you may borrow."

She flashed him a quick smile that made his heart thud behind his ribs. "I look forward to it. Good night, Radcliffe. I shall see you tomorrow at breakfast."

As absurd as it sounded, he disliked her calling him Radcliffe again. Hearing his first name on her lips was the next best thing to a caress. *Not* the thing to be thinking about right then. Swallowing, he nodded. "Until then."

He watched her as she turned and slipped from the room, her shoulders squared with that proud, confident bearing of hers. When he had first seen her before her performance, before he had known what a sharp tongue and bedeviling personality she had, he had thought her the most beautiful woman he had ever laid eyes on.

Remarkable to think, then, that she seemed even more so every time he saw her. He shook his head and leaned back against the edge of the desk. Should he have said he was too busy tomorrow to spend time with her? Absolutely. Was he sorry?

Not in the least.

No matter what, he was certain it would be a very eventful day.

Chapter Sixteen

"This is the part that must surely defy the laws of nature."

May eyed the odd-looking saddle perched atop the pretty black mare. The thing looked more like a torture device than a seat. Despite her efforts to be calm, nervousness swirled like a whirlpool in her belly.

William smiled, his golden eyes bright and warm in the burgeoning morning light. "I assure you, it is perfectly safe and normal, especially with a horse as docile as Blackella."

"Blackella?" She chuckled, knowing the children had a hand in that particular name. And for the first time, she realized that he hadn't named his own horse out of a distinct lack of imagination, but rather with brotherly indulgence toward his siblings. Though the nervousness remained stubbornly in place, the rest of her melted just a little. "Better than Orangey, I suppose."

He shook his head, a smile gracing his lips. "Naming animals is Clarisse's very favorite pastime. Unfortunately for the animals, she tends to go with the obvious. I'm just lucky none of the horses are pink or purple. Blackella is technically her horse, or will be when she's older. We've been training her with the sidesaddle with that in mind."

The groom finished tightening straps and checking whatever it was grooms were supposed to check. Giving a nod to the duke, he said, "She's right as rain, Yer Grace."

William nodded and turned to May. "We've already gone over the basics, and thanks to your routine, I'm confident you will have excellent balance. Just remember to use gentle, calm movements with the reins. And *relax*."

Right. Why wouldn't she be relaxed? She was only about to trust her life and limb to a stilt-legged beast she'd met not five minutes earlier. "This is as relaxed as I'm going to get. Now what?"

He gestured to the three-step mounting block the groom had positioned beside the horse. "Up you go."

This was when her blasted stubbornness tended to make trouble for her. She was sincerely regretting not swallowing her pride and agreeing to the carriage ride into town. But she was here now, and far be it from her to back down from a challenge. She expected the groom to get her settled, but William extended his hand, along with a welcome smile of encouragement. Though amusement still glinted in his eyes, he wasn't being flippant or careless.

Drawing a breath, she slipped her hand into his. His fingers tightened reassuringly and she savored the warmth and strength of his grip. He was in control, and he wasn't going to allow her to fall on her face. Yet, anyway. Once they were under way, all bets were off. She knew she was gripping his fingers too hard, but damned if she could make herself loosen her hold. Squaring her shoulders, she marched up the block.

"Excellent. Now, you really just turn and sit very naturally, as though into a chair."

Nodding, she turned, said a small prayer for safety and forgiveness for her foolish pride, and slowly lowered herself onto the saddle. The horse adjusted its weight, eliciting a gasp of alarm from May as she reflexively crushed William's hand in her own.

"You're fine, I promise. Well done, Miss Bradford." He didn't try to pull his fingers from hers. Instead he gave her a small, lopsided grin full of repressed amusement and something very close to pride. Her heart gave a little leap. The approval in his gaze was rather nice.

Resuming his role as instructor, he straightened his features and said, "Next, hook your, ah, lower extremity over the pommel, and take a moment to arrange yourself comfortably."

She bit back a grin. Couldn't bring himself to refer to her leg, could he? His prudishness was showing once again. "Lower extremity? Can you be more specific?"

He lifted a reproving eyebrow. "You are a clever person, Miss Bradford. I feel confident you'll figure it out."

Flashing a smile, she did as she was told. She was only willing to tease the man so much, seeing how his hand was her only link to stability. She tested her balance, leaning slightly forward and backward. The odd contraption was actually quite comfortable. It didn't feel nearly as awkward and unbalanced as it looked.

"Good?"

Good sounded like a relative term to her. "I'm stable, I believe. Time will tell whether or not I am appropriately positioned to avoid death." She was only half joking. It was odd to feel the power of the animal beneath her. Every breath, every movement, every shift of its body translated directly to her.

He gave her hand a little squeeze before pulling away. "Excellent. Let me mount up and I'll lead you about the yard a few times."

She waited, absolutely motionless, willing Blackella not to move as he mounted Gray in one swift, confident move. It wasn't fair, he being so at home, and she feeling completely out of her element. But really, wasn't that the way things had been with them from the beginning? She would love to see him aboard her father's ship, gripping the rail for dear life as they plunged from one wave into the next during a high storm. She enjoyed the mental image, even as she knew such a thing would never happen.

With the groom holding her reins, they started out into the center of the enclosed ring, moving roughly at the speed of cold molasses. Which, unfortunately, was still too fast for her comfort. She clutched the front of the saddle for dear life, and concentrated on learning the feel of the horse's gait. The duke might have called Blackella gentle, but as far as May was concerned, the mare walked with all the smoothness of a drunken monkey.

The lesson continued for an hour or so, first with the groom, then with William guiding her, until—miracle of miracles—she was finally riding alone, clenching the reins tight enough to make her fingers ache. When she had made her fourth circuit, she eased Blackella over to where William sat waiting patiently on his horse.

"I'm ready for the races, I believe. If you'd be so kind as to point me in the direction of the nearest track?" She lifted her nose in a parody of smug satisfaction, and was rewarded with a laugh.

"I'm afraid a ride through the estate will have to suffice." He gave a vague gesture with his gloved hand. "Silly rules about female jockeys, you know." There was a lightness to his voice that made her smile. This must be his true element, where he was at his most relaxed and confident. And he really did cut quite a fine figure atop his handsome gelding.

She sighed dramatically. "Oh, very well. But I do hope you can keep up."

"I suppose we will find out. Shall we?" He waved toward the gate, which would mean leaving this controlled little pen and unleashing Blackella into the world, with May completely at the horse's mercy.

The nervousness that had abated over the past hour surged back, and she adjusted the reins in her fingers. "Yes, of course. No time like the present."

With an approving dip of his head, he directed the groom to open the gate and led her into the yard. She stayed close to his side, trying to breathe past the pounding of her heart. Honestly, it was much more fun to make one's pulse race with a passionate kiss than with the fear of imminent demise.

Keeping the pace to a gentle walk, he headed for the open land toward the north, where the last of the summer wildflowers were dotting the hillside. The sky was bright blue between the frequent clouds, and the temperature just shy of warm. Good thing. The navy blue wool of the habit Lady Radcliffe had permitted her to borrow would have been miserable on a warmer day. At least it fit decently well, besides being a few inches too short and a bit too large in the bodice.

After a few minutes, he glanced over to her and smiled. "You're doing very well," he said, his voice warm with approval. "Are you becoming more comfortable?"

She was still as rigid as an iron pole, but the fear had begun to abate—slightly—as they maintained their slow speed. "I suppose. Although it may just be that after a while, one simply fatigues of terror." She gave him a teasing wink so he'd be certain of her humor.

"And here I was hoping you'd see there was nothing to fear. With proper respect for the animal and the environment you are in, it is plenty safe. Unlike, say, roaming the city streets at night, all alone."

She chuckled at his reminder of their very first meeting. "It's a wonder I've survived this long. I'm glad you are here to protect me this time."

"Indeed. No harm would dare come to you with me by your side."

He was teasing, just as she was, but for some reason, the protective tone of his pronouncement sent a shiver of delight dancing down her spine. Tossing him a mischievous grin right back, she said, "Lud, don't tell my father that. He'd likely insist I stay here forever."

He shook his head. "Surely your worst nightmare. Heaven forbid you be stuck in the most beautiful place in the world, with the most advanced civilization ever to have lived." His tone was slightly but unmistakably acerbic.

And there he went again. She arched an eyebrow as she sent him a sideways look. "Not that you are biased. Just out of curiosity, how many other countries have you visited in the world?" She knew the answer, but she was making a point, as she was certain he knew.

"Just one. That doesn't change the fact that this is the greatest country in the world." He cut a pompous glance her way and added, "Just ask Bonaparte."

She gave a long-suffering sigh and shook her head. "I pity you, really. To think you know something of a world that you have never really experienced is little more than conceit."

He pulled up on the reins, and she followed suit, careful not to move too quickly. When they were stopped, he swept out his arm, encompassing the vibrantly verdant, gently rolling lands around them. "Tell me this isn't the most beautiful view you have ever beheld."

May raised her eyebrows and glanced toward the duke. "This isn't the most beautiful view I have ever beheld."

He rolled his eyes. "Must you always be so contrary? Now you are simply trying to make a point."

"Who says I am being contrary? You asked me a question, and I answered it honestly." She paused before adding, "Unless that was one of those coded English questions that was supposed to be answered with polite agreement, no matter the truth?"

Crossing his hands over the reins at his thigh, he said, "First of all, there is nothing wrong with being polite. Second of all, where, exactly, have you been that was more breathtaking than this?"

There was genuine affront hidden in his defensiveness. Guilt plucked at her conscience. He'd been nothing but kind and patient today. She didn't want him to think she was disparaging something so obviously dear to his heart. "Allow me to clarify. This is a very lovely view. You must feel very proud to call it home."

The leather of his saddle creaked as he turned to face her more fully. "I think I prefer when you are brutally honest over patronizing," he said, his tone dry and rueful. "Please, enlighten me as to all the wonders I am missing in this world. What do you find more beautiful than the view before you?"

She knew he was a little exasperated with her, but she wanted him to know that she hadn't just been trying to be contrary. There was so much beauty around the world, and most people never experienced anything more than what was right outside their door.

Leaning forward as far as she dared, she said, "Off the very tip of India at sunset, when the sun merges with the horizon at the place where three oceans meet and sends shimmering pink light over both land and sea. The waterfalls in Sumatra, where the water is as clear as glass, and the spray stripes the rocks and big leafy foliage with rainbows. The Hai'an mountains of China. The turquoise beaches of Java, which in truth, is probably my absolute favorite. You've never seen a color quite so vivid and pure."

She sighed, remembering the last time she was there, her feet buried in the sand as she sat beside her mother, watching the low waves lap at the beach. She had been around sixteen, before Mama had fallen ill. Before May's whole life was uprooted and torn to pieces. Sometimes she felt that if she could just get back to the life she'd always known, to the places that were home and the people who had been her friends, she would feel normal again. The way she had felt on that beach.

William hadn't expected such genuine passion from her. She always seemed to turn her nose up at the ordinary simply to be contrary, or to prove how different she was from the norm. But clearly, that wasn't the case now. Her eyes reflected eagerness and sincerity, her voice nostalgia. Whatever she was thinking of at that moment, she seemed so wistful and full of longing, it almost made him ache on her behalf.

"The beach was your favorite?" he asked quietly.

She blinked and looked back at him, then nodded. "The beaches in the tropics are nothing like the beaches here—at least not the ones I've seen. The sand is as fine as sugar, the air as hot and humid as a baker's kitchen."

"That sounds . . . pleasant," he said, unable to keep the dubiousness from his voice. How did being somewhere baking in the sweltering tropical sun appeal to a person? Who wanted fine sand that got into one's clothing and seemed to line one's shoes for months?

She laughed and shook her head. "What were you just saying about honesty?"

"Very well, it sounds dreadful. Though picturesque, I suppose, which was the question."

Her shoulders rose in a Gallic little shrug. "It's hard to describe how wonderful it is when the breeze blows in from the ocean and caresses one's sun-warmed skin. Or how amazing it is the first time you see water so blue it hurts your eyes. It is hard to imagine God could conceive of such a color, let alone create it."

Looking at her eyes, it wasn't so hard for William to imagine. She possessed the most striking blue gaze, particularly when she was angry or excited. Her eyes positively sparkled now as she spoke of this place she loved.

Pursing his lips, he said, "I shall have to see if there are paintings somewhere that I could view."

She sighed and shook her head. "You'd do better to see it in person. No painting can ever properly capture beauty like that."

Deciding not to point out that there was no way he would ever see a tropical island, he said, "There are some very impressive mountains here in England. Scafell Pike in particular, which is the highest peak in the country. I'm certain they are substantially different from the ones you have seen in China, but they are still well worth the trip."

"I'm certain they are. There is much that is worthy of

a visit in this world, and I hope to see much more in my lifetime."

Clicking his tongue, he urged their horses into a walk again. "I wonder, is one born with such wanderlust, or is it acquired along the way?" It was hard to imagine feeling such enthusiasm for travel. Most of the time, it simply seemed like a nuisance to him. Not to mention dangerous when one added in ocean travel. How strange that horses were what she feared, when she'd traversed the unfathomably deep and wide seas.

As far as he could tell, only those dissatisfied with their lives would seek to escape it.

May stayed by his side, both reins gripped tightly in her hands. "Probably born with it, I'd imagine. My mother said she always wanted to see the world, but never thought she would have the chance. Meeting my father was a dream come true for her."

"She must have been a very brave woman. I can't imagine what her family must have thought."

"I gather they were not supportive. I've never met them, and have no plans to do so. If my mother didn't see fit to correspond with them—and vice versa—then I'm content to follow her lead."

Very interesting. Perhaps that had something to do with her aversion to this country. "Do they live here?"

"As far as I know, yes. Mama was from a small town near Portsmouth. But even when she was very ill, and knew she was not long for this world, she never wrote them."

Nodding, he allowed the silence to stretch between them for a minute. What had her mother been like? From what he gathered, she was likely a lot like May. Curiosity about the woman's life brought to mind the question of her death. "What happened to her?" It was a sensitive subject, but he wanted to understand more about what had happened in May's life to bring her to this point.

She pressed her lips together, looking up at the sky, though he doubted she actually saw it. "Malaria," she said at last. "We thought she had beaten it, but after the third occurrence, she finally succumbed."

He shook his head. It had to have been a horrible thing to go through for them all. "I'm terribly sorry. I can't imagine how hard that must have been on you."

"Can't you?" she replied, sending a curious glance his way. "You lost your own mother. And so dreadfully young."

True enough. The mood had grown somber, and he tried to think of something to lighten it. He settled on a question that had been on his mind since she'd introduced herself to Clarisse in the drawing room. "How did you come to have such an unusual name?"

That made her grin, which shifted something in his heart. It pleased him to see her smile. "Unusual here, perhaps. My mother was a great lover of Chinese culture. Mei-li means beautiful."

"How very fitting," he said beneath his breath.

She shot him a searching look as if attempting to determine his sincerity. Not wanting to linger over the compliment, he tapped a finger to his jaw. "I very clearly recall you telling my sister that your middle name is Britannia. So your name literally means 'Beautiful Britain.'" The irony of the moniker made him laugh out loud.

She scowled, setting one hand to her waist. "It was a compromise between my parents. My father wanted to be sure I knew where I was from, and I think my mother wanted me to embrace where I would go in life."

Say what she would, he still found it amusing. "And here you have been this whole time, acting as though you wanted nothing to do with this country."

"It's part of me, I admit. It's just not where I'm going. It isn't home."

Home. The word echoed through him. He looked out over the vista, wishing she could see it through his eyes. But why? Whether she stayed or left this country had no bearing on him whatsoever.

Only, it didn't feel that way. As much as he wanted to deny it, he couldn't lie to himself. Somewhere along the way, he had become invested in this woman. Though he firmly reminded himself that theirs should be a platonic relationship, friendship seemed to be the last thing on his mind.

He needed to put some distance between them. The conversation had become too personal, and he wanted to reestablish the boundaries that seemed to be crumbling.

"I think it's time we got a little more adventurous. Shall we try a trot?"

Her eyes widened and she clutched the reins with renewed vigor. "You're trying to kill me, aren't you? That's the point of this whole exercise. Lure me out here with false promises of glorious countryside, only so you can perform death by horse on your old rival."

He smiled with complete innocence. "I have no idea what you speak of. Have a little faith, Mei-li. In yourself and in me." He hadn't intended to use her name like that. It had just slipped out, as natural as breathing. He found he liked the way it rolled off his tongue entirely too much for his own good.

Clearly the slip had not gone unnoticed. Her mouth fell open as she blinked at him. "You've never called me that before."

He shrugged, attempting to portray nonchalance. "If the children can call you that, I suppose I can as well. Now then, will you be adventurous, or will you be fearful?"

"I think I shall be prudent," she replied, twisting the reins in her fingers.

"I think you are confusing the two of us. *I* am prudent. You are quite possibly the most *im*prudent person I have ever met." In that moment, it was a lie. If he were prudent at all, he would turn around and take her back to the house. She was proving herself to be brave and interesting. She was transitioning from odd to unique in the way he thought of her. That little switch made all the difference somehow.

Laughter crinkled the corners of her eyes as she lifted her chin in challenge. "No, you're thinking of *boring*, not prudent. In which case, yes, I am the most un-boring person you have ever met. So thank you."

"Oh? Then prove it. Just a gentle trot, so you can feel the wind on your face."

She bit her lip, looking out over the grassy meadow in front of them. He could practically see her shoring up her resolve. Looking back at him, she drew a short breath and nodded. "All right. Promise that Blackella won't throw me?"

"You'll be fine. Ready?"

She squeezed her eyes closed and let out a nervous little noise that was somewhere between a squeak and a groan. Opening her eyes, she said, "As I'll ever be."

William set off across the field, setting the pace to a brisk trot. The breeze felt good against his heated skin. May stayed close to his side, her gaze riveted straight ahead with great intensity. He kept a careful watch on her and was pleased with her form. Plus, her eyes were huge, her cheeks flushed, and her grin almost comically wide. It was impossible not to smile at her exuberance, especially knowing how terrified she had been only that morning.

"Anticipate your horse's steps, so that you may move with them," he directed, his voice loud enough to be heard over the thudding hooves. "You want to roll with the movement to help make it easier for both you and your mount."

She nodded, never taking her eyes from the terrain before them. He could tell the moment she figured it out, when her body began to move in rhythm with the horse's stride. She was no longer bouncing along uncontrolled, at the mercy of Blackella's movements; she was part of them. He could see glimpses of the inherent gracefulness she possessed.

When they'd made it to the crest of the next hill, he called to her to stop, and they both pulled up on their mounts' reins. She leaned forward, bracing her hands on her legs as she panted for breath. "Shiver my topsails, was that exhilarating."

He laughed aloud. " 'Shiver my topsails'? What kind of English is that?"

She gave a raspy chuckle, still trying to catch her breath. "The kind that gets the point across. Perfectly respectable among sailors, I assure you."

He prudently chose not to question the respectability of sailors. "Am I to assume, then, that you have conquered your fear?"

"No, not quite, which is exactly why it's so exhilarating." She flashed a smile as she breathed deep. "My father says that once a man loses his fear of the sea, that's when he makes mistakes. Maintaining a bit of the fear of God is what keeps us on our toes."

"Sounds as though he is a wise man."

William had wondered about her father. He must be a competent soul to have successfully maintained his career. Still, what kind of man would expose his wife and daughter to such an unorthodox and potentially dangerous life? Did he feel responsible for the way his wife had died? Perhaps that's how May ended up here, so clearly against her wishes.

"He is. *Most* of the time," she added with a sigh. Thinking of his decision to leave her in England, no doubt. She shifted on the saddle, stretching her back. "I don't suppose there's a way to get down from this beast, is there? I'd like to feel solid land beneath my feet for a bit."

Smiling, he jumped to the ground. He didn't bother worrying about securing Gray—he knew the horse would stay where he left him. Walking through the knee-high grass to Blackella's side, he offered May a steadying hand and said, "If you'll disengage yourself from the pommel, I'll help you down."

She did as he directed without comment, obviously eager to get down. When she was facing him fully, he held up his arms. "Using my shoulders for support, lean forward and I'll do the rest."

Though her hands must have been fatigued from holding the reins for all she was worth, she still clamped his shoulders tightly. As she leaned forward, he gripped her waist securely and pulled her from the saddle. All he needed to do was set her straight down and step away. It was simple and straightforward, yet as his fingers pressed against her flesh, he found himself pulling his elbows in, so that she slid down only an inch or two from his chest.

By the time her feet touched the ground, his heart was pounding. His whole being was overly aware of her closeness, of the subtle smell of her skin and the sudden widening of her fathomless blue eyes.

He knew he should step away. It was up to him to maintain the distance between them he had demanded. But for once, his feet wouldn't obey him. Just as his hands wouldn't release her and his heart refused to slow.

Swallowing, she looked up directly into his eyes. "Radcliffe," she said, her voice both stern and breathy. "I barely have the willpower for myself. I can't possibly bear it for the both of us." As proof, her pulse fluttered at her neck just above the high collar of her blouse. He knew she was trying to honor her promise to him. Hadn't he been the one to lay down the rules between them?

Calling on every ounce of willpower he possessed, he stepped back and allowed his hands to slide away from the curve of her waist. "Yes, of course. Just ensuring you are stable on your feet after your ride."

A single, knowing eyebrow arched high on her forehead. "Is that what we are saying?"

She deserved honesty. After all, she seemed to prize it above all else. "For the sake of prudence," he said, emphasizing the word with a small curve of his lips, "yes, that's what we are saying."

No arguments from her this time. She simply nodded and turned to look out over the land on the other side of the hill. "Another lake. Your land is certainly rich in resources."

He murmured his agreement, preoccupied with the delicate curve of her ear and the angle of her jaw. Shaking himself, he cleared his throat and said, "Indeed. We have several lakes and streams, and the River Wylie cuts through on the northeast quadrant."

"Will we see it today?"

He pursed his lips. He hadn't planned on heading that

far east. The mill was located on the river, and it didn't seem like a good idea to parade her in front of his workers. He didn't want for anyone to get the wrong idea about their intentions toward each other. Smiling to her, he said, "It's quite a trek from here. Perhaps we should play it by ear, given your newness to riding."

She grinned wryly in return. "In that case, I may never see it. Shall we take a short walk before resuming our ride?"

"Whatever you wish. You were brave enough to rise to the challenge of riding, so I am happy to give you the reins, so to speak."

Pride lifted her shoulders as she looked back over the lake. "Do you know? This land is rather growing on me."

The words pierced through his newly erected armor. He resisted the urge to slide a finger down the gentle curve of her cheek. "Thank you, May. It gives me great pleasure to hear it."

That, at least, was the absolute truth.

Chapter Seventeen

The man was going to be the death of her.

She hadn't been kidding when she'd told him she hadn't the willpower for the both of them. She was doing her damnedest to honor the vow she had made to him, but she'd never expected that he'd make it so hard.

The looks were bad enough. She could feel his gaze on her skin like the warmth of the sun. Each time it caressed the back of her neck or the side of her face, she flushed with the heat of it. But when he had lifted her down from the horse? That had nearly been her undoing. Feeling the possessive strength in his hands, the power of muscles that could hold her as though she weighed no more than a paper doll, was pure torture. Being that close to him was simultaneously thrilling and awful, since she knew she couldn't act on the desire thrumming in her chest.

The fact was, there was attraction between them. Pure, physical, honest attraction. She was attempting to maintain propriety for his sake, but if she was to make it the rest of the week, he needed to stop looking at her as though he wanted to pull her hard against him and kiss her until they were both breathless.

Or perhaps that was just what *she* wanted.

Regardless, she'd been relieved when, following their walk, the duke had found a fallen tree that she could use as a mounting block. One more time having his hands around her waist might well have been her downfall.

Despite the tension that hung between them like a taut thread, the ride had been quite tolerable. She was getting used to the feeling of being perched atop the beast, and was enjoying the easy conversation they shared as they headed continually north. The sun was higher in the sky, and she estimated they'd been riding for about an hour and a half when he'd pulled back on the reins and pointed to the tree line ahead.

"My northern border," he said, adjusting his hat to better shield his eyes.

"We made it?" Pride settled squarely in the center of her chest. She'd done it. She'd actually ridden all the way here without losing her nerve, her balance, or her breakfast.

"We made it," he confirmed, sending her a wide grin. Lord knew why it mattered so much, but she loved that he was so proud of her, too. She had met his challenge, and come out better for it.

"Thank you," she said, really meaning it. "I can't believe you convinced me to risk life and limb, but I'm so glad that you did."

His gaze was liquid amber in the sunlight. "I never doubted you would rise to the challenge. I can't imagine there is anything that would get the best of you."

"Careful," she said, valiantly fighting against a giddy grin. "I wouldn't want to throw off my balance thanks to an inflated ego."

"Don't worry. Were I to guess, I'd say it was already at its maximum limit."

She scowled at him in mock outrage. "Excuse me, you

barnacle-bottomed bilge swiller," she exclaimed, swatting at him with her long, slender crop. "I do believe that is the pot calling the kettle black."

He shook his head, biting back a grin. "If I knew what that meant, I'm certain I'd be impressively insulted. As it is, I'll simply assume you are appreciative of my observation."

He was actually playing with her, letting go of that stuffiness that had seemed to define him for so long. She rolled her eyes in teasing response. "Close enough. And if I am honest, I will admit that your diabolical plan may have worked."

"Of course it did. My diabolical plans always work. But just to be clear, which plan are we referring to?" He sent her an innocent look of query, making her laugh.

"Your scheme for me to experience your lands on horseback, so that I may better appreciate the subtle beauty of it all." She shook her head. "I'm not entirely happy about being made to enjoy a country I am determined to dislike."

She was teasing, but there was more truth in that statement than she wanted to admit. Part of her feared her father would force her to stay here, never coming to his senses and allowing her to rejoin him. Because of that fear, she couldn't help but rebel against everything about this place. To acquiesce to its charms was to admit that this might be where she ended up, and that was a fate best not contemplated.

He nodded gravely, mimicking his own stern, dukish nature. "As I said, my plans always work. I knew you would see the beauty if you but opened your eyes."

Glancing out over his lands, his features relaxed into what could be described only as contentment. "Should we turn back?"

"When we are this close to the border? I should think not. Why don't we race to the tree line? And by race," she added quickly, sending him a rueful grin, "I mean trot briskly while you very politely allow me to win."

"Just a trot? I bet you have a cantor in you yet."

"Just a trot," she said firmly. "I said I liked your lands, not that I wished to be buried on them."

He sighed. "Fine, fine. You set the pace, and I shall restrict my own speed accordingly."

"Perfect. And no making fun of my slow start. If you do, I shall force you to trade saddles so you can experience the disadvantage of the position."

He saluted, and she urged Blackella forward. She picked up speed until they were racing across the hillside even a smidge faster than the trot she had insisted on. William easily kept pace, watching her more than where they were going. The hill sloped gently down toward the valley, making it feel as though they were going even faster than they were.

The wind stung her eyes and pulled at her hat, but she ignored the discomfort and concentrated on maintaining her balance and savoring the ride. At this speed, it reminded her of standing at the ship's bow as they sailed into the wind. In a word, it was glorious.

"Superb riding skills, Miss Bradford," he said, smiling broadly as he called out the encouragement. "You possess a natural talent."

She grinned, adjusting her position as they reached the bottom of the hill. Mr. Horseman himself, complimenting her skills, such as they were. She opened her mouth to respond, but before she could form a single word, his horse stumbled and came up short. One second, he was smiling at her and the next he was catapulting over the gelding's neck, flipping in midair. May gasped, horrified yet unable to do anything to help. When he hit the ground, his momentum somersaulted him forward for another full rotation before he came to a stop flat on his back.

As fast as she could without suffering the same fate, she yanked back on Blackella's reins and wheeled around. He looked dazed but alert as he blinked up at her.

"Thunder an' turf, are you all right?" Her heart was in her throat as she raked her gaze over him, looking for signs of injury. "I'd get down to help if I bloody well knew how."

He groaned and sat up, rubbing the back of his head. "Well, that was unpleasant," he said, grimacing as he pushed to his feet and brushed off his sleeves.

Her relief was so great that she sagged in the saddle, blowing out a long breath. She would have sworn such a fall would have at the very least knocked the wind from him. Amazingly, he seemed none the worse for wear. He paused to stretch his back a few times, then rolled his head once before turning to see to his horse.

May took one look at his jacket and slapped a hand over her mouth.

His entire back was coated in mud. Liberally. From the bottom hem to just below his shoulders, he was one brown sodden mess. Mirth surged up from within her, but she valiantly held it back. The man had just been launched head over heels from his horse; laughing now would be wholly inappropriate.

Struggling for composure, she swallowed, lowered her hand, and said. "Are you hurt? That was . . . spectacular."

He glanced back at her, giving a small shrug. "I'm fine. I'm sure I'll feel it tomorrow, but I am at least in one piece." He paused, tilting his head. "*What* is that look for?"

"Nothing," she said, then quickly pressed her lips back together. There were several bits of debris sticking out from his hair, and his cheeks were both splattered with mud.

"If you are going to tell me you told me so, you can keep it to yourself," he grumbled, then went to check on his horse, which was waiting patiently as though it hadn't just thrown its master clear through the air.

"I wasn't going to gloat, for God's sake." *Yet.*

He ran his hands over the horse's legs, then pulled up each foot. He let out a frustrated growl. "Threw a shoe. I should have been paying more attention. Of course the ground would be muddy at the bottom of the hill after yesterday."

May marveled at his restraint. Any other man she knew would be liberally cursing right about then. *She* would have been cursing, were it her. "Is he all right?"

"Yes, thank God. Still, I can't ride him until I get that hoof looked at and the shoe replaced. It's hard to tell in this muck if there's injury to the hoof wall."

He shook his head, putting both hands to his hips. "I've never had this happen before. I mean, I've been thrown before, but that was the result of going too fast on a hunt when I was younger. You must think me a complete fool, assuring you everything would be all right."

Now that she knew everything *was* all right, the humor of the way he looked, standing there coated in mud and heaven knew what else, struck her all over again. She lifted her hand to stifle her laughter, not wanting to make a bad situation worse.

He crossed his arms, looking up at her suspiciously. "You do think me a fool. Fair enough," he said stiffly. Stalking a few feet away, he bent to retrieve his hat, giving her an exceptional view of his muddied backside.

She couldn't help it. The laughter sprang from her lips, shaking her shoulders and startling her horse. Even as she clutched the saddle, she couldn't stop. He jerked around, regarding her with the most spectacular display of indignant displeasure she had ever seen.

"I'm sorry," she gasped, trying to get herself under control. "It's just that, you have a little something, um, here—" She waved her hand in a huge circle, basically encompassing all of him.

He narrowed his eyes at her before looking down.

"No, not the front. The back. And your hair. And a little on your face."

This earned her another scowl, which made her only want to laugh all over again. He craned his neck, trying to see over his shoulder. When that proved fruitless, he ran his fingers through his hair, coming up with several pieces of muddy grass.

The look on his face was priceless as he flung the offending vegetation to the ground. "I'm so glad I could provide such amusement for you."

"Oh, for God's sake, lighten up," she said. "You scared the living daylights out of me. Now that you are fine, there's nothing wrong with being able to see the humor in the situation. Now, hand me down so I can help you."

He quirked an eyebrow. "No, thank you." He rubbed a sleeve across his cheek, which only served to spread the mud farther.

"You just made it worse. And you should see your jacket. You look as though you backstroked through a puddle."

Blowing out an exasperated breath, he unbuttoned his jacket and yanked it off. Clumps of mud fell to the ground as he did so, falling along the back of his legs on the way down. His white lawn shirt—no doubt the finest fabric money could buy—was now well-stained at the sleeves and the top of the collar.

Swallowing the fresh wave of laughter, she tried again. "Don't go cutting off that nose to spite me. At the very least, let me help you clean your face."

"A little mud has yet to kill anyone. You may stay up there on your high horse."

"Radcliffe," she exclaimed. "Let me down. You're being ridiculous."

"Yes, I know," he replied, sounding perfectly reasonable as he tossed his jacket over the saddle and turned back to face her, "but at the moment, I have no desire to correct it."

He looked so adorably stubborn, it made her want to wrap her arms around him, mud be damned. Not that she would—he had rules, and she had promised to abide by them. Still, she could at least wipe the smudge from his face. "Come over here and assist me, or so help me, I will attempt to dismount on my own, and if I break my neck, you will have only yourself to blame."

Ignoring her completely, he grabbed his horse's reins and started walking. "We are much too far from the house to walk back, but we are only two miles or so from the mill."

Obstinate man. Letting out an annoyed huff, she fussed with her legs, pulling the right one free of the pommel, and the left one clear of the stirrup. Right. It was basically like sitting on a tall platform at that point. If she could find a way to turn, she could do a controlled slide down to the ground. At that moment, Blackella started forward, following Gray's lead, but May quickly pulled back on the reins.

"What do you think you're doing?" The duke paused, sending her an incredulous glare.

"Handing myself down. Apparently if a woman wants anything done around here, she must do it herself." She slowly began twisting, holding on to the saddle for balance. She paused as she reached her side, clutching the edge of the saddle awkwardly as her legs dangled off to one side, and tried to determine the best way to proceed.

In hindsight, this was perhaps not the most elegant way to go about it.

As she completed the turn, she began to lower herself. She was doing just fine until a pair of arms wrapped around her waist. Startled—how the hell had he reached her so quickly?—she gave a squeak of alarm as her grip gave way.

Suddenly without purchase, she fell into his arms like a dropped anchor. He stumbled backward, and she knew in an instant there was no way he could compensate for the swing in momentum with May occupying his arms.

She was right.

With arms and legs flailing like a rogue octopus thrown back overboard, they hurtled backward toward the muddy earth. She had just enough time to tense and then . . .

Splat.

Chapter Eighteen

That had *not* gone the way he had imagined it would. Lying in the mud, breath knocked from his lungs, and backside sunk several inches into the mud, William gazed up at the puffy clouds above them, trying to figure out how things had gone so wrong. This was, for the record, the *second* time she had knocked him to the ground.

She squirmed on top of him, trying to disentangle their appendages from both each other and the huge swath of her skirts that had somehow wrapped around them. Grabbing her by the upper arms, he shifted her away and gasped for air, trying to refill his squashed lungs.

She twisted around to face him, already shaking her head. "Devil take it, are you all right? And I swear, that is the last time I am going to ask you that today."

Nodding quickly, he rubbed at his chest, making certain his ribs were still intact. "I would ask you the same, but I'm quite sure I took the brunt of it for both of us." How could someone who weighed so little in his arms weigh so much on his chest? It felt as though he'd been slammed with an anvil.

The comment obviously didn't sit well with her. Yanking her skirts from his legs, she sat up properly. "I was doing perfectly fine without you, thank you very much. You can thank yourself for whatever 'brunt' you sustained."

"You told me to help you," he growled back, pushing himself up to a sitting position and bracing his hands on the ground behind him. "So I was *helping* you."

"I *asked* you to help, and when you refused, I took matters into my own hands. If you decided to interfere after that, you have only yourself to blame."

"A gentleman does not leave a lady dangling from a horse like a fish on a line."

She lifted her chin a notch. "I was getting into position. I had it under control."

He snorted. "Until the horse shifted or spooked, then you would have been on your backside in the mud."

"Which is an improvement over this *how*?" She gestured widely with both hands, pointing out her prone position and mud-streaked skirts. Somehow, mud had splattered into her temples and across her right cheek. She looked utterly ridiculous and as mad as Medusa.

And for some reason, he suddenly understood what she had been laughing at earlier. He shook his head, letting out a rueful chuckle. "Point conceded."

She blinked, then narrowed her eyes ominously. "Don't you dare laugh." But he saw the way she pinched her lips together, fighting against a grin.

"Turnabout is fair play, Miss Bradford," he said before giving into the humor of the situation. He laughed aloud, not caring that it hurt his ribs to do so, or that the cold wetness of the mud had soaked clear through his clothes. What an absurd picture they must have made, wallowing in the mud like a pair of well-dressed pigs.

She smacked him square in the chest with the back of her hand, albeit lightly. "You weather-bitten sea bass," she exclaimed, but there was no mistaking the amusement in her voice. "How dare you laugh at a lady?"

He lifted his eyebrows. "Oh, so *now* you are a lady. All this time, you've refused the distinction, but now that you are covered in muck and cursing like a sailor it suddenly suits you?"

She grinned wickedly, giving up any pretense of outrage. "Precisely. I've never felt more ladylike in my life." Dragging a finger through the mud, she then swiped it across her left cheek. "See? I even have the same fashion sense as a duke."

He threw back his head and laughed, completely abandoning any hope of propriety. He couldn't remember the last time he had felt so free. If nothing else, she really could make him laugh. "You are beyond incorrigible," he said at last, shaking his head ruefully. What other female on the planet could have led to this moment?

"Good. Then you English haven't changed me yet."

Indeed. And heaven help him, but he was glad for it. He pushed his way to his feet and yanked off his ruined gloves. "We certainly have not." After tossing the gloves in the general direction of his horse, he turned and offered a relatively clean hand to May.

She pulled off her own gloves, threw them toward her own horse, then placed her slender hand in his. He quickly pulled her to her feet, allowing their contact to linger while she found her footing. She was an absolute mess, with fewer clean spots than dirty. "Come on," he said, his voice slightly rough. "The stream is just a few hundred yards from here."

He paused long enough to secure the horses to a nearby tree, then offered her his elbow. She ignored it, instead slipping her hand back into his. "My hands are clean and your sleeve is most certainly not," she said, giving him a little wink.

Another time, he would have protested. But right now, after all that had just occurred, it seemed perfectly natural to lace his fingers with hers. In that moment, all of their roles and rules had fallen by the wayside, and it was just the two of them, enjoying the company.

The water was higher than normal in the stream, which was for the best, given the amount of cleaning up they had to do. May glanced over at him as he pulled off his boots, set them aside on the mossy bank, and waded in. The water was bracingly cold, but spot cleaning would have been hopeless.

"Are you certain I didn't hurt you when we fell?"

He shook his head, conveniently ignoring the ache in his ribs. "I'm perfectly fine, I assure you."

She kneeled at the bank and dipped her skirts into the water. Thanks to the way they had fallen, she wasn't near as filthy as he was. She worked at the mud, rubbing the fabric back and forth over itself. "Your stepmother is going to swoon when she sees what I've done with her habit."

Vivian was the very last person he cared to think about just then. "She'll get over it," he said gruffly, trying to ignore the glimpses of May's leg that he kept catching. "It's a dreary fabric, regardless. I much prefer the colorful gowns you wear."

May glanced up sharply, surprise rounding her eyes. "Really? I had no idea. My aunt hates my gowns, and I rather thought you agreed with her on most things."

He didn't point out that her aunt was a woman, and he most definitely was not. He loved the way her gowns fit, and how the little touches, the embroidery and trims and unusual colors, made her stand out in a crowd. "Not everything. The gowns show your eye for beauty."

She dropped her skirts, staring back at him with the oddest expression. "Thank you. My father's trade provides me with the most exquisite of fabrics. Each one is special to me when I think of the place or person it came from."

Nodding, he smiled briefly. "It's good when we can have those reminders of people." He wondered how he would remember her when she was gone. Would he ever be able to look at the folly again and not think of her? Or at Blackella, or the nursery, or even the entire city of Bath? Everywhere he looked, she seemed to have left her mark.

Swallowing, he tried to refocus on his task. He was a disaster, and there was no way he could show up at the mill looking like this. Glancing down at his mud-streaked shirt, he sighed. There was no help for it. Taking a deep breath, he closed his eyes and dove underwater.

May watched, slack-jawed, as the duke emerged from the stream, water cascading down over his body. His white shirt clung to his chest and arms, the thin fabric nearly translucent against his skin. She could see hints of dark hair across his chest in between the vee of his waistcoat.

He scraped his hair back from his forehead then rubbed the water from his eyes. He looked himself over then, nodding in approval. "Much better," he decreed before glancing to where she sat kneeling on the shore. Oh, Lord have mercy, but the man was gorgeous. Particularly with his features relaxed and his lips curved in a soft smile. Having a nearly unencumbered view of his nicely muscled arms didn't hurt, either.

He tilted his head. "Is there a problem?"

She swallowed past the lump in her throat and shook her head. "No. I was just thinking that looked incredibly cold."

"It is," he said with a chuckle. He waded back toward her, his legs cutting easily through the swiftly moving waters. "Care to give it a try?"

There he went, teasing her again. Her heart gave a little flip as she shook her head. "I'm cold and wet enough as it is, thank you."

When he'd reached the shore, he held out his hand. "Are you sure? I promise to keep you from drowning."

She grinned, holding up both hands, palms out. "Your promises haven't worked out too well for us today. I think perhaps I won't tempt fate."

"I suppose you have a point," he replied with a rueful laugh. Wringing the excess moisture from his clothes, he came to sit beside her on the mossy bank. "I really do apologize. I never intended for either one of us to end up on the ground."

"Well, I should hope not," she said, sending him a teasing glance.

Rolling his eyes, he crooked a finger at her. "Come here. Your face is filthy. If you won't let me dunk you, at least allow me help you with that."

She readily obliged. Resting her hands on her knees, she leaned forward so he could have better access. Pulling a scrap of linen from a hidden pocket, he dabbed at her cheeks with one hand while holding her lightly by the chin with the other. There was nothing remotely romantic about his ministrations, but still her breathing kicked up at not only his touch, but his closeness. From this distance, she could see that he still had a faint trail of mud across his jaw. She dipped her fingers into the water and swiped it away. The hint of stubble abraded the sensitive skin of her fingertips.

He paused, his eyes meeting hers. She wet her lips. "Dirt," she said simply by way of explanation.

"Thank you," he said gruffly. Rewetting the cloth, he gently swiped it down the slope of her nose and along the creases bracketing her mouth. He lingered there, then slowly swiped the pad of his thumb over her lips.

She drew in a quiet breath, trying to slow the pounding of her heart. His eyes met hers again, and for a moment neither of them moved or spoke. She watched his Adam's apple bob as he swallowed, suddenly absolutely certain that he was feeling the same shock of awareness between them.

He lowered the hand with the linen, but kept her chin firmly tucked between his thumb and forefinger. Then slowly—oh so slowly—he leaned forward and pressed his lips to hers. It was a soft kiss, tender enough to make her weak in the knees. Thank goodness she wasn't standing.

He pulled away a few inches, his eyes flitting over her face. She didn't make a sound, didn't move an inch. She'd made a promise, and she wouldn't break it. Still, she had no intention of stopping *him* from kissing *her*.

He drew a long, slow breath, then leaned in again. Using his grip on her chin, he tilted her face and kissed her cheek, then the other one, then her forehead, then her temples. Each kiss was light but lingering, making her stomach dance with butterflies.

Again, he pulled back, his eyes searching. The wind rustled the trees above them as water gurgled over the smooth rocks in the stream. "I should stop," he said quietly.

"Yes," she agreed.

But neither of them moved.

His gaze fell to her lips again, and this time when he kissed her, he didn't hold back. Unlike their first kiss, *he* was in control. It was his hands that cupped her jaw and pulled her closer. This time it was his tongue that coaxed her lips apart and invaded her mouth with a moan of pleasure. It was his lead, his desires that drove the moment, making it utter perfection.

He kissed her deeply, passionately, toe-curlingly and heart-poundingly. His taste, his smell, his warmth—all of it filled her senses until it felt as though he was all there was in the world. Just the two of them.

By the time he broke the kiss, she was light-headed with exhilaration. His fingers lingered, holding her jaw as his golden gaze met hers. "You are one of the most incredible women I have ever met. I hope you don't mind my wanting to kiss you properly. Just this once."

A small, giddy smile lifted her lips. "I'll allow it. Just this once."

His mouth curled up at the corners. "I'm relieved to hear it." He kissed her again, then once more before releasing his hold and leaning back.

For as long as she lived, she doubted she would ever forget the way he looked, all wet and disheveled and handsome enough to take her breath away.

Nor would she forget the way she felt.

Whether she ever admitted it aloud or not, she was very, very glad for her summer in England.

Chapter Nineteen

Heaven help him, but she was gorgeous. She was more tempting than anyone he had ever known, and much more enticing. He could scarcely recall what it was that had so exasperated him about her when they first met. All those things that he had thought he disliked—her frankness, her humor, her ability to see him as a person instead of a duke—had somehow become the things he loved most about her.

And despite his intention not to allow his resolve to slip, he wasn't at all sorry.

As William and May walked toward the mill, their horses following along behind them, he knew that he could never regret that kiss. Those kisses. That feeling.

The look in her eyes.

It was against all the rules he had set for himself, all the careful plans he lived by, but that moment by the stream was one of the most meaningful in his life. It was honest, and real, and completely from the heart. There were no titles or social statuses or envy of money between them. No political gains to be had, or favors to be garnered.

They took their time walking. Yes, they wanted to dry

their clothes as much as possible, but there was also a sense of delaying the inevitable. When they reached the mill, there could be no more casual touches and familiar glances. The perception of the ducal estate rested on his shoulders, and that perception was particularly important when he was around those who looked to him for their livelihoods.

As they crested the hill that overlooked the mill, he slowed to a stop and gestured toward the building below. "Spencer Mill, the finest and most advanced mill in all of England." He was oddly nervous about what she would think. Would she appreciate the incredible amount of work that went into creating an industry from scratch? Would she finally see that he didn't simply spend his days lounging around his property?

She followed his gaze to the long, three-story stone-block building that rose from the valley with stately purpose. A single stack rose above it, while the canal flowed directly alongside it. The waters were still higher and murkier than usual, splashing against the stone retaining walls that had been constructed less than two years earlier, but thankfully it was still flowing unimpeded. Though most of the work went on inside, the grounds were busy with workers coming and going around the complex.

She raised an eyebrow. "*Spencer* Mill? You own this too?"

"Indeed. I had it built, as well. The greenhouse was my father's contribution to the estate. This is mine." It was the thing he was most proud of in his life, and he wanted her to see how much it meant to him. Her opinion shouldn't matter, but it did.

She nodded, seemingly impressed. "Ambitious. How long did it take to build? You couldn't have been duke that long, given your little sister's age."

Relaxing, he started forward again, leading the way down the hill toward the road. "My father died before Clarisse was born. I've held the title for almost six years, but I've been working on plans for building a mill since shortly after University."

"Really? I thought all young bucks fresh from University were required to spend their days aimlessly, gambling and sowing their wild oats." She sent him another of her wicked little grins.

Cutting her an arch look, he said, "Do you really know me so little? After all this time together?"

She brushed a fallen lock of corn silk hair behind her ear. "I know you as you are now, dreadfully responsible lord of the manor. I was rather hoping there was a bit of unruliness in your youth. I like to imagine you've had a little fun at *some* point in your life."

"I have." *Today*. But he didn't say what he was thinking. Best not to slide back down that slippery slope. "But I've always been focused on the future. My father encouraged me to be involved with the estate from early on. He wanted me to be intimately familiar with both its past and present, and to be involved in shaping its future."

Her smile was sweet, accentuating the rosy apples of her cheeks. "He sounds like he did a good job of preparing you for the title."

"Yes, and prudently so. He was already past forty by the time I was born. The men in this family are not known for having the longest of life spans."

"That's surprising," she said, tilting her head in thought. "With so much wealth and privilege at your fingertips, one would think you'd live longer than most."

They reached the hard-packed dirt road, which, with the exception of a few puddles, was fairly dried out.

"With great wealth comes even greater responsibility. It wears on a man."

Even at his relatively young age, he could feel that wear. He knew that he'd need to marry soon and get about the business of begetting an heir. He wanted to have time to properly raise and prepare the next duke. This next Season, he would have to apply himself to finding the sort of woman who would properly fit the role: upstanding, virtuous, biddable, and of impeccable breeding.

His brow furrowed slightly. At that moment, the thought did not appeal to him in the least. Those qualities had always been top on his list, but thanks to the woman walking beside him, they also sounded exceedingly boring.

Which was a *good* thing, he reminded himself. Boring translated to scandal-free and dependable. He needed a duchess who would take the role as seriously as its rank deserved.

May bit her lip, her eyes on the road ahead. "Do you ever wish that you had been born to a different life? One that may not have as much privilege, but in which you could do whatever you wanted with your life?"

Leave it to May to ask a question like that. Such a question had never entered his mind. Most people would kill for what he had, as hard as it was for her to believe.

"I have never once considered such a thing. My life is impossible to separate from my title. It's part of who I am, and I wouldn't have it any other way." He pursed his lips for a moment. "And really, I could ask the same question of you."

"But you should already know the answer," she said, smiling broadly. "I love the life I have lived thus far. I can't wait to return to it, in fact."

A pang of . . . *something* pulled in his chest. She

looked so beautiful, with her blue eyes bright in the sunshine, and her golden skin warm and inviting. Her habit was ill fitting, but it was testament to her remarkable figure that she still looked as regal as a queen. Was that why it was so easy to picture her in a different life? In one that played out right here in England?

As they approached the yard, some of the workers began to take note of their presence. Several tipped their hats, and a few others offered awkward bows. To a man, they all stared at May. A surge of protectiveness came from nowhere, and he had to force himself not to glare at the men and pull her to his side. It was natural that they would be curious. He'd never once been seen with a woman on the estate, let alone at the mill.

The main door thwacked open and Wallace Perkins hurried out. He was a brute of a man, short but built like a prize bull. His manner was always straightforward and to the point, one of the reasons William had chosen him for the job. A man who wasn't afraid to speak plainly to his superiors was a man who wouldn't be cowed by either his subordinates or his workload.

As he approached, it was easy to see that he had been on the work floor recently. His dark hair was dotted with the odd white cotton tuft, as were his brown coat and trousers. Grease smudged his fingers and sweat dampened his brow. "Your Grace. We weren't expecting you. Did you receive my note this morning?"

The man deserved a medal for his mild question and straight face. He had to be wondering who May was and what on earth had happened to the two of them. Though the dunk in the stream had helped, they still looked much the worse for wear.

"I did not. We've been out since breakfast. Is anything amiss?"

"Not at all, which was the point of the missive." He pulled a handkerchief from his pocket and wiped the sweat from his brow. "It was a near thing yesterday, but all is well thanks to your quick actions."

May sent William a curious look, and he gave a small shrug. "We had a fallen tree block the canal, which could have been disastrous if we'd flooded. But I had no more of a hand in the efforts than Mr. Perkins, or any of the other men who rushed in to help."

"You are too kind, sir. Is there anything that I can do for you now?"

Nodding, William motioned to his horse. "Gray threw a shoe while Miss Bradford and I were riding. The mill was closer, so we came directly here. Can you send for the farrier and a cart or carriage to get us back to the house?"

"Of course. If there is anything else you require, just let me know." He gathered the horses' reins and headed off for the stables.

Turning his attention back to May, William said, "Do you mind if we wait out here? I fear the noise and fibers inside may prove unpleasant. Additionally, I wouldn't wish to disrupt the workers with our presence."

"I don't mind at all. Lord knows I don't want to cause any more trouble today than I already have," she said with a rueful grin. "In the meantime, you can tell me all about this place and I shall pretend to know what you are talking about."

She was teasing, but he could happily go on for hours about the mill, the machinery in it, and the products they made. "Very well. Should I start with the spinning mule or the single cylinder condensing beam engine?"

"Oh, definitely the engine." She pursed her lips as though thinking. "Or, you could just start by telling me what it is you are milling."

* * *

It was amazing how differently he stood when he was speaking of something he clearly had so much pride in. May stifled a smile, happy to see the enthusiasm in his eyes. Yes, he'd always stood like a man in control, a man with the full knowledge of his power. But as he stood in front of the building he had envisioned, pursued, and created, there was a tangible shift in the way he held his shoulders and lifted his chin. Instead of standing tall and straight, he leaned forward just a bit, as though eager to discuss the fruits of his labor.

It was rather endearing. Particularly given how sweet he had been at the stream. Kissing him the first time had been lovely. Being kissed by him had been a thousand times better, and her head still buzzed with the pleasure of the experience.

Leading her to a low stone wall where they would be out of the way of the drive, he smiled and gestured for her to sit. She did—gratefully—while he remained standing. "This is the county's first cotton mill." Smiling, he gazed up at the building behind her. "We just received our first major shipment of American raw cotton, and using the very latest in steam-powered engines, we are able to create fabrics faster and cheaper, and in larger quantities than ever before."

She drew in a surprised breath, her enthusiasm slipping away. "Faster and cheaper? Does that affect the quality?"

Her father had been transporting imported fabrics for decades. She not only knew where the best fabrics came from, but she was familiar with—and even friends with— some of the people that produced them.

He didn't seem to pick up on the change in her tone. Pride lit his amber eyes as he met her gaze. "With such sophisticated machinery, the quality is both consistent and acceptable."

Acceptable? She screwed up her nose at the term. She couldn't help but think of her friend Smita and her family, all of whom worked to produce some of the finest India muslin in the world. Their craft was laborious and painstaking, but the quality was exceptional. In fact, more than half the village was employed by the mill there, and was therefore at the mercy of the textile market.

A stone settled in her stomach as she remembered the letter from Smita where she'd worried about the recent influx of cheap mass-produced but inferior textiles. Textiles exactly like what the duke was describing. "Acceptable? I thought a hand loom was the only way to guarantee a quality product."

"Hand-loom products are slower and more expensive to make. We are producing quality goods at a price more people can afford. More important," he added, gesturing down the lane to where workers were unloading crates from a wagon, "we've created over one hundred new jobs. That's one hundred more English men and women who can provide for their families."

Yes, of course—only Englishmen deserved to be able to work. Why had she allowed herself to forget the way he looked at the world? To him, his countrymen were far more important than any other people in the world. "Yes, but if you take four times that many jobs from others, how is that a good thing?"

Surprise registered on his face. As he realized what she was saying, she could practically see his gaze frost over like icy sea spray on a frigid porthole. "If you are suggesting that this, the business I have spent the last half dozen years working to create, is somehow a bad thing because it sees to the needs of those I am responsible for, then you have no concept of how seriously I take my duties to my tenants, servants, and employees."

Her pulse was kicking up, dismay blotting out the pleasure of the day. He had a point, she did see that, but there was a larger issue here that he wasn't considering at all. "And if a village's entire economy collapses because they can no longer compete?"

"Then they should have been paying more attention to the innovations in the market." He stepped away from her, the movement agitated. His affront was palpable, as an almost physical tension rose between them.

"Oh, really? And what would you suggest they do—buy the machinery that would turn their products into cheap facsimiles of what they have always been?"

His eyes narrowed as his jaw hardened. "The world is changing. England is no longer at the mercy of the East India Company and its pricing whims. There is a need for inexpensive textiles, and I am happy to be among those who fill it. If there is a market for high-priced, laboriously created textiles, then they are welcome to it."

She scowled at the mention of her father's employer. "Why are you bringing the Company into this? Because of them, England has a wealth of products it could have never hoped to enjoy otherwise. I've seen you enjoy your tea. I've seen the quality of your own fabrics, and you've readily complimented the quality of mine. Where do you think those things come from?"

Holding up his hands, he said, "You are obviously too emotionally attached to the Company to be able to speak of them with any amount of impartiality. And it is further obvious that we will never have an agreement on the subject at hand. I think it's best that we cease the discussion at once."

She crossed her arms. "Seeing how you are too emotionally attached to this mill to be objective, I concur."

He was right, though she hated to admit he was right about anything at that point. The mill was up and running, and nothing she said was going to change that. And really, she *shouldn't* change that.

When she pushed away her personal connection, she could see that he wasn't doing anything wrong or even amoral. But the problem was, her sympathies lay elsewhere. The people she cared about were elsewhere. Their disagreement was simply indicative of the huge chasm that separated their lives. When the air around them was so charged she could barely think straight, it had been easy to ignore.

Mr. Perkins emerged from the stables then. He hurried their way, having no idea of all that had just transpired. "I've located a wagon you can use, but I thought I'd offer my horse first, in case you wished to ride back."

Without consulting her, the duke nodded curtly. "Perfect. How soon can he be saddled?"

The man smiled, revealing a surprisingly charming smile. "He's already saddled and ready to go. I figured you might be wanting to be on your way."

Relief sagged May's shoulders. She would have never thought she'd be eager to ride, but the sooner they could head home, the better. Apparently, Radcliffe agreed. "Good man. I'll have him sent back to you before your shift is up."

The duke turned and stalked toward the stables, leaving her where she was, which suited her fine. Something told her the ride home would be much quieter than the ride there.

Chapter Twenty

The knock on his chamber door came shortly before midnight. William let out a low growl of displeasure. He should have known Vivian would ignore the rules. At least now he was smart enough to lock the doors. He hadn't always been that wise, unfortunately.

That particular thought only served to further darken his mood.

He would ignore it completely, but he couldn't be sure she wouldn't keep trying, which might wake May or her aunt. He was down to simply his breeches and his shirt, with the collar loose and his cufflinks long since tossed aside. Normally he would have been in bed an hour ago, but the events of the day had agitated him. He'd eventually sent word to his valet to retire for the evening, and said he'd see to himself.

Setting aside a book he hadn't really been reading, he padded barefoot to the door and pulled it open, scowl already in place. Only it wasn't Vivian standing there, mere steps away in the low light of the corridor.

It was May.

He stepped back, completely taken off guard. After the way they had parted, she was the last person he expected to see. Really, with the exception of his step-mother, she was the last person he *wanted* to see. "What are you doing here? Have you gone mad?"

He knew full well that she had little concern for pro-priety, but this reached new—and more dangerous—heights. It mattered not that she was well covered in her pale blue wrapper and night rail. One simply couldn't come to a man's bedchamber, period.

"I need to talk to you," she said plainly, as though they had just met in the corridor on the way to breakfast instead of at his bedchamber door in the middle of the night.

"Then I suggest you wait until a more acceptable hour to do so." He started to close the door, but she put her hand out, stopping the movement with a thud.

Her brows came together in earnestness. "Please, it will only be a moment. I can say what I need to say from here, in fact."

She really was mad. Fit for Bedlam, in fact. If some-one caught them now, there would be hell to pay. But with her physically blocking the door, there was little he could do that wouldn't cause an even greater scene. "Fine, but you'd best speak quickly." He crossed his arms over his chest and stared back at her with the cold, im-partial stare that he had mastered by the time he was ten.

Unimpressed, she met his gaze squarely. "I'm sorry. I know the mill is very important to you, and I should have been more respectful of that."

He lifted a brow. That was it? He waited for her to go on, to use the apology as an excuse to argue her point again, but she didn't say another word. Nodding once, he said, "Thank you. I appreciate the sentiment. Which, for the record, could have waited until morning."

It did take the edge off his anger. Slightly. He still

could scarcely believe she would attack both his mill's product and his motives, as though it were all some sort of nefarious bid to make the world a worse place. He had thrown everything he had into making the estate thrive, so that those who depended on him could be secure.

A ghost of a rueful smile slipped across her lips. "Not if I'm to get any sleep. I've been mulling it over for hours, and I've come to the decision that the way I reacted today was inappropriate, and even wrong. Whenever I am in the wrong, I find it impossible to sleep until I attempt to right things."

It might have been the first time he had heard her honestly admit to being wrong. How very novel. "Fine, good. You've apologized, I've accepted. Good night."

The squeak of door hinges down the corridor was unmistakable. Stiffening, he made a split-second decision. He reached out, grabbed her hand, and yanked her into the room. In almost the same movement he eased the door shut, then turned to May, who was clearly startled. *"Quiet,"* he hissed, putting a finger to his mouth.

She nodded, actually listening to him for once. He leaned his ear to the door and listened. *Footsteps.* They came closer and closer, and he grew tenser and tenser. May watched the door with wide eyes, not moving an inch. For a split second, he wondered if she had planned this, but he quickly discarded the idea. She wouldn't do anything that might result in her having to stay in the country a day longer than necessary, let alone an entire lifetime.

The footsteps didn't slow, thank God. They continued on, receding to silence. His brow furrowed as he pushed away from the door.

"Who was it?" May whispered, her hand gripping his forearm.

"I'm not certain. Someone walked past. I don't think it would be a servant, but that leaves only your aunt and my stepmother." Neither of whom he wanted prowling the corridors while May was here in his room.

She shook her head. "It wouldn't be my aunt. Her schedule is as regular as clockwork. She disappears into her chamber at nine o'clock at night, and won't emerge again for a full twelve hours."

He inwardly groaned. "That leaves Vivian. Perhaps she went to the library for a book." Unlikely, but what else would she do? At least she hadn't stopped here. Still . . . he reached over and turned the key, locking the door.

May's eyes rounded with clear disbelief.

Blowing out a breath, he sent her a stern look. "I am not risking someone accidentally opening the wrong door and discovering your presence. I am also not risking having you leave until I know it is safe to do so."

"I see," she said, releasing her grip on his forearm and putting a hand to her hip. "So you must be scandalous to avoid appearing scandalous. I do like the way you think." Her tone was teasing, as though the circumstances weren't at all alarming.

He narrowed his eyes. "Making light of a situation that is entirely your fault, are we?"

Lifting a shoulder, she said, "More or less. What else am I going to do while locked in a disapproving duke's bedchamber?"

As though he needed a reminder of where they were. Alone. In the middle of the night. He swallowed, suddenly realizing just how close they were, huddled together next to the door. But what were their choices? It was a huge room, with a seating area large enough to comfortably fit six situated between the door and the huge canopied bed that was placed against the back wall.

The problem was, any steps away from the door were steps closer to the bed, which was most certainly a *bad* idea. He really, really did not need to have May anywhere near the thing. Even with her innocent nightclothes and simple braid draped over her shoulder, something inside of him still responded to her. Never mind that, despite her apology, he was still displeased with their argument at the mill. He was nevertheless attracted to her in a way that made her presence here extremely ill-advised.

Gesturing toward the seating area, he said, "You may sit down. I'll stay here so I don't miss the footsteps when the person returns."

She glanced at his inner sanctum and nibbled her bottom lip, looking unsure for perhaps the first time since he'd met her. "Actually, I think I'll stay here. It may sound ridiculous, but I do have my own standards for behavior, and waltzing through your room is not included."

Of course it wasn't. If he was clever, he would have told her *not* to sit, at which point she likely would have gladly waltzed over and had a seat. "Why is it you always seem to know how to thwart me?"

"A talent, I suppose." A small smile crinkled the corners of her eyes as she looked him over. "Do you truly forgive me?"

He lifted a brow. "For the argument at the mill?"

She nodded. "I have a sneaking suspicion you were just trying to get rid of me."

"I was," he said, earning a light smack to his shoulder. He allowed a small grin before returning to the original question. "For what it's worth, yes, I forgive you. You and

I are opposites, Miss Bradford. No matter the issue, we will always have disparate views." Her name felt unwieldy on his tongue, but he was trying to force some distance in such an intimate setting.

It didn't seem to help.

She sighed and leaned against the wall, her eyes never leaving his. The lamplight was low, but it was enough to bathe her skin in a warm, golden glow. Her pupils were wide and fathomless, the blue around them almost lost to the darkness. "Yes, but it wasn't right of me to steal your moment of pride."

Why did she have to be so reasonable sometimes?

He wet his lips. "I have ample pride, as you well know. I can stand to lose some." His voice had fallen to little more than a murmur. The now-familiar desire to draw nearer to her squeezed his chest, making his pulse increase. She was wrong for him in a thousand ways—so why did she occupy so much of his thoughts? Why did his whole body respond whenever she was near?

She was quiet for a moment, her gaze flicking from his eyes, down to his mouth, then back to his eyes. She slowly shook her head. "What is it about you, William Spencer?" Her voice was low and the slightest bit breathy.

No one called him that. He was always Duke, or Radcliffe, or even William to a very select few. But no one ever just said his whole name, without the title that had defined him for so long. Even before he was duke, he was still known by his courtesy title, the Marquis of Salford. "What do you mean?"

But he heard the hint of longing in her voice. It was the same way he felt about her. Equal parts exasperation and desire. Knowing they were all wrong for each other, but having such powerful attraction, it was hard to be rational about it. She was strong and independent, two things he'd never looked for in a woman, but even as those were exactly the things that drove him mad at times, they also impressed him. She could hold her own, and he had to admire that.

She stayed where she was, her shoulders pressed against the wall as she looked up at him. Instead of answering his question, she said, "I told my aunt after dinner that I wished to go back to Bath tomorrow."

The thought of her leaving made his hands tighten at his sides. "You don't need to do that. You can certainly stay for the rest of the agreed-upon time."

"No, I can't. You and I are like two pieces of flint. When we're not beating each other, we're causing sparks. I need to leave before one of us really gets hurt."

Sparks. That was exactly the right word. He sighed and dragged both hands through his hair. "I suppose you are right."

She tilted her head slightly, exposing the left side of her face more fully to the lamplight. "There is a statement I never thought to hear from you." There was warmth in the words, despite her teasing.

He doubted he would ever forget her. Certainly he would never meet another like her. Stifling the desire to run his fingers down the smooth curve of her cheek, he said. "My siblings will miss you."

She chuckled softly, amusement flickering in her eyes. "Yes, and they will be the only ones."

"They *should* be the only ones," he said, shaking his head wryly, "but they won't." He shouldn't be saying such things. He should open the door, check the corridor, and send her on her way. But he didn't. He stayed exactly where he was, much too close to the woman who tempted him like no other.

One blond brow rose into a perfect arch. "I don't believe you." She pressed her lips together against a smile as she shook her head. "You Englishmen and your need for politeness."

Something inside of him gave way, a release of the tight rein with which he had been holding himself in check. He stepped forward, moving before he could change his mind. Her eyes widened, obviously not expecting the move. There were mere inches between them, close enough for him to detect that exotic scent of hers. His heart hammered at his own audacity.

Without a word, he reached out, slipped both of his hands into hers and laced their fingers together. He lifted their joined hands, sliding them along the wall in a smooth arc until they reached shoulder height. Her chest rose and fell rapidly as her eyes darkened further. Her lips parted as she watched him, surprised yet seeming to dare him not to stop.

He leaned forward, pressing her hands against the wall while he closed the distance between their lips, inch by tantalizing inch. When he was close enough to feel the heat of her breath against his cheek, he growled softly, "I'm not feeling very polite right now."

She met his gaze, desire burning in the indigo depths of her eyes. "Neither am I," she breathed, then leaned forward, eagerly meeting his lips. The kiss was searing, scorching . . . equally wanted on both their parts. Her fingers tightened against his as he leaned more firmly against her. The feel of her breasts pressed so perfectly against his chest was enough to drown out all common sense.

A last kiss, he told himself, even as he kissed a trail along her jaw to her ear. It had to be. She was leaving him, and his life would finally be returned to something he recognized. He scraped his teeth along the sensitive skin of her earlobe, eliciting a soft moan from deep in her throat. Tomorrow, he'd vow not to kiss another woman until he found his duchess. Tomorrow, he'd re-evaluate his rules of conduct, and chide himself roundly for ever breaking them.

But for now . . .

He returned to her mouth, kissing her briefly before nipping her bottom lip. He was rewarded with another soft sound of pleasure, and he couldn't resist doing it again. She seemed to melt against him, molding her body to his.

Untwining his fingers from hers for a moment, his skimmed his hands down the slender length of her neck, reveling in the silkiness of her skin even as he claimed her lips again in a bold kiss. When his fingers met the fabric of her wrapper, he paused, wrestling with his own desire, before finally giving in and slipping a knuckle beneath the fabric. Her hands slid along his lower back, pulling him closer, imploring him not to stop. It was pure bliss.

With his heart pounding, he further deepened the kiss as his fingers dipped lower, parting the silken lapels of her wrapper. The fabric slid like cool water across her skin, revealing inch by tantalizing inch.

A sharp knock at the door made them both freeze. Blood roared in his ears as his heart surged. A thousand emotions tangled inside of him as he forced himself to pull away and put a finger to his lips in a furtive plea for silence. May's eyes were wide with alarm and she nodded quickly, her fingers hastily righting her clothes. Gesturing for her to follow, he led her to the dressing room and shut her inside.

The knocks kept coming, escalating in loudness. Hurrying back to the door, he drew a few deep breaths before twisting the knob and pulling the door open. This time, it really was his stepmother on the other side, more unwelcome than ever.

"Go away, Vivian." The words were little more than a growl. He could have happily murdered her just then, even though a part of him recognized it was a good thing that kiss had been stopped. Lord knew where it would have led otherwise.

Actually, he was pretty sure he knew. His willpower when it came to May was apparently little to none.

Vivian looked unperturbed. "Please, William, there is no need to take that tone with me. I saw the light beneath your door and thought perhaps we could talk." She smiled at him, all innocence, but he knew her well enough to know she did not want to share a quick chat.

He crossed his arms, not at all in the mood for her tricks. "I've kicked you out of my house before. Please don't make me do it again."

Her nightclothes were much less modest than May's. The outline of her legs was just visible in the dim light of his room, and the neckline scooped far enough to reveal a wide swath of her cleavage. If she was attempting to be alluring to him, she was failing completely. There was *nothing* that could make her alluring to him.

She smiled commiseratively. "Judging by your mood upon your return today, I'm willing to bet you had a rough day with that charming little guest of yours. Since we've had so little time together since I arrived, I thought we could . . . comfort each other."

She was delusional. He had actually hoped that with the others here, she would back down, but clearly that hope had been in vain. "Good night, Vivian," he said quietly but firmly. He started to push the door closed, but her sharp voice stopped him.

"I don't know why you toy with her. We both know there is no possible way she could fill the role of duchess. Your standards are much too high to even consider it."

Anger chilled his heated blood. "Oh?" he said coldly. "Then why are you here?" Obviously she felt threatened by May, in one way or another.

Her eyes shuttered. "For company, of course."

Why did she keep pushing, all these years later? Was she trying to be permanently banned from his households? Yes, he wanted her children to have their mother, but he had his limits. "You know I will never be comforted by you."

"Really?" she cooed, raising an eyebrow. "When I remember your kiss and the feel of your hands on my body, I think perhaps that isn't true."

Fury speared through him. He set his mouth into a hard, straight line. "Be ready to depart by noon tomorrow. I don't care which house you go to, but you are not welcome in this one."

The curved lines bracketing her mouth deepened as she narrowed her eyes slightly. "But the children have barely seen me. Don't be rash simply because you had a bad day."

"It was your own choice not to spend time with them. If they've seen you once, that's once more than they have in the previous three months. That should do for a while." He didn't wait for her to answer this time. Closing the door practically in her face, he noisily twisted the key in the lock. His body was tense from the encounter, but his heart ached for his siblings. No matter what, they always seemed to be the ones who were hurt.

He waited, heart pounding, for her to leave. For a moment he feared she wouldn't, but at last he heard the receding footsteps. Drawing a fortifying breath, he hurried to the dressing room. The fury thinned, replaced by the dull weight of dread in his stomach. Would May have been able to hear any of that? He desperately hoped not. It was a good fifteen paces away, and the doors in this house were exceptionally solid. Swallowing, he pulled the door open.

May stood right behind it, her hands on her hips and her eyes narrowed. "What the devil was that all about?"

Surely she had not heard what she thought she heard. She watched him, incredulous, to see what sort of explanation he could possibly come up with. The knock had been a cold bucket of water to the burning heat of her desire only moments before. She had been lost to that kiss. *Consumed* by it. When she had told him they were like two pieces of flint, that's exactly what she had meant. They positively ignited when they were together like that.

But then she'd heard the knock, and then bits and pieces of that bizarre conversation, and now it was as though the ice water had made it into her veins.

William raked his hands through his hair, shaking his head. "That was my stepmother. I was counting on your presence — and that of your aunt's — to discourage something like this, but unfortunately I was wrong." He motioned for her to step from the dressing room and join him by the sitting area.

May didn't move as she stared back at him, aghast. "She . . . comes to your rooms? Often?"

Disgust twisted his lips as he shook his head decisively. "No, not often, because she isn't often here. But she has it in her twisted little Parisian mind that if she can land one duke, she can land another. There is nothing between us, and there *never* will be, but she never stops pushing."

May was quite sure her face was contorted with exactly the same emotion. "That's outrageous. And yet you still let her into your home?" She remembered when they had run into Vivian in Bath, how clear his dislike for the woman had been then. That he would speak as civilly to her as he did was impressive.

He lifted his shoulder. "The children. Whatever her issues with me, so long as she isn't hurting them, I will not rob them of their mother. I know how it is to live that way, and I would never sentence anyone, let alone my own siblings, to such a fate."

She stood there, staring back at him in amazement. What an incredibly honorable man he was. Well, besides the fact she was standing in his dressing room just then, shortly after having shared the most scorching kiss of her entire life. "That sort of kindness is ... uncommon," she said, unable to find a better word to encompass how truly amazing he was.

He quirked an eyebrow. "Do I need to come over there and check your forehead for a fever?"

And he even had a rare bit of humor that made her laugh. Her heart melted as she looked up at him. How on earth could the man she had argued so bitterly with in the past be the same man standing before her now? He was so much more than she gave him credit for. Yes, he was still a stuffy English duke, but he was *her* stuffy English duke.

She straightened abruptly, shocked by the direction of her own thoughts. No, he was *not* hers. He didn't belong to her, and she most certainly didn't belong to him. She couldn't. She didn't belong *here*. How could she have forgotten, for even that small amount of time, that she belonged half a world away? This was nothing more than a flirtation. A distraction, until she could return to her real life.

Hurrying from the dressing room, where the scent of him had surrounded her in the most delicious way, she rushed for the door. "No, but it really is past time for me to get back to my room."

"May, wait," he said, hurrying after her.

"Thank you for accepting my apology, I'm so glad that I can sleep well tonight." She was steps from the door when he caught her by the hand, spinning her around.

"Mei-li," he said, the word practically a caress. "Please, just give me a moment." When she didn't pull away, he relaxed a little, but didn't release her. "I just wanted to say that I'm sorry if things got a little out of hand tonight. I hope it didn't upset you."

Upset her? If only he knew how much she had relished it. She shook her head, doing her best to offer a polite smile. "Of course not."

"I'm glad." He gave her hand a light squeeze. "I want you to know that I meant it when I said you don't have to leave tomorrow."

She swallowed, resisting the urge to step into his arms and close her eyes, allowing herself to be lost to his touch once more. "I must. I'm . . . I'm anxious for my father's return, and I want to be sure that I'm there to greet him. Plus, I need to be ready to leave at a moment's notice, since I'm unsure of his schedule."

Lies. For once, she couldn't make herself tell him the truth: She was falling hard for him, and that scared the daylights out of her. If she allowed herself to fall in love with him, then what? Nothing good could come of it. This life was not for her, and it never could be.

His golden gaze met hers with unnerving intensity, as though he were attempting to divine what she was really thinking. "You haven't found anything to hold your interest here in this great country?"

Yes. "Don't be silly," she said as lightly as she could manage. "It turned out to be a nice visit, but I am eager to find my way home." And she was. She just needed to break free from his odd spell long enough to catch sight of it again.

He released her and stepped back, the warmth steadily leaching from his gaze. "I see. In that case, I wouldn't want to keep you."

Biting the inside of her cheek to keep from taking it all back, she nodded. "Thank you for your hospitality and . . . everything. I doubt I'll ever forget the time I visited a grand duke at his even grander estate."

Where the words would have once been a curse on her lips, tonight she said them with complete honesty and sincerity.

As she crept back to her room in the cool darkness of the corridor, she tried to remember the scent of the ocean on a calm, moonless night, but all she could smell was the crisp scent of sandalwood and the first hint of regret.

Chapter Twenty-one

"I still don't understand what all the rush is about. If you did something unseemly, by heavens you need to tell me. I won't have you besmirching my family's good name."

May stared blankly out the window, refusing to be drawn back into defending herself to her aunt. Suyin and Upton sat opposite them, both maids steadfastly maintaining their silence. They were likely wishing themselves anywhere but in this carriage. If there had been any other means by which to return, May would have gladly taken it, but unfortunately they were all stuck for the time being.

She had made the right decision, damn it, even if part of her ached with every mile closer they traveled to Bath. The carriage jolted again as they hit yet another rut on this endless ride. They were almost home, with only a quarter hour still left to go, and May was seriously contemplating walking the rest of the way.

Every half hour or so, Aunt Victoria would shake her head and fret about their abrupt departure all over again. The duke hadn't been there to send them off—something May was grateful for even while she was unaccountably hurt—so the older woman was doubly distressed about it. "What happened on your ride yesterday? That was when everything changed, I'm sure of it. Did you make an inappropriate remark to him?"

May couldn't hold her tongue any longer. Snapping her gaze to the older woman, she said, "Nothing happened! I've already told you that the duke is obviously a very busy man and there is no need to overtax his hospitality. Moreover, I'm anxious for my father's return, and though I know it shouldn't be for a week or so yet, I want to be there when he returns."

"I don't know what to think of such excuses. Particularly given the state you were in when you returned last night."

Taking a calming breath, May said, "One tends to be in a bit of a state when one falls from a horse or gets stuck in the mud. Please stop inventing nefarious deeds I may or may not have committed and just listen to what I am telling you."

Aunt Victoria narrowed her eyes. "I wonder, do you think me blind?"

May froze, her mind racing with the things her aunt might have witnessed. With the exception of last night's excursion into the duke's bedchamber, there shouldn't have been anything. Cautiously, she said, "No."

"I saw the way the two of you looked at each other. Absurd as it may seem, I began to have hope that you might somehow make a match. After all, if his father could marry that dreadful French woman, perhaps the current duke could tolerate an unconventional wife as well.

"Then, all at once, the hope is dashed and here we are, returning in an unseemly short amount of time." She pressed her lips together and shook her head. "If you can't succeed with a man who looks at you that way, you may well be hopeless after all."

May's temper flared hot, fueled by her already heightened emotions. "I'd rather be hopeless than a bitter old matron like you."

Her aunt reared back, her gloved and bejeweled hand going to her collarbone. Even the maids looked up at that before quickly diverting their gazes to their laps. Good. May really didn't wish for Suyin to suffer by association. This argument had been brewing for months, and it was solely between May and her aunt.

Finding her tongue at last, Aunt Victoria sputtered, "How *dare* you speak to me with such disrespect? You ungrateful girl. I've put my reputation on the line for you, and you have done nothing but trample it at every turn."

Frustration billowed in May's chest, making it hard to breathe. "*I* have trampled? What about your dozens of disparaging remarks toward me? Are you *trying* to destroy my confidence? Is it some sort of game to you to see how many ways you can try to cut me down?"

She had come here hurting, out of place and still mourning her mother's death, and all she had found was coldness and constraint. If it hadn't been for her friends, she would have surely gone mad.

Her aunt's affront was palpable. "This is exactly the insolence I have been 'disparaging,'" she exclaimed, lifting her chin with an angry jerk. "I have been doing everything in my power to help you fit in. I've done my best to mold you into a woman society will accept, and you have resisted my efforts at every turn."

"I'm not resisting; I'm being *me*."

"Then perhaps you need to change," her aunt retorted sharply. "I've been where you are, May. I thought everything was fun and games and that people would love me for the carefree girl that I was. Well, do you know what that earned me?"

"An earl for a husband, apparently," May said. The idea of her aunt ever having been carefree was beyond absurd.

But real pain flashed in her aunt's eyes as shook her head. "No. My naïveté led to a scandal that nearly destroyed my name. My parents sent me away for two years, and believe me, I shall never forget what that was like. Life outside of proper society can be a cruel, harsh place."

May could hardly believe what her aunt was saying, but the truth of it was written across her face. She couldn't help but be curious as to what sort of scandal her aunt had embroiled herself in, but it didn't seem prudent to ask.

Straightening her spine, Aunt Victoria seemed to recover her composure as she met May's gaze. "I was smart enough to learn my lesson. It was my impeccable manners that eventually won the earl's regard. I suggest you learn from my mistakes and change now, before you ruin yourself and your prospects."

As surprising—and enlightening—as the story was, it really had little bearing on May. Polite society was not part of her future. "I'm not going to change who I am to please people I hardly know. What is the point? Soon I'll be gone from this place, and nobody will remember anything about me."

And it couldn't be soon enough. After this week, she felt as though she was beginning to lose herself. To lose the memories of the way things were, back when Mama was well and the three of them had been so happy. She ached for the comfort of her father's arms. For the rocking of the ship and the hot winds in the tropics. She wanted those familiar and longed-for things so badly, it was all she could do not to close her eyes and cry.

"What makes you think that you are going back?"

Her gaze shot back to her aunt, ice suddenly pumping in her veins. "What do you mean?"

If she had looked victorious, or snide, or even angry, May wouldn't have been so alarmed. But Aunt Victoria merely looked matter-of-fact. She smoothed a hand over her voluminous skirts, pursing her lips as though weighing her next words. "Why do you think your father brought you to me? You cannot continue as you had without a chaperone. With your mother gone, it's time for you to find a husband and begin your own life."

May gaped at her, a thousand different thoughts buzzing in her mind, but not a single one that would come to her lips. Her gaze briefly collided with Suyin's, who looked equally as shocked. The steady pounding of the horses' steps and the creaking of the carriage as it swayed and shuddered filled the roaring silence as she tried to assimilate what her aunt was saying. "He told you that?"

She folded her hands primly in her lap. "He didn't have to. The situation spoke for itself."

But he hadn't said it. May clung to that one, clear thought like a lifeline. Drawing a deep breath in an effort to calm her pounding heart, she said, "The *situation* is that he was overwrought after my mother's death. By the time he returns, he'll have come to his senses and realized that he overreacted."

Aunt Victoria shook her head, her gray eyes sharp. "Someday, you'll realize that the world simply doesn't care what your plans are."

The carriage slowed then, and a look out the window

confirmed they were turning onto her aunt's street. *Thank God.* May started to fuss with her skirts, anxious to be ready to bolt the moment they pulled to a stop.

"Don't think this conversation is over," Aunt Victoria warned. "I am not satisfied with your lack of response over what happened with the duke."

May put a hand to her chest without conscious thought as her mind shifted to the memory of all that had happened the night before. "Then I suppose you will have to write him, because I have nothing more to say on the subject."

Not waiting a second more for a groom to come and assist them, May pushed open the door and rushed from the smothering confines of the carriage and the infuriating woman within it.

"Mei-li."

She froze, all the air whooshing from her lungs at the sound of her name in that beloved, gruff, longed-for voice. She looked up slowly, afraid she would find she had conjured it in her mind.

Before her stood the travel-weary, bearded, well-sunned image of her father, his arms as wide and welcoming as the great blue sea. All the anger, upset, and fear fell away in the blink of an eye, and before she even knew what she was about, she was running toward him like the savior he was.

Thank God Almighty, he had returned just when she needed him most.

The knock at the door of his study startled him. William glanced up from his desk only to find Vivian hovering in the doorway. The early-afternoon light flooded the room, illuminating her pale skin and wide hazel eyes. His mother's rubies sparkled against her bare throat.

"Leaving, I presume?" His voice was flat, just like the rest of his emotions.

She shrugged in that Parisian way of hers. "The carriage is packed." She paused before adding, "I noticed your guest left this morning."

"It's none of your affair." Regret was bitter on his tongue, but he refused to brood over it. May was free to make her own decisions, and if she felt the need to leave him, that was her prerogative. And what good would brooding do, anyhow? She'd be out of his life for good one way or another by the end of the month. Just as well that it was sooner rather than later. Given the knot in his chest, he had already allowed himself to become too attached to her as it was.

As for Vivian, he didn't owe her an explanation.

He leaned back in his chair, glowering at her. She had been a thorn in his side for years. It was a shame that *she* wasn't the one who was sailing away.

Sauntering toward him, she wrapped a fiery red tendril around her finger, her expression pensive. He knew it for the gesture it was: an attempt to draw attention to her most infamous feature. Where others might be shocked by such a color, she had embraced it. Used it to her advantage. "Mmm. I suppose she saw that you are not the man for her. And, I think perhaps you knew that she was all wrong for you."

This was exactly why everything had gone so wrong last night. She had interrupted with this nonsense, ruining the mood and obviously affecting May's attitude toward him. She had been understanding, but shortly after she had abruptly withdrawn from him.

"We are not having this discussion, Vivian. I suggest you don't keep your carriage waiting." He returned his attention to the ledger before him, pretending to study it just as he had been pretending to do when she arrived. His mind was a thousand miles away. No, that wasn't entirely true. His mind was forty miles away in Bath, with the woman he was doing everything in his power to forget.

Vivian tsked softly. "Poor William, always working so hard. You need to find the joie de vivre."

He glanced up in surprise. She rarely used French, at least around him. She always spoke so carefully, minimizing her accent, and she never referred to where she had come from or why she had come over. Shaking his head, he said, "You seem to have no trouble reaping the benefits of my labors for the estate."

"I'm very grateful. But I care that you are happy as well. In fact, Miss Bradford's presence made me see just how much I want to make you happy. One of these days, you really should take me up on my offers."

She definitely had his attention now. Why must she always push him? "For the love of God, when will you cease these unwanted advances? Have I not made it abundantly clear that they will *never* be welcome?"

Her fingers waved lightly through the air. "Only because you cannot see past propriety. It has always had its hooks in you. But you are duke! And I am a duchess. There is nothing to stop us from being together, if you would but see."

He shook his head, at a total loss of what to say. Had she gone completely mad? "You're speaking nonsense."

She stepped closer, her hazel eyes bright. "No! I have read about things much more scandalous. Look at the fifth Duke of Devonshire and his two wives. If he can live with two women, surely you can live with a young widow."

Revulsion tightened his gut. "My *father's* widow. That

is a tremendous difference, and if it's not illegal, it absolutely should be."

"Why? We are not related. You already are raising my children, and now we could raise them together."

It was all he could do not to physically remove her from the house, put her into the carriage, and send it away for good. "I am raising the children because of your distinct disinterest in them, not to mention your appalling behavior."

Her nostrils flared. "As though they could ever be mine. They, just like everything else, belong to the dukedom."

He blinked, taken aback by her words. "What are you talking about? They are your children! You are the one who chooses not to see them until it suits you." And he knew her pattern: She would flaunt an affair, he would go to speak with her, she would plead to see the children, then promptly ignore them as she set her sights on him. Shaking his head, he added, "As for the 'everything else,' you have your own allowance, as my father provided in his will. A generous one, at that." Much more so than she deserved.

Derision lifted her lip. "If there is one thing I learned in my life, *chéri*, it is there is no such thing as stability. We grasp for what we want and hope it will last, but there are no guarantees that it will not be taken away."

He spread his arms, at a loss. "Like what? What can be taken away?"

"Houses. Wealth. Food. Those we love. It is best not to become attached when they can so easily be taken from us."

Food? Loved ones?

In a sudden moment of clarity, understanding dawned on him. He could hardly believe it hadn't occurred to him before. She would have been a child during the French Revolution. If her family had been wealthy, there was a good chance they would have been caught in the upheaval. Had they been affected by the Reign of Terror? Was that why she'd never bonded with her children? For fear that they would be taken away?

He walked toward her, watching her carefully. "Vivian, why did you come to me that night?"

His father hadn't been gone six months, and Clarisse was barely three months old. It was the last time he had indulged in spirits. When he'd climbed the stairs to go to bed, she had materialized at his side, offering to help him. Together they had stumbled toward his room, and the next thing he knew she was kissing him.

In his drunken state, he was slow to react, slow to realize what was even happening. He had pushed her away, but not before he'd been branded with the taste of her. After that moment, he'd vowed never to allow himself to be so vulnerable again. He craved control much more than he did liquor.

He clenched his jaw against the familiar anger about that night. Perhaps there was more to her motives than he ever considered.

"As the new duke, you could be generous to me, or you could take everything. You never liked me, not from the first moment. I saw an opportunity to show you how much I have to offer, so I took it."

And when he'd rebuffed her, that was when she'd stopped seeing the children. Not that she hadn't always been aloof, but it was still a noticeable change.

He shook his head, compassion crowding out the anger. It was an emotion he would have never expected to have toward her. "Vivian, you are the widow of a duke. There is no more secure position than that."

"For now, perhaps. But only until you marry and have your own children. If you are with me, however, then Julian will be your heir, and then all things will be as they should."

A duke for a son would feel a lot more secure than a hostile son-in-law. He blew out a breath, bowing his head for a moment. He'd never seen the desperation before, not like this. He'd seen the manipulation, the posturing, the things she'd done for his attention, but never the fear behind any of it.

Raising his head, he looked her in the eye. "All of this has to stop. I will never, ever be with you that way, no matter what."

He straightened and clasped his hands behind his back. Despite the way he had always strived to live, things were not always black and white. If nothing else, this week with May had taught him that. With the power he held, he also had a duty to be merciful, when warranted.

Coming to a decision, he said, "But what I will do is buy you a house, in your own name, anywhere you want. You don't have to live there—you can simply know that it is yours. I will also transfer five thousand pounds into an account in your name only. This is in addition to your yearly allowance. No one can touch that money except for you, just as no one can ever take the house from you."

Her eyes went wider and wider as he spoke, until she was more or less gaping at him, her hazel eyes bright with cautious hope. "You would do that for me?"

He gave a brusque nod. "As for Clarisse and Julian, they are children of a duke, and will be raised accordingly, per my father's wishes. But you are their mother, and if you wish to live here in order to oversee their upbringing, that is your right.

"My only stipulation is that your chambers must be either on the nursery level, or in the east wing, and that you may not step foot in the west wing. Not ever. Is that understood?" He never wanted to hear her footsteps outside his door again.

She nodded, though he could see she still felt unsure. It would likely be some time before she could feel safe enough to open up to the children, and it was possible she might never do so. But regardless, he had done everything in his power to make things right.

For Vivian, at least.

With May gone, nothing at all felt right for him. Perhaps he should have done more to let her know that he wanted her here. The kisses they'd shared had spoken volumes, but he should have *said* more. Would it have mattered? Probably not. But if he had put forth the effort, at least he would not be left with the doubts he had now.

Chapter Twenty-two

It had been so long since May had been with her father and now that he was here she couldn't bring herself to leave his side. He felt like a real, solid connection to all she wanted and needed in life. To normalcy. He had brought the smell of the sea with him, its salty freshness clinging to him like an aura.

Settled beside her on the prim little sofa centered in the drawing room, he chuckled and patted her hand. "The stars aligned for us today, Mei-li-girl. I wasn't here but five minutes, long enough to know that the pair of you were gone. That barnacle-bottomed butler of yours, Torie, didn't seem too keen to tell me where you'd gone."

May bit her lip against a bubble of laughter. Hargrove often defaulted to silence. She didn't dislike the man, as he had certainly turned a blind eye to her early-morning escapes, she was sure, but they had never quite become friendly, as she had with many of the maids on staff.

Aunt Victoria was not nearly as amused. "It's easy enough to see where your daughter came by her manners. I'll thank you to have more respect when referring to my servants."

She'd already exchanged her traveling bonnet for her

lace mobcap and was sitting across from them in the uncomfortable-looking high-backed chair that she preferred.

Papa's pale blue eyes sparkled with mischief. "Yes, of course. I'm certain he is a perfectly superior butler, given his ability to look down his whiffer at a man. A very important part of the job, I understand."

May grinned. It was so nice to let go of all the confused emotions of the day and bask in the joy of his return. She leaned forward, eager to speak of things outside of this house. Outside of this *country*. "How was the voyage? What news have you?"

His expression softened, revealing the white lines creasing his weathered skin at the corners of his eyes. "The good Lord was smiling down on us this time. Excellent weather, minus a good squall or two, with winds at our sails like the hand of God."

Aunt Victoria set down her tea and stood. "I'm glad for your calm journey, Michael, but I'm quite exhausted from ours. I'll leave you to talk, and will see you both at dinner."

Papa stood while she made her way to the door. When she was gone, he turned and extended a hand. "Come, daughter. I cannot abide being inside on such a fine day. Let us take a walk."

She readily agreed. No one else seemed to understand her preference for the outdoors. Out of nowhere she thought of the duke, of how, in the beginning, he had tried to force her back inside, back down the straight and narrow. But then there was the time they had shared at the folly, and later on horseback. Alone out in nature, just the two of them. She clenched her jaw and shoved the thought from her mind, determined not to ruin this special time. She didn't want to linger on her decisions yesterday, not when her father was here at last.

As they headed for the park, they chatted about various things, enjoying each other's company. He shared details of the voyage and stories of some of the sailors that might or might not be true. Her father always could spin a good tale.

She told him of the festival, and of her new friends. He laughed at her story of how the trio met, and nodded his approval for how she had handled the meddling clerk, Mr. Green. Looking back now, with the security of knowing her time here would soon be over, she smiled with an unexpected hint of nostalgia.

It had somehow shaped up to be a very special summer, and she surely would never forget it.

"And what of any young men?" Papa's question was spoken mildly, but she could easily detect his sudden interest. She knew him better than almost anyone in the world, after all.

She decided to be deliberately obtuse, since this was the very last subject she wished to discuss. "There were young men aplenty at the festival. Sophie married an earl just a few weeks ago, and Charity is betrothed to a former army officer."

He sent her a chiding look. "You know well what I mean. Though I am happy for your friends, it is not their romances that interest me."

Curse it all, but she could feel a blush heating her face. All the chaotic emotions from the past week seemed to surge forth, and she ruthlessly tried to tamp them back down. It was ridiculous that she should be so preoccupied with a man who shouldn't even matter. Papa was here now, and soon this time—and the duke himself—would all just be a memory. "Nothing worth speaking of for me, Papa. What would be the point?"

Cocking his head in question, he said, "Why, to marry and have children, of course. Isn't that always the point of finding love?"

She very nearly choked. *Love?* She knew attraction, desire, and perhaps even lust, but she definitely did not know love. She tried not to think of the way her heart had soared when William's lips had touched hers, or the riot of butterflies in her stomach when he'd pressed her against the wall.

Drawing a fortifying breath, she said, "I can assure you, there is no one in this country I love." She spoke vehemently, as though that could make it true. No, it *was* true. She was obviously just oversensitive, given the freshness of the separation. "And when I say what would be the point, it's because I won't be here for long. Why begin to court a man when there will soon be oceans between us?"

The moment she looked back to her father, her heart sank. Something was wrong. All of the spark had fled his normally jovial eyes, and his mouth tugged down in a frown that disappeared into his pepper-and-salt beard. Outside of when her mother had died, it was the most ill at ease she had ever seen him.

The dread that had assailed her at her aunt's pronouncement in the carriage roared back with a vengeance. "Papa," she said, desperate to make her case before he could say what she knew was coming. "This is not the place for me. I'll suffocate if I have to stay here much longer. I want to go home. I *need* to go home."

"Mei-li—"

"Please," she said, interrupting him. She could already hear the inevitableness of his voice. "I know you are afraid that I'll contract some dreadful tropical disease like Mama, but there's risk no matter where you live. It may be influenza instead of ague, but the risk is still there. We can't live our lives in fear."

"Daughter," he said, more firmly this time. Damn it all, she knew what came after a tone like that. Disappointment. Heartbreak. Despair, even. All the things she had already had too much of this year. "We all have to face change in our lives at some point. I know you may be scared, but I thought long and hard before bringing you here. This is where you have the best chance for a good future."

She shook her head, over and over. The green leaves and grass and bushes seemed to close in around them, miring them in the moment as effectively as tar. "No, I can't stay here. Everything I know, everything I love, is half a world away from here."

It felt like a punishment for ever thinking she might be falling for an Englishman. That because she had dared to imagine it, the rest had been snatched from her hands in the blink of an eye.

Papa was silent for a few moments. He glanced toward the River Avon, though she doubted he really saw it, then drew in a long breath and turned to face her fully. "You don't understand," he said, his voice gruff. He stroked a hand over his beard, a mindless gesture he always did when he was troubled. "I wasn't just talking about you. I've sailed my last voyage, daughter. I can't take you back because I'm not going back."

She gaped at him, utterly aghast. "You *quit*?" How could he do such a thing without discussing it? They were a unit. First the three of them, and now just the two of them.

He gave a rusty chuckle, but no humor reached his

light eyes. "There's saltwater in my veins, Mei-li-girl. I'd planned to sail until I dropped dead at the helm, as old and crusty as ancient shoe leather. But the world is changing, and unfortunately I've gotten caught in the transition."

The world is changing. She clenched her jaw. Wasn't that what Radcliffe had said when he'd taken her to the mill? Shaking her head, she said, "But I don't understand. You work for the Company. They *own* the textile trade."

"Not anymore," he said with a shake of his head. "Parliament stripped the Company of its exclusive trading rights to all but China a few years ago, and that change is catching up to us now. The private free traders have been building momentum, and with new mills popping up in England, there are many who are anxious to do business with them."

May stood there, reeling, barely able to process the change to everything she knew. To everything she expected in her life. To everything she *wanted.*

Her father put his arm to her shoulder, the tired lines of his face reflecting deep sadness. She wasn't the only one in anguish. He too had just suffered a great loss, and her heart broke all over again for him.

"I'm sorry, May. I've put some inquiries in, but I'm a rusty old sea dog by now. Not likely to be many new opportunities out there for me."

Nodding, she turned and hugged him, grasping him tight as she fought to hold her composure. No matter how much she wished to the contrary, things would never again be the same.

There would be no going home for either of them.

"Are you leaving us, too?"

William started at the sound of his sister's tiny voice.

He turned from the window to find her standing several feet inside his study, hugging her favorite little doll to her chest.

"What are you doing down here? Where's Julian?" He'd been completely lost in his own thoughts, staring out at the path that led to the lake. Letting the curtain drop, he came around the desk to pick her up.

"He's playing with his toy soldiers," she said, clearly unenthused about the boy's choice of toys. "So I came downstairs to see the pinofort and your door was open. You look like you want to go away."

"Pianoforte," he corrected as he sat on the sofa and set her on the cushions beside him. "And you know better than to sneak away. To answer your question, no, I am not going away."

She looked up at him, her eyes wide and guileless. "Mama left, but she said she would be back soon. Mei-li left, too, but she said she wouldn't see me again because she's sailing far away. She gave me this," she said, pointing to the ivory comb in her hair that was shaped like an elephant. There was a tiny scrap of purple ribbon tied around its neck.

William sat back, his heart squeezing at the thought of May doing such a thing. He hadn't even realized she had told them good-bye, but in hindsight, he probably should have known. She might never follow the rules, but the kindness in her heart was unmistakable. Forcing a smile to his lips, he said, "She did? That was very nice of her."

Clarisse nodded in enthusiastic agreement. "Yes, I know. I told her thank you. She said it is very special, because it's good luck."

"Well, I suppose that makes you a lucky girl."

Her grin was huge. "I hope so. She gave Julian a compsess, but I don't know how to use it."

He raised his eyebrows, not sure about that one. "A compass?"

More nods. "She said it is so he won't get lost when he becomes a sailor."

These were not small gifts. They were thoughtful and of true value, and unbearably kind gestures to two lonely children that she would never see again.

A lump formed in his throat, just thinking of how much life she had brought to this place during her short visit. Had he ever laughed so much? Been more frustrated, or passionate, or exasperated? His title and his home hadn't impressed her, yet he felt as though she saw the true him. And she had certainly seen the goodness in his siblings. Somewhere along the way, she had truly earned his respect.

Not that she was without flaws. She had huge ones, glaring in their intensity. But then again, no matter what he tried to show the world, he did too. He was nothing if not imperfect, in fact.

Take, for example, the fact that he hadn't gone to see her off. Instead, he had brooded in his study like some sort of tragic literary figure. She hadn't deserved that. More to the point, there was not closure to their unconventional relationship. He hadn't wished her well, seen her smile, told her all the things he'd been too proud to say. *Don't go. Stay with me.*

"What did she give you?"

He blinked, looking back to his sister in question. "I beg your pardon?"

"What did she give you when she told you good-bye?"

Oh, the innocence of a child. He smoothed Clarisse's hair from her forehead and smiled. "Can you believe that I forgot to tell Miss Bradford good-bye?"

She tilted her head to the side and scrunched her nose. "Why did you do that? You always tell us good-bye when you leave."

"I know. Maybe I will send her a letter before she sails away." But even as he said it, the thought of putting to paper all the things he wanted to say seemed impossible. "Or perhaps I can go to Bath and tell her good-bye in person." The words were out before the idea was even fully formed, but he grasped it like a lifeline. The thought of having one more chance to see her made his heart slam against his ribs.

"You should do that. And then you can give her another hug for me." Her grin was wide and toothy.

He'd like nothing more, but that would be up to her. Nodding gravely to his sister, he said, "I shall pass along your sentiment. Anything else?" His mind was already racing ahead to how soon he could be there, and what he would say when he saw her. Of all the things he *should* have said before.

Clarisse bit her lip, then looked down at the doll clutched in her arms. Picking it up, she kissed it on its head and handed it to William. "Give her Dolly, too. She might get scared on the ship, and since I have her good luck elemphant, she can have this."

William carefully accepted the gift, giving her a sideways look. "Are you certain? I know she is your favorite."

"Mei-li is my favorite, too. Maybe if you ask her real nice to come back, she will."

His chest ached at the thought of bringing her back here. "Miss Bradford wants to go home, and we have to respect that." He'd tell her good-bye properly, but he wouldn't stand in the way of what she wanted.

"It never hurts to ask. That's what Julian always says."

He nodded. "We'll see. Now let's go find him so I can

tell him good-bye." As William clasped his sister's small hand and headed up to the nursery, her words rolled over in his mind again and again. *It never hurts to ask.* What would May say if he actually asked? What if she had a reason not to sail away? She had told him once that home was where the heart resides. What if he could show her that her heart was right here in England? It was a very, very long shot, but with the hope tugging at his heart that he could somehow change her mind, he knew he couldn't go on without at least trying.

An unfamiliar rush of nerves made his pulse pound at the idea. There might well be a lot more riding on this trip than he originally thought.

"You shouldn't have come so quickly." May tried to sound stern, but she knew she was completely unsuccessful.

Sophie rolled her eyes with the dramatics of an opera singer. "Of course I should have. What good is having friends if one can't drop everything and run to help them in their time of need? Just think how boring our lives would be otherwise."

May gave her friend a grateful smile. "Well, preferably one isn't on one's honeymoon when the call for help comes. I wish you would have waited a bit before rushing down here." She plopped down on the chaise longue, batting at an innocent lemon tree branch. "God knows I'm not going anywhere."

The look of sympathy from Sophie was as welcome as it was helpless. "I'm so, so sorry about this. I know how much you wanted to go home, and I know how little consolation it is for me to say so, but my heart still breaks for you. Of course, I'm selfishly glad that you will be close enough to see on a regular basis, but I think it may be too soon to point that out."

May gave a watery laugh. "It is. Quite. If I weren't so happy you were here, I would be tempted to kick you out for having said so."

"I was banking on that," she said with a wink. "As for the honeymoon, I plan for this entire year to be our extended honeymoon, so I can spare a few days. On second thought, perhaps I shall make it a lifetime honeymoon. I daresay Evan won't mind."

Cutting a wry smile toward her, May said, "That sounded shockingly close to a corrupting remark. I'd like to think I had a small part in adding a bit of scandal to your repertoire."

The day was exceptionally fine, which only seemed to mock her. A few nice days here and there would not make her feel any differently about this place.

Sophie chuckled, settling back on her own chair. "I'd say you are plenty responsible for any scandalous thing I may do or say. You gave me bravery. You were the one who made me think I was good enough to try for what I wanted, and I'm married to the man I love because of it. I owe you everything, and I will be here for you for whatever you may need."

May reach out and clasped Sophie's hand. "You and Charity are the best things that have happened to me in years. No matter what, I'm not sorry for coming here. Your friendships were worth it."

She was more grateful than ever for it now. She was adrift, and Sophie's presence was the only real thing that felt like an anchor. If Charity wasn't all the way back in Durham, May knew that she would be here for her as well. It was comforting, despite the hollowness that had opened up inside her ever since her father's reluctant announcement.

Blinking a bit of mistiness from her dark gaze, Sophie

sent her a huge grin. "Well, we'll figure out something to make things better." She sat up suddenly, her eyes going wide as she leaned forward. "The duke! Whatever happened with Radcliffe? That sounds like the perfect distraction from this mess."

May groaned, rubbing her hands over her eyes. "*Please* can we not talk about him now."

Even in the midst of all this upheaval, she couldn't quite stop thinking about him. She was so conflicted in her feelings. There could never, ever be anything between them. That much she knew without a shred of doubt. It had been a delicious distraction, a bit of fun that had made the end of her time here bearable. If she had known she would be stuck here for the rest of her life, she never would have indulged.

The truth was, as much as she found herself thinking of him, he still stood as the symbol of why she could never have the future she wanted. His mill may have only a small impact in the scheme of things, but it represented the changes that had led to her father's lost position, and to May's lost dreams.

And there she went, running in circles with it all over again. She was driving herself mad. The only thing she knew for sure was that, all other things aside, she bloody well *missed* him, and that was not all right with her.

Based on Sophie's suddenly keen expression, May had only served to pique her interest. "Right. Absolutely." She paused for perhaps a quarter of a second. "Except, what better way to get your mind off your father's dreadful news? Which probably would have been easier to do if I had not just brought it up again—sorry—but that's why telling me about the duke is a good idea."

Sometimes Sophie's logic could make a person dizzy.

May gave a great, long sigh and cut flat eyes over to her friend. "To answer the questions I know are coming: Yes, we clashed again, yes, we ended up kissing, no, nothing else happened. We learned in short order that we are simply not compatible, so my aunt and I came home."

Sophie deserved better answers than that, but May simply did not have it in her just then. Her heart was too raw.

"Goodness," Sophie said, obviously surprised by the new information. She opened her mouth as though to ask more, closed it, then gave a decisive nod. "All right, I promise not to push."

"Thank you."

"Even though I am ravenously curious what happened with the kiss."

"Thank you again."

May was quiet for a moment, staring up at the brilliant blue sky, but thinking only of that kiss by the stream. It had been her favorite. The one where he had finally given himself to her. Though the one in the room, where he had pressed so wonderfully against her, was a close second. Swallowing, she looked over at Sophie. "And it was kiss*es*."

Sophie nodded, her eyes wide but her mouth studiously shut. Knowing Sophie, that was quite a feat.

"But it wasn't what you think," May added, the words coming forth despite her resolve not to linger on the topic. "It was a flirtation, that is all. It was a little distraction while I bided time until I would leave this place."

"I see." More silence. Sophie must have been dying, saying so little.

"Good. Just so you know there was never any intent for something different on either of our parts. We are as incompatible as ice and hot coals."

"Mmhmm," Sophie murmured, nodding. "Kind of like Charity and Cadgwith?"

"Yes! I mean no," she said quickly, realizing that was not the best example, given Charity's betrothal to Lord Cadgwith. "We have no common ground. More important, we have no *desire* for common ground, which makes all the difference."

"But," Sophie said, drawing the word out as she reached forward for May's hands, "that was before either one of you knew you would be staying here. Things might look differently through that lens."

Despair washed through her all over again. She didn't want to look at the world through that lens. That lens was nothing but bitterness and disappointment at the knowledge that she would never find her way back to where she longed to be. Regardless, that lens couldn't change how incompatible they were. The exceedingly proper, tremendously wealthy, paragon-of-English-patriotism duke, and an outspoken, rule-breaking, travel-loving daughter of a sea captain would never mix.

Behind them, a throat cleared conspicuously. They turned to see Hargrove navigating the flagstone pathway. "Pardon me, Miss Bradford, but Lady Stanwix requests your presence in the drawing room. The Duke of Radcliffe has come to call."

Chapter Twenty-three

The announcement shouldn't have affected her quite so profoundly as it did. May's hand flew to her chest as the world seemed to momentarily blur around her. *Radcliffe?* What the devil was he doing here?

She knew Hargrove was waiting for her acknowledgment, but for the life of her, she couldn't seem to utter a sound. Sophie smiled and said, "Thank you, Hargrove. She'll be there in a trice."

The man dipped his head and turned sharply on his heel, heading back toward the house. May turned to Sophie when she felt she could speak with some amount of normalcy. "Thank you. I don't know what came over me."

"Shock, from the look of it, which may or may not have something to do with those kisses you spoke of. Clearly *they* were not incompatible," she said, offering an encouraging smile. "Now, do you wish for me to stay or go?"

May came to her feet, rubbing her suddenly cold hands together. There was absolutely no reason the duke should have come for her, but whatever he had to say, she wanted the strength of her friend by her side. "Stay. Please."

Sophie nodded, and the two of them made their way back toward the house. When they reached the drawing room, May paused, drawing a fortifying breath. Inevitably the question of when she was to leave would come up, and she absolutely dreaded admitting she was here for the foreseeable future. Would he regret allowing the liberties they had shared? Pretend sadness? Care at all?

Nodding to Sophie, she smoothed her skirts and headed inside. Her gaze found his at once, stealing the breath she had just taken. He sat perched on one of her aunt's ridiculously uncomfortable chairs, obviously ill at ease. The moment she entered the room, he rose to his feet and offered a short bow. "Miss Bradford, Lady Evansleigh, how good to see you again."

His hair was neatly in place, his charcoal jacket crisp and cravat neatly tied. He looked every inch the duke, including the look of determination in his dark golden gaze. He was clearly on a mission, which made her that much more uncertain. She straightened her spine, determined that he would not know how much seeing him again affected her.

"And you, Duke," Sophie said, a bright smile in place. She glanced to May and widened her eyes when May didn't speak right away.

Swallowing, she dipped her head. "Your Grace." Turning to her aunt, she said, "Where is Papa?" There was no telling how her father would react to the duke, especially after their talk of romance yesterday. The last thing she wanted was Papa getting his hopes up that she had found a suitor after all.

Aunt Victoria folded her hands neatly in her lap. "Your father is out walking." She flattened her lips in disapproval. "Again."

The duke glanced toward May before turning his attention to Aunt Victoria. "And a fine day for it. Perhaps I could interest the ladies in one as well?"

May pursed her lips, weighing her options. If they wanted to talk privately, a walk would be their best chance. But right then, she was decidedly unenthusiastic about finding herself alone with him. Already she could feel the damnable attraction between them, inexorably pulling her toward him. It only would serve to make things that much harder when he left.

Sophie glanced toward May, then turned back to the duke. "I think a walk sounds lovely. May?"

"I'm not opposed," she finally said.

"Excellent," he responded, his eyes surprisingly warm. He navigated his way through her aunt's overstuffed room to where they stood near the door. "Then it is settled. I think a promenade to the river would be just the thing."

Whatever had brought him here, it couldn't have been anything bad. His eyes held soft welcome, as though he were thinking of the times they had fit together so well.

May swallowed, trying to recall all the reasons he shouldn't be here. "Very well. Aunt, I'm certain we shall be back shortly."

As she led the way outside, she could feel his eyes on her back as they walked. She barely managed to repress a shiver, but gooseflesh still peppered her arm.

They stepped out onto the pavement and turned toward the park. Before they had walked five steps, he cleared his throat. "Lady Evansleigh, I wonder if you might be willing to allow Miss Bradford and me a bit of privacy."

Butterflies set flight in her stomach at the thought of being alone with him. She exchanged glances with Sophie, not even sure what she wanted. Her friend, however, had no hesitations.

"Actually," she said, her smile broad and knowing, "I'm certain my husband will be wondering what became of me. It was lovely to see you again. May, do send me a note later, if you please." She leaned forward and gave May a quick hug. "Be nice," she whispered, then hastily made her escape.

Drawing a fortifying breath, May turned to face the man she had thought she would never see again.

She was so, so lovely. Facing her again, alone at last, felt so completely right. William smiled, immensely glad he had come, and held out his elbow. "Perhaps we can take that walk to the park? I'd prefer not to talk in front of your neighbor's windows."

She looked down at his arm as though unsure of whether she wished to touch him, then blew out a quiet breath and settled her fingers oh-so lightly along his sleeve. After all they had shared, he was hard-pressed not to set his hand over hers. It was oddly foreign, being so polite with her. She was the one person with whom he never seemed to play by the rules.

As they walked along the pavement toward the park, his mind raced with what he would say to her. *I can't stop thinking of you. Come back to me. Let me show you what you could have here.* None of those sounded right. Yes, he wanted her to know that he wanted her here, but what did he have to offer her that might entice her to stay?

As they turned down the dirt path into the park, he stole a glance at her. She looked tense, worried even. What was it that she thought he was here to say? He slowed to a stop, and she looked up to him in question. "Is something the matter?"

Her sapphire eyes held a wealth of emotions as she gave an ambiguous shrug. "There is much on my mind since my father's return."

"Your aunt told me he had come back. You must be delighted to see him again." His words felt stilted, as though he were talking to a stranger. He had so much he wanted to say, and he had no idea where to start.

"Yes. Very." She gave him an unconvincing smile.

Could this odd reluctance mean that perhaps she wasn't as determined to leave as she once might have been? Hope flared to life, a small flicker that maybe, just possibly, she might want to be with him as well. As neutrally as he could manage, he said, "Do you know yet when you are to return?"

The dismay that knitted her brow and pinched her mouth took him by surprise. "No."

That was it. No elaboration, no explanation, just a very emphatic and displeased *no*. There was something wrong, he was sure of it. The change in her mood and even her posture was tangible. "May, what's the matter?"

For a moment, he thought she might not answer, but then she looked up at him, her eyes dull despite the bright sunlight. "I'm not going back."

Not going back? As much as a part of him wanted to rejoice, the larger part of him knew that this wasn't what she wanted. There was no way she would make such a choice of her own volition, particularly given the despair he glimpsed within her. He set his hand over her fingers, pressing them against his arm. "What happened?"

She shook her head, glancing down to the ground before meeting his gaze again. "I didn't realize at the time just how personal the discussion at the mill was. The Company has parted ways with my father in response to the decreased textile trade. He's not going back, and therefore neither am I."

The pronouncement was like a punch to his gut, stealing the breath from his lungs. All his work, all his effort toward breaking the Company's monopoly ... He'd never imagined it would ever hurt someone he cared for. He hated seeing the pain on her face, hearing it in her voice, knowing that he, in essence, was the cause of it. He squeezed her fingers in earnest. "May, I'm ... so very sorry." He didn't know what else to tell her.

What could he say? Everything she wanted had just turned to dust right before her eyes and there was absolutely nothing to be done for it.

She stepped back, pulling her hand from his. "Are you?" The words weren't angry, but the sadness in them was a thousand times worse. "For all your talk of progress and the Company, are you truly sorry for me?"

"Yes," he said honestly, forcefully. His chest ached, a dull, insistent pain that originated directly over his heart. He wanted her to stay in England, but not like this. Not because she was forced, especially when the fault could be laid squarely at his feet. He couldn't be sorry for all the work he had done in order to improve trade for England, but he hated that she had been caught in the middle.

"Yes," he said again, softer this time. Stepping forward, he reached out and grasped both her hands. She didn't pull away as he half expected she would. Squeezing gently, he met her gaze directly. "I care for you. Greatly. It's why I came here today. I had to tell you good-bye properly. More to the point, I had to tell you that I didn't want you to go."

She peered back at him, her eyes wide yet cautious. "Why are you saying this? Is it because you feel pity—"

"No," he said, not even letting her finish the sentence. "I'm saying it because it's true. The time we spent together was unlike anything I have ever experienced. You bring out a different side of me, a side that I wish to see more of."

He tilted his head, offering a small, honest smile. "I know this feels like the worst possible fate, and I'm not discounting your suffering. But perhaps there can be a silver lining."

Moisture gathered in her eyes, but she quickly blinked it away. "How could there possibly be a silver lining in being stuck in this country for the foreseeable future?"

He lifted his shoulders. "Because I'm here," he said simply. *And I want you here, as well.*

She shook her head, her eyebrows drawn together in a little v. "It's not that easy. You are a duke with a thousand duties and I am a woman who will never fit in, and who will always be pining for something she can't have."

The look on her face was like a knife to his heart. He hated that she couldn't have what she so clearly wanted, but at the same time, he wished she could see that this could be an opportunity. That maybe now, without the possibility of her going away, they could explore what was between them. There could be something so much better than the life she had once known, if only she would consider it.

He lifted her hands and kissed each one in turn, bringing her that much closer to him. "I am a duke who is just a man, and you are the woman who saw that all along. A woman who intrigues him. *Ignites* him. A woman who is more than just the place she lives."

Marriage.

The word came to him in a flash. It was insanity—could she be any more unsuited to the role of duchess?

Perhaps not . . . But in that moment he saw with perfect clarity that what she was suited to was the role of his wife. He, William, not the title he held. For perhaps the first time in his life, he could separate the two in his mind and see that he had needs and desires that were separate from the dukedom. He possessed the title, not the other way around.

And May possessed his heart.

She challenged him in a way he never thought he wanted. She was strong, and opinionated, and refused to bow to the dictates of others, and God help him but he *loved* it. She brought out a passion in him he never knew he could possess.

Her lips softened as her brow smoothed. She wet her lips and looked up at him, indecision showing in her eyes. "William—"

But before she could say more, a man approached, his footsteps startling them both. May's eyes went huge as she tugged away from William. "Papa!"

Dread surged through him as he turned to face the older man, whose peppered gray brows were raised halfway up his weathered forehead. Incredibly, he didn't look angry, but more stunned and curious.

"Well, daughter, what have we here? I was under the impression there was no young man who had captured your interest."

William straightened, offering the man his full respect. "My most abject apologies, Captain Bradford." This was what happened when he ignored his own rules. He could only imagine what the man was thinking.

The captain sent him an assessing look, taking in his clothes and manner. "I'm afraid you have me at a disadvantage, sir." To William's surprise, he actually looked pleased. His pale eyes glinted as he crossed his arms across his chest. The fact that he wasn't furious made it clear he was every bit as unconventional as May.

May stepped forward, her cheeks showing a hint of a blush. "My apologies, Papa. I was just explaining our circumstances and he was merely comforting me."

His eyes crinkled with a hint of an indulgent grin as he said, "Pray, introduce us, Mei-li."

Blowing out a long-suffering sigh, she gestured toward her father. "Captain Michael Bradford, this is my friend, William Spencer. Otherwise known as the Duke of Radcliffe." It was the least correct, most irreverent introduction William had ever had, but it served to relieve some of the tension from his shoulders.

Across from him, the moment seemed to have the exact opposite effect on her father. All the amusement drained from the older man's face as he took a step back and scowled. "The Duke of *Radcliffe*?"

There was such disgust in his voice, such vehemence, that William knew at once that May's father recognized his name. More important, he obviously knew the role William had played in the East India Company legislation.

A boulder settled low in his gut as he realized what was about to happen. Even as he turned to May, he knew there was nothing he could do to stop it. He should have said something sooner. He should have explained his role. It was too late now, and damn it all, he was going to lose her before he ever even had a chance to pursue her.

Chapter Twenty-four

May's brows rose in surprise. What the devil was going on? She had seen the delight in her father's eyes when he'd approached them. She'd heard the amusement in his voice as he had addressed the duke. He'd been pleased to find her showing interest in a man. But all of that was gone in a flash, replaced by a stony fury so unfamiliar to her, she took an unconscious step back. "You ... know him, Papa?"

How could that be? Her father was as far removed from English society as she was.

Or she had thought. Given the way he glowered at the duke, with his lip curled in disgust and his chin pushed forward, it was obvious he not only knew of him, but he held a very poor opinion of him. "Aye, I know him. A man should always know his enemy."

Enemy? Her fingers went cold as she gaped at him. "What on earth are you talking about?"

"Why don't you ask him? I imagine he knows exactly what I'm referring to if he was so kindly comforting you about your 'circumstances.' "

Alarm raced through her as she turned to face the man who had moments before been tempting her to believe there might be something here in this country for her after all. That perhaps there could be something more between them. Where once her heart had pounded with the possibility, now it thundered with the dread of what he would say. "What does he mean?"

William didn't flinch. He didn't look away or even avoid her gaze. But there was regret in his eyes. "Your father is referring to my role in spearheading the legislation to break the East India Company's exclusive trade rights. It was originally my father's project, and I picked up the reins after his death."

The words were like daggers, flaying her where she stood. How could he have not told her? The bitter taste of betrayal lay heavy on her tongue. She thought of their discussions, of all the times he could have said something. Of just minutes earlier, when he had pretended to sympathize with her over her devastation. God, but she had believed him. Believed that she mattered to him, and that they could somehow find enough common ground to stand on.

She shook her head, over and over, staring at him in disbelief. "Why didn't you tell me?" It was the question that reverberated within her, increasingly crowding out all other thought. How could he have let such an important detail go unsaid? He was actively going about dismantling her life, and never saw fit to let her know.

His eyes were shuttered, opaque to whatever he was feeling or thinking. It made her even angrier, after feeling that she had begun to really know him. *Love him.* She pushed away the thought almost as soon as it surfaced. Obviously she knew nothing of such a foolish notion if she could have thought to possess it for him, the treacherous bastard.

When he spoke, it was with careful control. "You were

leaving soon. It didn't seem relevant. You already knew of my position on the Company, and on trade in general."

Anger simmered hotly just below her skin, and she wished her father wasn't here so she could say all the things she wanted to. "Knowing your position and knowing you actively worked to bring my family to this point are two very, very different things. I believe you had to have known that. You owed it to me to be honest with me." That he would kiss her, knowing that it was under false pretenses, felt like a violation.

Some of his control slipped as he put his hand to his chest. "I was never dishonest with you."

She crossed her arms tightly over her stomach. "If that's what you think, then you know nothing of honesty. Or honor, for that matter." She said the words to hurt him, just as she was hurting. All this time he had pretended to hold the moral high ground, and in truth he hadn't a leg to stand on. Lying by omission was just as egregious as telling a falsehood.

His jaw worked as he met her gaze. "I regret that I wasn't more forthcoming. I cannot and will not apologize for my parliamentary actions, for I believe they resulted in fairness in trade and more opportunities in the industry at large. That being said, the collateral damage to your family is terrible, and for that I am truly and deeply sorry."

Collateral damage? Is that what one calls the destruction of one's whole life? She drew herself up, regarding him with her chin lifted and her spine rigidly straight. "You'll forgive me if I am unmoved by your sentiment."

He stepped closer, the first bit of real emotion flickering in his amber eyes. "I never intended to deceive you. I know this is all rather shocking and surely painful for you, and I wish that I could undo that. But please know that my feelings toward you remain unchanged. Whatever differences we may have, I care deeply for you and wish for you to be happy."

As if she could believe a word he said now. Her heart constricted, aching with a fierceness that she knew couldn't be assuaged. With hollowness swallowing her from the inside out, she turned to her father. "Take me home, please."

Home. As though there was such a thing. Thanks to the duke, she was little more than a rudderless ship, adrift in an unknown sea. Whatever brief hope she had had that her future might be salvageable dissolved into nothingness.

Her heart and her life would never be the same again.

Dering took one look at William and went straight to the liquor bottles lining his sideboard. He selected a bottle, poured generous portions of the clear liquid into two tumblers, and came to join William by the fireplace.

Handing over a cup, he said, "Pretend it's water and drink up."

William accepted the drink and sank into the nearest chair, not giving a damn about his posture. Or his brooding silence. Or the fact that he wanted to shout and curse at the top of his lungs. Nothing had ever gone so terribly wrong in his entire life. He could still see the look of betrayal on May's lovely face, hear the aching hurt in her voice.

Dering tapped his fingers on his own glass, watching him pensively. "Perhaps this will be easier if I tell you that I heard Captain Bradford is back in town. I also heard that it is unlikely Captain Bradford—or his daughter—will be leaving town."

Rolling his tongue over his teeth, William regarded his friend with a shake of his head. "I swear you have spies in every household in England."

Dering chuckled, though the humor didn't quite reach his eyes. It was clear he was concerned for William. "Only the ones that matter. Now, are you here to talk to me about something, or shall we sit here and hold our drinks pensively."

"I may have ruined everything."

Dering's mild expression never changed. "Can you be more specific?"

Swirling the drink around in the glass, William said, "What do you know about why her father isn't returning to the sea?"

Dering shrugged. "That I don't know for sure. Could be retirement, given his age. Could be unrest in the textile market. I hear tell the Company is cutting back their routes to all but China, which is apparently the only country for which they still hold exclusive rights."

William pointed a finger directly at him. "Bull's-eye. Care to put the pieces together, or do I have to spell it out?" All the pride he had once felt at that accomplishment tasted like ash in his mouth.

Leaning back in his oversize leather chair, Dering pursed his lips a moment. Realization quickly dawned. "Ah, I see. No good deed for the country goes unpunished, no?"

"Precisely." William clenched his teeth against the frustration and gnawing sense of wrongdoing. He had meant it when he told May he hadn't intended to deceive her, but that didn't change the end result. "It shouldn't have mattered. Nothing was supposed to become of my time with her. It was intended to be an enjoyable diversion for us both."

Dering took a long drink, then settled his dark gaze back on William. "So what happened?"

Wasn't that just the question? "I fell in love."

Dering's mouth literally dropped open. It was the first time in William's life that he'd ever successfully shocked the man. He wasn't surprised by his friend's reaction—William could hardly believe the words had left his own mouth. But they had, and more to the point, they were true.

God help him.

He dragged a hand through his hair, completely at a loss of what to do about it. When Dering finally picked his jaw up from the floor, he shook his head slowly and said, "Holy hell, my friend."

William raised his glass. "Cheers to that."

"So what now? I imagine she is aware of your role and more likely than not displeased, given the way you are draped across my furniture like a wet sack of flour."

Any other time, William might have reacted to such an undignified description. At that moment, however, all he could do was nod. "She is furious. Rightly so, I suppose. If I had anticipated where things between us might lead, I might have discussed it with her. Unfortunately, it was always a given that she would leave and, frankly, I never saw any of this coming."

Dering slowly nodded, his gaze still pensive. "Well, it is safe to say her leaving is no longer an option. The way I see it, you have two options."

"Those being?" Two options were already two more than he had come up with.

Setting down his glass on the side table, Dering leaned forward and extended his index finger. "One, you can realize that the situation is hopeless, and go home to your estate to live without her."

"That is not an option. Try again."

That old expression crossed Dering's wide features, the one he always got when he thought of the past. "Sometimes that is the only option, as I well know. Luckily for you, that's not the case here. You, sir, need to fight for her. Show her how much you love her, and that you want nothing more than to give her what she wants in life."

"I'd love to do just that. Unfortunately, I *can't* give her what she wants."

"You don't think she wants you? Love, babies, jewelry for Christmas?"

William rolled his eyes at Dering's flippant response. "It's possible she could want those things, but I don't know if she'll ever admit it. For her, the thing she wants most in the world is the ability to go home." The exact thing he had stolen from her. The one thing that was impossible for him to return.

"Then give her that."

William blinked at his friend, wondering if that drink had already gone to the man's head. "How exactly am I supposed to do that? Switch allegiances? Campaign for the reversion of the Company's monopoly?"

Crossing his arms and leaning back in his chair, Dering lifted an eyebrow. "Who said anything about the Company?"

"You're not making any sense," William explained, throwing up a hand in frustration. "Would you have me buy her father a ship and send them on their merry way?"

Dering smiled and raised both eyebrows this time. He didn't say anything, instead just sat there with an expectant look on his face.

Groaning, William came to his feet. "You have clearly gone mad. I should go."

"Your choice. But answer me this: How were you planning to export your goods once the mill is at full production?"

That stopped William in his tracks. He turned to face Dering fully, his understanding dawning. "You're speaking of investing in shipping," he said, his mind racing as he considered the implications. "Owning the vessel that transports the goods, charging others to ship, making use of a captain's decades of experience in both the routes and the trade contacts."

He sank down into the chair, working over the logistics. "It would be a fortune for the initial investment." After promising Vivian a house and funds, it would be an uncomfortable stretch to come up with the available capital.

Dering picked up his glass and held it in salute. "Lucky for you, you have a friend who is looking to invest in a new venture. Don't want to look as though I'm sitting around waiting for the old man to stick his spoon in the wall."

It could work. With the Company cutting their routes, they would have to be looking to sell some of their fleet as well. Not to mention cutbacks in decommissioned naval ships after the war.

If he did this, he could truly make right all the setbacks that had befallen May and her father. He could give her what she wanted most: the ability to return to the place she called home.

But where did that leave him? Exactly where it left him now: wanting her to choose him over her old life. The difference was, her happiness would be assured. Whether that happiness meant going away or staying with him, it would be her choice.

Drawing a long, bolstering breath, he smiled to Dering. "It appears we have much to discuss. I do hope your week is clear."

Dering gave him a wide, knowing grin. "For you, my friend, I have all the time in the world."

William smiled for the first time that evening. God willing, it wouldn't take that long.

Chapter Twenty-five

The sun had not yet crested the horizon when May arrived at the park. It was cool this morning, hinting strongly toward the coming autumn. She had never thought to be here for the changing leaves and waning days. It was lovely in its own way, though she never could bring herself to enjoy it. Just gilding to her cage, as far as she was concerned.

She wasn't angry anymore. She wasn't really anything. The only word that came to mind was *lost*. They hadn't even decided where to live yet. It had been weeks and they were still living with Aunt Victoria, waiting to see if any of Papa's inquiries would come through. She, at least, was finally showing a bit of compassion. After what she had said of her past, May imagined she understood something of what it was like to lose one's expected future.

Shedding her coat, May chafed her hands together to get the blood flowing. Soon she would have to find warmer clothes for her morning routines. She rolled her head back and forth and made her way to her normal spot. Closing her eyes, she breathed in and out several times, attempting to clear her mind and ground her body in the moment.

"You never did finish our lesson."

May's heart leapt to her throat at the sound of his voice. *William.* She spun in his direction, so eager to see his face she didn't even attempt to temper her reaction. He was so incredibly handsome, standing there in the murky morning light, his hair slightly mussed and his lips curled in a small, cautious grin. His eyes . . . She shivered, feeling his gaze like a physical caress. They seemed so warm and earnest, it was all she could do not to go to him.

She worked to get her breathing under control. To get herself under control, really. He had lied to her. Hurt her. Left her here to rot with nary a word for weeks. Weeks! She crossed her arms protectively over her chest. "What are you doing here?"

He walked closer to her, moving slowly but purposefully. "I wanted to see you. I was hoping enough time had passed that you wouldn't throw me over your shoulder the moment you saw me."

Lifting her chin, she said, "Let's just say I wouldn't suggest coming much closer."

He paused a few feet away, but it was close enough for her to feel the old connection between them. It was like a single strand of silk thread, gossamer thin but with an unseen strength that made it quite difficult to break. She steeled herself against her body's traitorous reaction, forcing herself to remember the pain of their last meeting.

He looked her straight in the eye. "May," he breathed, her name like velvet. "I've missed you. I never stopped thinking about you, never stopped regretting how I hurt you."

God, but she had missed him too. Or at least, she had missed the man she thought he was. The one who wouldn't have deceived her. "I'm surprised to hear you have wasted any time thinking of me."

It surely couldn't have been as much time as she had wasted thinking of him. Remembering his kisses, his touch, his beautiful golden eyes. The problem was, she always remembered the betrayal, the pain, and the hurt as well. How could she forget? Her whole life here was a constant reminder.

"I know you think I purposely misled you, but I swear to you I didn't. I also know that you hate the effect my actions had on you, and there is nothing I can do about it."

She shook her head. "No, there's not. Which is why you shouldn't have come."

He stepped closer, only an arm's length away now. "But the problem is, there is much more to us than that. When you came to the estate, it may have only been for a few short days, but you changed everything for me." Another step. Her heart raced faster still, and she had to force herself not to reach out.

Giving a helpless little shake of his head, he said, "I fell in love with you, Mei-li Bradford, without ever intending to. I had a vision for my life, and it did not include a tall, exotic blonde with the mouth of a sailor and the heart of a lion. It's just another thing I was completely wrong about."

Time seemed to have stopped at the words *I fell in love with you.* May stared back at him in utter shock. She shook her head, unable to believe what he was saying. "You can't love me. We're polar opposites. We would drive each other mad." Even discounting the matter of his deception, there were too many things working against them to even consider it. Still, her heart raced with the possibility.

He grinned. "You already drive me mad, and you

aren't even near me." He took another step forward, bringing his body entirely too close for her to maintain reason. "But there is one very important thing."

She swallowed, unable to take her eyes from his beautiful lips. "What?"

"Someone once told me that home is where the heart resides. I want you to find home, May, wherever that may be."

She was so overwhelmed by his closeness, she couldn't even make sense of what he was saying. "I don't know what you mean," she said, her voice little more than a whisper. The scent of sandalwood was like a sip of water in the desert, filling a need she didn't even know she had.

He lifted a hand and slid a single, featherlight finger along her jaw, making her shiver. "You will." He leaned forward, and she held her breath, waiting for the moment his lips would touch hers. But at the last second, he tilted his head and pressed a single kiss to the corner of her mouth.

"Good-bye, Mei-li. When you have everything you want, I hope you'll discover what you really need. And more important, where your heart truly lies."

Without another word, he turned and walked away, leaving her utterly bewildered and struggling to draw a proper breath.

Today was the day. The first shipment from Spencer Mill would have left England's shores on the newly christened *Anna Britannia*, a two hundred and eighty ton brig that Dering had found less than two weeks after setting out on his search.

William had named it in honor of the two most important women in his life: his mother and the woman he hoped would be his wife. The decision was in her hands. Which, of course, made him a nervous wreck.

He wasn't used to releasing control of things, and this was by far the biggest gamble he had ever taken.

"William, please, you're wearing a hole through the carpet." Vivian shook her head, clearly amused with his agitation. "Come over here and help Julian with his drawing. He can't remember what the sails should look like." She was living with them part-time now, and had made a noticeable change since William had purchased the home she had chosen, less than ten miles away.

Blowing out a breath, he pulled himself away from the windows he had been pacing between and lowered himself to the floor next to his brother. "How could you have forgotten already?" he asked, ruffling his brother's hair. "We were only there two weeks ago. And you say you want to be a sailor." He tsked teasingly.

It had been the most excited he had ever seen the children. They had run along the newly refinished deck, holding their arms out like soaring seagulls and laughing with abandon. They had toured the quarters and the various decks, continually getting in the workers' way as they put the finishing touches on the refurbishments.

Julian scowled up at him, obviously displeased with William's ribbing. "They couldn't let them out, remember? You can't put sails up at the dock."

True enough. As he leaned over and helped Julian draw them in, William couldn't help the fresh swell of anticipation that assailed him. He still hadn't heard a word from May. He had hoped she would come to him weeks ago when she'd learned of her father's new position. When she hadn't, he had waited, hoping she would show up when her father left for Portsmouth several days ago in preparation for the voyage. But even then, she hadn't.

It was impossible to know if that meant she was choosing to return with her father after all. The ship would have set sail today before the sun even came up, so one way or another, and with Portsmouth less than fifty miles away, he would have his answer by the end of the day.

Which was nearly at hand.

Even now, the sun was already slipping below the horizon, and he knew that the children needed to go to bed soon. He looked at Clarisse, who was attempting to place her elephant comb in Orangey's long fur. William hadn't said a word to either of his siblings, but they both knew he was acting strangely.

Vivian cleared her throat and looked at the clock resting on the mantel. It was after seven, and he couldn't pretend the day wasn't over. Doing his best to ignore the growing stone that had settled over his chest, he came to his feet. "Time to get ready for bed."

Clarisse looked up, confusion wrinkling her forehead. "But she's not here yet. I wanted to say hello."

William hadn't said a word to either of them. He narrowed his eyes at Vivian, who quickly held up her hands and shook her head. Turning back to Clarisse, he said, "Who isn't here?"

"Mei-li. You've been watching and watching, and since we are here, who else would it be?"

Who indeed. He forced a smile. "I'm just restless. Now, to bed with the both of you."

Nurse Plimpton rose and tended to the children as he and Vivian said good night and headed downstairs. They walked in silence all the way. His heart was heavy as he offered a shallow nod and started for his study.

"Radcliffe," Vivian said, making him turn. "I'm sorry for your disappointment. I think perhaps a walk in the garden will help clear your mind."

He swallowed past the lump in his throat, trying to maintain even an ounce of stoicism. "Perhaps I will. Good night."

She nodded and headed off toward the east wing, leaving him alone in front of the huge, empty drawing room. He looked around aimlessly, not even sure what to do with himself. Despite the enormous space, he suddenly felt closed in. Vivian was right. He needed air.

Stalking to the back doors, he let himself out into the garden, not bothering to bring a lamp despite the falling darkness. No matter how wretched it felt, he took solace in the knowledge that she had found her happiness. He had hoped, desperately so, that her happiness would have been with him. As much as he thought of her, dreamed of her even, it was difficult to swallow that she didn't do the same of him.

He had taken a gamble, and though he had lost, he took solace in the fact that she had won. She would have the life she wanted, and despite the almost overwhelming sense of loss on his part, he was happy for her. It wasn't what he had hoped for, but it would have to be enough.

As he walked along the stone path, his eyes on his feet, he realized that there was light out here after all. Faint, but definitely visible. He glanced up, confused, only to see the conservatory glowing with lamplight the way it used to when his father was still alive.

What on earth? Then, in a flash, hope flared to life, almost painful in its intensity. Could it be? It seemed far-fetched, bordering on ridiculous, but with even a slim possibility that she would be here, waiting for him in the warmth of the conservatory, he wasn't going to ignore it. He hurried to the fogged glass doors, his heart thundering against his ribs.

He was nearly jogging by the time he reached the entrance, and quickly turned the knob to let himself in. The warm, humid air immediately washed over him, dispelling the chill from outside. He breathed deeply of the floral, earthy scent, his eyes darting around for any signs of May. Nothing. No flash of jeweled silks, no hint of her smile, no sound of her voice. Only the flutter of birds' wings and his own pulse in the huge, forested room.

The light came from evenly spaced torches lighting the path that meandered through the overgrown space. Drawing a calming breath, he headed down the path, following the lights, hoping, *wanting* May to be there. To put him out of his misery, and let him know once and for all that she chose him. That right here, with him, was where her heart resided.

But as much as he searched for her sun-kissed hair and shimmering blue eyes, there was nothing there. He made it to the center of the conservatory, where the path ended at a small fountain surrounded by several half-moon benches. Still, he was alone. Was it possible that one of the servants had decided to light the space?

With his hope falling away, he blew out a long breath and turned to retrace his steps. And there she was. Like a figment of his dreams, she stood there on the path not ten feet away, swathed in shimmering jade silk embroidered with colorful birds that fit perfectly with the forest around her. She was perfection. More than beautiful.

Beloved.

Warmth that had nothing to do with the conservatory filled every corner of May's heart as she drank in the sight of the man she loved, staring back at her as though she were a mirage that might disappear at any moment.

She'd said good-bye to her father that morning. All

the way up until yesterday, she had herself so convinced that her happiness resided halfway around the world, she had intended to set sail with him. Even after the missive from Lady Radcliffe had arrived earlier in the week, explaining what William had done for her and imploring May to reconsider his suit, May still couldn't shake her stubbornness. But as she'd packed the last of her possessions with Suyin last night, she'd suddenly realized that her happiness had nothing to do with a place. It was with a person.

William.

Just as her mother had always said.

Her sudden announcement of her intention to stay had surprised no one but herself, it seemed. Papa had smiled and hugged her tight. Suyin had nodded knowingly. And when she'd arrived at Clifton House this afternoon and asked for Lady Radcliffe at the servants' entrance, the older woman had merely grinned and readily invited her inside.

May had wanted the moment she saw William to be perfect. The man who had made the grandest gesture she had ever heard of—buying a ship and hiring her father to captain it—deserved more than a simple knock at the door. He deserved something special just for him.

The truth was she loved him. Deeply. Honestly. Wholeheartedly. Whatever their differences, he'd proven that when it came to love, there would always be a way. She was nervous, but not apprehensive.

She smiled at him now, her heart so full of love and happiness, she could barely breathe.

"May," he said, the word a prayer and a plea at the same time.

She smiled, stepping forward one tantalizingly slow step at a time, drawing out the anticipation for when she could be in his arms once more. "It recently occurred to me that there was more than one place to find a tropical wonderland."

He stood completely still, his eyes piercing in their intensity as he watched her. "Is that so?" The hope in his voice made her bold.

She nodded, coming to a stop only a few paces away. "Just as there is more than one place a person can call home."

He surprised her, moving forward to close the distance between them and wrapping her up in an embrace tight enough to steal her breath. "You came," he said, the two words full of emotion.

Nothing had ever felt more right than being tucked in his arms, chest to chest, heart to heart. She had little thought for the life she had left behind, thinking only of the life she was choosing, beside the man she had fallen wholly and completely in love with. "I couldn't *not* come," she said, pulling away to meet his gaze. "You made it impossible to forget you, to imagine my life without arguing with you. Laughing with you." She licked her lips and said, "Loving you."

His lips curled at the corners. "I know exactly what you mean."

Squeezing her close, he kissed her with all the passion that had been building for weeks. A lifetime, really. She eagerly returned his kiss, wrapping her arms fully around him and holding him just as tightly. It was the best feeling in the world, knowing she was here, and that he was hers. The life that awaited her was not the one she had always imagined, but so long as she was by his side, she knew that it would always be happy.

Pulling away at last, he smiled down at her, his firelit

eyes glittering gold. "You do know that this is completely beyond the pale, us being here alone together. I'm afraid you have quite ruined me."

She lifted her eyebrows, grinning broadly. "Excellent. I knew if I worked hard enough, I could bring a little scandal to your life."

"Is that so? Well, I'm afraid I must demand you make things right."

"And how am I to do that?"

"Marry me," he said, emphatically, the words a plea and a declaration all at once. "Be my wife, my duchess, and the love of my life. Bring passion to both my days and my nights. Let me be the place that you call home."

The parts of her she hadn't even known were empty filled with a joy she hadn't known was possible. "Nothing could possibly make me happier."

Applause erupted from behind them, and they turned in unison to find the children, both in their nightclothes, jumping up and down and clapping, their small faces wreathed in smiles. Lady Radcliffe stood behind them, her hands clasped to her heart as she grinned back at them.

William laughed and shook his head, not loosening his grip on May one bit. "Spying again, are we?"

At that, Julian and Clarisse both giggled and pointed to their mother. "She made us do it!"

The older woman lifted her brows and shrugged in that Parisian way of hers, though there was no missing the mischievous glint in her hazel eyes. "She did just come from Portsmouth. We had to be certain she wasn't a smuggler."

Laughter filled the warm air as William's family—and May's family, soon enough—joined them for hugs and congratulations. She couldn't remember ever being so happy in her entire life, which was remarkable, given how far she was from what she thought she had wanted. Who would have thought that her love, her heart, and her future had been waiting for her in England all along.

Epilogue

Eight months later

A knock at the door interrupted the flurry of feminine conversation that had filled the small room that had been set aside for the trio's use. Raising her voice, May called out, "Yes?"

Mr. Green pulled open the door, his mouth pressed in a flat line as he gave a little bow. "Pardon me, Your Grace, Lady Cadgwith, and Lady Evansleigh. The committee respectfully requests your presence at your earliest convenience."

May offered a regal nod. "Thank you, Mr. Green. We shall be ready momentarily."

He nodded again, gave an awkward half bow, then slipped away, closing the door in his wake. May shared a devilish grin with Charity and Sophie. "That may have been the highlight of the entire festival thus far."

Sophie laughed as she rolled her eyes. "We are all of four days into it, so that's not really saying very much, but I know *exactly* what you mean."

Gray eyes sparkling, Charity shook her head. "Reluctant respect has never felt so good. I imagine he's heartily wishing he hadn't been so rude to us last year."

"Actually," May said, shaking her head, "I doubt he is. But knowing he has to be nice or face the committee's wrath must be the worst sort of torture for him. I'll readily admit—that alone is enough to make the hassle of being a duchess worth it."

She was teasing, of course. Becoming William's duchess hadn't been without its trials, but it had certainly been much less difficult than she ever would have imagined. There were those in the *ton* who had been appalled by William's choice to marry her, and though no one had been brave enough to say anything directly to her, she knew some felt she was quite unqualified for the role.

Not that she was at all bothered by the sentiment.

They might have had a point about her role as duchess, but there was no one more qualified to be William's wife. She loved him to distraction, and was secure in the fact that he felt the same way about her. He was so supportive, so willing to grant her whatever thing she wished, it had been an easy transition. He even joined her every morning for her routine, which even now made her smile to think about. Many of those sessions ended up leading to an entirely different sort of exercise.

Their days were full and busy, but in the best sort of way. May disliked idleness, and between the mill, the household, and the children, there was always something to keep her occupied. And as good as the days were, the nights were even better. The passion between her and William had only grown since their marriage last November. She had never known the kind of happiness and fulfillment she now enjoyed was even possible, and very soon that joy would be increased tenfold.

She smiled and put a hand to her middle. This year was sure to be even better than the last.

Sophie came to her feet, adjusted the canary diamond necklace at her neck, and looked around at both of them. "Well, do you suppose they are ready for the three Esses?"

Charity raised an eyebrow. "The what?"

"The three Esses," she repeated, grinning broadly. Pointing to each of them in turn, she said, "Baroness, countess, and duchess, of course."

May half groaned, half laughed. "That is terrible. Did you come up with that?"

She shook her head. "Actually, no. I ran into Mr. Wright, the vicar, yesterday at the Pump Room, and he told me that's what people had been calling us. It may be terrible, but it did rather make me laugh," she said, grinning that irrepressible grin of hers.

"Well," Charity said, reaching for their hands, "it's not everyday a trio like us comes along." There was no conceit in her voice, merely gratefulness.

May nodded as she readily joined hands with the others. "Indeed. I'm so happy to be a part of this with you. Although . . ." she trailed off, drawing a breath as she looked back and forth between them, "technically it's more of a quartet."

Two seconds ticked by before the others understood her meaning and erupted in cheers. Charity grinned hugely before saying, "Actually, that makes us a quintet."

May gaped, then let out a whoop of excitement. She hadn't thought her joy could be any greater, but she had been wrong yet again. After a moment, Charity and May sent identical looks of expectation to Sophie. She held up her hands, laughing. "Don't look at me! Perhaps someday soon, but at the moment, I'm still on my honeymoon."

They all hugged then, each grinning ear to ear with delight. Things had changed so much for them all this year, but thankfully, it had all been for the better. "Are you ready?" May asked when they had finally stepped away.

"Absolutely," Sophie answered, anticipation thick in her voice. They had all been looking forward to this moment for months.

They opened the door and headed into the Assembly Rooms ballroom, which was filled to capacity. As they made their way to the stage, May smiled to new and old friends alike. Lord Cadgwith stood against the back wall, with tiny, telltale tufts of cotton poking from his ears. His arms were crossed as he followed the group's progress toward the stage, a soft smile tugging up his lips.

They passed Charity's sweet grandmother, who sat proudly in the front row, Cadgwith's niece Isabella on her lap despite the festival's no-children rule. May had personally informed the committee that they wouldn't perform without their families present. Since theirs was one of the most anticipated performances, the committee had readily agreed. Beside the dowager sat Felicity, Isabella's mother, and beside her was her brother and vicar, Mr. Thomas Wright, followed by Lord Derington, whose oddly hooded gaze seemed focused on Felicity, interestingly enough.

To the viscount's right, Sophie's three sisters sat in a row, identical smiles on their faces. Lord Evansleigh grinned broadly as his gaze followed Sophie. May couldn't help but chuckle at the besotted look on his face—she adored him for loving Sophie so well. To his right sat his sister Julia and her husband, Sir Harry.

May smiled as she caught her father's eye in the next row over. His arm was settled around Julian, who waved at May when she winked at him. Vivian patted his knee and whispered in his ear, then pulled a giggling Clarisse a little closer to her other side. William sat on his sister's right, his amber eyes brimming with pride as May locked gazes with him.

Her stomach gave a little flip of awareness, even after all these months of marriage. He looked so blasted handsome, looking at her like that, it was all she could do to turn her attention to her guzheng as she took her seat. As much as he had claimed to dislike her playing when they met, he had quickly come around. There were many evenings when he sat by her side on her bench as she played the music of her heart, quietly sharing the moment with her.

She wasn't sure if she would make it back to the Far East anytime soon, especially with the baby coming, but she had made peace with that. She would always carry the influences of her upbringing close to her heart. In fact, she had even convinced William to hire Smita and her family to embroider a special line of trim for a higher quality range of fabrics they were selling to a dressmaker here in Bath, since May's exotic fashions were catching on with the *ton*.

The crowd seemed to hold its collective breath as Charity placed her hands on the keys, Sophie lifted her oboe to her lips, and May stretched out her fingers over the strings. Here with her closest friends, her dear family, and the husband she loved to distraction, she knew that she was well and truly home. For her, contentment was an almost physical thing. Her whole body was filled with it, and her heart grew a little more each day.

As the first notes sang forth from their instruments, May closed her eyes and smiled. This was the life she never knew she wanted, and she couldn't have been any happier to call it her own.

Read on for an extract from the first book
in Erin Knightley's PRELUDE TO A KISS series . . .

The Baron Next Door

Hell and damnation. Was he to have no peace at all? Hugh Danby, the new and exceedingly reluctant Baron Cadgwith, pressed the heels of his hands into his eye sockets, pushing back against the fresh pounding the godforsaken noise next door had reawakened.

"Go to Bath," his sister-in-law had said. "It's practically deserted in the summer. Think of the peace and quiet you'll have."

Bloody hogwash. This torture was about as far from peace as one could get. Not that he blamed Felicity; clearly the news of the first annual Summer Serenade in Somerset festival hadn't made it to their tiny little corner of England when she offered her seemingly useful suggestion. Still, he'd love to get his hands on the person who thought it was a good idea to organize the damn thing.

He tugged the pillow from the empty spot beside him and crammed it over his head, trying to muffle the jaunty pianoforte music filtering through the shared wall of his bedchamber. The notes were high and fast, like a foal prancing in a springtime meadow. Or, more aptly, a foal prancing on his eardrums.

There was no hope for it. There would be no more sleep for him now.

Tossing aside the useless pillow, he rolled to his side, bracing himself for the wave of nausea that always greeted him on mornings like this. *Ah, there it is.* He gritted his teeth until it passed, then dragged himself up into a sitting position and glanced about the room.

The curtains were closed tight, but the late-morning sunlight still forced its way around the edges, causing a white-hot seam that managed to burn straight through his retinas. He squinted and looked away, focusing instead on the dark burgundy-and-brown Aubusson rug on the floor. His clothes were still scattered in a trail leading to the bed, and several empty glasses lined his nightstand.

Ah, thank God—not *all* were empty.

He reached for the one still holding a good finger of liquid and brought it to his nose. *Brandy.* With a shrug, he drained the glass, squeezing his eyes against the burn.

Still the music, if one could call it that, continued. Must the blasted pianoforte player have such a love affair with the brain-cracking high notes? Though he'd yet to meet the neighbors who occupied the adjoining townhouse, he knew without question the musician was a female. No self-respecting male would have the time, inclination, or enthusiasm to play such musical drivel.

Setting the tumbler back down on the nightstand, he scrubbed both hands over his face, willing the alcohol to deaden the pounding in his brain. The notes grew louder and faster, rising to a crescendo that could surely be heard all the way back at his home in Cadgwith, some two hundred miles away.

And then . . . *blessed silence.*

He closed his eyes and breathed out a long breath. The hush settled over him like a balm, quieting the ache and lowering his blood pressure. Thank God. He'd rather walk barefoot through glass than—

The music roared back to life, pounding the nails back into his skull with the relentlessness of waves hitting the beach at high tide. *Damn it all to hell.* Grimacing, he tossed aside the counterpane and came to his feet, ignoring the violent protest of his head. Reaching for his clothes, he yanked them on with enough force to rip the seams, had they been of any lesser quality.

It was bloody well time he met his neighbors.

Freedom in D Minor.

Charity Effington grinned at the words she had scrawled at the top of the rumpled foolscap, above the torrent of hastily drawn notes that danced up and down the static five-lined staff.

The title could not be more perfect.

Sighing with contentment, she set down her pencil on the burled oak surface of her pianoforte and stretched. Whenever she had days like this, when the music seemed to pour from her soul like water from a upturned pitcher, her shoulders and back inevitably paid the price.

She unfurled her fingers, reaching toward the unlit chandelier that hung above her. The room was almost too warm, with sunlight pouring through the sheers that covered the wide windows facing the private gardens behind the house, but she didn't mind. She'd much rather be here in the stifling heat than up north with her parents and their stifling expectations.

And Grandmama couldn't have chosen a more perfect townhouse to rent. With soaring ceilings, airy rooms, and generous windows lining both the front and back—not to mention the gorgeous pianoforte she now sat at—it was a wonderful little musical retreat.

Exactly what Charity needed after the awfulness of the past Season.

Dropping her hands to the keys once more, she closed her eyes and purged all thoughts of that particular topic from her mind. It was never good for creativity to focus on stressful topics. Exhaling, she stretched her fingers over the cool ivory keys, finding her way by touch.

Bliss. The pianoforte was perfectly tuned, the notes floating through the air like wisps of steam curling from the Baths. Light and airy, the music reflected the joy filling her every pore. Here she had freedom.

Free from her mother and her relentless matchmaking. Free from the gossip that seemed to follow her like a fog. Free from all the strict rules every young lady must abide by during the Season.

The notes rose higher as her right hand swept up the scale, tapping the keys with the quickness of a flitting hummingbird. Her left hand provided counterbalance with low, smooth notes that anchored the song.

A sudden noise from the doorway startled her from her trance, abruptly stopping the flow of music and engulfing the room in an echoing silence. Jeffers, Grandmama's ancient butler, stood in the doorway, his stooped shoulders oddly rigid.

"I do beg your pardon, Miss Effington. Lady Effington requests your presence in the drawing room."

Now? Just when she was truly finding her stride? But Charity wasn't about to make the woman wait—not after she had singlehandedly saved Charity from a summer of tedium in Durham with her disgruntled parents. "Thank you, Jeffers," she said, coming to her feet.

She headed down the stairs, humming the beginning of her new creation. Her steps were in time with the music in her mind, which had her moving light and fast on her feet. The townhouse was medium sized, with more than enough room for the two of them and the handful of servants Grandmama had brought, so it took her only a minute to reach the spacious drawing room from the music room.

Breezing through the doorway with a ready smile on her face, Charity came up short when the person before her was most definitely *not* her four-foot-eleven, silver-haired grandmother.

Mercy!

She only just managed to contain her squeak of surprise at the sight of the tall, lanky man standing in the middle of the room, his dark, rumpled clothes in stark contrast to the cheery, soft blues and golds of the immaculate drawing room. She swallowed, working to keep her expression passive as her mind raced to figure out who on earth the man was.

Charity had never seen him before—of that she was absolutely sure. It would be impossible to forget the distinctive scars crisscrossing his left temple and disappearing into his dark blond hair. One of the puckered white lines cut through his eyebrow, dividing it neatly in half before ending perilously close to one of his vividly green— and terribly bloodshot—eyes.

He was watching her unflinchingly, accepting her inspection. Or perhaps he was simply indifferent to it. It was . . . disconcerting.

"There you are," Grandmama said, snapping Charity's attention away from the stranger. Sitting primly at her usual spot on the overstuffed sofa centered in the room, her grandmother offered Charity a soft smile. "Charity, Lord Cadgwith has kindly come over to introduce himself. He is to be our neighbor for the summer."

Kindly? Charity couldn't help her raised eyebrow. The

man had come over without invitation or introduction, and Grandmama had actually allowed it?

Correctly interpreting Charity's reaction, the older woman chuckled, clasping her hands over the black fabric of her skirts. "Yes, I realize we are not strictly adhering to the rules, but it is summer, is it not? Exceptions can be made, especially when the good baron overheard your playing and so wished to meet the musician." Her gray eyes sparkled as she smiled at their guest.

It was all Charity could do not to gape at the woman. Yes, no one was more proud of Charity's playing than her grandmother, but this was beyond the pale. Good gracious, if Mama and Papa knew how much Grandmama's formerly strict nature had been changed by her extended illness, they never would have allowed Charity to accompany her to Bath without them.

The baron bowed, the movement crisp despite his slightly disheveled appearance. "A pleasure to make your acquaintance, Miss Effington," he said, his voice low and a little raspy, like the low register of a flute.

Despite the perfectly proper greeting, something about him seemed a little untamed. Must be the scars, the origin of which she couldn't help but wonder about. War wounds? Carriage accident? A duel? Setting aside her curiosity, she arranged her lips in a polite smile. "And you as well, Lord Cadgwith. Are you here for the festival?"

"Please don't mumble my dear," Grandmama cut in, her whispered reprimand loud and clear. Charity cringed— the older woman insisted that her hearing was fine, and that any problem in understanding lay in the enunciation of those around her.

"Yes, ma'am," she responded in elevated, carefully pronounced tones. "Lord Cadgwith, are you here for the festival?" Heat stole up her cheeks, despite her effort to keep the blush at bay. She had never liked standing out—when away from her pianoforte, of course—and practically shouting in the presence of their neighbor was beyond awkward. One would think she'd have come to terms with the easy blushes her ginger hair and pale, freckled skin lent itself to, but no. Knowing her cheeks were warming only made her blush that much more violently.

It certainly didn't help that the man was by far the most attractive male to ever stand in her drawing room, scars or no. She swallowed against the unexpected rush of butterflies that flitted through her.

For his part, Lord Cadgwith did not look amused. "No, actually. I had no knowledge of the event until my arrival." He made the effort to speak in a way that Grandmama would hear, his dark, deep voice carrying easily through the room. A man used to being heard, she'd guess. A military man, perhaps?

"Well, what a happy surprise it must have been when you arrived," her grandmother said, smiling easily. "Charity is planning to sign up for the Musicale series later this afternoon. There are a limited number of slots, but I have no doubt our Charity will earn a place."

And . . . more blushing. Charity gritted her teeth as she smiled demurely at her grandmother. Music was the one thing for which Charity had no need for false modesty, but sharing her plans with the virtual stranger standing in their drawing room felt oddly invasive. "I'm sure Lord Cadgwith isn't interested in my playing, Grandmama."

"On the contrary," he said, his voice rough but carrying. "It is, after all, your music that prompted me to visit in the first place."

Her mouth fell open in a little "Oh" of surprise before

she got her wits about her and snapped it shut. Still, pleasure, warm and fizzy, poured through her. Her music had called this incredibly handsome man to her? Not her looks (such as they were), not her father's station, not curiosity from the gossip. No, he had sought her out because her playing touched him. Pride mingled with the pleasure, bringing an irrepressible grin to her lips.

Grandmama beamed, her shrewd gaze flitting back and forth between them. "Well, I do hope you'll stay for tea, my lord."

His smile was oddly sharp. "Unfortunately, I must be off. I just wanted to introduce myself after being serenaded this morning. Lady Effington, thank you for your indulgence of my whim."

She nodded regally, pleasure clear in the pink tinge of the normally papery white skin of her cheeks. He turned to face Charity, his green eyes meeting hers levelly. "Miss Effington," he said, lowering his voice to a much more intimate tone as he bent his head in acknowledgment. "Do please have a care for your captive audience in the adjoining townhouses, and keep the infernal racket to a minimum."

Lost as she was in the vivid dark green of his eyes, it took a moment before his words sank in. She blinked several times in quick succession, trying to make sense of his gentle tone and bitingly rude words. He couldn't possibly have just said . . . "I beg your pardon?"

"Pardon granted. Good day, Miss Effington."

And just like that, the baron turned on his heel and strode from the room. It was then that she caught the fleeting hint of spirits, faint but unmistakable, in his wake. A few seconds later, the sound of the front door opening and closing reached her burning ears. *Of all the insufferable, boorish, rude—*

"My goodness, but he was a delightful young man." Grandmama's sweet voice broke through Charity's fury, just before she was about to explode. The older woman looked so happy, so utterly pleased with the encounter, that Charity forced herself to bite her tongue. It wouldn't do to upset her—not after she was only just now recovering from her illness. The currish baron wasn't worth the strife it would cause.

Forcing a brittle smile to her lips, she nodded. "Mmhmm. And you know what? I think I'll go play an *extra*enthusiastic composition just for him."

With that, she marched from the room, directly back to her pianoforte bench. The baron could have been pleasant. He could have kindly asked her to play more quietly, or perhaps less frequently. But, no, he had chosen to go about it in the most uncivilized, humiliating way possible. It was his decision to throw down the gauntlet as though they were enemies instead of neighbors.

She plopped down on her bench with a complete lack of elegance and paused only long enough to lace her hands together and stretch out her muscles. Then she spread her fingers out over the keys and smiled.

This, Lord Cadgwith, means war.